# UNION
# SQUARE

# UNION SQUARE

### ALBERT HALPER

1933

THE LITERARY GUILD
NEW YORK

Published by Viking Press

COPYRIGHT 1933, BY ALBERT HALPER
PRINTED IN THE UNITED STATES OF AMERICA
DISTRIBUTED IN CANADA
BY THE MACMILLAN COMPANY OF CANADA, LTD.

# TO
# THE FOUNDRY

# UNION
# SQUARE

# ONE

I

UNION SQUARE is surrounded on all sides by mountains. To the north are the Alps, to the east the Caucasus, to the west lie the Urals, while southward stand the Ozarks, with the plains of Texas just beyond. And south, further still, lies the heavy sea, which heaves and rolls like oil.

This is no idle dream. Through the passes and steep canyons swarm, all day long, Finns and Tartars, Poles and Italians, a few on swift running ponies, many afoot, but all with gleaming teeth; and the bulges in their clothing hide old hammerlock pistols and shiny, deadly, heavy-handled knives. They come from all four directions, with fine white dust ingrained between the tiny wrinkles of their skin and joints, some with fierce eyes, others with an old, hollow hunger in their bones, and all in silence.

Here, in this little plot of ground, hemmed in on all sides by high, dark shadows, the dust is ten inches thick and, when rain falls, the mud comes up as high as a pony's belly. No one speaks because there is no common tongue; the dribbling files of horsemen stare straight ahead, their tangled hair upon their tired shoulders, while the fetlocks of the animals, in quiet rhythm, make little lanes between the sifted dirt.

Toward the south, at the Ozarks, the grass grows lovely green in spring, but in the Alpine north wind rages all year round, with cold, white nights to break the pauses. Here no man dares live, the snow piles high, and even the heavy Teutons, those heroic gentlemen with muscled limbs, turn back their chargers and ride away, the horses blowing as they climb the trail, hooves ringing hard against the rocky, frozen ground.

Now, with the years, this valley has been trodden bare. But though men come, there is no house or tent, or common marking-post to nick with shiny axes. The earth in winter cracks in jagged lines fifteen feet deep, in spring the soft loam heals over. Wind rushes through the gorges, and whirling puffs of smoke rise briskly from the ground, like vapor from a winded stag, or little clouds from musket fire.

In June, when nights are calm, the stillness, like a sheath, hides the knife-flash of far-off, summer lightning. Over the floor of the valley hang stars and clouds and floating summer moons. Then autumn comes, and the sky grows cold—cold and blue as steel. Hail hurries from the east, advancing in swirling, pelting curtains; and it comes with fury, driving in behind a sixty-mile gale, and lashes the sides of the canyons, whose naked shoulder-blades, scarred with the whippings of countless storms, beatenly endure, like the patient backs of Chinese coolies, the stinging lashes and hate of time.

There are no trees, no beds of flowers. Seasons roll round like huge wagon wheels, each spoke a month, each revolution a year; the thick, fat hubs are as stolid as fate.

This is a land of waste and doom. The cold comes when the night falls and the wind rides on a storm.

> —*From the manuscripts of James Nicholson, demented printer, student of philosophy, worshiper of Roman culture, a little, skinny gent who goes around scattering cards printed from old-fashioned type from his basement quarters over on Thirteenth Street. The above was written in October 1931, on a day when the communists demonstrated and were dispersed by the police.*

The square was calm after the riot. At five o'clock, when the lamps along the walks lit up, there were no more banners, the shaky temporary speakers' platforms had already been knocked down by the police, and the only people about were a few shabby women and children who had come to gather the thin boards which lay strewn upon the ground for firewood. They came wheeling battered baby-buggies with knock-kneed axles, and under the lamp-light, as they stooped, they looked like peasants digging potatoes, or sowing the earth in spring.

By half-past five the wobbly baby-buggies were loaded with the scattered boards, and the women and children pushed them along, going up the side streets. Two or three buggies broke down, the axles caving in, so the children and their mothers had to gather the wood in their arms while the smallest kids dragged at the buggy handles and followed behind.

At the main B.M.T subway entrance Grandma Volga —this nickname bestowed upon the ancient dame by Officer Terence McGuffy, who was famous up and down Fourteenth Street for his classic utterance: "I have met the enemy and he is now in jail"—Grandma Volga, the stocky old woman with the shawl over her head whose grinning mouth slit her wrinkled face as she sold you pretzels, cast a searching eye over the autumn scene and saw, aloft, the thin, piercing point of the gigantic flagpole which stood like a tremendous carpet tack in the center of the square. Slowly swinging her glance around, her broad, aggressive, Slavonic face taking on a look of hardness, her stare finally came to rest coldly upon a hot-chestnut vender who stood but a few feet away and who was her fiercest competitor. She glared so hard that the chestnut vender, a little fellow, coughed gently and looked the other way. His name was Mr. Feibelman, and every morning he rushed toward the main entrance of the subway, hurrying with all his might, because whoever arrived first stood closest to the stairs, and that was the best position.

Staring the other way, Mr. Feibelman began counting the money in his pockets, by the feel of the coins. Business had been pretty good today, on account of the riot. There had been many people in the square, the press said thirty thousand, mostly onlookers, and twice Mr. Feibelman had had to go home for additional supplies of chestnuts.

"No Tovarich!" the old woman finally shouted toward him, spitting, then made off, wheeling her buggy over the curbing and going up Fourteenth Street, her last few unsold pretzels joggling loosely on the tall thin sticks like bracelets on the bony arms of skinny women.

Mr. Feibelman, still busy counting the coins in his pockets, watched the old woman cross Fourth Avenue, saw her nervously dodge between the heavy traffic and, when she had been sucked into the crowd like a seed in the wind, he stared up at the big clock in the tower of the public utilities building, and waited a few more minutes. Then, sighing and giving little mournful grunts, he looked up and down the street for a last customer and, finding none, finally began putting out the little charcoal fire in the tin bucket.

He was almost finished when someone came up, asking for a ten-cent bag. The vender, nodding, dug down into the warm pail without looking up, but as he raised his glance he saw who it was—a young fellow of slight build who stood there with finely shaped head tilted sensitively to one side. The young man wore no hat; he held out a dime, smiling a little. There was something gentle about him.

"Oh, it's you," grinned the vender and put two extra nuts into the bag. He was glad to see him and took the dime. Then, spitting briskly into the tin bucket, at a last flicker of flame, he turned up his collar, pushed his little wagon, and began going up the street, heading for the crowd on the other side. Raising the front wheels of his wagon there, he pushed over the curbing, shoving it off, and, like a seed in a sudden wind, was instantly sucked out of sight.

The young man, left alone, began walking around the square, edging away from the lights and the crowd. He put his hand in his pocket to feel the warmth of the chestnuts and covered a full block before he ate the first of them.

## II

ON THE Fourth Avenue side of the square the traffic was the heaviest; it tore along like two lengths of whistling chains, scraping hard against the car tracks and the street, urged on by the motions of the traffic cops. One length hurried toward the south, the other speeded northward, both checked and prodded by the stop-and-go of traffic lights.

The young man had plenty of time; he turned north and began following the low thick wall and, while his fragile feet trod the pavement, he glanced sideways occasionally to view the statues in the dim dark, nibbling rabbit-like at the chestnuts as he strolled. Behind him, on a large pedestal, was George Washington firmly seated upon the broad back of a powerful charger, bigger than life, with bronze brow as calm as a cheese-knife, one hand extended in a vague gesture which was pretty hard to figure out. The young man, starting on his third warm chestnut, then passed Lafayette, the gallant Frenchman who helped this land in time of stress, and noted how the Frenchman's sword was graceful in a pointed pose. Then came Lincoln—a little to the left—Lincoln, mighty man of the people, standing with a strong humbleness, his bronze brow also as calm as a cheese-knife, viewing sadly from the gloom of the park the crashing bustle of Fourteenth Street. On the west side of the square, facing Broadway right near the Free Milk for Babies Fund hut stood a sculptured group, a woman with a couple of children, a dreamy piece of work that you had to pass a hundred times before you really noticed it was there.

After going all around the empty square, the young man (his name is Leon Fisher, he's a photo-retoucher by day, an artist at night, and a member of the Communist

Party of America at all times!) crossed over to the south side of Fourteenth Street and turned south down Fourth Avenue. Inserting a hand into a pocket, he felt the chestnuts growing cold.

The chimes of Grace Church over on Broadway and Tenth Street struck the hour, the musical bongs floating in the thin, chilly air. When they died away—six stately bongs, all solemn in tone—the dull roar of the Fourth Avenue traffic was paramount again.

Leon Fisher turned east on Eleventh Street. He passed the garbage cans in front of the corner Coffee Pot, walked by the cooks-and-waiters' employment agencies, saw the wide front of the Catholic school in the distance, the lights of Webster Hall just beyond and, still strolling, finally came up to an old five-story tenement, a tall narrow building squeezed tightly between two other structures, a crazy scrawl of fire-escapes across the face of it.

A frightened cat darted out of the hallway. The artist (at night), sniffing at the stale odor coming from the building, entered the hallway and began walking up the narrow passage. Inside, a small gas light burned high near the ceiling, the flame wavering in the draft coming from the doorway.

The stairs wound sharply upward, in a spiral. On each floor lived four families—two in the rear, two in the front, each pair sharing a common toilet out in the cold, windy hall. There were five floors, four flats to a floor, twenty small, dark apartments in all. Little ten-cent locks hung from rusted staples on the doors of the toilets out in the hall, called by Jason Wheeler the "old guard" or "locked, we stand against the whole wide world."

Going up, passing the second landing, Leon Fisher heard, through a crack of a misfitted door, the sound of loud talking. A husband, a staunch father of four kids (three big enough to walk, the fourth a six-months-old infant) was hollering his head off about something, shouting with his head cocked toward the smelly hallway. "I tell you it's the limit! These foreigners, if they can't lock the toilet when they're through, if they can't snap the lock shut, why they ought to go back to the old country." . . . Hank Austin speaking, a big brute of a fellow, but he's merely letting off steam, merely showing who's boss around the house. His good wife, a short plump dame with a powerful bust, stood with lowered glance, her limbs quivering proudly at the timbrous voice, her stare straying occasionally toward the stove where food was cooking.

"Now, Hank," she said softly. "Now, Hank," she murmured quietly. And Hank, good old Hank (he was young), who worked in a warehouse down on Lafayette Street, sank his six-foot Yankee bulk into the old rocker while the eldest of his kids pulled his heavy boots off.

Leon Fisher's legs were growing weak and tired at the third landing and, when he reached the fourth, his brow felt a bit damp and a small, whistling sound was coming from his throat. He stopped, drew in a dozen deep breaths, and once more began climbing, wishing that his friend did not live so high up. Finally he reached the top floor and, looking toward the rear, saw a dim glow on the dirty transom window above the door. He walked back there and knocked three times. Someone shouted inside. Turning the knob, swinging the door back, he was already smiling his sad, warm smile before he had entered the room.

"Hello," he said, the goodness of his soul pouring from his large dark eyes.

Jason Wheeler, ex-poet and ex-communist, pot-boiler writer for the cheap sex-story magazines and former student of world affairs, grunted back an answer. He was half drunk again. Sprawled out on an old, broken chair, a bottle in his hand, one on the floor, his grim mouth loose and sloppy from the gin, he raised his glance and stared harshly at his friend.

"Well, come in. What the hell's the matter with you?"

With slow, hesitant steps, his eyes full of sympathy, the little fellow entered and closed the door.

Jason wiped his damp lips. Then, lifting his hand and nodding seriously for emphasis, he spoke to Leon as if before a solemn jury. "Knowest thou, my friend, that today, yea today, I didst sell another of my filthy yarns and have already received a check for twenty bucks for it? Aye. So all is well again, my yeomen ride, the wolf goes slinking from my door, and along Fourteenth Street the Revolution goes marching on."

"Maybe I'd better come around tomorrow," said Leon, hurt because Jason was making sport of the communists again.

"Sit down," said Jason. "Rest your weary can. No bands play as I sing my weary lay." The ex-poet was at it again.

Leon, keeping his overcoat on, sat down on a chair and stared thoughtfully about.

Jason's room, long and narrow, had bare brown walls, gone unpainted for many years now. In one corner stood an old iron cot, in another a small table upon which reposed a portable typewriter and close by, on the floor, kicked and cuffed about, was a battered phonograph, which did not work. Sheets of paper lay scattered on all sides, and the ten-cent waste-basket under the table had long since overflowed with crumpled-up copy, like a huge bud bursting dirty cotton. Everything was untidy here, dust lay along the woodwork, and where the walls met the floor were rolled-up accumulations of old sweepings, resembling closely the huddled bodies of small, gray mice; these were fluffy looking. One corner of the bed sheet, like the tip of a handkerchief, peeped from under the worn covering.

"Well," said Jason, "say something."

"I'm glad you sold the story," Leon said quietly.

Jason set the bottle he held in his hand down upon the floor; the bottom of it hit the wood with a dull sound. "I know you are, you're the only friend I've got in this town. All the others stink like last week's socks."

The little fellow shifted in his chair.

"I mean it. All the others stink; I've dropped them all."

Again the little fellow moved uneasily in his chair. He liked Jason, but did not like his friend to speak so bluntly. With strained and sympathetic eyes, he watched as Jason reached down for the bottle again and turned his head the other way at the sound of a prolonged gurgle.

"You ought to stop," he finally said, after he heard the bottom of the bottle hit the floor again.

Jason, thin-faced and pale, his mass of dry, light brown hair standing up on all sides, stared hard through the thick horn-rimmed glasses he wore and made a bitter, sourish face, turning down the corners of his mouth. He was of medium height and had a rather lanky build.

"They got me, Leon, five shots above the heart, the sixth square in the rectum, all six barrels used. Good gin, fifty cents a pint."

The ex-poet was at it again. He watched narrowly as Leon squirmed on the chair and hated himself with all his soul as he continued to bait his best friend, who had climbed five flights to see if he were short of funds. Reaching down, Jason picked up the evening newspaper from the floor. He turned a few sheets, his eyes roving up and down. Leon knew what he was in for, his friend was about to indulge in his favorite pastime, called "scanning the news."

"Well, Leon," said Jason briskly, clearing his throat like a schoolteacher, "we will now take up the automobile business and ascertain how the motors are going, whether there are any blow-outs along the automotive industrial front." He turned another page and began reading from a full-page advertisement, getting a bright, perky note into his voice: " 'I'm not famous but my car is. My Chrysler beats any car I have ever owned. . . . Mine isn't a front-page name. I'm not wealthy, I'm not poor, just go along enjoying myself in my own little world of neighbors and friends. But just because I'm not famous myself is no reason why I shouldn't drive a famous car. I *do*. I drive a Chrysler—with that patented Floating Power everybody is talking about.' How's that, Leon? I'm not wealthy, I'm not poor, just go along enjoying myself in my own little world of neighbors and friends. Not bad, eh?" He turned another page. " 'Brotherhood would make wonderful world. By Henry N. Kost. If the people of this world would realize that we are all brothers and sisters and really do love each other what a wonderful world this would be! Liberty, N. Y.' That's from the readers' column, Leon, from a guy who lives up in Liberty."

With his stiffened glance and firm, tiny lines at the corners of his mouth, Jason smiled at his friend, his eyes hard and bright from drinking.

"The trouble with you communists, Leon, is that you don't fall for the wrong women and you don't drink enough. You've got to get cock-eyed every once in a while or you can't appreciate straight vision. That's the trouble with you, you've all got one-track minds. Look at me, prosperity is in the wind for me, if things keep up, if the checks keep on pouring in for these masterpieces I hammer out, why I'll have to rent that little back room across the hall as a storeroom for my gin. I've got to plan, to think about the future. Well, what do you say, am I right or am I wrong, Leon? That is the question which confronts us here."

Leon, his glance still toward the bare, brown wall above the ex-poet's head, did not stir, did not say a word. Inside his chest, his heartbeats, like bird-wings, fluttered for his friend.

Jason stared hard at the bottle on the floor.

"I got paid today," said Leon. "And I quit my job besides. How are you fixed for funds?"

"You go to hell," said Jason quietly.

"Did you pay your rent yet?" Leon questioned.

"What did you throw up your position for?" Jason demanded. "You did the same thing last year. Who told you you could paint?" He frowned at his friend, but now Leon was smiling, he sat there staring warmly at the ex-poet.

"If I nurse my cash along, I'll be able to hold out until the middle of winter maybe," he told Jason.

"Then what?"

"They might take me back, I spoke to the foreman about it."

"Well, I say you're crazy to do it, I say you're shaky in the brain to quit a job to paint and do work for the Party. On the other hand, maybe you're right, just go along enjoying myself in my own little world of neighbors and friends." He gave a mocking smile. From the floor, staring up at both of them were photos on the front page depicting scenes of the afternoon riot in the square. Jason read from the large type without picking up the paper: "Reds routed, cops beat radicals, crowds watch, story on page 2."

Leon, stirring on the chair, rose to go.

"You're teasing me again," he said softly.

The ex-poet ran a hand slowly through his dry massed hair. He looked down in the mouth, his front fell quickly away.

"Did you hear from her?" asked Leon, standing near the door.

"No," said Jason. "I guess she got transferred and left town."

"Well, good-bye then. I might drop around tomorrow, I've got to go to a meeting now. You ought to put the gas-heater on, it's getting chilly in the room."

Jason sat there.

Leon closed the door silently and stood out in the cold hall for a while, then began walking quietly down the stairs.

The smell of cooking assailed his nostrils, cold air blew in through a smashed windowpane on the third landing, and all the way down he was conscious of the faded smell of old cats' droppings. Pieces of talk came through the cracks out into the hall. A dog barked twice and a kid bawled for food; someone was allowing the water to flow full force into the zinc tubs used for bathing and laundry purposes.

Leon reached the ground floor, walked out upon the street, and turned west. He passed the building next door which was a remodeled high-class apartment house now called the Glen Cove Apartments and saw a well-dressed, middle-aged man coming from the doorway, leading a small dog by the strap. They passed each other under an arc lamp, and in the harsh light Leon noticed that the man had an iron-gray mustache and a worried look around the eyes.

## III

THE MEETING of the comrades was called earlier than usual. By seven-thirty the hall was already hazy with cigarette smoke, the folding chairs were set into place, and, when the chairman finally took charge, a dozen small arguments were going hotly and a few speakers were shouting at each other.

The chairman hollered and pounded with his gavel. "Comrades!"

The hall settled slowly, one voice dying out at a time.

"Comrades!" the chairman said again, cleared his throat, and looked calmly about the place. All heads were turned front.

In the rear, looking about alertly, sat Leon Fisher, taking in the situation. Going to meetings made him a trifle agitated and restless and, as he stared about, he sensed tonight's meeting would be stormier than usual. Here and there sat men with bandaged heads and toward the front he saw a girl with her right arm in a sling—the marks of battle from the afternoon's riot. The cops had struck out brutally.

"Comrades," said the chairman, "the meeting is called to order. Today various events have happened, there will be conflicting opinions given from the floor regarding the demonstration that was held this afternoon in Union

Square, but I beg you not to interrupt any speaker who has the floor, I beg you to allow each comrade speaking to have his say." He pounded with the gavel.

The meeting started. At first everything was orderly; a few speakers rose to discuss the demonstration which had ended in confusion and a riot. One or two criticized the line of march, a few more found fault with the organization of the event. Someone, a girl, jumped up and, speaking heatedly, stated that the speakers had been too widely scattered in the crowds.

More talk followed. Then came discussion of the riot itself.

"I saw the plainclothesmen myself," shouted a man from the floor. "They came from the north of the square and began shoving, and the cops who were in on the dirty business began shoving back. Pretty soon the riot started, the whole square was pushing and jamming. Comrade Feeny was kicked in the face after a cop clubbed him to the ground, I saw it with my own eyes!"

The chairman had to pound with his gavel again.

"We have been tricked again," someone shouted from the left side of the hall. "We have been taken in like a lot of kids. The newspapers have made fools of us again."

Fools?

The house came down on the last speaker, he was shouted and stormed from the floor. From then on, the meeting was in turmoil. The chairman, waving his arms despairingly, hollered in a flat tired voice, pounded again and again for order, but got nowhere. He had been one of the speakers in the square, and his voice was about gone now.

Leon Fisher, sitting in the rear with tense, tightened body, had his little jaw set. A fury was seething in his chest, he clenched his small, slim hands between his knees and sat all knotted up, a damp sweat forming on his brow. Arguments were going on on all sides, whoever had the floor was drowned out, and above them all, his hands pleading and waving like a tired windmill, stood the worn-out chairman, trying to make himself heard.

"Comrades, comrades!"

Suddenly Leon felt like rising and shouting down the whole floor, telling them all to come to order. He sat rigid, more perspiration gathering on his brow. A good hot argument was going on right in front of him, two rows away.

"So the big cop began shoving me, using his hands too freely, so I told him where to get off at. I spat square in his face!" Bessie Silvers speaking, a stitcher in a sweat-shop over on Twenty-Eighth Street, a big, husky girl with a solid build.

Leon swung his glance toward the left, and started. He saw a couple of newcomers, strangers, a man and a girl. His heart began pounding as he stared at the girl. Large, blond, and with a full, softly rounded figure, she sat there dreamily and calmly, listening. Who was she? He had never seen her before. He could hardly take his eyes away to look at her friend, at the dark-complexioned fellow who sat low-browed and brawny at her side, his black stringy hair hanging in his eyes; the fellow looked to be a Mexican. Leon stared at the girl again, he was an artist and saw her beauty instantly; her skin, milk-white and unblemished, shone in the hall, and upon her head lay her piled-up blond hair, falling softly into waves.

Bessie Silvers, having let off steam, having gotten something out of her system, stared left and saw the newcomers; her face changed, grew harder. "There she is again, she created quite a fuss at the lecture Friday." The other girls looked. "She's a Party member from New Orleans," someone said, a girl. They lowered their voices and talked it over. There was something spiteful in their speech now. Leon understood. Most of the female comrades were plain-looking, homely girls who did not relish keen competition. "She's with that Mexican again, they say he was run out of Mexico for Party activities."

Leon, looking toward the left again, saw the fellow begin scratching at his head; he had a huge paw.

"Like an animal," Leon thought, shuddering.

The meeting broke up at last, broke up with Comrade Edward Lukotas giving one of his customary orations, only tonight he was a bit more fiery than usual, calling upon all and sundry to join in on the overthrow of capitalism. His speech sounded hollow and strident in the hall; in a meeting of this kind, where most of the members had a wide understanding of economics and had been in the movement for years, Comrade Lukotas's words rang flatly. But no one interrupted the tall, lanky fellow. Lukotas, who had worked in a New Jersey canning factory for years, had learned all he knew about socialism after reading a few ten-cent pamphlets issued by the Party. He halfscreamed at the close of his speech, then sat down, panting and red-faced. The chairman, looking fatigued, closed the meeting.

Chairs scraped against the floor, comrades rose, small groups formed and began talking.

Someone came over to Leon, who had risen. "Well, Leon, you weren't there in the afternoon, were you?" The comrade asked the question amiably, smiling at the little fellow. Everybody liked Leon Fisher.

"No," answered Leon. "I couldn't get off. But I quit

my job tonight. From now on, I'll have plenty of time for the Party."

A few more comrades turned around and smiled at him.

"Have you met the newcomers?" one of them asked, a fellow who had noticed Leon glancing off toward the left.

A flush crept into Leon's face. "No," he said.

So he was taken over, taken over to the strangers and introduced.

"Comrade Helen Jackson, Comrade Leon Fisher; Comrade José Morales, Comrade Leon Fisher. Comrade Fisher does our posters, the good ones."

The girl turned her blue eyes pleasantly upon the artist. Leon stammered a disconnected answer. The comrade who had made the introduction returned to the group, while Leon stood in his tracks, digging his nails into his palms, thinking hard and fast.

"You're from New Orleans?" he finally blurted out.

The girl nodded. "How did you know?" She smiled at him.

"I heard someone speaking about you, I just happened to overhear."

"Comrade Morales is from New Orleans too, he worked for the Party there for a while."

The swarthy fellow, his round, blank face as stolid as a good-sized cantaloupe, stared off to one side, no friendship in his eyes. Finally he yawned, clamped his mouth shut, addressed the girl in a low guttural, and took her arm. The girl, frowning for a fraction of a second, turned her glance away from the Mexican and for a fleeting instant smiled at Leon and, before she went off with her partner, held out her hand. Leon took it, his heart pounding violently. Her hand was soft—soft and warm. His head swam.

When they were gone, he wiped his forehead. To cover up his confusion he blew his nose violently into his handkerchief, joined a group, listened to the discussion, his mind wandering, and finally, when the comrades began leaving (it was late now), he too went down the steps. Comrade Lukotas was walking beside him, the ex-cannery man from Jersey, muttering to himself. "The goddam bosses, the dirty bosses . . ." mumbled Comrade Lukotas, a smoldering gleam to his stare.

Leon went out upon the chilly street, walked to the square with Lukotas, where Lukotas took a subway train, then headed east toward his rooming house on Fifteenth Street. Around the square big electric signs flashed on and off on all sides, blinking at each other from the tall tops of buildings. Leon walked fast, his hands in his pockets, his shoulders hunched. The cold air stirred his dark, soft hair.

When he reached his rooming house, he slipped his key into the lock, went inside, and glanced at the small table near the foot of the staircase to see if there was any mail for him.

He was about to start climbing the steps when a door under the staircase opened and a young girl came out, walking with a serious little frown on her face toward the bird-cage which hung near the lamp.

"Hello," said Leon.

"Oh, is that you?" answered the girl, stopping, as if surprised, as if caught off her guard. "I was just coming out to look at the canary, I just wanted to make sure the cage was properly covered, it gets cold in the hall sometimes."

"But what are you doing up so late? And you haven't your coat on either."

"I'm not cold. You're not to worry about me." Her fingers fussed with the cloth covering the bird-cage. She was a small girl, smaller than Leon; he was fond of teasing her.

"I ought to tell your aunt," he said sternly, speaking in a low voice because the house was quiet. "It's after eleven and here you are out in the cold hall without your coat on. What were you doing up so late?"

"I was reading a book," she answered meekly.

A book? No, she had been listening for his footsteps.

"What was the name of it?" Leon demanded, getting a certain note of authority into his voice.

Her fingers fluttered about the cloth, she turned her head aside. "The book is about Paris," she said quietly. "It tells of student life there."

"Well, you're too young to read such stuff," said Leon. "Girls of sixteen should read cook-books."

He received no answer to this.

"I ought to tell your aunt anyway," he went on. "Suppose you caught cold, suppose your aunt had to pay doctor bills? What do you say to that, Celia?"

"I'm eighteen," she answered. "You know very well I had my eighteenth birthday only two months ago. You yourself bought me some linen handkerchiefs."

This set Leon back a foot or two, but he recovered quickly. "Anyway, you stay up too late, maybe I'll tell your aunt about it, I'll have to think it over."

At the bird-cage, her small, slight figure half-turned away from him, she did not move. The splendid coil of heavy black hair on top of her head caught the light from the hall lamp. Then Leon thought about something, he cleared his throat.

The girl turned about, facing him frankly, and gave him a shy, pleasant glance.

He told her he had given up his position earlier in the day and asked her to pose for him for a portrait. "From now on, I'll have plenty of time to paint. I'll be able to sleep longer, too. That means you won't have to rap on my door at seven-thirty any more." He frowned. "Well, I'll speak to your aunt about your posing for a portrait, I'll think about it."

Clearing his throat, still frowning, he looked at her closely. She was smiling faintly, a dimple showing in each cheek. Her face was smooth, like pale ivory, and for the first time he noticed what a fine forehead she had. The light from the lamp came from the right and, unconsciously, he began studying the planes of her face. The only thing wrong with her was a certain frigidity about the mouth because she was very careful not to allow her lips to go all the way back when she smiled; one of her front teeth was broken off and the jagged stump of it glared right at you if she allowed it to show. Leon, at one time, had made a casual remark about the tooth and from then on, when she smiled at him, she only half-smiled, and this made her face appear a trifle frozen; it also gave her mouth a childish, appealing twist.

"Well, good night," said Leon. "If you want, you can ask your aunt's permission to pose for me. But you should have had your coat on this evening."

"Yes," she said, looking down. Her hands hung idle at her sides. When she heard him close his door on the floor above, she turned quickly and went into her room.

Leon lay in bed in the darkness, a free man, no job for a while. He had a strange, free feeling. Pretty soon he began thinking about the new comrade from New Orleans, that girl with the full figure and fine, blond hair, recalling the soft pressure of her hand and her blue, pleasant eyes, but before falling asleep his thoughts swung toward his friend the ex-poet, who he hoped would stop drinking, because cheap gin was driving the fellow to wrack and ruin.

## IV

AFTER LEON had left, Jason sat staring at a crack in the wall for a full five minutes, an empty glaze to his eyes. Then he pulled out his dollar watch and saw that it was after seven already. He put his old gray hat on, shoved his arms through the sleeves of his worn overcoat, stuck a cigarette between his lips, and clicked the light out.

On the second landing he lit his cigarette and tossed the match aside. A fellow lodger passing him, going up, called attention to the burning match, speaking sharply, and, with his own foot, stamped the glowing end out.

"Don't you know this house is a fire-trap?" he said, sore. "What do you want to do, burn us out of house and home?"

Jason walked down sullenly, paying no attention to the fellow. Reaching the street, he turned east, heading for his "source of supplies," the Crystal Lunchroom over on Third Avenue, where he had a charge account. The dull roar of the elevated thundered overhead. He hummed a rhyme:

"Roar, trains, roar away. The cow's in the pasture, the mice are in the hay."

Ahead were the lights of the Crystal Lunchroom. He came up and went inside. The smell of old frying hung low in the store. It was a long, narrow place, none too clean, a row of stools at the counter and fly specks all over the damp walls. Jason took a stool near the big twin coffee percolators.

Hearing the door bang, Pete eased out of the cook's quarters in the rear and came up. He was a little pockmarked Serbian, with dry, hanging mustaches, bowed in the legs and knock-kneed in the pocketbook. He had a special on tonight—liver and onions for 30c, two vegetables, tables for ladies. But no ladies ever came in. Still the sign outside inviting them was good advertising. In the day his trade was made up of laborers and casual passersby, in the evening the élite of the higher class Bowery gentry came in, sniffing at the food, just enough change in their pockets to pay the check, everything all figured out beforehand, before stepping into the place.

Pete poured a cup of coffee for Jason without waiting for an order. He shoved a dull, oily-looking spoon across the counter, then ran a thoughtful hand vaguely across the pockmarks of his leathered face. The pocks were about the size of small Swiss-cheese holes.

"How much do I owe you?" Jason asked, his mouth close to the warm thick rim of the cup.

Pete took a slip of paper from a nail, scratched his head, frowned, counted, and finally gave the amount. He never was very fast at addition. "Twenty-three dollar and eighty cents. It was twenty-three sixty-five last night, but you take a pack of Camels last night."

"All right," said Jason and tossed a yellowback on the counter. "This makes it ten dollars less."

Pete did a little more figuring, a little more scratching, took the yellow bill, straightened it carefully, put it into the cash register and stuck the paper on the nail again. He shoved a second cup of coffee across, grinning. "On the house," he said, wiping a greasy hand against the front of his greasy apron.

Jason, dumping two full spoons of sugar into the second cup, wondered how the hell he could kill the evening.

"What would happen," he said, "if a sudden wind would blow into this ancient tavern, whisking that slip of paper into oblivion? How about it, Pete?"

The Serbian laughed and clawed thoughtfully, gently at the cheese holes of his leathered face. "No such wind she strong enough, Mister Wheeler. This New York, not Balkan mountains. Ha, ha, ha." He had a sharp, dry laugh, like a bark.

"I'm just warning you," frowned Jason. "I'm not rich, I'm not poor, just go along enjoying myself with my small circle of friends. What kind of a car do you drive, Pete?"

"Ha, ha, ha." The skinny, little Serbian laughed again, sniffing meanwhile to find out if the cook back in the rear was allowing the onions to fry too long.

The front door opened, and James Nicholson, the cracked printer, came in, carrying a new sign under his arm. The left side of his face was twitching slightly, he stared a trifle pop-eyed as he handed the package to the Serbian.

"I'll be back later," he said hurriedly. "I'm working on a document, I'll be back later." The door banged behind him, he was going up Third Avenue already.

With slow, thoughtful fingers, the Serbian opened the package and at last, taking the string and paper away, bared to view a fine square of pure white heavy cardboard. Lettering in old-fashioned type stood out sharp and clear:

> **Eat Today
> Tomorrow You Die**

Standing on top of a box, the Serbian drove a tack into the dirty wall, hung the clean card near the stack of coffee cups, then stood off ten paces or so to get a view of it. He grinned proudly at the ex-poet.

"That man, maybe he a bit nuts, but he make fine signs, Mister Wheeler. He make this lunchroom what you call the class!"

Jason, still sitting on the stool, stared at a big fat cockroach crawling toward a bowl of doughnuts, finished his cup of coffee, waved his hand at Pete, and headed north for Fourteenth Street.

Harsh lights blazed on all sides there. The shrills and the shouts of hawkers, the rattle of the venders' carts blended hoarsely. In the stalls fountains were squirting orange juice, flapjacks turned somersaults in lunchroom windows, and the big banners above the vaudeville show billowed in the wind. The ex-poet hummed a tune: "On Fourteenth Street the bugles blow; blow, bugles, blow, oh, blow."

In front of the Academy of Music, a towering building specializing in feature pictures accompanied by eight big-time acts of vaudeville continuous from morn till midnight, matinee 25c, evenings 50c, someone slapped Jason briskly on the back and, turning, he saw who it was—Sam Kugel, a pulp writer, a lad who wrote under the high-class name of Gerald Pennington.

They stood talking awhile, discussing the literary racket, getting the lowdown on ways and means of their trade and craft.

"I'm writing wild westerns now," said Kugel. He was a fat-faced young man with a plump nose sticking saucily forth at you like a little bulge on a big potato. "I get a cent a word, but you gotta knock the stuff out fast, the editors change quick these days."

"What's your latest opus?" asked Jason, his glance straying. In front of the pool hall entrance a girl was talking to eight fellows, two of the boys had their faces close to hers, arguing, urging; she had fine legs.

" 'Gunsmoke on the Range.' A good title, I calls it."

"Aye. Good enough," said Jason and hardly listened while his friend rattled on. The smell of mustard was in the air, the wind swept the aroma swiftly from the hot-dog stand a few doors east. Finally Kugel (Gerald Pennington to his vast army of loyal readers) hooked Jason's arm and, still talking about the literary racket, sandwiched in the remark, "I'm on my way to a little blow-out down on Bleeker Street, I'm taking you along, you don't need an invitation."

Jason did not want to go. "I'm not rich, I'm not poor, just go along enjoying myself with my small circle of friends."

Kugel didn't get it. He argued some more with his friend, but Jason had long since tired of Village parties. Finally Kugel walked off alone, waving his hand, looking back over his shoulder, smiling and half-shouting something which Jason failed to hear.

Jason strolled on, passing the lobby of the theater. He kept near the curbing and every so often spat out slime and phlegm; he was all choked up inside. The big bulk of the new Salvation Army Building cast a shadow three blocks long, covering all the buildings in its path with a black swath.

At Seventh Avenue and Fourteenth Street, Jason, feeling more clogged inside than ever, struck his breast four or five times, little, thumping blows. He swallowed slowly and exploringly, alert for any new sensation. He turned south, walked down Seventh Avenue and at Twelfth turned east because Eleventh was a blind street at Broadway. He was going past the second entrance of Saint Vincent's Hospital when he saw a large, empty, lighted room with a nurse in uniform sitting at a desk. Without thinking, he opened the door and went inside.

The nurse raised her eyes.

"Can I see the doctor?" Jason asked.

"Doctor who?"

"Something is wrong with my chest or lungs. I came in to see the doctor," Jason said.

"But this is no clinic," the girl explained, looking at him.

He stood quiet.

"What's wrong with you?" She saw he looked a trifle shabby. A cigarette dangled from his mouth and, when he raised a hand to take it out, she noted the fingers darkly yellowed from the nicotine.

"I've been spitting a lot," he told her. "It's my chest."

"Here, wait a minute," she said and picked up the telephone receiver. She called up the charge-nurse and spoke quickly into the mouthpiece. "A young man here wants to see a doctor about his lungs, it may be an urgent case."

Jason stood by listening. The large bare room was clean and silent as the charge-nurse at the other end of the wire answered. Jason could hear, faintly, little murmurs coming from the receiver. The nurse hung up, reached in a drawer, took out a card and began asking questions.

Jason gave her his name, his address, and, when she

asked his occupation, he answered queerly. "I'm not rich, I'm not poor, just go along enjoying myself with my small circle of friends."

The nurse, a healthy-looking, lively-eyed kid who was new at nursing, let out a laugh. It was the first let-down of her professional front.

Just then the phone rang. "Yes?" she said, her face going business-like again, her voice rising briskly. Jason, feeling a huge, wet, sagging knot somewhere in his chest, swallowed painfully. The nurse hung up. She looked very sorry.

"The charge-nurse just phoned me that no doctor is available. She said if it's a lung case it can wait until morning."

"But for crissake, I'm sick!" said Jason. "I'm a sick man!"

"But what can *I* do?" the nurse said, getting agitated, biting her lip. "I only work here."

Then Jason calmed down. "I guess I'm all right," he said quietly and started for the door.

The nurse jumped up and called him back; something about the fellow moved her very strongly. She was a young girl from upstate, and as yet the chill brutality of a big hospital did not have a powerful grip upon her. While Jason stood waiting, she went over to the cabinet, reached for wooden spoons, swabbing sticks, cotton, and a liquid she said was good for slime-clogged throats. She shoved the supplies into his hands. "Here, take them, go before someone comes in."

"I guess I'm all right now," said Jason and started for the door again. It closed quietly behind him. At the curb he spat out a large, heavy piece of slime. Then, looking up and down the silent hospital street, he let the supplies fall downward into the gutter.

At the window, her faced glued to the glass, the nurse saw everything, and she almost felt like crying.

Jason headed east, reached the tenement, and started climbing up the five flights of stairs to his quarters, the "ex-poet's abode," as he jokingly wrote in his "memoirs," which were the backs of rejection slips he received from various magazines.

# V

NEXT DOOR, at the Glen Cove Apartments, Mr. Andre Franconi, who lived on the floor below the young "Russian" couple, was sitting at the table, writing to Florina who was out in California getting beaten up regularly by her husband who, she wrote, was making more money than ever in the grape business but was growing shorter of temper day by day. For the third time Mr. Franconi read Florina's letter. Back in Italy, many years ago, he and Florina had once been betrothed.

Andre, I cry five times a day, give the priest all my money, say twenty Ave Marias every morning, and pray to the blessed Virgin all night long. I pray to the Virgin that Joe will change, that he will be a good man from now on, that he will not beat me and the children any more. Andre, back in Bessano it was not like this. Remember how we used to follow the carts to Roveredo and Filtres. Sometimes we even went as far as Vittorio. Your uncle was a good man, Andre, but he should not have looked down on our troth. He had plenty of land, but my parents did not ask for fields. Two of the bambinis are crying and the sun is very hot here. We have been here in California for three years now, and every day Joe speaks your name and he says it with a curse. I tell him you are thousands of miles away, that you live in New York and that you don't know where we're at, but still he swears. Mother of God! Ten devils are in his bowels. He gets drunk on his own grapes and goes through the house breaking up the furniture we got from the mail-order house in San Francisco. Ai, Andre, back in Bessano it was not like this. Even if we could not marry there, it would be better than this. Don't wait so long to answer my letters, Andre. At the post office no one suspects. I tell the Mexican girl to ask for mail for Rosa Pinorio and the clerk gives her your letters. Rosa Pinorio, remember her? She was the oldest lady in the village when we were little children. I send the servant twice a week and pray that you will not stop writing. Andre, say more in your letters. It is six years since I am in America and thirteen since I have seen you. You did not meet me at the boat, I have never been able to understand it. I think about Bessano every hour of the day. I pray all night long to the blessed Virgin. A mother of three children should not feel like this, but it is fate, Andre. If it were not for your letters I would throw myself down the mountains. Tomorrow, when the priest comes again, I will give him all the money I have saved during the week. I have already given him my mother's ring, my sister's crucifix, and the gold earrings from my grandfather. All I have left is the silver medallion you gave me before you left Bessano and that I shall never part with. It hangs between my breasts every minute of the day when Joe is not in the house. Andre, answer this letter soon. My tears have formed a stream going down the mountains. Write more pages to me. I have cried so many nights now. God will forgive me, a sinful woman, for thinking of you night and day.

With respectful wishes,<br>
FLORINA.

He stared at the written Italian, at the fine flowing hand, and for a long while sat there trying to write an answer to her letter.

In the end he wrote the old, old words, repeating almost phrase for phrase what he had written in previous letters, telling her to be patient, that he thought often of her, that her three children could not be cast aside now. He tried to make his letter very sensible, but not too matter of fact. He knew she was a patient woman who wrote impatient letters and told her that with time many things could happen.

He himself, though only thirty-five, was already a spent man. And as he wrote he wondered what she would think of him if she knew how recklessly he had squandered his youth, if she knew that, though he still made a fine appearance and dressed in well-cut clothes, he made weekly visits to a doctor and only a month ago had received an injection of mercury at the base of his spine.

He sealed the letter and fixed a stamp upon it. So many words, so many years now lay between them. Standing up, he went into the bathroom, where he stood a long time before the mirror over the sink, feeling the sides of his face. It was an old habit that many barbers had. He stroked the sides of his face slowly, exploringly. He was a tall, handsome man, a little distant about the eyes, and had fine black hair combed smoothly back. He looked like a gentleman. His eyes were black and shining—the perfect Latin type—but when you looked closer you saw that the pupils burned steadily with a strange, dull fire.

Down at the Wall Street barber shop, where he worked, the manicure girls wondered why he did not look their way like the other boys in the place, until one of the girls said that Andre must have a sweetheart back in Italy and "some wops, they're pretty straight when it comes to things of this nature, sister."

## VI

OUT IN THE HALL, passing Mr. Franconi's door, the young "Russian" couple who lived on the floor above were returning from a little East Side shopping tour.

"Forgive me, Natasha," said the husband as he dropped a round loaf of black bread before the apartment door. He was a fat little man, very short in the leg but big in the face and was slightly afraid of his slim blond wife. When they entered their flat, Natasha (this was not her real name but an acquisition of some eight or ten months, ever since they had passed a Russian *objets d'art* store, read *The Cherry Orchard* and had gone bag and baggage over to the Russian front) set the groceries smartly down upon the table and stared hard at her little hubsand.

"Forgive me, Natasha," he said again, trying to get a good Russian feeling into his voice, trying to talk like a character out of Gogol, "forgive me. I shouldn't have dropped it, I was very clumsy, forgive me, my own."

Natasha frowned. She was a little Nordic about it because she came from Scandinavian ancestry, but she did the best she could.

"All right, Vanya, I forgive you. Now put the tea to boil."

The fat little man took his coat off briskly, struck a match, had the gas stove going, and reached for the black tea purchased at the Russian store over on Second Avenue, not the tea on the first shelf bought at the chain store.

Then they got set to spend a "Russian" evening together—Mr. and Mrs. Otto Drollinger at home, Vanya and Natasha to each other, in their snug retreat away from the harshness of the bustling world.

They nibbled on caviar sandwiches, drank hot tea from tall glasses, and later on Natasha, reclining upon the sofa, started reading from Turgenev, from a tale called "Knock, Knock, Knock." She was a copywriter for a Bronx department store, writing copy for the bargain basement, and sometimes had a yearning to do real literary stuff. Reading on, savoring the rise and fall of the flawless prose, she sighed in the pauses and stopped to gaze into space, drinking in the beauty of the Russian scene. On the mantelpiece were arrayed Russian knickknacks, a pair of wooden candlesticks direct from Khartov, and above that an ikon hung against the wall. There was also, the latest addition, a miniature troika, with man and horse and all, the forelegs of the steed flying on in silent thunder, the muzhik swinging and cracking his whip in the air. The thing was about twelve inches long and brightly painted.

Vanya, seated on a small three-legged stool direct from Odessa (that's what the salesman had said, but on the bottom of the stool some writing had been scratched out), stared dreamily ahead, thinking of his job. From deep within his large Teutonic heart there flowed the waters of his mild nature.

"Natasha," he said, finally thinking of the events of the day, "Natasha, my boss Mr. Cushing is a nonentity." The surging speed of the flying troika upon the mantelpiece gave his mind a heroic pace. "A nonentity," he repeated, remembering how fond the Russians were of that honored word. "Just think, Natasha, he had me make a layout in three colors, I worked at it like a peasant all day, and in the afternoon, when I brought it to his desk, he smiled and said it was too artistic. 'What I need is an advertisement for this new model ash-can,' said he. So what was I to do, Natasha? After all, he is the barin of the place, a stupid one, my love. So I worked another drawing out, in charcoal, made it in fifteen minutes but didn't take it up to him until it was time to go home. And what do you think he said of the new drawing, Natasha? Ah, you should have been there, he even placed his hand upon my shoulder, the fine barin did. 'Great,' says he, 'I'll send it to the engravers the first thing in the morning,' and then he gives my back a pat."

Natasha, half-listening, half-thinking of Turgenev's flowing prose, whispered softly, "You are a great artist, Vanya."

But Vanya, hearing, puckered up his lips and frowned. "But what does it gain me, Natasha? My good work they smile at, the trash I do, they like. Believe me, my dove, that Mr. Cushing, for all he's the barin of the place, he's just a nonentity." And with his hands moving for emphasis he made his point again.

"Listen, Vanya," said Natasha, and she read a passage from the book . . . winter in Moscow . . . snow on the streets . . . the bells of troikas ringing . . . students home from school . . .

But Vanya continued to mumble. "Nonentity."

In the square the radios were still going in the doorways, there was no more competition because the phonographs from the 9c record shops had shut their horns. The blazing lights flashed on and off: "THE FLAVOR LASTS," "SAVE NOW," "4%," "KLEIN'S, ON THE SQUARE." At the north side of Fourteenth Street the windows of the darkened buildings caught the glare and gave back dull reflections, like the filmed eyes of the blind beggars who trod the sidewalks during the day. The airways beacon on top of the public utilities building stuck like a horizontal needle into the sky, warning or informing our faithful aviators that Fourteenth Street was no landing field. Doors banged and slammed, the taxi-dancing jazzbands blared away. In the big armory over near Sixth Avenue (two old cannon out in front, their black muzzles pointing to the sky), the National Guard lads were taking off their uniforms and going to the showers after a two-hour drill; some of them discussed the coming boxing bouts, soaping up their armpits.

"Natasha," Vanya said in bed, talking to her Nordic back, "that assistant manager, that fellow who you said works in the next department to you, does he still look your way, does he still try to talk to you?"

And Natasha answered, it was the old, old plaint. She was tired and sleepy and the tea had given her a nice warm feeling.

"It's you I love, little Vanya," she said, her words running together, her eyelids sticking fast. "It's you, little Vanya . . ." but did not finish.

Vanya listened for more, but no further words came. So, giving a soft, little grunt to himself, he rolled over in a comfortable position, heaved a drawn-out sigh, and closed his faithful eyes and went to sleep. If the people of this world would realize that we are all brothers and sisters and really do love each other what a wonderful world this would be.

Across the hall, in the Boardman apartment, an argument was springing up.

## VII

MR. BOARDMAN, the man with the iron-gray mustache who took a small dog out for a short walk every night, stood silent as the young woman he lived with dragged him thoroughly over the coals. Watching her trim figure as she strode nervously up and back, he endured in silence, wondering, in a small corner of his brain, just why he went on living with her. After their six months of fairly quiet living together, she was now beginning to show the shadier side of her nature.

"You should have wrapped that woolen covering around Dodo before you took him out," the young woman said harshly. "I suppose you wanted the pup to die, to kick the bucket, so that I'd be all alone in the flat and go nuts just hanging around. Maybe you could collect on his life insurance then, Boardie." She smiled grimly and stood hard and firm, facing him.

Mr. Boardman went to stare from the front-room windows, his back toward the young woman. Across the street the lights of Webster Hall were blazing, a big ball was being held there. Drawn up in a long file, like a line of hearses, stood a row of cabs, and, as each taxi received a fare, rolling away, the long file moved forward, creeping slowly up the street.

As he listened to the words spoken at his back, Mr.

Boardman felt very old, although for fifty he was a finely preserved man and made a rather distinguished appearance; he had good, trim, wide shoulders, was of medium height, had a head of cropped iron-gray hair, and wore conservative clothes. His gray mustache, neatly clipped, gave him the look of a broker, or a vice-president in one of the smaller banks. He had a good position with a large manufacturer of marine engines.

"The next time you take Dodo out, see that he's warm," the young woman said, and when he half-turned toward her she placed the burning end of her cigarette against the polished arm of a fine, expensive chair, extinguishing it. "Do you hear me?" She raised her voice.

To keep her quiet (he was afraid the neighbors were already talking), he answered, turning his back toward her again, thinking of his sixteen-year-old daughter whom he had sent away to a Massachusetts finishing school almost a year ago.

"All right, Margie," he said quietly.

"All right, and don't forget it." Reaching down, starting to murmur, she lifted up the small dog, cuddled it, and began whispering into its silken ears. She stroked the dog's soft, brown, curly hair. "My 'ittle Dodo, my 'ittle, 'ittle Dodo, is you warm now, is you 'ittle better-better now, Dodo?" The dog responded with a sharp, tiny yap and was kissed upon its moist nose for reward.

Down upon the street an auto honked, and the long file of cabs moved slowly forward again. A big Negro doorman, dressed like an admiral of a South American navy, stood near the entrance and blew his whistle for another cab to move on up. Mr. Boardman, watching from the window, wondered how it would all end. Sometimes he wanted very much to be free of her, she was the devil incarnate, but at other times she could be sweet and nice and it was a pleasure to have her at his side. He had met her at a swanky speakeasy, where she had been employed as a hostess, and when he had first started taking her out she had been sweet and melting enough for anybody.

He stood there thinking, his back toward her, staring down at the tops of the taxis. Pretty soon she began to relent; she started talking baby-talk, addressing the dog in her arms, but in reality aiming her words at him. He understood. He saw through it but felt hollowed out and did not care to show an iron front. Speaking with a sugared sweetness, patting the small dog and stroking back its ears, she finally coaxed Mr. Boardman next to her upon the sofa; and only when he was sitting beside her, only when he held her in his arms and began kissing her passive face, did he realize how strong a hold she had upon him, how much he really needed her. The firm feel of her youthful body, the quiet expertness of her kisses, the smell of her drove everything else from his mind. She held his face between her cool, calm palms and kissed him slowly.

He knew he was a fool; he was fifty years old and had had a wife who had been an angel compared to this hard, brittle, young woman. But the fires of his autumn were flaring up in him, the last fuel was burning in his body; he was a widower in good health who had always led a quiet, well-regulated life, and now he had taken a gamble.

To taunt him a bit, the young woman took his gray, aristocratic head between her hands and pretended, in a soothing voice, that she was really sorry he was growing old. He was sensitive about his age, because he was not really an old man, but he sat quiet in her arms, hoping she would stop her game. She murmured on. She spoke about his white hair, about the fine lines at the corners of his eyes, kissed him gently on each cheek, and in the end pulled his ears playfully, waggishly.

"It's not really white yet," she said with feeling, running her hand slowly over his hair, stroking it. "It's not really white." She kissed his cheek again, gently.

No, it wasn't white. It was gray, iron-gray, she knew that well enough. Lately her game had taken on a more calculating and well-timed cruelty. He sat in silence, something inside of him going dead and dry.

"Where are we going to eat tomorrow evening?" she asked.

"Anywhere you like," he answered. "We can go to that place on Fifty-First Street, I still have the card to admit us."

"But I'm tired of that joint, darling. We were there twice already, dear."

"We'll find some other place to go," he said.

Then she began talking about a pair of shoes she had seen in a Fifth Avenue shop window, an eighteen-dollar pair, but they were so fine to look at, really. She stroked his ears, using the same gentle tug and pull she used on the dog. He told her he'd give her the money for them, and she cuddled closer, patting his face, calling him a dear and giving his cheek small, quick kisses.

Then she got up and stretched her arms. It was getting late, it must be near midnight, she said. He himself rose from the sofa, thought a while, then said he was going out to buy the morning paper. "I won't be gone long, dear," he said. She objected a little, murmuring that she did not want him to leave her, but there was no conviction in her voice.

"I want to get a look at the *Times*," he said, putting on his hat and reaching for his coat and cane. As he was with a big manufacturing company whose stock was quoted on the curb, this reason sounded fairly reasonable. He turned the doorknob carefully and went out. In the last few weeks he had started taking short walks late at night, to quiet his nerves.

Opening the entrance door below, he met Mr. Franconi who had just returned from mailing a letter. Both men greeted and nodded neighborlily at each other.

"The night is fine," said Mr. Franconi, his words faintly tipped with an Italian accent.

"The afternoon paper said it might be cloudy," answered Mr. Boardman.

Mr. Boardman strolled up the empty street toward Union Square. The lights from Webster Hall shone on his back until he turned the corner. He wore a fine, dark overcoat. Breathing the cold air, walking up a deserted street with only an occasional auto hurrying up Fourth Avenue, was very pleasant and, as he drew in a few deep breaths, he had a feeling of health and well-being. His stride took on a brisk jauntiness and he tapped the sidewalk with the tip of his cane now and then. No, he wasn't an old man by any means; his eyes were clear and alert, his step was strong. His glance, swinging from right to left, took in the view of the second-hand book stores, noted the piles of volumes stacked inside the darkened shops, and before one or two of the store-fronts he stopped to read a few titles. Then he walked on.

The square was quiet. A few of the advertising signs were still lit up, but most of them were already dark. He took a turn about the square, following the low, thick wall. Then he retraced his steps toward the apartment and only when he stood before the entrance, fishing for his key, did he remember that he had forgotten the paper.

He turned and walked toward the square again, a trifle irritated.

Then he returned for the second time, the paper under his arm. He slipped the key into the lock and climbed the stairs and, as he came closer and closer to the apartment door, the thoughts of his sixteen-year-old daughter crowded him and he wondered what she would think of him, if she knew the truth, if she knew he was living with someone.

Finally he stood before the door. The climb had tired him just a little. He shuffled the sheets, mussed the paper a little, then came inside. He was careful to click on the small table lamp, the one in a distant corner, because Margie did not like a sudden light to shine into the bedroom. He took his hat and coat off, laid his cane aside, and crinkled the paper so that it made a slight sound.

"Is that you, dear?" came from the bedroom, vague and dreamy, like in the talking pictures.

He answered, taking his shirt off, walking quietly about the room as his fingers tugged at the firm knot of his necktie. He was standing near the rear window when he raised his head and saw, in the next building, a light burning on the fifth floor; the figure of a man sitting reading near the window was outlined there.

It was Jason, but he was not reading. He was sitting in a chair with a newspaper on his lap and was coughing almost silently, spitting slime upon the printed sheets he held.

# VIII

A HALF-HOUR LATER the long file of cabs in front of Webster Hall had dwindled down to three. The tall Negro doorman took things easy and went to stand at the curb, talking to one of the taxi drivers, laughing with a cackle at the white man's jokes. Then he went inside the hall, surveyed the scene, saw the orchestra putting away their instruments, and went outside to tell the lads at the wheels that the ball was over.

Two cabs drove away, one remained. In a few minutes a couple in evening dress came out and stepped into the waiting taxi. The driver looked straight ahead, in the Park Avenue manner, while the Negro held the door open; before the cab rolled off the doorman poked his head up in front of the car, as if to tell the chauffeur the passengers' destination, and whispered quickly about a private matter: "That's another two bits you owe me, brother, for chasing those two cars away."

The driver, his head still straight ahead, nodded stiffly, shifted gears, and the cab swung away from the curb.

Fifteen minutes later the front of the building was dark, all lights had been extinguished. In the middle of the block a lone arc lamp shone down the street. A few blocks south, men were sleeping on the Bowery, huddled in the cold doorways.

Fog came in from the harbor. On the river, boats began calling to each other. You could faintly hear the foghorns in the square. The bronze statues became a trifle damp and a small drop of moisture gathered at the tip of Lafayette's heroic sword. The dim lights from the scattered lamps shone dully on the broad brow of Lincoln and gave off subdued highlights from the staunch, swelling buttocks of George Washington's powerful charger. Time wore on.

The cop walked his beat, following the low, thick wall, none other than Officer Terence McGuffy, who was famous up and down Fourteenth Street for a certain classic utterance and also for his thorough knowledge of the Russian situation in general.

The square was silent, he walked along. Coming to the south end of the little park, he crossed over and covered the Fourteenth Street side, ever mindful of a certain statement in the book of the Policeman's Code: "At all times a patrolman should discharge faithfully his duty." He flashed his searchlight into the doorways of shops and stores.

But when he reached the Acme Theater he paused a while, to gather more knowledge about the Russian situation. The Acme Theater (matinee 15c, evenings 30c) was a small show devoted to the showing of Soviet films, and it was by careful glancing at the photos displayed in front and also the reading matter tacked onto the billboards that Office McGuffy had first begun acquiring the extensive knowledge of Russian affairs which made him highly respected by his fellow officers.

He scanned the billboards, flashing his searchlight upon the prints displayed. "TEN DAYS THAT SHOOK THE WORLD, *continuous from 11 a. m. to 11:30 p. m.*"

Then he resumed his beat. He was patrolling the east side of the square when he noticed a little, hurrying figure moving in front of him. At first he became suspicious and alert, then he chuckled to himself. He knew who it was—just another nut, a little geezer with a few screws loose in the head.

McGuffy strolled on, his glance on the figure which was moving rapidly in the fog. When he had come a ways, still following, he looked a bit sharper and saw what appeared to be large, square snowflakes fluttering to the street.

The little gent ahead was throwing handfuls of cards

into the air—white squares the size of good-sized marshmallows. He threw with energy, his arms going like an excited speaker's addressing a large audience.

Officer McGuffy came up to the first card and picked it from the street. He began frowning as he read.

> **There Can Be No Peace**

The cards were finely printed, the old-fashioned type stood out sharp and clear from the white background.

"A nut," pronounced McGuffy, flipping the card away, peering into the fog ahead. "Just another nut." Last week the cards had said: MAN'S DESTINY IS WAR.

McGuffy frowned again. "A nut, that's all he is, maybe I ought to run him in." He swung his nightstick, just for the exercise of it, and as he began covering the north side of the square again he saw the small, hurrying figure of the demented printer far ahead, and then he lost him in the fog.

By this time it was half-past one and the ninety-eight clocks in the windows of Ross's Klock Korner (formerly Korn's Klock Korner) began striking the half hour, the big metal ones bonging away in a stately fashion, the tiny wooden ones going pick-pack-puck in a very modest manner indeed.

# TWO

**I**

THE MORNING broke damp and chill. The gray fog which had settled down during the night did not lift as usual. Traffic swept around the square. Long before the doors of Klein's Dress Store opened, crowds of women and girls had gathered. Private policemen in gray uniforms tried to keep order at about nine-thirty, because at that time all the doors were unlocked and the women swept forward in a powerful surge, grabbing at the dresses on the racks, searching and clawing for bargains. It was cash down here, "on the Square," each woman held her money in her fist.

Near the curbing, along Fourth Avenue, ran the subway grating, with dank heat flowing up. Women did not like to stand there, as the warm draft blew their skirts up, but the men did not seem to mind; there was always a gang of them gaping and grinning and nudging, waiting for unsuspecting dames to walk across the ironwork.

With the first crack of daylight the parade of the Fourteenth Street beggars began. There were legless fellows; blind men who held onto small, faithful dogs; deformed, cleanly shaven fellows who wore army shirts and overseas hats to give a good "ex-service" effect; an old hag with scabby cheeks; a Negro boy who twitched horribly, allowing saliva to dribble over his chin, and all kinds of wrecked bits of humanity.

It was a busy thoroughfare, but there was room for all. The bootblacks—old men and young men—stood two or three yards apart, leaning against the low wall surrounding the square, and as you passed they called out (some briskly, others in a hollow, tired tone of voice) and pointed toward your shoes. "Shine 'em up five cents, shine 'em up five cents," they said. There were also young men and boys who peddled songs printed on big, square sheets of paper, songs that told you all about the silver lining and how to chase the blues away. And further down were the high-pressure boys, the lads who spat and hawked their wares at you, offering, for your consideration, socks, bars of candy, twenty-five-cent neckties ("they're worth two bucks apiece, mister, honest to Christ!"), shoelaces, needles for the lady of the house, and little Japanese toys to tickle the kiddies' fancy. But the cleverest lads of all were the fellows who sold worthless watches out of small, black leather bags, one eye out for passing suckers, the other on the policeman down the street.

The noise was terrific, everything was bedlam. Folks crossed the street against the traffic and were shouted at by our vigilant police. Everywhere you turned a vender shoved an object under your nose, yelling, screaming, urging you to buy. Some even clutched you by the arm, others followed you a way with whining voices; and on all sides stood the pretzels, stacked up on long, upright sticks, trundled along by old women and men wheeling mangled baby-buggies.

Barkers stood in front of almost every store, like at a circus, rattling off the bargain prices of fur pieces, shoes and dresses hot from the marts of fashion, pointing to the goods in the windows. In their second-floor windows one of the bigger fur stores had six or seven manikins walking around in small circles, young girls with heavy make-up on their faces, modeling cloaks and fur pieces. A small crowd of idle men stood on the street below and made comments concerning the scenery above.

At ten o'clock most of the movie houses opened up, greeting the citizenry with a burst of electric lights in the box-office windows. Bargain prices were offered before noon, at the "early bird" matinee, and long lines of people, mostly men and girls out of work and a few who had night jobs, shoved their dimes through the "How Many?" window and went inside, into the warmth and the darkness.

Later on, on the corner of Irving Place, which was just a short distance from the square, the barker from the burlesk show swung into action. Every day he donned another costume. He was a small, hook-nosed gent and had a dry, hoarse way of shouting, as if his throat was lined with coal dust. Yesterday he wore a pirate costume, now he stood in a clown's outfit, his cheeks painted a sickly white, his great red grinning mouth standing from his face as raw as a fresh veal cutlet.

"Girls, girls," he shouted, "fifty bee-ootiful girls, men . . . dancing, singing, shaking . . . all young and easy to look at . . . smoking in loges, get along, folks, the show starts soon, you can't afford to miss this great, glittering, stoo-pendous array of bee-ootiful girls . . ."

The damp wind blew through his flimsy costume, he stuck another cough-drop into his mouth. "Girls, girls . . ." and his words go floating toward your back as you pass him by.

Down the street the radio-phonograph feud had already started up, an everyday occurrence. Over the doorways stand horns and from these horns the news and racket from the world goes forth—blaring out upon the street, prize-fight returns, Spanish music, and how to make a pudding out of two cups of flour and a pound of Sonny Boy oatmeal.

This is no place for quarter. Each man steps upon his comrade, some tread lightly, others crush you with their heavy boots. And centered between the sets of car tracks stand the policemen, the officers of the law—big fellows with white gloves on their mitts, their outdoor faces the color of a good grade of juicy beef, and when they raise their regal palms the traffic halts, stands still like a slack conveyor belt, awaiting the sharp slit of the whistle.

Swarm after swarm of heads pass, wave on wave, all kinds of nationalities, the true melting pot of the town. Little dark Cuban women, big black Negresses from Jamaica, tony little kept women from West Side apartment houses, tall lanky Swedish girls with washed-out faded eyes, sturdy Polish housewives carrying big shopping bags —all crowd into the bargain stores and shove and push and jam near the counters. The salesgirls, kids who get twelve dollars a week, stand tired against the onrush, answering questions about the merchandise with dead, slack mouths, glancing at the clock often, putting on a brisk, alert front whenever the floor manager takes a casual stroll up and down the aisles.

Six days a week the swirl goes on. But within the square itself, it's quiet. A few bums and seedy unemployed sit huddled on the benches, staring at the cliffs of buildings, gazing at the sea of passing heads. From a cold, gray sky a wind comes sniffing at their bones. 4%, says the sign over the Amalgamated Bank. The flavor lasts.

And the flagpole, like a tremendous carpet tack, sticks its point into the windy sky.

## II

JASON WHEELER, ex-poet and former student of world affairs, walked down the five flights of the tenement to find out what the mailman had brought today. When he reached the doorway, where a long file of rusty tin boxes stood in a crooked row, he stuck his fingers into one of them, found nothing, looked at the others, and decided to wait until the mailman arrived.

Across the street the kids were already lining up in front of the Catholic school, their books in their hands. They stood in a long file, two deep, the boys on one side, the girls on the other, while a few sisters, in trailing black habits, kept order and smiled gently at the kids. A few minutes before nine o'clock, when the school bell was ready to ring, a young father in long black robes came to stand at the top of the flight of stairs, the damp wind ruffling his garments. He was a very tall young man with a long, sleek face and had narrow shoulders. The wind, pressing his robes against his body, showed you he was pot-bellied; and this was startling, he was so tall and thin. The bell finally rang. The kids moved meekly up the stairs into the school, the black-hooded sisters following gently in the rear. The last one shut the door.

Jason, standing in the doorway of the tenement, stared up the street toward Fourth Avenue, where a horde of men were collected in front of the cooks-and-waiters' agencies. They were standing along the curb, talking and smoking, though they knew there were no jobs upstairs.

A man came out of Webster Hall, a business-like gleam in his eyes. He was the porter, and he knew a thing or two. He came lugging a ladder, spread its legs, propped it solidly against the sidewalk, and climbed up to the top like a nimble monkey. He was a little, wiry fellow. In his hand he held a slip of paper; it was his duty to change the changeable sign for the new ball to be held tonight. From a long wooden box he took out some letters, shuffled others on the sign, glanced often at the paper for reference and at last cocked his head to one side, regarding his handiwork with a bright, proud eye: "FIRST ANNUAL DANCE OF THE SECOND AVENUE ARISTOCRATS MUSIC BY PROFESSOR A. B. NUDDLEBAUM AND HIS GOLD COAST BOYS."

A train of elevated cars roared by on Third Avenue. The janitress of the tenement (she called herself the housekeeper) hove into sight, a fat old dame with a heart as big as her bulging stomach. She waddled forth from the dimness of the hallway and stood alongside the ex-poet, a bright, expectant gleam in her ancient eyes, waiting for him to say good-morning. She was fond of Jason, the old girl was. Once she had offered to sew buttons on his shirts, and the last time he was sick she had puffingly climbed the five flights to his quarters carrying hot chicken broth for him.

"Good morning," she said at last, her old cheeks shaking like an alderman's.

And Jason answered.

"Waiting for the Jolly Postman?" she asked, smiling or grinning (take your pick).

The ex-poet frowned. That Jolly Postman business had been of his own invention, he had nicknamed the flat-

footed mailman on a morning when he had received a
thirty-dollar check, with the old dame standing by. She
stood there now, leaning on her broom, her old shoes
cracked, her left stocking coming down. On her chin was
a bit of the yellow from a fried egg.

In the next building the door of the Glen Cove Apartments opened and Mr. Boardman came out, gray-faced,
hurriedly, a worried look under his eyes. He had shaved
a bit too close this morning and had put too much talcum
on his cheeks. The janitress, in admiration, stared at his
trim, well-tailored back.

"That's the fine-looking gentleman who takes a little
doggie out for a walk every night," she told Jason. "He
don't seem so happy, does he, Mister Wheeler?"

The ex-poet spat toward the curb, aiming thoughtfully.
"Maybe he hasn't got a small circle of friends," he said.

The old janitress, who could never figure out just what
Mister Wheeler was saying but who liked him just the
same, giggled a couple of hee-hee's and shifted weight as
she leaned upon her broom.

A few minutes later Mr. Franconi came forth from the
same door and again the old woman, in admiration, stared
after him. She was fond of trim-looking gentlemen, the
old girl was. "Another fine man," she said. "He looks
something like Rudolph Valentino, don't you think?"

But at this juncture the big garbage truck came up
the street, with a crew of men heaving and slinging cans,
grunting as they lifted, sighing as they tossed the empty
cans down with an offhand bang. When the crew emptied
the cans of the tenement, the old janitress, puffing, took
them down into the basement, using the sidewalk entrance.
She lifted the wooden lid which gave out upon the street
and dragged the cans down. Then she came up again

and stood next to Jason, waiting for the Jolly Postman.

Up the street came a young couple, glancing at the fronts of buildings, looking for rooms—a swarthy, low-browed fellow and a tall, well-built girl with blond hair. They had passed the tenement when the janitress suddenly remembered that she had some rear rooms for rent; she called, but the couple were too far away. Then she went back into the hallway, came out with a "For Rent" sign and hung it on a nail. "Maybe they'll come back," she said.

Again the door of the Glen Cove Apartments opened. The young "Russian" couple came out. Both looked business-like now, the little fellow had to hurry a bit to keep up to his slim, blond wife who had longer legs than he had. He moved his stumpy legs rapidly and clutched at his large black hat, a hat fit for a swashbuckler, a lid with a lot of dash to it. From the rear, his coat tails flying, he made a comical appearance.

"Artists," snorted the janitress, a sensitive soul. "That black hat of his! There was a time, Mister Wheeler, when this neighborhood had only working people, now it's lousy with phony folk. Artists, phony people, I calls them. No red blood in their veins, the neighborhood is going down, Mister Wheeler."

"Aye. It'll hit the basement any minute now, Missus Atkins."

At last the Jolly Postman came, a heavy man getting old, his wide, flat feet slapping the pavement as he trudged, plowing on. Where the strap from his back rubbed against the left shoulder the cloth of his jacket was worn away. He came up the street, stuck letters into boxes, bringing good news and bad, doing his bit in the world. He was a loyal soul, he was.

In front of the tenement, seeing Jason and the old janitress waiting, he paused and frowned, his wide, good-natured face taking on a look of sternness.

"Is this the famous Twenty-Door City?" he inquired, a bunch of mail in his right fist.

"Aye," said Jason. "That it is."

"Then I have some mail for it," the Jolly Postman reported. "I have two letters for Jason Wheeler, Esquire."

"I happen to know that man," said the ex-poet solemnly. "He and I shot corned beef together on the steppes of Second Avenue. He was a fine shot, I must say. He was that."

The Jolly Postman chuckled. His scowl fell away like water. "Here they are," he said and handed Jason the two letters, a long one and a short one. In his other fist he held electric bills; these he stuck into the boxes, jamming them in.

Jason climbed the five flights to his room. One of the letters was a rejection from a sex-story magazine, the other was a second request from a non-paying poetry journal for material. Jason had stopped writing poetry over a year ago; he laid the letter aside. The other envelope he picked up again and read, for the second time, a personal note from the sex-story magazine editor. "You have failed to make the heroine as warm and alluring as you have done before for us, Wheeler. See if you can't send us a yarn as good as your last one, 'What She Told Him on Their Wedding Night.' That was a corker. Yours truly."

Jason pulled up a chair to his typewriter, opened up the case. The keys, catching the pale light from the windows, glittered dully up at him. He sat before the silent machine and began whipping up his mind, trying to cook up a red-hot plot. A sluggish feeling flowed through his brain. He hated his hack work with every drop of blood in his body. Bending over more, crouched in a determined pose, he made up his mind not to look at the bottle on the floor, not even to think about a drink. He forced his brain to become alert and flayed his thoughts unmercifully. His eyes, hard and stern, glared grimly at the little, lettered keys. But finally, choking back a lumpy feeling, he reached down, grabbed the bottle, and took a long drink. A hot, fiery feeling began immediately to burn in his belly. He put the bottle down upon the floor, cursed himself, and sat more determined and rigid than ever, as if strapped to an electric chair.

But he could not write, could not get going. He swung his jaw around to stare out the dirty windows. Clotheslines—old, sagging lines of knotted rope—swung gently in the gray, damp air. Across the way an old gouty woman was coming from her kitchen window onto the fire-escape, a bundle of wet garments in her arms. Jason watched her. Even from the distance across the yard he saw her red, swollen hands, her tired, flabby face. The wind whipped up her heavy skirts revealing cheap cotton stockings with holes in them the size of twenty-five-cent pieces, and suddenly, as she reached up to hang the first wet garment out upon the line, one red, bony knee showed, a pitiful thing.

Jason swung into action, this was all he needed. Whirling around, facing the keys again, he started hammering for all he was worth, his gray eyes hard and fixed upon the paper, the muscles of his jaw set grimly. He pounded out the first page of copy in record time: "It was a cold, raw, windy day on Riverside Drive and as pretty Patricia Manning turned into Seventy-Fifth Street the frolicsome breezes blew her Parisian dress playfully about so that a handsome, fast-walking young man could not help but stare at a luscious area of rosy thigh above two dimpled, silken knees. . . ."

In the pale rear room the sound of the sharply struck keys steadied into a hard rattle like machine-gun fire.

Over on Fifteenth Street his pal the artist was taking life at a more leisurely pace, however.

## III

LEON had taken his time about getting up today. This was his first day of freedom, and he meant to make the most of it. For a while he lay quiet under the quilt, just feeling good, but later on he couldn't stand it any longer and jumped out of bed and began dressing.

He picked out a soft flannel shirt which was a bit frayed around the collar, shaved, and stroked his small, smooth jaw and walked humming about the room as he knotted his necktie carefully.

Then he went out to eat, shopping around on Fourteenth Street for a breakfast, finally settling down to two fried eggs and coffee at an armchair cafeteria. When he returned to the rooming house, he met Celia on the stairs, her hair hidden in an old house-cap. She was hard at work, shining up the banisters, sweeping the stairs, going at it strong. Along the hallways all the doors were opened, the windows were raised. She turned around when Leon came in.

"I got up earlier today," she said. "Most of the rooms are done already, I've been working fast." Her face was shiny, the hair above her ears was slightly damp; it clung curly and moist against her pale forehead.

Leon, looking up at her as she stood near the top of the staircase, wanted to know why she was driving herself so hard.

The girl colored. "I want to pose for you today."

Leon, feeling pretty good, feeling comfortable in his old soft flannel shirt, having a lot of time on his hands, could not keep from teasing her again.

"No," he said, "I can't take you from your work. What would your aunt say? No, I shouldn't have asked you to pose for me."

"But I'll be finished in a half an hour," Celia said. "You can just see how fast I'm going."

"I don't want you to hurry yourself," said Leon and, looking thoughtful, he climbed the stairs, passed her, and went into his room. He closed the door. Celia stood upon the stairs, not doing anything for a while. Then she heard him hammering, he was stretching a canvas, and she smiled to herself and worked faster than ever.

A half hour later she knocked softly on his door. He swung it open.

"Oh, it's you," he said.

Through the opened door she saw that the canvas was already stretched, a tall clean canvas, and it stood ready upon the easel near the window.

"My aunt said it would be all right," said Celia.

Leon, looking around for his paints and brushes, finally glanced at her.

"But you've got your red dress on," he said.

"Well, it's my new one, I was saving it."

"You're to put the other one on, the dark one," he told her.

"But this is my new one," she said. "It fits me better than the other. The other is worn at the cuffs."

"You're to put the dark one on," he said.

Wrinkling her little forehead, standing helplessly before him, she bit her lip and at last left the room. When she returned, she had her dark dress on.

"It looks so old," she said quietly.

But Leon was already sketching her in charcoal; he told her to sit quiet, not to move her hands in her lap. "You're to look natural, perfectly natural. Don't pose."

She tried to look pleasant and moistened her lips.

"Don't smile," he said.

Then, hurt, she gave up and stared hopelessly before her, the joy of posing gone, the loneliness of her young life flowing from her eyes. In a flash Leon began squeezing paint from tubes and started painting furiously.

Gray light came through the window at his back. He did not want sunshine for such a picture. As he painted, he worked the figure and the background together, remembering certain phrases from the instructors down at the art school he had once studied at.

He painted for a long time, staring at her with the cool, hard eyes of a surgeon, no warmth to his gaze. The smell of paint was in his nostrils. He wiped the tips of his brushes quickly, stirred the color and mixed it on the palette and where a highlight shone upon the model's forehead he took up his palette-knife and with one sure, strong stroke applied a slash of pale paint in exactly the right spot. The room was not long enough for him to walk back and look at his work in progress, so he cocked his head, squinted, stared at the model, and emitted little, active grunts now and then.

Around noon, after a few short rests, he suddenly

noticed that the girl's face was going gray. He hurried out into the hall for a glass of water, came rushing back, and after she drank a few sips began bawling her out, frowning and shouting at her.

"What if you would have fainted?" he said.

She sat there meekly, looking toward the windows.

"You would have fallen from the chair, you would have hurt yourself," he almost shouted. "Think of it!"

She told him at last, speaking humbly, that she was sorry. He was cleaning his brushes, fussing around the palette. Pretty soon he calmed down, his breathing became more regular.

"That's all for today, thanks a lot. I think it will be a good painting."

"Isn't it finished yet?" she questioned simply.

"Finished? Why it'll take four or five more sittings. Don't look at it now, you'll be only disappointed."

Finished? What did she think he was, a barn painter?

Someone was walking up the stairs. "Celia." It was the girl's aunt.

Leon opened the door quickly. Mrs. Chapman, a tall, gaunt lady in her middle fifties, stood at the threshold and inquired how the painting was coming along. Her nose wrinkled—the strong smell of paint filled the little room. Leon opened the window. He was a little afraid of her.

"I put paper under the easel," he said quickly, "there's no spots at all on the floor."

## IV

IN THE AFTERNOON Leon paid a visit to his friend the ex-poet. Before climbing the flights he stuck his fingers into Jason's mail-box to see if the postman had brought anything on his second trip. He drew out a small pink letter bearing a Philadelphia postmark; there was no return address. Leon took it upstairs with him.

Jason was lying on the cot, staring at the ceiling when Leon entered after knocking three times. The ex-poet has just finished a tale called "Patricia Pets Her Way to Happiness." He was all fagged out. Leon placed the letter upon the table, and Jason, rolling his head to one side, saw the pinkness of it, but made no move to pick it up.

"I was just going by," said Leon, sitting down.

Jason did not answer; he looked to be a very sick young man and stared with slack eyes toward the ceiling.

After a long silence Leon said, "You ought to see a doctor."

"How was the meeting last night?" Jason asked, changing the subject.

Now it was Leon's turn to sit in silence. Jason, because he had once been a Party member, knew very well how the meetings went; they had not changed since he had dropped out. He prodded the little fellow until Leon, against his will, found himself answering the ex-poet.

"The meeting was a bit stormy," said Leon.

"Did Comrade Lukotas get up and shoot his gab off?"

"Comrade Lukotas spoke a few words," came the answer.

Jason cackled. In the end, because his chest pained, because he was tired out from writing hack and did not want to think about anything, he tore into his little friend and, as usual, did it very skillfully, using communism as his scalpel. Lately all their talks were ending this way.

Every time Leon came up to visit Jason he resolved beforehand not to be ensnared, not to talk communism with his friend, but little by little, goaded and prodded, he found himself sucked into the whirlpool. He was no match for Jason, and he knew it. Jason had the cool, calculating mind of a fiend when it came to forensics, he could make black look white, he had won prizes in economics in a large midwestern university and had once wanted to write a book on social science. At the Party meetings he had caused all sorts of rows, tangling up the chairmen and the speakers, shooting his bitter barbs from all angles of the floor, accusing the sub-committees of short-sightedness and mismanagement. Everybody felt relieved when he dropped out of the Party.

Right now he used the same old tactics on Leon. He agreed with everything the little fellow said at first, nodding his head as he lay there flat on his back. But as soon as Leon made one vague remark he started slashing. Both agreed on generalities, both were in favor of a social revolution; they agreed on a number of things.

Then Leon, branching out, let a few words fall concerning the Party here in America. Jason was ready for him. From then on, the little fellow was on the defensive.

The first thing Jason did was to inquire about the membership. How many comrades had the Party now?

"Ten thousand," answered Leon.

"All right. Let's make it twelve thousand. With this handful you're going to overthrow capitalism here. Fine. Now, comrade, a few questions. Is it true, or isn't it, that every year forty per cent of the comrades drop out? Is it true, or isn't it, that there is such a big turnover?"

No answer.

"Is it true, or isn't it, that most of the membership is among the foreign-born workers? Is it true, or isn't it, that these comrades are located in New York, most of them, in the most European city in America? Do you really think, Comrade Leon Fisher, that a movement appealing to the American masses can be successful as long as the agitators of the movement are not Americanized themselves and have not de-Russianized the propaganda they're trying to hammer into the heads of American labor?"

"You distort the facts," said Leon, savagely.

"Do I? All right. But don't forget that the Russian revolution was strictly a Russian movement, engineered by Russian revolutionaries and applicable only to the old imperial regime." A pause. "However, tovarish, if these prosperous times continue, I predict that the communist movement here will gain in strength in spite of the Communist Party."

No answer.

"And what about the solidarity they're always preaching about, Comrade Leon? Look at all the splits you've had in the past few years. You've got the left-wingers, right-wingers, left of the left, Trotzkyites and other factions. And each piece fights the others; they hate each other worse than they hate the capitalists. How about the solidarity they're always preaching about?"

But now Leon came to life, he had his back to the wall.

"It shows the Party at least is alive!"

"No," said Jason. "It shows that the Party has small men at the helm. There are no leaders big enough, strong enough to weld the factions. If the Party here didn't have Russia to look up to, the whole movement here would be laughed off the map."

Leon struck out as well as he was able. "Do you favor the Socialists then?" he demanded.

Jason gave a snort. Socialists? No.

"Well, what then?"

"I am in favor of being neither rich nor poor, just having a small circle of friends, that's all." The ex-poet was at it again.

"You're dodging now," said Leon. "We're gaining strength, look at the good work we've done at the strikes at Gastonia, Passaic, and Kentucky."

Jason waved these comments aside. "The Party had no competition there. It had the whole field to itself and naturally the strikers took whatever help was offered."

"And in the last few years most of the promising writers and artists have swung over to our side," Leon said.

Again Jason waved the words aside. "That's only natural. Any young artist, if he's any good at all, is a radical, and the most radical movement in the limelight now is communism. Anyway, in New York it's getting to be known as a Jewish movement. I come from the west and I know my people. I'd like to see a lot of brawny American workingmen following these Jewish agitators over the ramparts along Fourteenth Street. No, frankly I can't picture it."

Leon winced and turned his head aside. Through the windows which were covered with film, gray light filtered and lay across the ex-poet's tired face.

"You're too hard on the Party," Leon said, feeling sorry for his friend.

"I merely state the facts," answered Jason. "How much progress has the Party made among American unions? Take the great Railroad Brotherhoods for instance. Take the carpenters, plumbers, and brick-layers."

In the end, however, Leon remained unshaken. He was a visionary and felt that in time all obstacles would be swept aside before the march of communism. He felt also that Jason would re-enter the Party. He knew his friend.

They sat in silence a long time after that.

Later on, just before he got up to go, Leon spoke a few words about his plans concerning the future, how he was going to paint and do a lot of Party work now. He spoke about the meeting last night again and said a few new members were present. He dropped a few words about a new blond comrade who came from New Orleans.

Jason, rolling his head on the pillow, looked at the little fellow keenly. Leon, still talking, said a Mexican had come up with her.

"Did the girl wear a brown coat, did she have a brown coat with a black belt?" asked Jason.

Leon's heart began to pound. Was Jason making fun of him again? He didn't answer, didn't say a word.

"But I tell you I saw them," said Jason. "They walked by looking for rooms this morning."

Leon, his heart still hammering, said he'd have to go now. "I put a letter on the table for you."

"Thanks," said Jason and lay quiet on the cot. So much talking after hacking out the story had hollowed him out; his face seemed to have fallen inward.

At the door Leon hesitated and stared toward the bed. "Jason," he said slowly, ". . . Jason, you ought to see a doctor. I've got some money . . ."

"Got a match?" asked Jason. He lit another cigarette, inhaled deeply like a spent runner, the bones on the upper part of his face drawing through the flesh, and seemed to revive a bit. His legs, slack upon the cot, lay dead as sticks. The soles of his shoes faced the windows. The bottoms had holes in them.

"I don't suppose you heard from her?" said Leon, his hand on the knob.

Jason blew out smoke and frowned toward the ceiling. "She must be in another city, she was speaking about getting transferred."

They were speaking about a young lady whom Jason had lived with some time ago. She had a good job with a large manufacturing company which had sales offices in various cities.

After Leon left, Jason got up from the cot and came over to the letter. The letter was from the young lady; he recognized the handwriting immediately. He tore it open. A five-dollar bill dropped to the floor.

After he read the short note, he shined his glasses slowly and lay down quietly upon the cot again. She wrote that she hoped he was well and would not think about her any more. She made no mention of the money enclosed. She had tried to reform him, had tried to get him straightened out, and had tried to cure his love for gin, but she made no mention of this in her note. No, she said nothing about it. She wrote that she hoped he was well and would not think about her any more.

Fifteen minutes later Jason went downstairs and paid the five dollars against rent due.

The kids from the Catholic school across the street were being dismissed; they came across the street in a noisy flood, swinging their schoolbooks, shouting, their voices dying in the gray, damp air.

## V

THE CRACKED LITTLE PRINTER sat in the Crystal Lunchroom that night, drinking a cup of hot coffee.

"The point is," he said to Pete, who ran the beanery,

"the point is, there can be no peace." He was emphatic about it.

The Serbian, running a knobbly-knuckled hand over the cheese holes of his leathered face, stared toward the street, where the higher-class Bowery gentry were now walking northward to panhandle a few dimes on Fourteenth Street.

"How can there be peace when men are made for war?" asked the printer. He stared a trifle pop-eyed at Pete and chewed gingerly on a hot roast-beef sandwich. "In Rome the phalanxes under Cæsar marched across the plain, each warrior in time, whole legions of them swinging along, shields at rest, spears in their right fists. The dust of the earth came up like steam under their feet. How can there be peace? How?"

Pete poured the man a second cup of coffee and turned to gaze toward the windows and the street again. He scratched his left elbow, where a rash had just broken out.

The printer bit into the sandwich again, very carefully, avoiding as much as possible the left side of his jaw where his teeth were bad.

Darkness had long since fallen upon the town. The fog had thinned a good deal, but the air was still damp. If this cracked little fellow did not make such high-class signs for the lunchroom, the Serbian would have sent him flying long ago.

"When will that new sign for me be ready?" he asked, staring hard at the fellow.

Mr. Nicholson swallowed and wiped his mouth with his ink-stained hands. He had slim, well-formed fingers. "I can't say, Mr. Garolian. At the present moment I am busy writing a historical document. I don't know when I'll have the time. The world spins around like a heavy wooden top, but the glory of Rome flows on like a river of song."

Pete grunted and once more stared toward the windows and the street.

The printer set his second cup of coffee down, empty. He sat on in silence, staring pop-eyed into space, one side of his face twitching. An old, gray, battered hat sat high upon his head, and he hadn't shaved for four days. Long hairs grew from his chin, but his cheeks were smooth and hairless as a boy's. Along each side of his small, bony nose were fine lines, running up toward his eyes, which were gray-green in color and just a trifle glassy. At the temples his hair was going dirty gray. His clothes were baggy and untidy, but he did not appear shabby.

In the rear of the lunchroom the cook rattled the pans. The dish-washer at his side, who was getting more nervous and fidgety each day, dropped a dinner plate, but caught it just before it hit the floor. The cook grinned. He was a man with a sense of humor. He was waiting for Pete to fire the fellow for his carelessness.

"Try it again," he grinned at the old dish-washer.

But the old man sat upon a tin can and tried to calm his dry, hoarse breathing. He shot his head meekly through the wicket and saw that Pete had his back turned. His skull was clean-shaven and had a bluish tint to it.

"No," said the cracked printer, speaking to the wall, "there can be no peace."

Getting off the stool, he started to declaim an ode, speaking like a Roman senator, but Pete was getting pretty tired of the business and turned his back to see how the coffee was coming along.

The cracked printer threw out his left arm in a jerky gesture, headed for the door and hurried up the street.

When he reached his basement quarters over on Thirteenth Street, he shut his door against the street, against the town. Then he turned on the light and stared about. Against one wall was a long, crudely hammered-together bookcase filled with old histories, well thumbed, *The Decline and Fall of the Roman Empire* by Gibbon and other standard works. A big unpainted desk stood under the electric bulb, and upon this desk were stacks of paper and folios of manuscript. The printer's face grew alert and alive as he pulled a chair up. He cocked his ear toward the north, listening to the drone of the city outside.

In the square the crowds were melting. Grandma Volga caught the last few customers and grunted at them in her meager English. Mr. Feibelman was busy making a few sales, sticking chestnuts into paper bags. He had repainted his little wagon last night and now there stood, against the side of it, the hallmark of his trade. "HoT CheTnutZ," the slogan read and the passing citizenry turned to stare.

Across the street a new show was playing at the Acme: THE POWER OF DARKNESS, rendered by the Moscow Art Players, titles in English, taken from Tolstoy's immortal drama for three days only, matinee 15c, evenings 30c.

James Nicholson, in his basement quarters, opened a bottle of ink, stuck his pen inside, bent over a bit more and began writing, one side of his face twitching more than ever, the thinning fog at his back, the city roaring all around.

> NOW IN the fall a chill comes from the plains. The sentries at the river beds peer eastward toward the hills. Gray mist like gas comes settling to the ground.

In half an hour the fog grows dense, a scout goes riding out ahead, digging in his heels against the charger's ribs. Two miles away the fog is dust. Ten thousand sheep and goats and rams are traveling slowly across the plains. To greener grass, to better water. The shepherds stand there meekly, no weapons hidden in their clothes. The scout rides back and stands before his Captain. "Sire, the sheep are lean, the meat will boil out tough and stringy." The Captain opens up a keg of beer. "Bring me the fattest, a cut of lamb will not taste bad." Four scouts go off and shove the shepherds gruffly aside. They sort and choose and lift upon their horses a dozen of the fattest sheep, a hearty load. They ride away, and climb a rise of ground. The shepherds stand and stare and hear the fading hooves while the growling, faithful sheep-dogs start to whine, and beasts stand humbly all around. . . .

*—This from the fourth volume, from the home and print-shop of a man of parts.*

# VI

DOWN in a warehouse on Lafayette Street on that same foggy October evening (a few hours earlier) the foreman of the hustlers stood looking the boys over. There were eleven of them, all brawny brutes with hard legs, good shoulders, healthy hearts, and skulls like ivory. They shoved and wheeled their loads along, each worker's glance upon the man ahead of him, all thinking of five-thirty and a nice, hot meal at home.

The foreman, appearing casual, looked them over. Business was due to drop off soon, maybe in another month or so, and a few men would have to be knocked off the payroll. The workers walked by, rolling the loaded handtrucks along, their heavy boots ringing against the iron, fireproof floor, their caps on cockily, shoulders swinging, back muscles expanded as they shoved the loads along. There were eleven of them, all faithful brutes, with heads like ivory.

In the inner office the foreman took his hat off, and stood before the boss, the Big Chief—Old Running Water, as the hustlers called the boss among themselves.

"They're all good men," the foreman reported, "every one of them. They're workers, too. I don't know which ones to tell you to let go, every man of them is pretty good. I hired 'em carefully."

The Big Chief—Old Running Water—took the stump of cigar from his loose damp lips and growled back an answer. He was a broad, powerful man sitting down, sitting in that wide chair of his, but when he rose you saw he was old and beefy; and when he grew violent, his heavy cheeks shook from side to side, like the withered hindquarters of an old Panhandle steer. He had kidney trouble, Old Running Water had.

"We'll have to let about four go," he said. "Keep your eye peeled, watch for the guys who kid around or slacken down, but keep your mouth shut. You say they're all pretty good, hunh?"

The foreman nodded. He was a man who had come up from the ranks himself, a hustler from the days of yore, and his word could be depended on, he knew what he was talking about.

"All right—bring out the records," the Big Chief said,

barking over his shoulder to the kid who worked in the office, to the squirt who was always reading mystery novels. The kid jumped, Old Running Water had spoken, his cigar stump in a meditative but firm position between pudgy thumb and forefinger.

The records were slapped down upon the broad table. The binding was of faded green corduroy. Old Running Water ran his eye up and down the absentee column, looking for check marks. All the lads had fine records. As the wages were pretty fair, only the pick of Manhattan's hustlers worked within these walls.

The roving eye came to rest, a glint shone there.

"Henry Austin, he was absent once about six months ago," the Big Chief said, frowning at the ledger.

"Hank? Why Hank is one of the best," the foreman answered quickly, a fair man, a fair remark. "His wife had a kid then; he phoned in and took a day off."

Old Running Water grunted, shifting his buttocks two points north by northeast in the wide chair. The kid, standing, went back to read that mystery novel of his, the Chief's back toward him; the lad had a drawer of his desk opened handily, so that the book could be instantly dropped into it out of sight.

The glint went away and came back, it shone.

"Well, Hank was absent, he put us in a hole then," grunted Old Running Water.

"We wasn't very busy then," said the foreman. "I stepped in to take a hand toward quitting time, but it wasn't hardly necessary, sir."

Once more the Big Chief gave a thoughtful grunt. Hank's name, like a sharp spike, was driven in his brain.

"Well, we'll see," the Big Chief grunted and closed the ledger with a ponderous hand. His sleeves were rolled.

Golden hairs, like fuzz, frizzled all along his beefy forearms. He lit a match and blew a fine blue cloud of smoke, sending it toward the mouthpiece of his phone. "We'll see," he said, and the spike went driven deep into his brain.

The foreman walked out.

On the wall the big clock read five-twenty-six and still the men worked on, they were faithful slaves indeed, all good men and true, hard times, they were afraid to bat an eye, each man knew what he was up against; when they got hot around the collar, they thought about their kids. That cooled them down. All had iron backs and shoulders, strong rigid legs, and heads of ivory. They rolled the loaded trucks along until the bell rang.

Hank punched his card and put it in the OUT rack.

"If I were you, I'd watch my step," the foreman told him quietly, when no one else was looking.

Hank dropped his jaw like a hod of bricks. What's that? Ho, you can't scare me, and he stared into the foreman's eyes, looking for laughter there. But the eyes he saw were as sober as hell—clear and dark as a couple of bottles of cold beer. The foreman said no more. His gaze wavered and he walked toward the right to check up on a shipping ticket hanging from a nail.

Hank went out, walking down the iron stairs. He took the subway home. He bought a tabloid paper to drug his nerves, read the love-nest headlines, was pushed in the sardined train by girls, men, boys, women, and packages and finally reached his stop.

He climbed the stairs with thoughtful eyes. As soon as his hand touched the doorknob, his kids threw wide the panels and ran at his legs, grabbing at his knees. They were all under nine years old. It was his habit to drag them over the floor, moving their dead, limp weight like seaweed. They were proud of their father's strength. But now he stood stock-still. They let him go.

"Hank," his good wife said, that wife who whined and gurgled by turns. "Hank." She questioned with her stare.

"I'm hungry," came the answer. He threw his tabloid down and washed his hands. Then he sat down before a plate of hot food, a big slab of juicy meat bought at the market-place on First Avenue, under the thunder of the elevated. Missus Austin shopped around, she stretched the family's dollars.

The others ate. In the bedroom the six-months-old baby bawled. The wife got up and put the dish-mop in its fist. The flat was quiet.

"Hank," she said, staring at him over the heads of the eating, guzzling kids.

And Hank, why he had lied, he wasn't hungry at all. The food lay calm upon his plate, he had shoved one forkful between his jaws and had chewed and chewed, but the stuff was hay to him. His tongue was thick and dry, that was the trouble. He gulped a glass of water.

To get away from the stare of his wife, he shoved the tabloid in front of her face, shoved it high, hiding from her eyes. She saw some black print staring at her: GALA CRUISE TO HAVANA, MUSIC AND DANCING. There was a picture of a long graceful boat and on the decks were lanterns. Underneath the announcement was an advertisement for children's underwear: YOUR KIDDIES DESERVE THE BEST. The kids ate on, the meat was juicy stuff indeed, Missus Austin continued to stare at the paper hiding her husband's face.

As soon as the meal was over, the kids went downstairs to play. Then the wife rose and put the paper down— short and powerful and healthy she was, with a bust fit for a wet-nurse. She took the paper from his hands, she ran her soft damp palms over his Yankee face (his ancestors had fought at Valley Forge), she tried to rouse him just a little. His stare was hard.

"Hank," she said, almost a whisper.

And Hank, good old ivory-headed Hank Austin, there he sat with his six-foot Yankee bulk and roused himself at last. Under her questioning stare he finally spoke—just a few words, listening for the bawling of the brat in the other room, the kid, his heir (fourth in line).

"We'd better start and try to save more money," he said, and said no more.

A hot pain stabbed her heart. She started whining, her little soft nose puckered, he stared at her blouse which was bursting with the health of her. She was living down to the bone, she whined; she shopped at the stalls of the Jews, she haggled over pennies, she couldn't do any more.

Hank raised the paper again and stared, but did not read. The print, like black ants before his eyes, like dead cockroaches with rigid legs, stood harshly from the paper.

To stop her whining, he shot some fire into his eyeballs and glared toward the door when he heard a banging out in the hall. He thundered to his sturdy dame: "Those foreigners, those folk across the hall, do they leave the toilet door unlocked yet when they're through, do they still leave the door open?"

The wife gave an answer, half gurgling now.

"I guess they do," she said.

She stood squat before him. He frowned at her. "I guess they do," she said again, wiping her hands on her apron, her pale hair shining under the kitchen light. She turned quickly to the sink, to clear things up.

"They ought to go back to the old country," Hank

roared. "What do we want with foreigners here? There's not enough jobs the way it is."

Then he saw her startled eyes, her indrawn mouth—he had given himself away, the fool. To cover up his tracks he roared again. "They ought to go back to the old country!"

He was still shouting when his kids came in—bellowing is the right word, and the oldest kid knelt to pull his boots off, grunting as he strained in toil.

That poor toilet door, it had suffered again, it was a thing buffeted by fate and the wind in the hallway, a bit of carpentry with a ten-cent lock on it. But now Hank was satisfied, he had shot off steam; perhaps the whole picture in his brain had been thrown upon a false screen. What had the foreman said? Hardly anything. Old Running Water wasn't such a bad scout, he and the foreman both. Hank half-grinned as he sat now, the kids went to bed. Missus Austin closed their bedroom door softly and came to stand before him, wiping her soft hands rather nervously on her apron again.

But out in the hallway, when the door banged once more, the metal lock rattling a bit from the impact, Hank's Yankee face grew resolute and stern for the second time and he rose up to his six-foot bulk. Now the hands of his wife fluttered more than ever, it seemed she would never get them really dry.

But Hank finally sat down again, glaring toward the hall, his bronze jaws as firm as bank-vault doors. His face softened gradually, it was getting late.

Oh, that toilet door!

# THREE

## I

ALL DAY LONG, all night long the phonograph-radio feud went on, the music from the horns over the doorways blaring out upon the street. Folk stood before the loudspeakers, the lamps were lit, signs blazed and in the square Comrade Irving Rosenblum (Rosie to his pals) gave the citizenry the lowdown on the graft of Wall Street, telling how every governmental order came from a well-known house of bankers. Rosie stood upon a soap-box, swung his arms (the night was cold), and those who stood directly in front of him, received a spray of spittle now and then.

Rosie was a little feller—black hair, a big, militant nose, a screaming mouth, and a four-dollar overcoat bought at a second-hand joint over on Third Avenue. He called for action, Rosie did. His jaw wobbled, rattling like a small machine-gun, his throat wriggled as if a live fish were flopping inside near the throttle. He had the goods, that orator had, the citizenry stood around and listened.

Officer Terence McGuffy swung his nightstick, just for the exercise of it, and caught a phrase or two. Then he sauntered on, one of the city's finest, a lad who knew the Russian situation from A to Z. The low, thick wall running around the square bulked dim in the dark, sixteen or eighteen inches thick (the square was elevated a bit too, you had to walk up a small flight of steps to tread the historic earth there), and as Rosie's arms shook and waved, the big electric signs blinked back: "SAVE NOW," "GUARDIAN LIFE," "WRIGLEY'S CHEWING GUM," "UNION SQUARE SAVINGS BANK," "CENTRAL SAVINGS," "THE AMALGAMATED," and other staunch and reliable banks. The square was fairly sprinkled with places to dump your money, there were plenty of takers for the cash, earn while you sleep, the pile grows with us.

In the brief pauses, when station announcers stopped to get their wind, you could hear the taxi-dancing jazzbands in the middle of the block blaring strong, urging the couples on. Ten cents a dance . . . pick your hostesses, boys, here they are, lined up and waiting for your manly arms. The girls, mere kids with painted faces, stood around in long, three-dollar, sweat-shop dresses, giving the lads a dreamy, Greta Garbo glance, looking the boys over, trying to find out who had the most tickets (the girls went fifty-fifty with the house). Some of the men gripped the girls too tightly, pawing a bit, but that was to be expected; the men were mostly foreigners, dark fellows with little, dancing flames in their eyes, and the blond hostesses were grabbed up the fastest. On the dinky platform the jazzband blared—hot, slow music, the wailing, sobbing blues. The numbers were short, a couple of squeezes, a whirl, and another ticket please. The saxophone player, a fellow with a glass eye, squinted every time he was due for a solo number, for if he didn't, he'd stand a chance of having his artificial optic pop out upon the floor. As it was, his eye popped from the socket two or three times a week.

Side streets cut across the town. Rows and rows of rooming houses, tenements, basement speakeasies, small

Jewish and Hungarian restaurants, candy stores which did no business dotted the section, with here and there an Italian grocery, bologna hanging in the front windows. The smell was fierce in summer, in the fall the air was cold.

At eight o'clock Rex Bingo came on the air, king of the crooners, singing his sad, sad love songs. His fluted wails floated over the East Side rooftops, into the autumn night.

"This comes to you through the courtesy of Mowitz Brothers, makers of custom-built furniture designed in the famous Mowitz manner, station W K P, please stand by for a few seconds, folks."

## II

MR. FRANCONI came home from the barber shop at half-past eight, right after the famous Mowitz hour, and found another letter in his mail-box from Florina. That made it two already for the week. He was a little tired of receiving her letters and a little tired of reading them and did not quite know himself why he kept the correspondence up.

He entered his apartment and put his hat and coat away. His feet felt tired. Standing up all day, giving shaves, shampoos, haircuts, and singes, was a weary job. Taking off his shoes, he inserted his feet in cool, leather house-slippers.

Then, with slow, careful fingers, no hurry in his brain or eyes, he opened up the letter and started reading.

> Andre, you have not written to me for over a week now. I have sent the Mexican girl four times within the last three days to ask for mail at the post office and always she comes back with empty hands and shakes her head. I

have sent up my prayers to the Blessed Virgin and have prayed that you are not sick and I have given the priest money to light two candles near the altar. The grapes hang heavy from the stems and the fields are full of people. This will be a big harvest. Joe also has given money to the priest, but his prayers are mixed with liquor. I have been thinking and thinking and I tell you plainly, Andre, that I cannot go on much longer. In your letters you say nothing and give me no hope. Sometimes I feel like taking a train and coming to see you right away. It is thirteen years since I have seen you, six years since I have been in America. I am a young woman yet, Andre, but I will not always stay young. I read your letters over and over and try hard to find out what you think. Maybe all my tears have run down my face for nothing, maybe I have passed my nights in prayers in vain, but I cannot believe this. Andre, when you write to me, tell me something definite. Sometimes I think that I will not live very much longer. I have spoken to Father Tortinas, who has been in the mountains a long time, but I cannot tell him of my love for you. I am a sinful woman. Mother of God! Father Tortinas is an old man and is going away soon to his people in Spain, he says he wants to see them before he dies. Joe bought a new truck and has already driven many loads of grapes to the railroad. My children are all well. The empty crates are all around and yesterday a hired man tripped and fell across one of them and tore his cheek open. I put a bandage around his face. Everything here is sunny, but so sad. We are near small mountains, but the bigger ones are forty miles away and when the sky is clear they look close. If I could not write you letters, Andre, I would go crazy. I cannot help myself. In the next farm there is a young widow, a Swedish woman, and I know that as soon as I am gone or die, she will move in here and take care of the children. Already the neighbors are talking. Joe goes away in the evenings and meets her in the fields. When he comes into bed late at night I can smell her smell on him. He thinks I know nothing. I have not said a word. I am sending you a picture of myself in this letter as I have often promised you and you must send me one of yourself. No one will find it, I will keep it in the crack behind the clock I brought from Italy with your medallion. I close this letter, Andre, full of tears, a sinful woman, and pray to the Virgin that you are well and strong. I pray that you will write me soon.

With respectful wishes,<br>
FLORINA.

He took the photograph from the envelope and looked at it. He hardly recognized her. When he had seen her last, she had been slim, thin-waisted, and full-bosomed. Now she was full-faced and sturdy, she frowned from the picture at him. Her eyes were large and thoughtful and had slight hollows under them. She posed stiffly. He laid the photo aside.

At nine o'clock, after trying to write a letter in answer, he finally had to tear up two unfinished sheets and postpone the matter again. He glanced at his watch, put his shoes on again, and started humming to himself. There was no gayety in his voice. He went outside.

The night was fine. He walked east until he reached First Avenue and came up to the Italia Club, a social organization composed, mostly, of Italians of foreign birth. The club was on the second floor and from the street, before he began climbing the stairs, he saw the lights and heard the loud talking and laughter. Looking pleasant, setting his shoulders jauntily back, he ascended and at the threshold stood poised there, flashing his well-known smile. He really was a handsome man. He had a fine, quiet way of smiling.

His comrades shouted to him, several came over and clapped him on the shoulder and, half leading, half following him, they walked the length of the smoke-filled hall.

"Andre," they said, speaking rapidly in brotherly Italian, "you are a stranger here. Two weeks it is or so, two weeks now, Andre."

He waved his arm and answered pleasantly. His comrades laughed, nudging each other, winking.

"Who is it now, Andre, a blonde or a red-headed one?" They laughed obscenely.

He smiled quietly, feigning modesty. "I have been very busy," he said simply.

His friends roared and laughed and clapped him hard upon the shoulder. "You dog, you. You lucky devil. See how quiet he is. Ai, ai, it is the quiet ones who are the most dangerous, you've got to watch them closely. They say nothing, but they are wolves. Tony, two beers and four wines. . . ."

There in the noise and the cigarette smoke, the card playing and the sound of laughter, Andre's eyes burned darkly bright, and to the nudges and winks of his friends he gave no answer, sitting pleasantly among them, smiling faintly, tasting the bitter sweetness of the cool, white wine and their good, honest comradeship.

## III

LEON painted every morning and at the end of the week had the portrait finished. He wiped his brushes, stood as far back from the easel as the room permitted, and squinted his left eye slightly. Celia came to stand near, giving him her little frozen smile.

It was a good painting, he knew that. It was the best he had ever done.

"But it makes me look so sad," she said thoughtfully.

He cleared his throat and went on wiping his brushes. "What was I going to say?" he said frowning.

He said nothing.

There she stood, waiting for him to say something about the painting, something about her perhaps.

"Well, you can have it," he finally said, sticking his brushes into a jar of turpentine. "It'll have to dry first, it's too wet now to carry."

But she wouldn't hear of it, in fact she grew quite worked up about the matter. "Isn't it worth a lot of money? It's hand-painted," she said. "You should try to sell it, to send it to a gallery."

He had to smile a little, but when she stood there, stood there looking hurt and meek, he frowned and said he'd think the matter over.

Later on, she heard hammering down in the basement, and when Leon came up he was carrying a packing box he had made.

"What's that for?" Celia inquired, coming out into the hall.

"I'm sending it away to an exhibition. They won't take it, but I'm sending it away just the same."

There was something grim about his mouth. She said, "Oh," and went back into her room.

In the afternoon Leon called on Jason. Jason was sitting near the window reading an old back number of a sex-story magazine, trying to hunt up ideas for future plots. The little painter came in smiling. He saw that Jason was looking pretty good.

"I just sent a painting off to Philadelphia," Leon said. Jason's face changed slightly at the name of that city.

"What for?" he asked.

"They're holding a show there pretty soon, a big exhibition. Maybe I'll get in."

"Whoever told you you could paint?" said Jason dryly and turned another page. "How's this, Leon? 'Then she came into the bedroom from her bath with only a silk robe on and when she turned the light on found Bruce Pemberton sitting calmly smoking his pipe.' My pal Sam Kugel wrote that yarn two years ago, he was using Jack Dillington as his nom de plume then. Not bad, eh? The lad shows promise."

Leon said nothing. He knew that Jason knew that as yet he had had nothing to do with women. He did not like his friend to speak about such matters crudely.

Jason changed the subject. He scratched his jaw with his dirty fingernails.

"Say," he said quietly, eyeing Leon keenly but unobtrusively, "that blond comrade of yours, that blonde from New Orleans and her Mexican friend are moving into this building, into the famous tenement known to all as Twenty-Door City."

Leon didn't believe it at first. He was accustomed to Jason's taunts by now. He sat there stiffly, stared ahead, and finally wet his lips.

"What's that got to do with me?" he finally asked, his voice cracking a little.

"Nothing," said Jason. "I'm just telling you. That buxom maiden, that girl of your golden dreams, is moving into this building, I thought you might be interested.

Listen: 'What are you doing here, Bruce, you cannot be with me alone in this penthouse apartment. We are not married, Bruce, she said. Bruce sat there calmly, smoking on his pipe. There was something self-confident, self-reliant about the young man. He was the heir to millions. I will not budge, Gloria, until you promise to marry me, he said firmly. The janitor was monkeying with the fuse in the basement and just then the flat went dark. Gloria screamed, Bruce leaped forward. Was this a trap, she thought, as Bruce's arms protected her, enclosed her?' Well, Leon, that lad Kugel sure wrote a swell yarn there. Shall I read further, do you want to hear the climax?"

Leon, still sitting rigid, was thinking rapidly about the new neighbors due to move in. Jason read his thoughts.

"The old janitress told me they'd move in right away, maybe they're moving in right now, I don't know. Maybe I can get to know her, Leon, and get you an introduction, eh?"

Leon said nothing, hoping his pal would change the subject. Know her? Why, he knew her now, hadn't they been formally introduced, hadn't they spoken a few words together? He remembered the soft pressure of her hand.

"Shall we go out for a walk?" the ex-poet said.

Now it was Leon's turn to stare keenly at his friend. Since when was Jason going out walking during the day? Jason spent his days drinking, writing, and brooding, taking occasional walks only during the evening.

Jason stared out the windows. The truth was that he was taking a few afternoon walks now for his health. That young nurse whom he had met in the hospital, that healthy, lively-eyed kid, had mailed him a card asking him to call at the hospital, and when he had arrived she was waiting in the doorway for him, waiting to go walking with him. She had on her street clothes. She said she had thought so much about him since he had left the hospital that night that she felt she had to see him again. He couldn't shake her off. So they went walking. He was shabby and his shoes looked kicked and cuffed about and for the first time he felt sensitive about his appearance, but she made it a point not to notice. In the end they had gone into a lunchroom and because he had no funds she paid the checks. She said it was all right. Something about him, the bitter twist to his mouth and the queer way he had of talking perhaps, moved her very strongly. He tried to chill her, to hold her off. She was the same type of girl as the young lady who had had herself transferred to Philadelphia just on his account. But when he had walked her back to the hospital door, she had made him promise to get in touch with her often. She told him what afternoons and evenings she had off.

Leon was still wondering what had come over his friend as they started walking down the flights of stairs of the tenement together. The smell of old floors and moth-eaten woodwork was in their nostrils.

When they reached the doorway they stopped. Leon stood quiet in his tracks.

"They're moving in right now," said Jason.

At the curbing stood an old white horse between the shafts of a small moving van. The driver and two young fellows were unloading some second-hand furniture. The old horse had swelling knee joints and kept pawing at the pavement.

Then Leon recognized the two young men on the wagon. They were the Turner brothers, Harry and Sid Turner, Party members and active in the Red Drama Group. He half-shouted to them. Sid looked around; he was the older brother. Jason knew them, too. Both young men came off the wagon and shook hands, and Sid explained everything. He told Leon and Jason that he and his brother were moving in with two new comrades they had met at a Party meeting last week, a girl from New Orleans and her friend, a Mexican. Leon began breathing hoarsely, and over his head, frowning all his might, Jason caught Sid's eye and gave him a hard, stern look. Sid glanced at Leon's face and understood immediately; he stared back at Jason, when Leon was looking toward the furniture on the wagon, counting with his eyes the articles there.

"How many beds did you say you had?" Leon asked at last, his face frozen.

"Three," said Sid Turner. "We got them at a second-hand store cheap enough. We'll save by living together."

"Three?" repeated Leon, his eyes taking on a strange light.

Sid had his mouth open ready to answer when Jason motioned quickly behind Leon's back.

"Three beds, yes, sure. One's a double bed, José and I will sleep on that. The other is for my brother Harry, the third for Comrade Helen." He went back to the wagon with Harry and resumed unloading the stuff.

A chill November wind drove up the street. There was a thin, shiny sweat on Leon's brow, but he looked relieved.

The two brothers and the driver made a few trips into the tenement with the furniture. They worked fast, it didn't take long to get rid of the little load. At the curb the old white horse kept pawing slowly at the pavement. His head was hanging very low.

When the last load had been carried inside, Sid came out and spoke to Leon and Jason. "It's all inside now," he said. "José and Helen are back there now, want to come back and meet them?"

He stared at Jason.

"Sure," said the ex-poet, and they all went back.

When they entered the flat (it was on the ground floor, rear west, three rooms and pretty dark ones, too) the Mexican had his shirt off and was shoving the stuff around in place. He was a powerful-looking brute and had fine-muscled shoulders, smooth, hairless, bronze skin. He looked up as Jason and Leon entered. The girl came forward from another room. She smiled at the little fellow right away.

"My friend Jason Wheeler lives here in this building," Leon stammered quickly. "We were just coming from his room when we saw Sid."

Jason was introduced. The Mexican hung around, not saying much. He looked as if he were used to taking things easy. The girl looked the same way; she had on an old dress and there were a few smudges on her cheeks.

Before they left, Leon said he'd come over maybe and help straighten things out and fix things up in another day or two, maybe. He was smiling and his eyes shone as he stood looking at the girl.

Then they were out upon the windy street—Jason and Leon—and walked slowly northward. Jason was frowning through his glasses and did not have a thing to say.

"They say Morales has done good work among his fellow peasants down in Mexico," said Leon. "He had to leave the country, the police ran him out."

When they reached the square, the last of the late afternoon sunlight was slanting off the statues. Lincoln's head and shoulders were sunny, but his legs and shoes were shady. A small mass meeting was in progress, a man was shouting down upon a hundred upturned faces. Thirty feet off stood the trim little hut used by the United States Recruiting Service, a stall just a trifle bigger than a telephone booth. A sign in front stared toward the haranguing orator: JOIN THE COLORS, GO PLACES, DO THINGS.

A shivering kid of eighteen without an overcoat was talking to a husky sergeant there.

## IV

JASON sent off letters: one, two, three of them. He wrote them in his own hand and did not type as usual. For so many weeks, months, and now years he had thought, worked, and written upon keys that the pen between his fingers felt strange to the touch; he was accustomed only to signing his name: Jason Wheeler, after yours truly, or sincerely yours.

The letters were sent off to Philadelphia.

Replies came, worded exactly the same as the first letter she had sent him. She hoped that he was feeling well and told him not to think about her any more. Jason laid her letters aside. He strolled over to his "source of supplies" and sat at the counter while Pete poured him a cup of coffee.

Darkness had fallen. Turning, he stared toward the street, where the squat supports of the Third Avenue elevated threw shadows into the front of the store. A slow wind stirred the arc lamp outside and the zone of light swayed gently from side to side. Jason sat. When he moved, he heard the faint crackle of her letters in an inner pocket. He stared back toward the swaying zone of light again. Already the jetsam was beginning to float by, wreckage from down the way, fellows in rags, fat women with baggy eyes, drunks who staggered up to you and pawed your coat lapel whining for "a dime f'r cuppa o' coffee G' blessya." There were also a few men who walked stiffly like wound-up toy sentries, their eyes bright and popping, the corners of their mouths jerking; these were the "hoppy" boys, lads who went in for "Chinese stuff," but it cost something to get coked up and most of the drunks had no urge to try and change their luck.

Two old bums mooched along outside, staring inside the store. Both stopped, dug into their pants, and, looking down, counted carefully a few sweaty coins upon their palms. They held a conference and wagged their shaggy heads. One of them pointed to a sign Pete had stuck against the glass and argued hotly with his pal. His pal swore and held out, then gave in. They came inside.

Pete eased up, six years of Third Avenue experience in that cagy dome of his.

"How much you got?" he asked right away.

They slapped the damp coins upon the cracked marble of the counter.

"All right," he said, "I fix you up, I give you both the corned beef hash with mashed on side, also peas."

They said it was all right, then Pete went back and told the cook to warm up that small batch of hash left over from the special he had run noontime.

The two old bums at the counter were talking: "So he comes up to me . . ." "Who?" "Why, the guvner, of course, the old gent whose son sends him ten bucks a week, and he comes up to me and he says, 'Lay off the hookers, take a shot of daisy.' So I plays dumb and I says, 'Daisy? I ain't never tried a shot of dope yet.' And he says, 'My boy sent me the allowance today, come with me, I'll blow you to your first Daisy.' So nacherly I goes along. Well, we goes up two doors south of Uncle Beagle's Pawn Shop and he knocked four times, three fast and one slow, and a fat guy leaves us in. 'Try the pipe first,' says the guvner to me, but I'm an old hand, so I asks for the needle. Better than a hooker of smoke any day, say I. Just knock four times."

The hash arrived. Both sniffed at it, then tore in, shoving the food down. After the repast one of them asked Jason for a cigarette. The ex-poet handed them his pack. They took two apiece and lit up, got off their stools, and left like Park Avenue gentry, blowing cigarette smoke over their shoulders, chatting socially, their bellies warm with food.

The wind died down, the zone of light outside lay like a hoop of silver flat against the pavement. Jason stirred.

"Say," he said to Pete, "I hate to ask you, but can you let me have two bucks until Friday, I've got a check coming."

The Serbian coughed, thought in a flash, then pinged the cash drawer open. Jason took the two damp bills, Pete marked it down upon the slip of paper.

"Thanks," and Jason was off the stool and went outside, walking south toward Uncle Beagle's.

In the store Pete stood staring at the NO SALE sign just registered. A few plates dropped in the rear, he whirled about, heard no accompanying crash. Through the wicket shot out the aged, steamy face of the dish-washer, a crushed and sorry gent, his bald, bluish skull shining in the light.

"No breakerage, boss," he reported and bent to pick the broken crockery from the floor. They had cracked neatly, silently.

Jason, his chin down, his eyes swinging from left to right as he walked, was going south on Third Avenue, wondering how a shot of dope could stack up to a pint of fair-grade gin.

In Cooper Union the lights were lit, the porters were busy mopping there.

Three golden balls swung and swayed, informing the world that Uncle Beagle was here to help in times of stress. In the window (ironwork screening placed before the plateglass for protection after hours) were old guns, fishing tackle, accordions, monkey wrenches, an ivory-handled fancy doorknob, camping knives, a book whose title page read *How to Cure Warts,* nickel-plated wristwatches, fountain pens, and a second-hand fur coat with its good side turned toward the street.

The building two doors south had a brown door. . . .

## V

THE ITALIA CLUB ran their annual dance that night. Mr. Franconi came home from the barber shop a little later than usual because he had paid another visit to Dr. Morrison over on Madison Avenue after getting off from work. Dr. Morrison had taken another blood test to find out how things were going and said he would learn the results within a very few days. He said he was quite confident that a definite improvement had been obtained and, averting his gaze and staring at his calendar, stated that the treatments would have to be continued.

"We can arrange so that they will not cost so much," he said quietly.

Mr. Franconi stood there listening. The doctor's office had a thin, clean smell.

When he came home, Mr. Franconi was all tired out and did not really care to go to the annual dance of the Italia Club but the affair was the biggest social event of the year at the clubrooms and he knew he was expected to attend.

He sat down in the easychair in the front room, all the lights of the apartment extinguished, and rested quietly in the dark for a half hour or so. He sat fully relaxed and let his face sag. His breathing was calm and restful.

Then, feeling better, he pressed the light on, changed into his dark gray suit, picked out a blue silk tie, knotted it carefully, and spent a long time brushing back his smooth, black hair. All the lights of the apartment were lit, there was something festive in the flat. For five minutes, after he had finished dressing, he stood in front of the bathroom mirror feeling his face exploringly with his hands. His eyes were deeply sunk, the flesh covering his cheekbones was thinly firm, but in the cheeks themselves slight hollows were forming. This brought out the bone structure of his face, accentuating the good points of his features.

One hand stroking the sides of his face, the bright lights of the living room at his back, he hummed a tune. Just before leaving, he sprayed perfume on the right lapel of his coat, inserted a handkerchief into the outer pocket of his jacket, then put his hat and overcoat on.

Walking leisurely, looking occasionally at the pleasant sky (the stars were out), he covered the few blocks to the Italia Club in ten minutes or so. As he climbed the front stairs he saw the lights and at the topmost step started humming again, a snatch of a song he remembered the wagoneers sang on their way to Vittorio. There was a long pause in one of the bars of the song, when the singer was supposed to snap his fingers or make the sound of a whip cracking over the backs of the oxen, but Mr. Franconi made a silent, inner cracking to himself, pausing, then hummed the succeeding bars.

He was still humming softly as he approached the entrance. At the door he was greeted boisterously, as usual. Several of his friends had had three or four drinks already. They walked him back to the hat-room, where he took off his overcoat and hung up his hat. After that they came out upon the floor.

The place was filled already, the members believed in arriving early. All the card tables had been shoved away, chairs had been lined against the wall, and far down the narrow hall a small Italian orchestra was seated. At the windows the dark shades were drawn, pulled down behind the curtains. The place was hazy with cigarette smoke, full of noise and loud talking. Almost all the members had brought their wives or sweethearts.

Then the orchestra began playing. Short men, tall men, middle-aged fellows from the other side and young American-Italians, all swung out into a dipping waltz. Every year it was the same—at first they swung round to Italian tunes, then came the fox-trots and the one-steps.

Mr. Franconi, smiling and bowing to his many friends, wandered toward the other end of the hall, where the punch table was. Tony had an assistant tonight, a fellow who took care of the punch, because Tony himself was run off his feet bringing out the other drinks for the members.

"Andre," someone called in Italian. "Andre, you devil, come over here."

Three couples stood off, drinking punch at the other side. He did not know the women.

"Andre!"

He went over smiling. Two of the women were very pretty, the other was plump and extremely healthy-looking. As he was introduced, he sensed at once that their partners had told them all about himself, bragging. He bowed slightly, smiling pleasantly. The men, dew on their honest foreheads, looked at him proudly. The place was stuffy.

"Tony! Tony, this punch is water. Make it seven wines, Tony!"

Tony, plenty of sweat rolling down the plump sides of his face, was rushing all around, clinking glasses, knocking bottles together, pouring out the stuff.

Mr. Franconi smiled pleasantly toward the healthy-looking woman, directed a jest at her partner, and asked for the honor of the next dance. The woman, round-faced, health bursting from her cheeks, her eyes shining, answered rapidly in Italian, dipping her head. Her escort flung out his left arm in a heroic gesture.

"Tony!" he bellowed, but Tony was already coming on the run.

Mr. Franconi swung out on the floor with the young woman, dancing easily. Had he picked one of the prettier women, the other would have felt slighted. He knew his people. He did not want to offend anybody. He had no strong urge to do good, but neither had he the inclination to cause friction. When he came back (the woman perspiring, her face slightly flushed, her body tingling pleasantly, her head dizzy from the perfume on his coat lapel), seven glasses were standing on a tray; they had waited for the dance to finish. Then they all lifted up the wine, the women looking at the men, the men glancing at Mr. Franconi. All took the first sip together. Two more couples came over. Someone passed cigars around, and, as Mr.

Franconi bent his head slightly to compliment a woman on her dress, the men winked broadly and laughed obscenely.

"Andre," they said, "be careful, she is already betrothed."

The fiancé winked the broadest, the girl colored.

"Ah, a dog he is, a wolf, Maria!"

Clapped on the back, introduced, whispered about by the women, he mingled easily with the crowd. All the men felt sure Andre was a practiced heart-breaker. In the club it had long been an accepted fact.

All during the evening he acted the pleasant, polished gentleman, flattering the women, dancing with the plainer-looking ones, treating his friends occasionally to wine.

The musicians, when the hall grew unbearably hot, peeled off their coats and played with sleeves rolled up. By this time many of the members walked about with wilted collars, their hair hung in their eyes, the loud talking grew louder, good-natured arguments sprang up, and toward midnight there was a scuffle which was skillfully turned into a friendly affair. Andre looked cool and at ease all evening. He was the first to leave. As he went toward the checkroom, his friends followed him, laughing, winking, speaking with double meanings.

"Why don't you bring her around sometimes, Andre?" they said. "Is she a blonde or a red-head? You dog, I bet she's waiting in your place now, she has a key of her own!"

They clapped him on the back, helped him into his coat. The halo they threw about him warmed the women toward him. One or two of them said something with their eyes. He answered back, parrying expertly with his own glance.

As he went out the door, three or four men walked with

him into the hallway. It was cool in the hallway. Through the opened door came American music, a one-step.

"Don't be a stranger, Andre," they said. "You always pay your dues, you should come up more often."

They spoke to him in Italian. It was nice listening to real friends in your own language. He began walking down the stairs, hearing his friends, the dull blur from the hall and strains from the small Italian orchestra.

When he reached the street, he began walking home. His face felt stiff and dry now, from smiling and looking pleasant all evening. Along the curbs at the garbage cans, cats were stepping, crouching, nibbling. The street was quiet. He drew in the autumn air and blew it slowly from his lungs and felt himself a tired man. The last bars of the wagoneers' song eddied in his brain, filtering through the dance music and loud talking of the whole evening now left behind: "Ho, how the wheels roll, pull on down the sunny mountains . . ."

Then he made that inner cracking of the whip again.

When he reached the Glen Cove Apartments, he met Mr. Boardman, who was coming back from the square with a newspaper under his arm. They stood in front of the building, acknowledged each other's greeting, and hesitated, as if they had something to say to each other. Both had a certain respect for each other, though they did not know just why.

# VI

THREE O'CLOCK the next afternoon. . . . Inside the hallway of the tenement, on the ground floor of Twenty-Door City, Leon looked toward the rear and saw light coming through the transom window toward the left. He stood there thinking, staring down the hall. Well, after all, he had been introduced, they weren't perfect strangers, were they? And besides, they were comrades, members of the Party together. He dug his nails into his palms. And hadn't he volunteered to help her fix the place up? He cleared his throat, stood there thinking hard, and continued to stare up the long, narrow hallway. Out in front was the old janitress, standing in the sun. She turned about, smiling.

"Waiting for Mister Wheeler?" she asked.

"No," said Leon and strode to the rear and knocked upon the door, rather softly, but it was knocking just the same.

Comrade Helen, large, well rounded, blond, opened it. The hall was dark, at first she could not make out who it was.

"It's me, comrade," said Leon, stammering a bit. "I promised I'd help you fix the rooms up, you know, but I was busy painting."

"Oh, yes." Leon saw a flash of strong, white teeth. She opened the door wider, he went inside where she looked at him warmly.

All the rooms were in disorder, the beds weren't made, though it was afternoon already. Comrade Helen Jackson from New Orleans made no excuses, she was a Southern girl and let things slide. She said Sid and Harry Turner were working, José was out doing some organization work for the Party, out among some Long Island candy factories which were paying slave wages.

"Come on in," she said when he was already inside. He stood there with his overcoat on, undecided what to do, what to say.

"I was just going by," he said. "I was up to see my friend Jason, but he's not in."

His eyes roved about, those sharp artist's eyes of his, taking in the details. Three cockroaches were crawling up the wall above the sink, big fat ones with swollen backs. On Comrade Helen's feet were old felt house-slippers and for the first time Leon noticed she had rather thick ankles; however, they were strong legs, staunch, proletarian legs, ready to plow America for the Revolution, as the saying goes.

His uneasiness wore off. After all, why should the place be clean? They slept here, that was all, the rooms were temporary quarters, why fuss and bother? His mind grew tolerant, his eyes, wandering, did not criticize any more. The first thing he knew he had his overcoat off (the place was warm, a small coal stove was going), and they were talking together. He sat down in a chair and looked at her healthy, pleasant face and just to be in her presence was like receiving charity, he felt. He was far gone on her now. In some uncanny way this girl, this young woman with the blank face of a smiling milkmaid, had already sucked him to her without an effort. There he sat, his large eyes glowing like furnaces, his slim, sensitive hands on his knees, and every word, every look he gave her betrayed his heart and thoughts.

They talked about the Party. They discussed activities among the striking miners. The girl knew a great many names and seemed to be well informed. Leon became animated, his words came out, as from a gusher. He had no friends, no close friend expect Jason, and Jason was always making sport of him; so now the thoughts and dreams flowed out like oil, he had never talked like this before. Little by little, caught up by his warmth of feeling, the girl found herself answering sentence for sentence, conscious of the little fellow's goodness. He talked so warmly and sincerely. The minutes flew.

Then Leon caught himself. He laughed, and he himself was surprised at the new note in his laughter. "I was going to help you fix things up," he said, laughing.

She got up, shuffled about in her large, sloppy house-slippers, and made the beds. She made them rather untidily. As she bent over, drawing the sheets taut, her hips strained through the dress. Going about in house-slippers without heels gave her a solid way of walking. Parts of her body shook and quivered. She was like a large, healthy, female animal.

Leon got up and began putting things in order. While he stood upon a chair, Comrade Helen handed him things. They hung old curtains at the windows. The beds they rearranged. Moving them was work, Leon grew warm and took his jacket off. Helen, who was stronger, did most of the heavy lifting and shoving, while Leon, burning in the face, grunted as he helped and pushed things about. Both began to perspire, the thin dress of Comrade Helen stuck to her back.

But the place took on a kind of order. In half an hour the flat looked different. They sat down to rest, smiling at each other, telling one another they looked warm and perspiring. Leon took his tie off and wiped his face with his handkerchief. Then Helen stood on a chair, reached up into the shelves over the sink, and brought down a bag of apples. They sat there eating them, talking.

At four-thirty, while they were still eating apples and talking, the doorknob rattled. Leon stiffened. José came in; he grunted when he saw the little painter. He had been distributing leaflets all day long in the cold, had been turned down by the very people he had wanted to help, and in the end had been chased off by the police. He came in and took his coat off, threw his old misshapen hat on the bed, and hunted around for bread to make sandwiches. He had brought a dime's worth of cheese along. Sitting down at the table, his back to Leon, he sliced the bread in thick hunks, slapped them together against the cheese and started eating, his powerful jaws going up and down like pile-drivers. His broad, firm back stared hard at Leon, he made no move to turn around.

No one spoke for a while. Leon, uneasy in the chair, re-knotted his necktie. José was sitting on the little fellow's jacket. Leon noticed how Comrade Helen looked at the Mexican, at the hard way in which he sat; he saw now who was boss around the place and his heart started hammering. Finally he stood up to go. He went over to the table and gave a tug at the corner of his jacket. José went on eating. Leon tugged again, José lifted one side of his rump and the crumpled jacket came forth. The little fellow put it on quietly. He went toward the door and started to say something, but found he couldn't talk. Helen rose and stood at the door with him. José was making another sandwich and, looking at him, Leon saw the broad, firm back again, the thick, strong neck bent forward as the fellow sliced the bread.

As he opened the door Helen thanked him for helping. She was a little business-like about it.

"There's a draft," said José, without turning around.

"All right," said Comrade Helen shortly. "I'm sure you won't catch your death of cold. Good-bye," she said to Leon. "Thanks."

The door closed, he stood out in the hallway. Well, why didn't he move, why wasn't he on his way? Did he want to overhear something, had he turned spy? He stood there rooted, his legs unflexing. Pretty soon he heard an argument start up, he heard a chair go scraping back. Then came the guttural of the Mexican. And Comrade Helen answered. Leon, stock-still in his tracks, heard. How her voice changed! She could be shrill as a fishwife, she hollered José down. In two minutes a hot argument was going, epithets flew up and back. Leon, his soul vised, rushed up the narrow hallway. He heard a crash like smashing crockery, a woman's scream, then was on the street and heard no more.

He was all the way to Thirteenth Street when he reminded himself that he hadn't seen Jason. He stopped, whirled about.

Then he remembered he had nothing special to see Jason about anyway.

## VII

BIG CHIEF RUNNING WATER, his wide bulk filling the doorway leading to the office, stood looking at the hustlers rolling the merchandise away, stood listening to the small, well-oiled wheels of the trucks going over the smooth iron floor. The eleven hustlers, at first unaware that he was watching, went their carefree way, wheeling, bending, stopping, slamming the boxes and crates down with a noise, yet with an experienced expertness that did the stuff no damage. Each bang, each dumping was calculated by the micrometers within those loyal ivory skulls; each man knew his task, how much pressure to exert at a turn, when to lean against the load, when to heave ho, as the saying goes.

Old Running Water, standing there within the boundary lines of his shanty of an office, surveyed the scene from his poop-deck, cocked his eye to left and right, for signs of sun or rain, saw only the dull iron floor and the burning electric bulbs and took a puff from the stump of cigar between his teeth. The eleven hustlers heaved off again, the Big Chief stood in the shade.

Hank Austin, good old Hank, whose ancestors battled for freedom and the right to drink tea without English tax-stamps glued on the boxes—old Hank (he was young) was second in line, shoving a load along. The man behind, a pal of his, whipped a few words forward, a wise-crack, and Hank, returning the humorous quip, slung a few words back himself, his head jerking as he laughed, his mouth wide open carelessly. At that moment Old Running Water, still in the shade, narrowed his eyes (movie fashion), clenched the cigar butt firmer between his teeth, and the nail was driven deeper within that brain of his.

The Big Chief went into the office and settled his solid, very hefty bulk into the chair. Then he called for the ledger again, slapped the wide book open, turned the sheets and looked them over—and after Henry Austin's name he put a thick dot, making it with his big, soft pencil, a careful dot. The pencil point worked round and round, nice and black and perfect to look at. Before he knew it, Old Running Water, moving his ample hindquarters two points east by southeast in the wide chair, had quite a dot there—it stood out like a small, circular piece of soot from the whiteness of the page.

Cocking his head, he still could hear the smooth roll of wheels over the iron floor. The foreman came in, laid a sheaf of shipping bills down, sheets which were marked up in blue, red, and green pencil, strode out, and told the men where to put the new load, that big shipment of unmixed paint just come in from Milwaukee, via ship and rail.

"Over there," he ordered, pointing to the forward wall.

The men obeyed, and once more the trucks rolled by, each hustler passing the office door, eyes upon the guy's shoulders ahead, arms hard and rigid from the load. They went up and back like mine-workers in a shaft five hundred feet below.

At the east wall of the warehouse the big freight elevators hauled up load after load, slamming their big, wide doors. A cold draft blew up the shaftway, the men wore two sweaters under leather vests; on their hands were yellow, rawhide gloves. If a man shouted, his voice bounced off all the walls and had a hollow, metallic ring; a whistle went a long way, circling around the trucks and boxes.

In the office Old Running Water, his mind flowing on like heavy honey from a jar, sat thinking slowly, his pencil in his fist, his old eyes staring into the hollow of the mouthpiece. The phone rang. The kid at the small desk dropped his mystery novel into the ready, opened drawer and shut it smartly. The ring was on his extension.

"Consolidated Warehouse. Yessir. Two loads at Pier 43, Cunard Line? All right, our trucks'll call in the morning. Bye."

The receiver jiggled into place, the drawer below opened craftily, the lad dipped down and pulled up his book again. He started reading, resumed where he left off . . . "Just then Professor Farrington, late of Scotland Yard, swung his lean, muscular body over the iron fence of the mansion on the hill and in the flash of lightning that followed saw sprawled out in the tall, wet gress the body of Lawyer Brown. The professor crouched beside the fallen figure. 'Dead!' he gasped. A long, narrow, evil-looking knife lay at the body's side, with no blood on it. Professor Farrington, wrinkling his brows, straightened up at the sound of whirring wings, and at that moment from the sycamore tree on top of the mansion hill an owl hooted three times softly. 'Dirk again!' said the professor and stood up and looked sharply all around. . . ."

The phone rang. The kid dropped the book into space again. This time the call was for Old Running Water, who lifted up a beefy arm, took the receiver off the hook, and, listening, began playing with his soft, lead pencil as he answered, making the round dot opposite Henry Austin's name bigger and bigger, until the dot was as large and black as a good-sized bullet hole.

# VIII

IN THE DAYS that followed, Leon (at first timidly) came over many times to help Comrade Helen straighten things out, starting out from his room with the hope in his heart that Comrade José Morales would not be around. When he arrived, the flat was always in disorder, the three comrades, José and the Turner brothers, did not lift a hand about the flat. Leon, with one eye on the artistic possibilities of the rooms and the other eye on Helen's figure (his soul torn between the two), put things straight, rearranging the furniture almost every time, making an excuse for his visits. In a short time Comrade Helen grew accustomed to seeing him coming over often and would allow the rooms to remain in a disordered state, until the little fellow put in an appearance. He always stood quietly out in the hall a while, before he lifted up a hand to knock. A few times, as he waited, he heard squabbles, and went away without rapping.

December came on—gray days, cloudy days, nights of rain and chilly wind. No snow had fallen yet, but the rawness of the weather was worse than a storm.

In the slums life crawled on, dragging itself along. Long lines formed hours before the charity headquarters opened up, lines of the living dead, and bundles were distributed to the holders of cards, heaved over the counters. The people stood outside pressed against the wall, slowly moving forward. At the corner a policeman was on duty, but had nothing to do. All was humbleness, all was meekness; there was no flare-up at all. Folks took their packages and left, cutting down side streets, each man or woman going his own way, hoping they wouldn't meet any of their neighbors.

In the tenements the little coal stoves burned only in the early morning and toward nightfall, when it was coldest. Fuel was sold by the bag, a dollar for a short, squat sack of hard coal, bringing the rate up to twenty dollars a ton; there was no way to check the weight either, by expert packing a sack could be made to look fuller than it really was. The small-time venders, wheeling their handcarts up the streets, shouted: "Coal-man, Coal-man . . ." Kids ran downstairs to tell the Italian what floor to come up to.

And at five o'clock, when darkness fell, women with their kids were foraging for firewood, wheeling their babybuggies or even carrying old ropes or rags to tie up the sticks. They hunted around the rear platforms of furniture companies, factories, drygoods stores; and if a box was sighted, the fastest of foot got the booty, with the others hating the winner. On First Avenue, where the outdoor markets crowded each other onto the street, stale fruit and half-rotted vegetables were sold toward nightfall, and by careful plucking and picking a housewife could occasionally get a downright bargain.

Every family handled its own washing. Clotheslines were strung inside the rooms, up and back, zig-zagging; the steam from the damp garments covered the windows with mist, making the place look warm and cosy, but when you blew, vapor came from your mouth in a long column.

Every day, every night, the leaders of our country gave this serious situation their undivided attention. Bigger and better organized charity drives started, teas were held in the finer hotels, representatives of big business gave reassuring talks over the radio, financial journals made bi-weekly predictions, quoting graphs and charts; and politicians, their eyes on coming elections, faced the problem frankly, but when they were through talking you found they had promised nothing definite. A few of them ended their speeches with staunch, heroic words: "The American people, bravely facing this severe and prolonged crisis, are coming out of this darkness into a new dawn, with the customary ruggedness that has always been our heritage since those hardy days when the pioneers, in the face of overwhelming odds, pushed westward in their covered wagons, opening up this glorious country of ours. . . ."

Along Fourteenth Street shivering men stood in the doorways of radio stores listening. The music from the taxi-dancing jazzbands blared out upon the street.

In the square Comrade Irving Rosenblum harangued the multitude, giving them the lowdown on the whole rotten situation here at hand. Each oration he opened solemnly with the time-honored salutation:

"Fellow workers!" (no spittle flying yet, his face still calm) "—fellow workers" (looking the citizenry over), "here in America, in the greatest, the richest country in the world, with warehouses filled with food and clothing, ten million people are unemployed and hunger stalks the land." (A glance around, allowing the words to sink in, waiting for a Fourteenth Street trolley to rattle by, watching a few shabby geezers ambling over.) "Fellow workers, you are living in the United States, in a land of liberty and freedom. You have a voice in the Government. Yes, you have. As a member of the Unemployed Council, I, with a group of other comrades, journeyed up to Albany, the Capitol, and demanded unemployment insurance, lower rents, and a fifty-million-dollar appropriation for unemployment relief." (Some figures, that'll wake 'em up.) "And when we got there, fellow workers, when we reached the Capitol, when we walked up the tall flight of stairs to talk to the Governor, we were met by the police. We came unarmed, but were given no quarter, we were beaten and clubbed, four of my comrades so badly they are still in hospital. I myself was hit over the head and stunned and was sick for three days. This, comrades, was our answer." (A pause, now the little fellow swallows, he's getting warmed up, Rosie is.) "Fellow workers" (the sarcastic touch coming, the bitter-humored stuff), "you need not worry, everything will be all right. Just sit home and take things easy, toast you toes at the stove. With the right men in office as we now have" (a knowing, sour smile flecking his lips), "it will only be a matter of time, maybe a hundred years, maybe two hundred, but don't worry, my friends, everything will straighten out. If you don't live to see better times, your grandchildren will, so what's the difference?" (No applause, a few grim smiles, some of the citizenry shift slightly in their tracks.) "Comrades, you may not know it, some of you may be entirely unaware, but the fact is, there is a great war going on—the Class War, capitalism against the working class. Which side are you on?" (He stares at the shabby geezers who have wormed their way up front.) "Which side? There can be no compromise, it is a battle to the finish. . . ." (Here another trolley rattles by, Rosie takes in a good deep breath of air.) "The Communist Party of America fights for the working class, protects the workers, it is the only party in America with a militant platform. Fellow workers, I tell you that . . ." (Now he has hit his stride, from then on the little fellow's mouth rattles like a machine-gun.)

December still came on, chilly nights on the East Side. Jason Wheeler, ex-poet, ex-communist, former student of world affairs, bard of the famous tenement known to all as Twenty-Door City, sold another sex-story and received a check for eighteen dollars. Some of the money he spent on gin, some against his rent bill, the rest he donated to Pete, who ran his "source of supplies." The lights of the Crystal Lunchroom burned brightly. "An army crawls on its belly," said Jason, sipping a fourth cup of coffee. The cook in the rear rattled his pans.

But Jason forgot to pay his gas bill, his quarters were cold. He sat in his overcoat and hammered out his stuff on the typewriter. And now those letters, those small pink envelopes post-marked Philadelphia came to a stop, the Jolly Postman did not bring any more to the tenement. Jason waited and waited, but none came. Whenever his friend Leon came over, the ex-poet turned the conversation toward a certain point. "I'm getting tired of this town," he told Leon. "Maybe I'll check out for a few days, the change will do me good."

And Leon, going through his own wilderness, getting

up stiff and dry-eyed after tossing about in feverish dreams all night, said a few words to his friend to show he was really interested. "Where'll you go?"

"I don't know, maybe a bus ride, maybe Philadelphia, it doesn't cost much and it doesn't take long, you know."

"Yes, it's only about a hundred miles," said Leon vaguely, thinking about something else, wondering.

Aye, December, a chilly, gloomy month. In the square the bronze statues discolored more, taking on a greenish tint. The show running at the Acme was now CRIME AND PUNISHMENT, a throbbing drama by Feodor Dostoievsky, rendered by the Moscow Art Players, matinees still 15c, evenings 30c.

At Webster Hall "The Girls From Sweden" ran a dance, a Swedish ball, stamping, whirling, dancing their peasant Scandinavian dances intermingled with jazzy American numbers. In the pauses a fellow with a Finnish accordion jumped upon the platform and pressed out a tune, a sea-chanty, and all heels hit the floor; the fellow worked and sweated at the song.

The African doorman, gold braid all over his cap, upon his shoulders, and heavy against his chest, spoke in conference with a cab driver at the curb. "Brother," he said, "a lot of poor folks is dancin' tonight, just trash, no business in sight as far as I kin see. Them is workin' people there, the tips at the checkroom has been lousy from what I gather after looking over the situation." The cab driver stared straight ahead, his gaze hard up Eleventh Street. Behind him a file of cabs, not so long tonight, waited for fares. Couples came out, but walked the few blocks toward the subways, business was plenty bad. Cold air hurried on, no stars were out, no moon. In the middle of the block the owner of the small Hungarian restaurant thought about selling a little booze across the counter, business was so rotten by him too; he stood in the rear of the deserted store, surveying the empty tables with a gloomy eye, noting lonely-looking salt-and-pepper shakers, old cane-bottomed chairs, and his face took on a hang-dog, beaten look. Over the fire was cooking, slowly, some goulash, the smell hung heavy above the stove.

In the second week of December Jason sent two letters off to Philadelphia, waiting four days before he sent the second. No answer came. A few days later, when Leon came upstairs to see his friend, Jason was stretched out upon the cot, his eyes bright, thin lines etched across his forehead. The ex-poet pulled the left sleeve of his shirt down hurriedly.

"Is that a rash you've got there?" asked Leon, quick of eye, quick of mind, before the sleeve was pulled down all the way; and just before he left, when Jason wasn't looking, he took the gas bill from the nail. It wasn't big, only two dollars and ten cents.

Miss Allen, that young nurse Jason had met a few times since he had paid a visit to the hospital, sent him a card again, asking him to call, and when he called, why, there she was, all dressed in her street clothes, standing modestly in the doorway waiting for him. She took his arm and they started walking up the street and, glancing from the corners of her eyes, scanned him closely. In a doorway of a large furniture store on Fourteenth Street she felt his pulse, glancing at her wristwatch. "What have you been doing, your pulse is so fast, what have you been doing?" she asked. He stared out upon the street with old-man, empty eyes and then looked deadly at her, blankly is the word.

They walked up Fifth Avenue, going north toward

Twenty-Third Street. Big buses hurried by, hugging the curb, passengers on top and bottom, the heavy autos farting light blue gasoline fumes from the exhaust.

The traffic lights changed, the citizenry stepped across.

"You forgot to call me at the hospital last Monday as you promised," said Miss Allen, said the young nurse who was now fighting for a losing cause.

Jason walked on, no brightness in his eyes. The second door south had a brown door. . . . In the cold he fished out a smoke and lit the cigarette like an expert, puffing at it like a hungry man. The young nurse from upstate looked the other way, he was so worn and thin. She took his arm when they reached the corner and, as the ex-poet looked sharply toward the right to see if traffic was approaching, he saw that her eyes were wet. He inhaled a great draft then.

At Twenty-Third Street they turned back, walking slowly. The wind shifted, driving in from the east. They stopped in front of the hospital entrance. Jason was now shivering, trying to hide it. Then he said something, said a few words in that quiet, dead voice of his that made up for everything. He stared up the street as he spoke.

"I would have taken you to a show," he said, "but I'm broke." He kept staring up the street, frowning, as if something interested him there. He took his glasses off and shined them slowly. Miss Allen bit her lip, her eyes were going wet again. She gave his arm a squeeze.

When he had walked a half a block she was still standing near the entrance, watching him strolling up the street. He had narrow shoulders and looked so boyish from the rear. The sole of his left shoe slapped the pavement gently at each step, cold air blew in upon his socked foot.

A few days later the mailman brought Jason a package,

a pair of shoes. They were a trifle too wide for him. No note was inside, nothing at all. Jason put them on and began wearing them. The old ones he tossed out the window, dropping them down upon the small yard below.

And the next time Leon arrived, Jason, who heard his footsteps, had his feet hoisted upon his typewriter table, so that the little fellow could see the brown, sturdy shoes he now had on.

"Where did you get them?" Leon asked, wondering if his friend had received another check.

Jason took his time about answering, he was even a bit arrogant about it. Leon had to ask again.

"Where?" said Jason. "Why, I bought them in one of the swankiest dumps on Fifth Avenue," and he gave the name of the store. "The pair set me back fourteen dollars, but they're worth it. I'm careful about my feet."

He sat there gazing at the staunchness of the shoes; they had wide toes and would wear well—English shoes perhaps. He stared so fondly and so long that he did not notice that Leon stood there smiling.

"Well, what are you grinning at, don't you believe me?" Jason said, half-shouting. "Do you think I'm a liar?"

Leon stood there, still smiling. From his large, dark eyes there flowed the warmth of his generous nature. "I was smiling at something else," he said. "Here you sit in the cold, when you have a gas-heater in the room. Why don't you light it?"

Jason glared at him. Was the little fellow making sport of him, was the worm turning? "I'll not answer to that," the ex-poet replied. "Besides, the room is warm enough."

"Is it?" Leon opened his mouth and blew vapor forth, gray steam. Then, still smiling, he crossed the room, struck a match, and bent down in front of the little gas-heater. Jason grew hot around the collar, this was going a bit too far. Didn't the little fellow know very well that the gas was shut off, the bill wasn't paid? He cleared his throat and glared hard at Leon's bent-over back. A spurt of flame shot from the burner, then the gas flowed brightly, burning evenly. The room became filled with glowing heat.

Leon turned about, holding the blackened match in his hand. He stood there smiling, waiting for Jason to say something.

The ex-poet sat there frowning a long while.

"Oh, yes," he said at last, matter-of-fact, not yielding an inch, "I was going to light the burner just before you came in, but I was all out of matches."

## IX

TOWARD the middle of December Mr. Boardman, the gray-haired, gray-mustached man who lived with the trim young woman across the hall from the "Russian" couple, began to look more worried about the eyes than ever. Even the old janitress of Twenty-Door City noticed it. Every evening she saw him leading Dodo by a leash, taking the dog for a short walk up the street, then back again. He was a fine-looking gentleman, he had an air of breeding, and his clothes fitted him well, the old girl thought. She wondered what the matter was, what was troubling him. Then she thought about hanging out a sign for that little room across the hall from Mister Wheeler, the one that had been vacant for over a year now; the agent of the tenement had said something about it.

Every day the Jolly Postman came up the street, making his rounds, walking in his wide, roomy shoes, but he did not always bring jolly good news. He brought Mr. Boardman the news that his sixteen-year-old daughter who was studying in a Massachusetts finishing school would like to come to New York for the Christmas holidays to visit her papa. She wrote the letter in her girlish, virginal hand, signing her name with a girlish swirl at the end, like a mousie's tail: Milly, the signature was, with a curly swirl at the end of it.

The postman plodded up the street with his load upon his back, stuck the daughter's envelope into the Boardman mail-box and went his way, recalling that sturdy epic dear to the hearts of all mail-carriers: "Neither snow nor rain nor heat nor gloom of night stays these couriers from the swift completion of their appointed rounds. . . ." This legend, carved over the wide staircase of Indiana limestone of the main Post Office was duplicated in a modest cardboard sign which reposed inside the door of the employees' lavatory of Station "D" over on Thirteenth Street.

Mr. Boardman, home from the office, waiting for Margie to finish dressing before they went out for the evening, wondered what he'd do about the matter. He hadn't seen his daughter for over a year now and, though he wanted her with him during the holidays, he knew it couldn't be done—it wasn't "practical." He held his hat in his hand, walked the room slowly, waiting for Margie to finish dressing. She was in the bathroom, and through the half-opened door he heard her humming to herself, in that low, throaty voice of hers, that sad, vigorous way she had of humming the blues. He caught some of the words . . . "Da-da-da-Daddy, why do you spank your little Ma-ma now . . . ?"

"Ready?" he said when she clicked the light out there.

"Nope," she answered, turning brightly, giving his cheek a playful tap. He placed his hat down and hooked her dress from the back for her. She had doused plenty of expensive scent on her clothing tonight, the flat smelled like a florist's shop.

"Where we going, daddy?"

"Anywhere you like," he answered quietly, picking up his hat again, reaching for his cane. He helped her with her coat, the new one he had given her as a gift only a month ago. It had a fine fur collar.

"There's a new place just opened up last week," she told him. "Over on Fifty-Fourth Street, they say it's a real joint."

"All right, we can go there," Mr. Boardman said and clicked the living-room light out. She kissed his cheek, kissed it lightly in the dark, standing on her toes, pursing her lips baby-fashion. He closed the door quietly, they walked down the stairs. When they reached the street, they stood looking up and down until a cab came along.

In the taxi she sat playing idly with his fingers, acting very happy and glad to be with him. The hum of rubber tires against the pavement, the feel of her cool fingers toying with his, lulled his brain. They got off in front of an old-fashioned brownstone front, he paid the driver, and the cab rolled off. Early evening traffic went up the street, a few people walked by. At the corner a drugstore sign flashed on and off: Venida Hair-Nets, Soda & Prescriptions.

At last they were inside, after Mr. Boardman had done a little smooth, quiet talking through an opened panel of the thick front door. To clinch the argument he showed a few cards from other speakeasies. The heavy door swung back.

Small round tables lined the walls, middle-aged waiters who served silently and knew their business went in and out of the kitchen. The conversation of the guests was low-pitched and refined, this was no noisy joint. Most of the women, smartly dressed, were no longer young, and their male escorts were well on in years themselves. The place had an air of class.

The head waiter gave Margie and Mr. Boardman a table to the left. The food was warm and good, they took their time. The drinks were all right too, everything was fine. Sitting back, turning his fine gray head, Mr. Boardman surveyed the scene, allowing his glance to wander here and there. A few women looked his way, he was quite attractive. Margie, after the soup, wiped her lips with her napkin and carefully rouged her mouth; she took out a new stick and tore the cap off with her fingernails and afterwards, when the entertainment began, Mr. Boardman saw how her mouth flamed, it looked like a dexterous smear of blood.

Three girls came out in tights to warble a bit, singing the blues. They swayed slowly, moving in unison, each face the same, mouths forming the same voweled words, heels tapping the floor, powdered thighs quivering slightly as they tapped. They were the Harmony Sisters, God's gift to Broadway. The guests gave the girls a warm hand, the kids had it coming to them. Afterwards a master of ceremonies, a tap-dancing lad who tried hard to break his neck, stepped out upon the floor in an encore number and, with two small green spotlights playing on his face, lifted a small megaphone to his mouth and sang a sad, sad love song. Mr. Boardman, thinking of his sixteen-year-old daughter and how he could get out of seeing her during the Christmas holidays, wondered why all the songs had to be so sad. Turning his head, he saw Margie and a tall man three tables away looking at each other. He lit another cigarette and stared down at the gold-plated matchbox. Margie tapped his wrist quickly across the little table.

"I saw you watching," she said, smiling. "You're jealous, I do it just to make you jealous, you daddy-daddy."

"I was looking the other way," Mr. Boardman answered. "I didn't notice."

They had a few more drinks, it was nice and quiet here, not like the other noisy places. Still, the prices were rather steep, you paid plenty for it. Mr. Boardman paid. They went out, the head waiter bowing in the French tradition; he was a gent who had taken in a few continental movies and knew just how the farewell was executed.

Outside the air was cold again. Margie turned her fur collar up, giving her rear a more aristocratic look. At the corner the drugstore sign still flashed on and off: Venida Hair-Nets. Mr. Boardman didn't stop to read it all, it was not important enough.

In the cab, riding home, he spoke to Margie about his sixteen-year-old daughter, how his daughter wanted to see him during the coming holidays. The taxi hurried up the street. He spoke quietly, staring at the driver's neck. There was a small pimple there. Mr. Boardman told Margie that, if his daughter really wanted to come to New York, why he might have to stop at a hotel for a few days; he might have to stop there alone.

"I could tell my daughter the decorators are repainting the apartment, or that I moved. It would be perfectly easy to explain it that way."

"But what about me, daddy, what am I to do when you're gone, when you're living at the hotel?"

"My daughter will stay for only a few days, a week at the most, that's all. After that it will be the same again," Mr. Boardman explained.

"But I'll be all by my lonesome," Margie answered poutingly, toying with his fingers, thinking of the tall man who sat three tables away, thinking of any tall man who was fairly handy. "I'll be all alone, daddy."

"It won't be for long, dear."

She continued to toy with his fingers as the cab sped on, humming over the pavement.

"It won't be for long," he repeated, listening to the steady drone of the rubber tires as the taxi hurried them back to the Glen Cove Apartments, wondering vaguely how it would all end.

"I don't know what I'll do," murmured Margie sadly, still thinking of a tall man, still playing with Boardie's fingers.

Mr. Boardman, his stare fixed upon the pimple on the neck of the driver in the seat ahead, tried to reassure her all during the ride.

His words were clearly spoken, but had a dead ring to them.

# X

FOR SOME WEEKS now Celia had been saving her pocket money, putting the small change into a narrow tin box in the upper left-hand drawer of her dresser. There were mostly dimes and quarters in the box, but as the days passed a small pile began accumulating. Every evening she read the dental advertisements in the paper, leaning over the sheets, wondering what dental parlor did the best work at the lowest price. In the rocker, erect and quietly stern, her aunt held a travel book about the Orient in her hand. Mrs. Chapman was very much interested in India lately because she had received, two months or so ago, a letter from a friend up in Boston who had a brother-in-law who was a missionary near Bombay.

The light above the table shone upon Celia's black coiled hair. Her chin cupped in her hands, her eyes lifting to stare vacantly at the faded flowers of the wallpaper, she wondered why Leon had that bright, hurried look in his eyes lately and why he passed her on the stairs with only a brief word or two. Only today she had reminded him, as he was rushing out, that she was ready to pose for those five-minute pencil sketches he had talked to her about a few weeks ago, but at her words he had stood stock-still for a long time, before he remembered just what he had said.

"Oh, yes," he had finally said, coloring slightly, "I'm working on a new canvas now. As soon as I'm finished, I'd be glad to have you pose for me." She stood there until the door banged.

But when she cleaned his room, she looked about and saw no work in progress, only a roll of canvas in a corner, a few wooden stretchers, and a few hazy pencil studies of people walking past Union Square. She started cleaning his room very vigorously, working hard at it, doing a thorough job because she knew he liked his quarters neat and clean. But just before she finished, her chin trembled and she had to sit down in a chair and blow her nose softly. She sat there staring at the wall, her hair in the old house-cap, the broom in her girlish hands. Later on, in the afternoon, she bought a red flower from a peddler going up Third Avenue, spending a dime from her hoarded pocket money, and when Leon returned he saw the flower standing in a glass of clear water on his dresser.

He felt a little funny around the throat as he stood there looking at it.

The next evening, as he was going out for supper, he walked quietly back behind the first floor staircase and knocked softly on Celia's door. When she opened it, her face flamed. Leon stood there ill at ease.

"Thanks for the flower," he said, pitching his voice low. "Thanks, it was nice of you."

"I happened to find it," she said, one hand trembling on the knob. "It wasn't anything."

"Well, thanks just the same." He stood there, his throat harsh and hot like a wooden plank under a summer sun. "I was going for a walk later in the evening, I'm going out to eat now, and I thought, if you had nothing to do, you might care to walk with me." He had finally gotten it out. He stood there expectantly, as small and slight as she. And Celia? Her heart was throbbing, her fingers clutched the doorknob. Go with him? What would her aunt say to that, going walking with a roomer? She had never gone out with a young man yet, she was only eighteen, and of course she did not attend dance halls or go walking alone along Fourteenth Street looking back over her shoulder.

"I don't know . . ." she said. "My aunt—you see . . ." But he was standing there. They heard someone walking on the stairs a few floors above. "All right," she said hurriedly. "Knock twice at my door at eight o'clock, I'll be ready."

At eight o'clock the stars were shining over Fourteenth Street, shining in a dark December sky. On the corner of Third Avenue the vender selling Turkish *halvah* stared with his small, greenish eyes at the passing throng, then barked a low, sad bark, urging the folks to patronize his push-cart. "Five cents a cut, five cents a cut. Mister, missus, five cents a cut . . ." A small knot of men stood at the curb, listening to the jazzy music coming from the Diana Gardens. Two gents from the lower Bowery stopped to listen, too. The Diana Gardens were on the second floor and they could see dim blue lights, Chinese lanterns, and streamers. A big sign stared: DANCING IS A SOCIAL NECessity. The sign wasn't long enough, the printer did the best he could.

At eight o'clock (chimes ringing all around the square) Leon walked down from his room, that funny feeling at his throat again, and knocked twice upon little Celia's door. She stood there waiting, all dressed up already. They went out the building quickly.

"It's not cold tonight," said Leon, after they covered the first block.

Cold? No, it wasn't. Celia had read the weather forecast, it would be fair and pleasant tomorrow, too. The report stated fair and warmer tonight and tomorrow with fresh southwest winds shifting to southeast. On the seaboard moderate to light north to northeast winds from below Hatteras to Block Island would blow, driving in north or northwest from Nantucket to Halifax or Sable Island.

"I suppose your aunt was surprised when you told her you were going walking," said Leon, taking her arm at the corner.

Celia stared straight ahead. She had feigned a headache only a half-hour ago and had told her aunt she was going straight to bed. "Why should my aunt be surprised?" she said, quietly, firmly, her small mouth taking on a determined look.

Leon coughed gently.

"I don't know," he said.

They neared Second Avenue and Seventeenth Street and entered the small park there. A tall black iron fence was around it, old-fashioned ironwork.

"Well," said Leon as they started walking up a deserted path, "no one seems to be around." He laughed a little.

"I'm not afraid," said Celia, feeling suddenly daring, her heart pounding at her words.

Leon laughed again. He stuck his hands in his overcoat pockets and whistled a few bars of a tune.

"I once studied the violin," he said, "when I was very young."

They walked all around the little park three times, going up every path. The night was rather springish, no chill in the air, and when Leon spied a newspaper on the ground he picked it up and asked Celia if she would like to sit on a bench for a while.

"If it's too cold, why of course we don't have to sit down," he said.

Celia sat down, spreading the paper for him, too. There was plenty for both, she said. She put her hands in her pockets, to keep them warm.

Pretty soon Leon was talking. The fine night, this young girl at his side, his afternoons with Comrade Helen —all fused, and the darkness of the park helped him along. He threw caution to the winds, he told Celia he was a communist.

A communist? What was that? She had heard and read about some demonstrations and how the police had dispersed paraders several times—but communists, what were they? She sat there puzzled.

Leon told her all about the movement. She was no sneering audience such as Jason, she sat watching his face as she spoke. Down the path a little arc lamp stood casting light their way. The light fell upon his brow, the air stirred his hair, he brushed back a lock as he started talking. He told her all about the brotherhood of the movement, how labor produced all wealth, therefore all wealth should go to labor, how women were at last to have equal rights in the new scheme of things. He also spoke about Russia. Now he was going strong, talking quietly, earnestly, his words and thoughts tumbling from him as he spoke. All of his own dreams, his half-formed ideals and ideas took shape now and came pouring from him in long, running phrases. He had the right word for everything, he linked his sentences perfectly. Celia, sitting small and quiet as a squirrel, listened. The wind shifted from east to northeast. Leon spoke for a long time, maybe a good half hour or so.

Finally he saw she was chilly, she was even shivering a bit. He asked her if she were cold. She said, "No."

But he saw she was lying. He himself felt very warm now, he stared up the path. Finally he said: "Come on, let's walk, I'll talk you to sleep pretty soon." He laughed.

So they rose from the bench and took a few more turns about the little park. In a dark spot they saw a sailor kissing a girl; the sailor had the girl backed up against a tree. Leon and Celia walked faster, staring ahead and only when they were out of the park and passing street lights did they talk to each other again.

But now in the light and with street noises all around Leon became aware that in the park his words of fire had been meant for someone else. This girl was walking with him at his side while in his brain another face was printed. Celia tried to rouse him, she attempted to discuss what he had just spoken to her in the park, and Leon tried to respond. He listened to her faltering, disconnected sentences (he saw at once she had failed to grasp a single Marxist statement he had made on the bench) and called himself a fool. Now he knew for sure that all the glowing thoughts had flowed from the furnace of his mind toward someone else all evening. He answered lamely and they walked in silence toward the rooming house.

Finally Celia, sensing his mood, stopped talking, stopped trying to say something that might please him, and walked at his side as silent as he, her little heels rapping against the sidewalk. They passed Fifteenth Street before they knew it, came up to Fourteenth, and, obeying a whim, Leon stopped in front of a vender with greenish eyes who was barking a low, sad bark. He bought a ten-cent cut of Turkish *halvah*. The old gent put it into a bigger bag.

"Here," said Leon, holding out the bag to Celia. "Take some."

She reached into the sack and broke off a piece. The stuff was rich and oily, heavy.

"This is supposed to be Turkish stuff," said Leon, wiping his fingers, chewing. The first mouthful was all right, the rest tasted like straw. Above their heads a jazzband blared, they lifted their eyes and saw the opened windows. DANCING IS A SOCIAL NECESSITY. They strolled on, Leon holding the paper bag. The stars were still shining above Fourteenth Street, shining in a dark December sky. At the curb a few venders had their wares spread out, three pairs of gen-u-ine silk socks for a quarteh, you cannot go wrong, Japanese jumping toys for the kiddies at home and a razor-blade sharpener for a dime. On the seaboard the wind drove in from below Hatteras to Block Island

and continued to blow in that direction. At half-past ten Celia, who liked walking along Fourteenth Street with Leon, suggested that they go home, her aunt might be worrying, she said. They retraced their steps, walking toward the east again. Leon opened the front door with his key. Celia walked quickly back behind the staircase and didn't stop to talk to Leon very long; in fact, she was a bit short with him.

"Thanks very much," she whispered, one hand on the knob, her ears listening for footsteps.

Leon stood there smiling at her. Thanks? "What for?" he said.

"Well, I enjoyed it," she answered quickly, listening for footsteps, tightening her grip on the doorknob. "I mean your talking and the walk. I enjoyed it very much, Leon, you know that."

His smile grew warmer and he said he had enjoyed it, too.

Then she closed the door. She got inside, trembling all over, hugging the evening to herself tightly. She took her clothes off and lay in bed with the light on for a long time, so that she could jump up and see herself in the mirror often. The flat, oily taste of the *halvah* was still in her mouth, no, she wasn't dreaming. She clicked the light off at last and snuggled into bed.

## XI

THE CONSOLIDATED WAREHOUSE down on Lafayette Street was so busy with the Christmas rush, there was so much stuff coming in and going out of the huge building that Hank Austin stopped worrying about the foreman's warning or the stare that Old Running Water had once cast his way. All the boys worked overtime up to the nineteenth of the month, the hours piled up.

When he got paid off on the nineteenth, which was a Saturday, Hank felt so good he stopped into Hearn's on Fourteenth Street and bought his youngest kid a colored rattle for a quarter. Afterwards he walked along Fourteenth Street, shouldering his way through the crowds, looking at the shops. All the stores were dressed up for the holiday—wreaths in the windows, cotton and false snow decorations to make the displays look wintry, cranberries and mistletoe; and in the window of the small Hungarian restaurant (Hank is now plowing up Eleventh Street) there hung, in sad dejection, a shabby rope of high-grade garlic.

Hank Austin went home, into the hallway, clumping up the historic stairs of Twenty-Door City, swung his apartment door open and, as his kids ran growling at his legs, why, he dragged them across the floor like so much seaweed. Then he dug into his pocket, bent over the eight-months-old infant (time has passed), shook the rattle, and teased the kid as a chubby Austin fist stretched out for it. In the end he placed the toy in the baby's hand, smiled a while down at his heir who was fourth in line, then took his hat and leather jacket off. He washed up, pulled a chair toward the kitchen table, and when the kids weren't looking nipped his good dame's buttocks nippily.

"Hank," she said, her eyeballs rolling, giving him his soup. He scowled down at it, lifted up a spoonful, blew upon it and swallowed it down. Good stuff. All the kids ate, aping the old man, holding their spoons in their fists with a full, tight grasp, shoving the food down.

"I made eighteen hours extra this week," said Hank,

turning to the roast beef. "Lots of stuff came in this month, loads and loads."

"How long will it last?" His wife speaking, standing short and sturdy over the stove, placing food in a plate for the eldest of her brood. The kid, watching, squealed; she gave another spoonful.

"Well, don't know," says Hank, hot food in his mouth, warm soup in his belly. "Old Running Water was busy running all over the floor with shipping sheets in his hands. He was quite excited, the old boy was. He's not a bad scout, the foreman neither," says Hank, chewing his food, his jaws going up and down. "Nope, they ain't bad, it's the depression."

But on Monday, which was the twenty-first, there were no extra hours, no overtime at all. The loads dropped off, dropping off a hell of a lot. In the office Old Running Water's desk was almost bare of sheets. The truckmen, looking seriously at the floor, took the corners more carefully and settled the stuff to the walls a little slower, stretching the work out. Old Running Water stared thoughtfully at the mouthpiece of his phone. There he sat upon his ample bottom, a cog in a big wheel himself, thinking of smaller cogs, pondering and frowning, chewing his cigar stub slowly. Finally, reaching out with his beefy arm, scowling and wrinkling his brows, he brought the point of his soft lead pencil across the ledger sheet and worked the point against three more truckmen's names.

Then he closed the ledger, four would have to be shaved off the force after the holidays. The kid, sitting at the desk behind him, lifted up the heavy book with a grunt and placed it back into the safe.

Later on, the foreman came into the office and stood idly about, an uneasy look under his eyes. He stood chewing on a toothpick and stared at the long, light brown hairs that grew out of the Big Chief's fatty ears. Old Running Water had been a blond in his youth.

At five-thirty the boys checked out, punching the clock—eleven husky men with caps pulled over their loyal skulls. Hank checked out the last, he had plenty of time, he was in no special hurry, he never got a seat on the subway anyway. As he placed his card into the OUT rack on the left-hand side of the clock, he caught sight of the foreman standing in the office door, saw the foreman staring into space. The man was still chewing on a toothpick and, as Hank headed for the stairway, the foreman's eyes swung round, staring at the broad, leathered back that swung along. A draft blew in as the door was opened, but was cut short when the iron latch clicked into place again.

And that night, that chill December night, when Bill (he was another truckman working for the Consolidated) came over to Hank Austin's place, paying a social call, the atmosphere was just a trifle gloomy. Neither man knew a thing about four dots after four hustlers' names. They sat in the kitchen (the other two rooms were used as bedrooms) and in a loyal, American fashion discussed loyal, American topics. Their good wives sat and listened; Bill's dame was hefty, too, only not so short as Hank's missus.

"Take Hoover, for instance," said Hank, clearing his throat, "take Hoover, now he's doing the best he can, no man can say he ain't. Take Hoover, for instance . . ."

And Bill nods, nods that loyal skull of his. The two wives nod also, the kids sitting around with their elbows on the edge of the big kitchen table nod too, nodding from fatigue. At nine o'clock Missus Austin, wearing her green Sunday-and-company dress (which is a bit tight under the armpits, but it's too late now, she can't change it)—

Missus Austin packed her young ones off—but first they made a trip out into the cold hallway, holding the key in their childish fists, one after the other. Then the grown folks sat alone, two pairs of them, the men hustlers, the women housewives. Now Bill was talking, he had a word or two to say.

"Take the Government, for instance," he said, frowning as he grappled for the right words, "take the Government, for instance, they're doing the best they can, you can't say that they ain't. But things are tough, it's a bad year, we got to be patient. Take the Government, for instance . . ."

And Hank nods, nods that loyal skull of his. His missus nods also, Bill's wife nods too, all of them nod as the speaker has his say.

At nine-thirty, the political situation cleared off the decks, they sat around and had a playful game of rummy, no stakes, no hard feelings, just a round or two. Years ago, right after the war, after America's triumphant emergence from the storm and strife, when factories were humming and the sky was the limit, Hank and his missus had played for stakes, Hank puffing on a perfecto, wearing a fifteen-dollar silk shirt with broad zebra stripes. But now he sat playing for the fun of it, it was better that way anyhow, no hard feelings, no arguments. Bill, who thought along the same lines, who had made plenty of jack in the good old post-war days, shuffled the deck and flipped the cards around. He was a big man, going just a bit beefy around the hips, and he had a bald spot on the top of his crown. When that spot had first appeared his good wife had kissed it in fun, now she slapped it every week or so and teased him that he was getting on in years.

Missus Austin, looking classy in her tight green dress

("Christ, she's got a build as solid as a rock," thought Bill), made coffee after a while and brought out a pound bag of chain-store cookies. The men were not hard drinkers, that is, er, drinkers of, er, hard stuff, so the coffee had to do. Four bottles of nice cold beer would have gone over big, but then, er, beer cost something and, er, the Austins had a lot of mouths to feed.

The cookies and the coffee were all right, big cups of strong coffee—that's the way.

"Take the unions, for instance," says Hank, scowling at a cookie held in that big fist of his, "take the unions. Now some of them are pretty strict to get into, but as a whole most of them are doing the best they can. Times are tough, you can't get away from that. But by spring things should get better, that's what the papers say. . . ."

"What about the commoonists?" Bill's good wife asks, sticking her hand into the fire. "They go around making trouble, they ought to be run out the country."

Communists? That meant foreigners; and instantly Hank's thoughts swung sharply toward the family across the hall, a den of Italians, co-sharers of the third front toilet, they ought to go back where they came from, and he remembered that banging toilet door.

"Commoonists?" he said, aping her pronunciation, shoving his underlip out. "They're foreigners, they ought to go back where they come from. This country should be for Amerikins." And his powerful jaws crushed the chain-store cakes into a powder.

"Take the commoonists," says Bill agreeing, also getting worked up. "Now that's another matter. Take the commoonists . . ." and he shot off his gab, spilling out all he had to say in sixteen words.

Now Bill's wife was sorry she had started things, the

men were going at it like hammer and tongs. Missus Austin, reaching carefully across for another cookie, so as not to put too much strain upon the cloth under her armpits, hoped the men would change the subject and would talk about the weather.

"They say that in Russia a wife can dee-vorce a husband in fifteen minutes," Bill's wife put in, adding spice to the boiling broth.

Now Missus Austin grew curious, she was a woman and naturally was interested in the feminine movement all over the world.

"All a woman has to do," went on Bill's wife, "is to go up to some kind of an office and fill out a sheet . . ." and she told them all about it. "I seen it in last Tuesday's paper . . ."

When she was finished, her husband looked at the whole thing from a man's viewpoint, from an American's standpoint. "What about the kids?"

"Oh, the kids . . ." his wife grunted. "I don't know about that . . ."

"Now take Russia," Bill said, barking his words out, a small vein beating in his forehead, "take Russia. It might work out all right there, but over here it's different. Over here it's . . ."

But now both women were nodding and he found himself talking to only Hank. Hank, his empty stare fixed upon the rim of the coffee cup, sat as if listening, but his thoughts were very far away, far away to that evening when the foreman had dropped a word into the slot of his brain.

"Now, take Russia," Bill was saying, whipping himself up, scowling at the ten-cent sugar bowl, at the taut silk under Missus Austin's armpits, "take Russia . . ."

He was still taking that great, wide sprawling country when the chimes of Grace Church struck eleven strokes, tolling eleven times in their classic, tolling manner.

## XII

WHEN THE ELEVENTH CHIME died away, melting into the frosty, East Side night, Officer Terence McGuffy came on for duty, swinging his nightstick as he came. He glanced across the square, looking toward the north, and saw, above the Guardian Life Insurance sign, a lot of stars shining in the dark December night. To the west was the Amalgamated, to the east the Union Square Savings Bank, and to the south was the gigantic Wrigley sign, which of course towered above all. McGuffy, surveying the scene, looking over his territory with the eye of a king's lancer, swung his nightstick again, and sauntered across the street. Autos slowed down as they approached him.

For a few minutes he stood talking to Officer Frank Hajek, another stalwart cop with a face like a hunk of juicy beef fresh from the butcher's ice-box, only Hajek wasn't a Celt, he was a Lithuanian and had high, grinning cheek-bones—a sturdy lad. He had once been a truck driver's assistant, but that was a long time ago, maybe three years back or so.

"How are things, colonel?" inquired Officer McGuffy, swinging his club as he came, wiggling it behind his broad Irish back, making circles in the dark December air.

"Fine, major," came the answer, and the big, white-gloved mitt of Officer Hajek lifted slowly in a gesture of regal authority. The east-west traffic spurted and started to flow by, trolleys bumping over the tracks, autos humming along.

The two fellow officers stood a while together, discussing current topics in the current manner. By glancing across the chilly square McGuffy had a good view and could spot a sergeant all the way to Seventeenth Street, but, of course, no inspectors went cruising about as late in the evening as this. Still, you could never tell; he swung his glance about, like a stalwart lancer in the king's service.

"I hear Kelly got taken on the carpet today," said Officer McGuffy as the traffic flowed smoothly by, as a wind sprang up in the square.

"Kelly, Mike Kelly?" and Hajek's palm rose slowly up again, giving the north-south traffic a chance to get going.

"He was caught boozed up in Joe's basement joint over on Sixth Avenue," said McGuffy, twirling his stick behind his back again.

"Oh," said Hajek, motioning at a slow moving car, "I thought it was something serious."

There was no more news then, nothing further to talk about. From the car tracks where they stood the decorated shop windows looked bright and cheerful. The cotton really looked like snow from the distance.

"Only a few more days left," said McGuffy, thinking of Christmas.

"Hey!" hollered Hajek and started bawling hell out of a driver who had attempted to make a left turn against the lights. Officer Hajek, walking over, stuck his jaw out, narrowed his left eye a little, put one foot on the running board and started his sarcastic faucet running, a wide-open tap. He shoved his head inside the automobile. "Are ya color-blind?" he asked, talking loudly, getting a harsh ring to his words. "Can'tcha see the red light, are ya wearin' smoked glasses, buddy?"

The driver, a young man, his hands on the wheel, a stream of cars behind honking and squawking for a clear road, looked funny about the gills.

"Here, pull over, pull over," commanded Hajek.

The car pulled over, there was a girl inside. With short toots and backward looks, the drivers of the other autos started passing.

"I ought to run you in," said Hajek, shoving his head inside the car again, right near the speedometer light, highlights shining on his grinning cheek-bones. "The least I can do is to give you a ticket. Yah." But he made no move, did not take his white gloves off.

Out on the street, centered between the sets of car tracks, Officer Terence McGuffy was at the helm, directing traffic in his comrade's absence, while his fellow officer faithfully discharged his duty. The rule-book said (this in bold-face type), "Co-operation between fellow officers in the line of duty is but one of the many rules the policeman must faithfully observe."

Finally Hajek allowed the car to move on, he gave the lad at the wheel no ticket even; he had a good cop's heart after all. Besides, the young girl sitting next to the driver was a good-looker, lifting and crossing her left leg as Hajek bawled out the meek young man. She stared wistfully at the big cop, and he saw she had a well-turned calf. "I ought to run you in," says Hajek, righteousness in his heart but forgiveness in his roving eyeballs. He looked less stern. "I ought to run you in," he said. A pause. "Well, get going, get a move on, what are ya waiting for?" The driver, looking grateful said: "Thanks, officer," and shifted gears. The girl smiled toward him and as her friend shifted into second uncrossed her leg.

"The public!" Hajek said, coming back to McGuffy.

"Sure, sometimes they get your goat," McGuffy said. "Well, so long, Frank, I'm shoving off," and he started strolling northward around the square.

He took his time. When he made the rounds of the south side he crossed over to Fourteenth Street and paused a while to scan the reading matter and photos in front of the Acme Theater. Another Russian picture was playing, this time, THE OLD AND THE NEW, the great epic of mother Russia's struggle for growth. The billboards were covered with pictures of tractors, stacked wheat, smiling workers, and scythes against the sky. McGuffy, swinging his club behind his back, wiggling it playfully like a doggie's tail, looked the photos over, posting himself thoroughly on the Russian situation. When he crossed over to talk to Officer Hajek, he cleared his throat and, of course, had to boast a bit about his knowledge, and you couldn't blame him.

"Those Russians," he said, and gave his comrade the lowdown on the whole Soviet system. "Dumping goods, having a big army, even training young girls to shoot, making stuff cheaper, now take those Russians . . ."

He told Comrade Hajek all about it.

A few blocks southeast another speaker was going strong, haranguing a workers' audience—none other than Comrade Irving Rosenblum speaking on the subject of trade unionism, telling the lads how to go about organizing. "Now in Russia," he said, warming up, putting shrapnel in his eyes, "take Russia, for instance . . ." and he told the workers all about it.

Aye, they were all talking Russia somewhere on that dark, December night. Stars shone in the sky. The whole

East Side was growing Russia-conscious, what with the Acme Theater, the comrades selling the *Daily Worker*, *The Moscow News*, and other Russianized sheets. Right near the corner a store had recently opened up, selling *objets d'art* from the Soviet Republics: blouses, basté shoes, candlesticks, jugs, dishes, and towels. People who came in to buy were mostly Greenwich Villagers, arty-looking young couples who lived in small "studio" apartments below Fourteenth Street and had lately swung over from free love to communism.

Gray air hurried by, driving in from Sable Sound. In one of the pauses, when the radio announcer stopped to get his wind, you could hear a phonograph record tinkling away, playing a merry *metilitza*. Over on Second Avenue the Russian cafés were jammed; there was a swanky, uptown crowd filing into the Russian Art Café and even the Original Moskowitz (half-Hungarian, half-Russian) had a goodly throng, with the last tables near the smell of the kitchen filled up before the night was over. Balalaika music strummed away, the chefs opened many tins of caviar.

"Here is a very fine Russian dish," said the waiters, bending low over the guests, allowing their tunic sleeves to billow out. "In Moscow it is a favorite. . . ."

The guests order, just a little bit of Russia, heigh-ho, see that man playing the balalaika, why he's a Tartar, I'll betcha, a real Caucasus face, ah, the Russian soul!

The cooks do not rattle the pans. It is quiet here, subdued.

At a quarter to twelve Mr. Quincy Boardman began packing his suitcase. He was leaving for the hotel and Margie, blowing her nose softly and looking sad and sorry, stood by watching.

"Oh, Boardie, Boardie darling, I'll be all by my lonesome, I don't know what I'll do without you."

Mr. Boardman, carefully shaven and thinking of his sixteen-year-old daughter who was due at the railroad station early in the morning, said it was only for a short time, and went on packing. He placed his things into the grip with care, then locked the leather bag.

At the door Margie clung to him. He went down the stairs quietly, hailed a cab at the street, and registered at a family hotel on a side street.

In the flat across the hall the young "Russian" couple were making plans for Christmas Day. Vanya, his nose pressed to the glass, stared down upon the street and wondered if it would snow by then, if he would have a white Christmas, just like in northern Russia. He talked it over with Natasha, who was getting a little tired of acting Russian, but, of course, she couldn't back out now because she had so many knickknacks and pieces of Russian furniture in the flat.

The air grew cold and raw outside. It blew into the hallway next door, through that shattered windowpane on the third floor, rattling the little ten-cent locks on the doors. But Hank was sleeping, he did not yell or holler out at all.

On Thirteenth Street Mr. Nicholson, the cracked printer, got up from his bed after lying thinking for a long, long while. He was about to start on another volume and had been thinking up an opening sentence. Finally he had it. He jumped out of bed, threw the covers aside. There he stood, excited, his eyes glassy, standing in his bare feet, in his long, dirty suit of winter underwear. He thought about the Roman legions, how they swung along. He ran his eyes over the books in the shelves, Gibbon's *Decline and Fall of the Roman Empire* and other standard works. Going over, he pulled a tome out, still thinking of a good first sentence, still hunting for an epic phrase.

He thumbed the pages. Victories stared up at him, how the crashing phalanxes swept all before them, how homeward, on the seven hills of Rome, shout upon shout rang out upon return. Men—men were made to fight, men were made for war! He thumbed another page . . . women coming rosy from the baths, slaves following, matrons walking full-bosomed past the marble columns. Women? The left side of his face began to twitch. Women? He knew what they were for. He strode over in his bare feet to the case of type, gripped a galley stick and started setting. Under the bright electric bulb his fingers flew on nervously.

Southward, in the middle of the block on Eleventh Street, the owner of the small Hungarian restaurant, late as it was, stood watching in his doorway and when he saw a big man in a cap come up, he opened the door and the man came inside. They closed the deal in fifty seconds. The Hungarian was going to sell booze, business was rotten, he had to live, there were mouths to feed. "I'll be around Wednesday," the big man said. "We'll see how the stuff goes."

The door slammed, the Hungarian stood in the rear, feeling queasy on his pins for a while. Then he put out the lights and went home. A man's got to live, there were mouths to feed.

Far away, on the Jersey City side, a ferry boat shoved off for Manhattan, Skipper Jim Hawkins at the front rail. He was thinking about that item he had read in the papers lately, how folks had begun to hoard money and not take it to banks. Jim felt a bit bad about it, he had sixty dollars stuck away in the White Owl cigar-box under his alarm clock in his Jersey City room. He was still thinking about it when the front of the ferry gently bumped the slip and settled snug against the wooden bulk of wharf-front.

On the return trip the wind began to rise a little, shifting from north to northeast. It continued to blow that way, driving in from Halifax.

# FOUR

## 1

CHRISTMAS MORNING stole along Fourteenth Street like a gray wolf slinking into a dead prairie town at dawn. The sky was overcast, the damp wind sniffed at every lamp-post and deserted hallway. Just before the sky cracked open, it looked like rain—cold, pelting, lashing rain—but shortly after 4 a. m. the temperature began rising, some of the dark clouds hurried southward toward the harbor, and from then on the day was dull and gloomy.

No Yuletide snow lay banked against the curb. In the Bowery missions the cooks rose early and started slicing potatoes, carrots, onions, and half-rotted turnips for the daily stew. To be up to snuff, to keep abreast of that happy Yuletide feeling, the manager ordered a couple of cans of green peas and sliced red beets to be opened, a little change in the menu, which he felt would go over great with the boys—and also with the board of trustees which was due to visit the place today.

In the windows of all the stores along Fourteenth Street the MERRY CHRISTMAS signs still hung, their silvered lettering staring out upon the street. Every church around the square began ringing out their bells. Some bonged, some clonged, others banged and clanged. Life must go on. The public must be kept informed. The presses roared, quivering the buildings. Trucks drew up and dropped their loads of papers at the newsstands, like trumpeting elephants dropping heavy pancakes on a jungle track. The early morning editions carried the customary Yuletide greetings from the customary people: bishops, cardinals, baseball managers down in Florida, movie stars, prize-fighters, heads of big department stores and steel mills, senators, real estate development promotors, and other stanch supports of our mighty commonwealth.

Transportation report. Long files of empty coaches stand at the sidings, after delivering metropolitan passengers to the folks back home. Traffic pretty heavy, reported the manager of the eastern division. But we have taken care of the holiday rush very efficiently.

In the city proper, long lines of pilgrims stood in front of gray cathedrals, waiting for the first mass to start. Inside, candles burned, plump priests walked up the main aisles, swinging heavy censers. A pale glow was spreading softly in the sky. Over the radio came early organ music, tones swelling, and a trained chorus joined in, hallelujahing mightily—strong, full-chested voices. In one of the East Side boarding houses, where some of the lodgers, subway track-walkers who worked on the early shift, had to get going before the day was fairly started, bacon and eggs sizzled merrily in Missus McCarthy's pans.

The municipal bath-house on East Eleventh Street was closed, no baths today, Antonia. So the little ten-year-old girl walked sadly homeward, hugging her towel and skinny bar of soap to her bony breast.

Then the bells began ringing again, in greater and greater volume, rising in crescendo. The priest began chanting the first prayers, while the long file of pilgrims, like a soup-line on the Bowery, moved slowly forward, carefully climbing the cathedral stairs, passing the big, wide iron doors. The pews were shiny in the dim half-dark.

Peals kept thundering out upon the town, rolling up the chill, gray streets. The tones died above the harbor, where a line of barges, towed by a couple of puffing tugs, drew by like a link of sausages pulled through mire by a pair of panting bulldogs. The skipper of the first tug, hearing the fading tones, leaned over the rail and spat thoughtfully into the mighty waters of the broad Atlantic. Then he stared toward the skyline of Hoboken and wondered how long it would take to get over there.

Sniffing at the doorways, the cloudy morning slunk along, a gray wolf sneaking into town.

## II

AT EIGHT O'CLOCK Mr. Boardman rose from his bed in a quiet hotel in the east Thirties, put his leather bedroom slippers on, and walked to the window to peer down upon the cloudy street below. In the next room (he had taken two rooms with adjoining bath) his sixteen-year-old daughter lay sleeping, her loosened, light brown hair lying in a soft mass above her pillowed head. Mr. Boardman, crossing over to stand in the doorway, stared upon her sleeping figure, saw her regular, even breathing (one smooth, slim forearm exposed outside the quilt), stood there looking for a while, then went back to bed, where he lay under the covering, staring at the dull tone of the ceiling. He lay like that for a long time.

When at last he heard his daughter stirring, he got out of bed, yawned loud enough so that she could hear, and called to her in a cheery, good-morning voice. "Up, Milly?" he said, putting on his leather slippers. "Yes, papa," came the answer, the voice pure and clear, with a fresh sixteen-year-old ring to it.

He walked to the windows and lifted the shades, one by one. The morning outside was still gloomy. When he turned to speak to his daughter who was in the next room, he set his facial muscles self-consciously, setting them in a cordial, fatherly manner, and asked if she wanted to take a shower now, or later. "Or will you wait for me to take a shower, Milly?"

This made his daughter angry, in a playful way. Who did he think he was (her voice playful, little bits of love for him hidden behind the chirping words)—who did he think he was, taking a bath before his daughter took hers, making her wait? "I thought you were a gentleman, papa, I thought you believed in chivalry."

And her father made answer, a warm flow of feeling driving out the gloom in his bones. "I just asked you, Milly, I just wanted to find out if you were going to shower now or later."

"Well, I'm going to bathe now," she answered sharply, and told him to close his door while she entered the shower. "I'm not a little girl any longer, I'm sixteen years old, so you're not to look," she said. And while she was getting ready, while she placed her bathrobe on the rack inside the shower-room, she kept talking crossly to her father, hiding little bits of love behind her words. Her talk came through the door, muffled by the stout wood of the hotel—girlish twittering. "Do you remember, papa, how you used to bathe me when I was small, right after mama went away? Do you remember, papa, how I used to call you Pika then? It was Pika this and Pika that, I sure made you hustle, papa." Now she was doing up her hair, so that it wouldn't get wet. She spoke toward the door again. "Do you remember that, papa?"

Mr. Boardman remembered. He remembered, suddenly, that his wife had been dead for eight years now.

"You used to get soap in my eyes," his daughter went on, her words coming through the door, "and one time my eyes smarted so much I cried all morning. Do you remember that, papa? No, I suppose you wouldn't."

Mr. Boardman went to stand near the windows, where he could look down upon the street as his daughter's words came to him. The gloom was going slowly from his bones, but something equally heavy was settling into place.

"Thanks for answering my questions," his daughter said. "I bet you've taken out your watch to see how long I'll be. Well, papa, you can stand there looking at it, because I'm going to take my time about it. I haven't seen you for over a year now, so if I treat you badly you have yourself to blame. Do you hear, papa?"

He cleared his throat at the window.

"Do you hear, Pika, do you hear?"

"I hear, Milly."

"Well, now I'll start, I've found a nice pink bar of new soap. It has such a nice smell, too."

Then he heard the shower, the water hissing against the tiles. Setting his facial muscles again, working up the old feeling, he walked quietly to the bathroom door and knocked sharply. "Milly."

"What is it?" Her voice was shrill, to rise above the spurting water.

"Should I soap you up, can you do it yourself?" he asked, mockingly.

"I won't answer such a question," she replied and went

on washing, loving her father more than ever. When he knocked again, she pretended not to hear him and did not answer. Afterwards he did not knock any more but went to stand near the windows again, his stare once more down upon the street below, his hands clasped thoughtfully behind his back. Later he heard the shower stop.

"I forgot the towel," she cried sharply. "Papa, reach me a towel!"

He walked over to the sink and took a heavy towel from the rack above. She stuck a slim, smooth, dripping arm out the half-opened door while he handed her the towel. As he gave it to her, she turned her wrist cleverly and pinched him on the forearm. "That's for being so mean as to want to shower first," she said and banged the door shut.

Five minutes later she called from her room, telling him he could now take his shower. She was sitting on her bed, dressing. She did up her hair in a soft, light brown pile and wondered if her father would feel bad if she applied lip rouge. She had never used it before—the authorities at the school forbade it—but at the station, coming to New York, she had bought a lipstick. While her father bathed, she kept up a chatter, speaking to him as she pulled her stockings on, rolling them tightly above the knee. She was a tall, slim girl, just beginning to blossom out. Sometimes Mr. Boardman had to shut off the shower to hear her. Finally he was finished, came out in his bathrobe, and began dressing. They continued to talk to each other, from room to room, the words coming through the opened doors of the shower.

"Where are we going today, Pika? Remember, it's Christmas. We've got to do something nice today."

"We'll go anywhere you like," he answered, knotting his necktie, looking at his face in the mirror. His stare was too thoughtful, he reset his facial muscles again. "What would you like for breakfast, madame?" he asked, a foil to her mood and manner. "The tongues of humming birds or just a glass of orange juice?"

"Bosh," said Milly. "You know what an appetite I have in the morning, papa. Well, I can still eat a hearty meal."

"All right, we'll order a steak then."

A steak? No, that was too heavy. "Remember how you used to cook my breakfast just before I went to grammar school, papa? At first you always burnt the toast. Then we got Agnes, that fat Polish woman. She was a good cook, only her puddings were spiced too much. Remember her, papa?"

Mr. Boardman, looking at his face in the mirror, remembered.

"I wonder where Agnes is now, papa. She wasn't so old when she came to us, was she? I don't think she was sixty yet. But she was so fat, wasn't she? I remember she had no ankles hardly at all."

Later on, dressed and hungry, they went out to eat, going into a small, quiet place on Madison Avenue. The coffee was good, Milly ordered a second helping of wheatcakes. "I'm growing tall, I need plenty of food," she said. Once or twice she gently kicked her father's foot under the table and asked him why he looked so sour. "Isn't the bacon good?" she asked, looking at his eyes. He got a grip on himself and from then on she could find no fault with his manners. From then on, he was a cavalier, his manners were perfect, he said the proper phrase at the proper time and had her smiling and pleased with him.

After breakfast they walked up Fifth Avenue for a few blocks and, hearing church bells, turned east on Twenty-Ninth.

"Let's go in," the daughter said, and they went in.

It was a small church, the congregation composed mostly of theatrical folk, and they took a bench in the rear. They sat through the service. The place was dim, cool to the eye, and restful. Toward the end the organ music, swelling, came out in a fine, rolling flood; someone opened the wide doors and, when they walked out into the air, they felt new and uplifted, and Mr. Boardman no longer had a worried look about the eyes. When a shabby man approached him he took out a dollar bill and gave it with a smile. The fellow lifted his hat and started to sputter his thanks. Milly, her eyes going misty, looked up at her father and held his arm tightly. Without speaking, walking silently together, they continued up Fifth Avenue. Occasionally Mr. Boardman tapped the sidewalk with the tip of his cane. Cars hummed by on the wide, smooth street. The air was still gray, but the weather was not so cold. It was pleasant to pass deserted shops, office buildings, window displays, and see only Christmas strollers walking up the street.

When they reached Thirty-Fourth Street Milly wanted to know what her father intended to do with her after the spring term of school was finished. "Will you ship me to camp again, like you did last summer, papa? It was nice there, but I would rather stay here in New York with you."

He told her it was hot and sticky in the city. "New York is terrible in the summer, no breeze or wind at all," he said.

"I won't care. I could cook your meals for you, we could go to the movies together. You'll see, I'll be so good to you, papa, you won't want me to go back to school in the fall."

He did not tap the sidewalk with his cane for over twenty paces.

"Well, Pika, what'll you do with me in the summer?"

"I think you'll go to camp again, Milly."

Then she took her arm away. "But I don't want to go there, papa. I want to be in the city with you."

"We'll pick out a different camp then. If you don't like a camp in the mountains, maybe we can find one along the seashore up in Maine."

"No," she said, taking his arm again. "I want to stay here with you."

They walked on, silent.

"Why did you have to have your apartment cleaned when I came here for the holidays, papa? You're so mean to me sometimes. Why couldn't you have waited until afterwards? We could have lived together in your own apartment and then I could cook for you. This way we have to go out for all our meals. And anyway, I don't care much for hotels, there's nothing homy about them."

"The management couldn't clean my rooms at any other time," he told her, thinking fast, tapping his cane sharply against the sidewalk.

"Bosh. If I were living with you I'd tell them when to clean my place and, if they didn't like it, I'd move."

He laughed shortly.

"I would," she said. "You bet I would."

He patted her arm as they crossed Thirty-Sixth Street.

"Anyway, I want to see what kind of an apartment you live in. Before I go back to school I'm going to look your place over."

"But they're cleaning there, dear."

"I don't care. I want to see what kind of rooms you've got and if everything is comfortable enough."

He smiled, terror hiding behind his eyeballs. He tried to dissuade her, talking to her like a child, but this made her all the more determined, and by the time they had covered another block she was really angry with him. Tears stood in her eyes, she was almost crying. "But don't you see I love you so much, papa, don't you see I only want to look at the place and then go away? All I want to do is to see it and leave, that's all, papa, really. I want to see where you live."

Now, though his face was calm, his heart was hammering. He didn't know what to do. How could he explain the young woman living there, how could he explain the whole affair? He cleared his throat while his thoughts raced hard.

"I haven't got the keys," he said. "I had to give them to the house-painters."

"Then we'll see the janitor," she answered promptly. "He'll have a duplicate set."

He had to tell his daughter the janitor had no keys for the apartment. "A month ago I lost my set, so he gave me the only one he had."

She set her small jaw, her eyes still misty. "Well, anyway, I want to see what kind of a neighborhood you live in, then," she said and in this he was unable to budge her. So at Forty-Second Street they stepped into a cab and, before he could lean forward and tell the driver the destination, Milly bent over and told the fellow. She knew the address by heart and was proud to tell the driver where to go, to her father's apartment house.

The taxi rolled down Park Avenue, into Fourth Avenue, crossed Fourteenth Street, and pulled into Eleventh. Milly, her eyes alert, kept glancing from left to right out the windows. Old tenements and remodeled apartment houses stood side by side. They passed a few small churches. Turning to her father, smiling at him, she said she liked the locality, it was interesting. "So many bookshops around the corner," she said.

At last the cab came to a dead stop before the Glen Cove Apartments. Mr. Boardman, sitting stiffly, felt his heart pounding harder than ever. What if Margie should walk out? He took out his handkerchief and blew his nose quietly for a long time, holding the square of linen up to his face so that it practically hid all his features. Milly, who grew excited, wanted to get out and make sure the janitor hadn't an extra key ("They always have, papa, but they're too lazy to look for it."), but Mr. Boardman finally persuaded her not to be so foolish, and so at last the driver finally shifted gears.

Standing at one of the windows on the second floor Mr. Franconi, who was spending Christmas in his flat, saw Mr. Boardman and a young girl sitting in the rear of the cab and wondered why they did not get out and enter the building.

Finally the cab rolled off. Milly, staring back at the building, saw a little fellow walking excitedly up the street, no hat on his head, fire in his eyes, happiness all over his face, and wondered who he could be. Just as the cab whirled around the corner she saw that the young man had entered the doorway next to her father's apartment house. Then the taxi was humming northward, passing Union Square.

## III

LEON FISHER had been shot up to heaven, he had been treading soft-boiled clouds all the way from Fifteenth Street. Just a little while ago (he is now walking through the hallway of Twenty-Door City), the doorbell of his rooming house rang and, when Celia's aunt answered it, she found a special-delivery boy before the door with a letter for Leon Fisher, esquire, the little artist who had the third floor rear room east. She walked up the stairs with the letter, knocked on his door and, because he was not fully dressed, slipped the envelope under.

Leon, just dressing, stooped, picked the letter up and tore it open. He read the brief note twice, his eyes racing across the typed sheet: "Dear Mr. Fisher," the letter read and went on to say that owing to a clerical error in the offices the announcement of acceptance of his portrait of a young girl entitled "Celia" had been delayed in getting mailed to him. To remedy this, this special-delivery letter was being sent to inform him that the Pennsylvania National Academy was happy to include the picture in its forthcoming annual exhibition to be held in Philadelphia.

Leon Fisher tore out of the house, treading soft-boiled clouds. He hurried up the musty tenement hallway, all excited, his thoughts disarranged, his brain whirling. The exhibition, opening soon, was national in scope and attracted huge press notices; it was a feat, his getting in. His heart fluttered pleasantly, like a silken banner in the breeze, as the saying goes. As he half-ran up the street, the first thought in his head was to inform Comrade Helen of this stroke of luck.

He stopped dead in his tracks, however, as he stood before her door. After all, this was Christmas morning, folks were sleeping yet. But his heart was still fluttering pleasantly like a silken banner in a buoyant breeze.

He knocked. No answer, too soft a knock. . . . He knocked again, waiting, his heart picking up a beat or two. Still no answer. Could it be possible that they were still sleeping, Comrade Helen and her three comrades? Why— it was almost noon, eleven o'clock anyway.

He knocked again, louder. He heard a sudden creak of bedsprings, heard José's guttural mutter, cursing in Mexican no doubt, then the lock clicked, and Sid Turner poked a sleepy head out. Sid's eyes were red, he was very tired and sleepy-looking. At first he did not see who it was in the hallway and his voice was gruff. Then Leon spoke.

"Oh, it's you," said Sid and his voice changed. He smiled.

"Is Comrade Helen there? I came here to tell her my picture has been accepted by the Pennsylvania National Academy."

"That's fine, say, that's fine," said Sid and smiled again. "I'm glad to hear it." And then he turned, speaking to Comrade Helen, whose bed was in the smaller bedroom next to the kitchen. Leon stood out in the hall, waiting, feeling excited, joy rushing from his throat in a flowing, silent shout. A minute passed. He stood closer to the crack of the door, nervously waiting for the girl to appear. As he fidgeted, his forehead bumped the door gently and swung it open a few inches more and he saw, with a start (good Christ, his eyes must be playing tricks with him)—he saw Comrade Helen sitting on the edge of the double bed, dressing herself, hooking on her dress; and in the same bed, his broad back and coarse black hair toward the door, lay the Mexican! Sid, yawning at the door, saw Leon's eyes. He clamped his jaws shut instantly, took in the situation. The little fellow out in the hallway began shivering. Helen and Morales? Helen and the swarthy, stocky Mexican?

Sid poked his head out the door, no longer sleepy now. "Helen's dressing," he said. "She just went into José's room to get her other dress. She hangs her things there, we've got no other place for them."

Leon, hunched in the dim hallway, stopped shivering.

Within his body a whimper died away. He swallowed hard, then cleared his throat. Sid shut the door a little more, Leon could see very little of the inside of the flat now.

In another minute Comrade Helen, her hair not yet combed, her face smooth and rosy from sleep, came toward the door, and at that moment José turned over sleepily in bed and grunted at her that a draft was coming in.

So she closed the door and came out to stand in the hallway near Leon. Sid went back to bed.

"I just happened to drop by," said Leon, his eyes shining in the half-dark, his nostrils alive as he smelled her. He could smell she had just come from bed. "A picture of mine has been accepted by the Pennsylvania National Academy."

When she asked when he had received the news, he blurted out the truth, it came from his lips before he could stem the words. "I just got the letter, they sent a special delivery and I just got it a few minutes ago."

"And you came right over to tell me?" She was pleased to have so much power over the fellow, he was putty in her hands and she knew it.

"No, I just happened by," he stammered quickly, "I just happened by, so I thought I'd tell you."

In the hallway, her eyes growing accustomed to the light, seeing his large, blazing eyes on her, she smiled sweetly and stood looking at him. What a power she had over this little fellow, this one-hundred-and-ten-pound communist! She was a large, warm hearth-fire and he liked to be near her all the time.

"Do you know what day it is?" she asked, smiling at him.

He nodded. "But, of course, Christmas means nothing to us; we're Party members."

Still, he felt as if he should have brought something

along, anything, a small gift. He stood there rigidly, thinking fast.

"What I really came over for," he said, snatching at the first thought that tore along, "was to ask you out for dinner and maybe to a show besides. I thought you would like that."

The special-delivery letter which he clutched in his hand and which he had figured on showing her, he now shoved out of sight, into a pocket of his coat.

Comrade Helen accepted, she said she would be glad to go out with him. It was chilly in the hallway, she had no coat on. "Call for me at about four," she said to him. "I'll be ready then. Then we can go out together."

She spoke the last words softly. Christ, how his heart was going now, throbbing like a pond pump. It was still pounding hard even after she went inside.

He stood in the hall alone, collecting his thoughts, pulling himself together, and as he started walking toward the street he thought of Jason; his excitement about the accepted painting leaped up again, and he started climbing the flights to the ex-poet's quarters.

He came in without knocking. Jason was fully dressed and had just finished shaving. He was sitting reading the paper.

"I just got a letter from Philadelphia," said Leon, all excited again. Jason looked alive at once. Philadelphia?

"You're a liar," he said. "The mail isn't delivered today. Today's Christmas, the church bells have been banging away all morning."

"I've got a letter from Philadelphia in my pocket," said Leon, hugging his secret, smiling at his friend. He dug his hand into his overcoat and clutched the letter there.

Then he noticed how strange Jason began to act, how

Jason's face changed. The ex-poet's mouth was twitching. Leon started.

"Well, hand it over, then!" said Jason. "Good Christ, man, do you like to torture a fellow? Hand it over, I say!"

Leon's mouth hung open. Hand it over? He looked at Jason's face again. Why—the fellow's cheeks were actually gray! Reaching into his pocket he took out the letter quickly and placed it in Jason's hands.

He stood quiet, watching the life die out of Jason's eyes, seeing the face go blank and dead again.

"Oh," grunted Jason, reading the typed note. "Yes, that's fine, so you got in the show?" He handed Leon the letter back.

"It'll be a big exhibition. Maybe I'll get a write-up in the papers."

Jason was himself again, it didn't take him long. "You ought to win the first prize," he said dryly. "How big is it, a thousand dollars, or a million?"

Leon stuck the letter into an inner pocket. He should have known better than to come up here feeling excited.

"What are you doing today?" he asked, changing the subject.

Jason, picking up the paper again, pointed toward the old mantelpiece. Standing there, like a deadly-looking anti-aircraft shell, was a tall round bottle of clear fluid—gin. "I'm getting drunk today. In that bag in yonder corner repose five oranges, waiting for the pressure of my godlike hands. Celebration, ring out ye cock-eyed bells, ring out."

Leon stood there with the letter hidden away. He knew Jason had not received a check for some weeks now and wondered how he had been able to purchase the gin. The ex-poet read his thoughts, and laughed mockingly.

"Leon, I hereby inform you that yesterday I didst receive another check for one of my filthy masterpieces, this time for the sum of fifteen dollars. And further, my good lad, I am thinking seriously of renting that little room across the hall for a storehouse. I intend calling it the Gin Chamber of Mount Parnassus. How's that? The Gin Chamber of Mount Parnassus."

"I saw a sign hanging downstairs advertising the room," said Leon, "but the janitress will never rent it. It's too small, and besides no one would care to live there."

"They'd better not," said Jason. "That room is reserved for me, I'll tell the old dame to take her sign down right away. I'll tell her I intend to transform it into a gin chamber."

"But you'll have to pay her rent for it, and you owe her two months now," said Leon. "What about the money?"

"Oh, money," grunted Jason as he picked up his paper again.

## IV

A HALF-HOUR LATER Comrade Helen was serving her three fellow comrades breakfast, and helping herself at the same time. In a large crock she stirred batter, scooped some out and let fall a ladle on the hot, grease-covered pan. The wheat-cakes didn't taste so good, but the comrades were hungry and made no complaint. All ate in silence, chewing, picking up the soggy pancakes, staring at the table, drinking their coffee. The three young men sat with trousers and underwear—no shirts on.

Afterwards Sid and his brother left, swallowing full glasses of cold water to drive down the breakfast. They had some Party work to do and would be gone all day, they said. As soon as they were gone, the Mexican's eyes took on a catlike gleam and, as Helen reached across the table for the sugar, he grabbed her wrists.

"What was that fellow doing outside the door so early?" he asked, holding her hard, hurting her. When she began clenching her teeth, wincing, he let her go.

She told him, speaking meekly, that it wasn't her fault, was it, if the little fellow had fallen for her? And besides, what harm was there in it if he did hang around her? "He never swears or hits me like you do. What's the harm if we're friends?"

Harm? The Mexican laughed sneeringly. "No harm," he said, "but I'm getting tired of him snooping around. Every time he comes here I got to pretend you and I are merely friends. Anybody can see how it's with us, but the little fool must be blind. The next time he comes here I'll fix him, I'll tell him right out. I'll tell him we sleep together every night."

Helen went to the sink and began washing the dishes. He knew he had her cornered and knew also she did not want him to tell Leon. Why she did not want to lose the little fellow's friendship and adoration she did not just know herself.

"I'll tell him all about it," José was saying to her. "I'd like to see his face. Maybe I'll even tell him about that other man down in New Orleans."

She turned full around and worked at the dishes, not answering him. He sat staring at her back. Finally he got up from the table and stood next to her at the sink, sneering at her, watching her hands fumbling with the dishes. Leaning toward her he grinned wider, then inserted his hand downward from the top of her house-dress, working his palm slowly, insinuatingly against the bare flesh. She shivered and wrenched his hand away. He gripped both her wrists again, viselike. His pressure was terrific. Shoving his smooth, round, golden face close to hers he grinned catlike, breathing hard and hot upon her face. His grip was painful and she began whimpering. "José," she said, "José," and a warm, drowsy wave of helplessness flowed over her.

He began speaking softly in Spanish, still gripping her hard. The pain increased until her mouth fell slowly open, until she leaned against his chest. She grew weaker and weaker, tasting the bitter sweetness of his strength, flowing toward him, her eyes closing, no fight or hate in her body. She slipped her arms around his waist with a moan as soon as he released her. Bending his head, lowering it over so that it stood harshly forward from the column of his powerful neck like a bull's, he bit her on her left shoulder, working her house-dress away from the naked flesh with his teeth first. He bit her twice.

Then, because she was so helpless now, he had to lift her up to get her into the small room off the kitchen. He carried her there as if she were a damp, limp bag of sand.

## V

AT FOUR O'CLOCK Leon knocked on the door, rapping softly. Comrade Helen, alone, thinking, sitting at the table looking at her hands, got up and opened it. There stood Leon, smiling. She smiled back, though her eyes were rather slack and her face pale.

"Everybody gone?" said the little fellow brightly, glancing about, feeling good because José was not around.

The girl nodded. Sid and Harry had gone out right after breakfast, José had left a little over an hour ago, he was going to see some of his countrymen in the Bronx.

While Comrade Helen went into the bedroom to change into another dress, Leon sat at the table. He drummed his fingers happily upon the top of it while he waited, and stared at the closed door, listening as she moved around there. Finally she came out, looking a bit more cheerful, her hair in order, color on her cheeks, a black silk dress snug against her body. Leon's eyes were furnaces again. Comrade Helen stood there smiling.

"You've got a new necktie on," she said, looking at him quizzically.

"No," he answered, lying, "it's an old one," and he smiled back, still feeling that inner breathlessness he felt every time he was troubled by the soft contours of her figure. He stood up, helped her with her coat. On the street she took his arm, his heart started throbbing.

"Where are you taking me?" she said.

He told her, clearing his throat first. "I thought we'd go some place for dinner first and afterwards take in a show. Maybe the vaudeville at the Jefferson Theater, I haven't seen vaudeville for a long time. Would you care to go there?"

She pressed his arm, and at that moment liked him very much. "But it'll be expensive," she said.

He puffed his chest out, beginning to sweat at the firm feel of her arm. Expensive? What difference did that make? Besides, his picture had been accepted for a big exhibition. "No," he answered, "I can manage it," and he stared ahead like a young rooster just learning the thrill of mighty crowing.

They walked toward Second Avenue. It was only four

o'clock, but already the sky was pale and dirty-looking and dusk was coming on. Before a small Italian restaurant in a side street they stood talking, discussing the prices, the food, and if they really wanted an Italian meal. Finally they went inside. Leon, standing behind Helen, helped her with her coat and hung it up, and after they sat down he ordered for both, his voice quavery, his heart fluttering like a silken banner in the breeze.

The place was empty. It was a small restaurant that ran 60c specials and had spotted tablecloths. The waiter, a tired fat fellow, nodded his bald head sleepily and shuffled up and back with the food, which was not so hot.

When darkness came on, the waiter reached up a fat arm and clicked the light on. He grunted. His shirt had worked loose as he had raised his arm and now he fumbled with the ends of it. Leon and Comrade Helen, the only customers, all alone, sitting on opposite sides of the table, eating together, the little fellow raising his eyes often and smiling, took their time.

Two cold slabs of apple pie came out, the dessert. The waiter came forward when they were almost finished and, shaking a tin can, sprayed powdered sugar upon the pieces left. Then he walked slowly back to the kitchen, his damp service-towel swinging on his crooked arm.

In Leon's pocket some rolled-up papers rustled—charcoal drawings he had done in school. They finished their coffee, the waiter took most of the dirty plates away.

"Do you want another cup?" asked Leon, when the waiter was standing near, when the fat guy was absently scratching his ear.

"It will cost a nickel extra," the waiter said, easing up, his face as alive and alert as the cold slabs of pie he had brought out before.

"Can I have some more water?" Comrade Helen asked.

The waiter hove off, his nose pointing due east toward the kitchen in the rear, and returned, carrying two overflowing thick glasses sloppily, setting them down with his damp, plump hands.

Leon, after the fellow was gone, started talking about this and that, and by degrees swung the conversation around to art, to painting, to art schools, and other allied topics. Then, reaching inside his coat, he pulled out his roll of drawings, his drawings that the art instructor down at the school had been genuinely enthusiastic over. He laid them on the table.

"Oh, yes," he said and reached into a pocket and brought forth cigarettes.

Comrade Helen knew he rarely smoked. He opened up the box, an expensive brand, cork-tipped. He struck a match and lit his own after hers, puffing quickly, blowing out the smoke in rapid clouds. The little fellow felt like an aristocrat. Comrade Helen, feeling good after the meal, no dishes to wash and wipe, no forks and knives to clean, smiled across the table. She picked the roll of drawings up.

"What is it?" she asked, toying with the roll.

"Oh, some drawings. I thought maybe . . . I thought maybe you might care to see them, so I brought some along."

But the waiter, hovering around, snooping about, wondering what kind of a tip would be left behind, put a damper on and Leon said they could look at the drawings later, and stuck them back into his pocket. No privacy here, none at all, and the restaurant empty.

Again he helped Comrade Helen with her coat, put his own on, fished around for money, and left a quarter tip. The waiter opened the cash drawer quietly, closed it quietly, and smiled by lifting up the corners of his mouth just enough so you could notice it.

The air was getting chilly outside. Fourteenth Street came up to them, lights blazing, good old Fourteenth Street, the Broadway of the East Side, where east meets west and the twain struggle, kiss, groan, and step upon each other's faces.

Before the lights of the big vaudeville house Leon dug deeper into his pocket again and extracted money. Helen stood off to one side while he got the tickets; a few lads in the lobby gave her the eye, looking at her shapely parts.

Beside the vaudeville there was a full-length feature picture, a good three-and-a-half-hour show, your money's worth all right. They came inside when the animal act was starting, dogs whirling, jumping, walking on their forelegs, the trainer standing off to one side with a tight, set smile on his face, flicking the floor smartly with his whip whenever a dog relaxed. Bows and hand-clapping. More acts. Singing the red-hot, mama blues, bring back my great, beeg, lov-a-bllle da-dy-ie to me.

Leon, sitting in the dark, in the close, hot dark, every seat in the house taken, did not like the show. He had been in the Party movement too long, he couldn't stand the happiness songs, the smile-your-blues-away numbers, the smutty wise-cracks, the way the chorus girls rolled their bellies toward the house. He sat deep in his seat, a taste of straw in his mouth. Comrade Helen applauded at the curtain, she sat leaning forward when the tenor sang out his soulful melody, how he had walked the road alone until at last he had found yo-ou.

Then came the picture, a gangster film. Again Leon sat squirming, enduring. Finally it was over, all over, and they walked up the aisle and outside, where the fresh air was good against the face and wonderful going down your lungs. Toward the west the lighted-up clock in the tower of the public utilities building pointed to half-past eight. Comrade Helen said it was still early yet, happy words to Leon Fisher.

So they walked a bit. They went along Fourteenth Street, into the broil of the East Side. Crowds milled slowly, men stood slackly against the sides of stores and buildings, looking the janes over, waiting and hoping for a pick-up. And now, even though it was Christmas day, the venders still were on duty, shoving their toys, shoe-laces, rayon socks, candy-bars, and other truck before the passing faces. More beggars than ever sprawled, stood, shuffled, and croaked for alms.

Comrade Leon and Comrade Helen continued west, walking slowly. They passed Union Square and saw the sky, like a pale sheet of muslin, hanging above the little park. No stars were out, no moon. When they reached Fifth Avenue, the long line of arc lamps coming closer and closer together in the distance was nice to look at; the lamps shone against the black asphalt, cars hummed along. It was quiet here, few folks. They stood before the bright windows of Ross's Klock Korner and studied the tiers of clocks, all kinds of them, metal ones, wooden ones, clocks made of Dutch saucers, windmills, and candy-boxes.

And when they returned slowly eastward, it was still early. They looked aloft and once more saw the time in the tall tower. Comrade Helen said it was still early, music to Leon Fisher's ears. They crossed over and walked on the other side of Fourteenth Street, and, as they came up to the Automat, Comrade Helen had a hankering for a cup of nice, hot coffee.

They went inside. Leon hunted around until he spotted

a table away back in the rear, off to one side. He brought two cups of coffee over, asked Comrade Helen if she wanted something else, a piece of pastry, a baked apple, anything? She shook her head, smiled at him. The little fellow was all warmed up by her, he sat down and asked how many spoonfuls, and poured the sugar in.

Then, glancing around, looking here and there, hither and yon, he brought out the roll of drawings again, spoke about art, art school, and three or four well-known painters. He mentioned, casually, that he had done a few drawings from life in his student days. He said nothing about the instructor who had told the class time and again that Leon Fisher was the best student enrolled.

The girl, sipping her coffee, urged him to show her the drawings. He took the rubber band off, spread the sheets out carefully.

The work was good, studies from the nude. Indifferent to things artistic as she was, Comrade Helen sensed immediately that the fellow had power. His shadings were clean-cut and concise and by the use of a few strong, harsh lines he had the curves powerfully drawn, sure and firm. All the models were young women, reclining, standing, three-quarter facing, profile and back poses. The drawing of the back pose was startling, one single line taking care of the deep, narrow spinal groove.

She looked at the last of them, then glanced at them all over again. Leon, his lips against the coffee cup, sat happily. He saw that now she was impressed.

And when he walked her back to the tenement, when they stood alone in the damp, narrow, dim hallway, she was still impressed by his drawing and remembered how several Party members had spoken of the striking posters he had made for parades. Before her door she thanked him for the afternoon and evening. She said she had enjoyed it very much. She meant it. He stood there with a thick, happy feeling in his throat. And just before she opened the door, she held her hand out and he took it, feeling her pressure, hearing her murmur something in a low voice because she thought José or the Turner brothers might be back by now.

"Some day I'll pose for you," she said, her hand on the knob. "I'll pose for you . . . in the nude if you want me to. . . ."

Her words still hung in the hall after she was inside. He stood there like a stick, still hearing them . . . in the nude . . . if you want me to. . . .

Well, what was wrong with that? What the hell was wrong with that, he demanded of himself? Hadn't he painted hundreds and hundreds of nudes from life down at the art school? But he stood there conscious of the floating words still hanging in the dark, quiet hallway . . . if you want me to. . . .

He found himself walking alone around the square. The chill air cooled his brow . . . if you want me to. . . . Did she really mean it, would she take off her clothes and stand before him as he sketched her? . . . if you want me to . . . He kept walking around the square, the teeth of his brain chewing nervously and biting at his thoughts. He must have walked around the square six or seven times, his thoughts tumbling, pro and con arguments shuttling through his mind, speculating, visioning, imagining, wondering.

Far ahead someone else was going around the square, following the low, thick wall—a little fellow who walked jerkily: James Nicholson, cracked printer, student of Roman culture, a first-rate typesetter in his rational days. At the south side of the square the nut began tossing cards in the air, flinging them out like handbills to a starving public.

Leon, his eyes ahead, saw the squares of paper flutter to the sidewalk. He trod on them, going on, following the wall. The little bluish lamps had a misty haze about them, dampness hung low over the Yuletide town. Finally, bending over, Leon picked a card from the pavement. He stopped to read. In old-fashioned type, beautifully spaced and set up, the print stared forth like a bold command:

> **Men Are Made for War
> and Women for Procreation**

The printer, his pockets depleted, broke into a half-run and hurried southward to his rooms on Thirteenth Street.

# VI

AND THE EX-POET, what was he doing on this merry holiday? Well, Jason was getting a headache from the continued bell ringing of the neighborhood, and to cure this feeling, why of course applied himself to his healing "balm," or, in other words, he plied the bottle, that tall bottle that stood upright like a wicked anti-aircraft shell.

The bells eased off, the "balm" worked sure as prayer. In a short while he was lolling at ease on his old worn cot, one hand holding a glass, the other making wobbly circles in the air. In celebration he turned on his poetic spigot and allowed the flow to splash and tumble where it willed.

"Blow, bugles, blow," he mumbled sloppily, "and answer, hot dogs, answer, wharking, jarking, karking. On

Fourteenth Street the mustard's green, in Union Square the mob is queen. Blow, bugles, blow, set the wild echoes barking. And answer, comrades, answer, harking, larking, farking."

Finally, sitting up, he took a pencil in his fingers and tried to write the ode just composed, but the paper blurred before his eyes. It didn't matter, he wrote the piece down anyway, his hand strangely heavy and slow-moving against the sheet. "This should win the grand prix at the Pennsylvania National Academy," he mumbled to himself.

He tossed down a few more hookers, the liquid sliding down his throat like smooth, warm silk; hot ribbons spread out all over his belly, a good, nice feeling. He started to feel drowsy. Then the bells came on again, Grace Church now, striking the half-hour in loud, sonorous tones. He sat up, aroused. He reached over and picked up a postcard from the table received in the mail yesterday from Miss Allen, the nurse. She wrote she would be waiting in the hospital vestibule at four o'clock on Christmas day. The chimes ended, half-past four now.

Jason got up hurriedly, put his hat on, shoved his arms into his overcoat and went on down the stairs, his thoughts confused, his legs jerking, feeling weak.

When he reached the hospital, Miss Allen was still waiting, looking lonely and disappointed.

"I'm a hound," he mumbled drunkenly, standing before her, his hat on wrong, his mouth loose and full from the gin.

She took his arm in silence, and they began walking south along Seventh Avenue. Darkness settled down upon the city, the dusk was going gray with fog. "I forgot about your postcard," he muttered, heavy on her arm. She had to hold him a little as they crossed the street, his knees felt so watery.

They kept on walking. "Where should we go?" he asked.

The girl suspected he had no money and was afraid to offer to pay admission to a movie; she was afraid also that as soon as they'd enter a show Jason would fall asleep immediately in his seat. She led him eastward, listening to his mumbled babble, holding his arm at the crossings, staring straight ahead.

"Ever hear of Philadelphia?" he mumbled. "I gotta pome there, it's gonna win grand prix there. And answer, comrades, harking, larking, farking. Blow, bugles, blow, send your wild echoes out above the windy town. Keep on blowing, O hearty notes."

He received no answer from the girl at his side. Walking erect, head straight as a soldier's, stride firm, she continued to hold his arm. Crossing Sixth Avenue at Eighth Street they had a train of elevated cars rolling over their heads. Jason stopped and looked up.

"There's thunder in the air," he sputtered blearily. "Thunder. Roar, world, keep on roaring, a hundred and thirty million cacklers give us back reply. How's that, Miss Allen? I'm going strong, aye, mighty strong indeedy. Roar, world, keep on roaring. Thunder away!"

She pressed his arm and, leaning heavily against her, he allowed her to walk him on. And as they walked, his weight against her side, another weight started pressing on her heart.

He told her Philadelphia was a great town, that it **was** the greatest place in the whole wide world, only too few people were aware of that important fact, that was the trouble. "A young lady I know lives there," he went on, babbling to himself. "Until a few short months ago I occupied a strong position within the fortress of her heart. Then she tossed me down into the moat, out of the barricades, into the crool, crool world. In plain language, she gave me the air. Her name was Sylvia, she has wavy hair like yours."

The nurse allowed him to babble on. He told her all about it, speaking of moonlight and roses, lovers and cotton-candy, slurring his words, beating his breast in mock futility. "She says I was a weakling, that I broke too many promises on the liquor issue, so I says, I says to her, well, what of it, what thahell of it and she says nothing, not a word, says she. So she got herself transferred to Philly, a place in God's country and here I am and thassa way it is, my friend. Say, your arm is heavy. Is my arm heavy, dearie?"

The nurse, looking ahead, shook her head. After another block was covered, silence fell upon the ex-poet. The chill, damp early evening air revived him a bit, his mouth grew firm, he drew his lips together, and his eyes plunged on into the coming darkness. The street lamps came on. "I'm a hound," he muttered savagely, and said no more.

Then they came out of the end of a street full into Washington Square. Near the Arch of Triumph stood a huge Christmas tree with lights blazing in all the branches, giving out a merry Christmas atmosphere, causing people to view pleasantly and state smilingly, "Ah, the Christmas spirit, see the pretty tree."

A few buses, like old cows standing near a lonely fence, stood four-fifths empty near the rail at the south end of the chilly square. Chauffeurs were pulling at a last few drags of their cigarettes before rolling northward in the cars again. The walks were deserted. A few autos hurried along the curving drives into the side streets. Above the Judson Tower a little cross perched against the dark sky was lit up with electric bulbs, while toward the east the buildings of New York University stood stark and gray like limestone masonry, like blockhouses, all their windows dark. Miss Allen took her arm away and stood quietly with her hands in her coat pockets. Jason stared toward the big buses to the south.

"I'm a hound," he repeated.

Miss Allen took his arm again, gave it a gentle pressure, and they started walking up one of the empty paths. The big circular fountain held no water, no spray shot up. For the next half-hour they walked the paths in silence, the brilliant lights of the huge Christmas tree at their backs.

Jason started gagging gently, he had the urge to spit big, heavy pieces of slime upon the pavement. He had the feeling it would be nice to lie quietly on his cot right now.

"If I had a decent place I'd ask you up," he told Miss Allen. "I know you're tired of walking. But I live in filth, I'm lazy and unambitious, I have no urge to grab the jack, to be one of the go-gettum, there's-big-opportunities-waiting boys. You're wasting your time going with a guy like me, I'll never amount to anything."

"You go home and rest," she answered. "I've got to be back on duty soon."

"But I'm telling you," he argued hotly, stopping and looking at her, "I'm telling you I'm just a drunk, you're wasting time in even talking to me. I'm a bum!"

"Oh, don't talk like that," she pleaded. "God, don't talk that way."

"But you've got to know!" he shot back. "I'm telling you for your own good!"

Then she saw his face was feverish. She took his arm

again and they started walking. The lights of the tall Fifth Avenue apartment houses were twinkling, wreaths hung in some of the windows. More autos, like squat, military bowling balls rolled along the groove between the curbstones of the street, going almost silently.

They walked north and cut west at Twelfth Street. In front of the hospital she stood looking at him, at his burnt-out youth and talent. Her mouth trembled. She asked him to promise her that he wouldn't drink any more, that he'd try to get a grip on himself. The words rang faintly, with a familiar echo in his mind. He stared hard up the street.

"Rats!" he said. "To hell with it. No promises for me. Rats!"

Then, when he saw her face, he mumbled something in an undertone. He told her he might walk over the coming Thursday afternoon, he said he'd think about it. He spoke in a mutter.

"I wish you would," she answered. "I'll wait in the vestibule anyway."

Then he walked off, going near the curb. A half a block down he started spitting slime. He had to lean a hand against a lamp-post, he felt so weak from coughing. But when he reached Fourth Avenue, he was all right again, he drew in great drafts of the damp, raw air.

"Rats!" he said out loud, speaking viciously. "I make no promises to anybody. To hell with them all!" And with a determined stride he walked on toward the tenement.

# VII

MILES TO THE NORTH, somewhere near the Bronx, Old Running Water, belching as he rose, finally left the dinner table and sank into the big, soft Cogswell chair. About him was his family; today the Big Chief was at home.

In the parlor, standing near the front windows, was the family Christmas tree purchased for the grandchildren, the kiddies, with lights and toys in the lower branches (the Big Chief couldn't reach very high without straining himself—and his wife was old and short). His four grandchildren, small kids, itched to take the baubles down; one of them was two years old and kept on bawling, reaching out his little fists. Old Running Water grunted cheerfully, he would give the command when he was ready.

The two sons-in-law, two young up-and-coming Americans, tall lanky fellers who had married Old Running Water's virgin gals, sat with white collars and pale hands (both were office-workers), glancing with servile smiles at the old man, thinking of his bank account. They took the old boy's fifteen-cent cigars and both, at once, offered burning matches to the Big Chief's face. Old Running Water, bending forward and grunting, puffed until he had the perfecto going good, a nice feeling in his heavy, aging bones. In the kitchen his two daughters, their kids at their skirts, were helping the old woman with the dishes. The sound of clattering plates, small talk, splashing water, drifted toward the front room.

The two sons-in-law, long slack hands upon their lanky knees, cigars sticking from their mouths, puffing on the old man's fifteen-centers, talked about conditions, working themselves in (thinking of the old gent's bank account), discussed the times, the coming elections, and the fact that only yesterday a prominent banker was quoted in the press as saying that the darkest corner had already been rounded and now the dawn of better times was surely breaking. In a rather sugary way they sat there talking to the heavy old man.

Old Running Water, thinking of four dots after four men's names (one dot as large as a good-sized bullet hole), puffed in silence, his eyes half-closed in thought.

"It's bound to come, but the good Lord only knows when," he said, speaking of better times, of the cornucopia of plenty, of the mural oil paintings showing a calm-faced, high-bosomed dame holding out both arms, books in one, wheat, corn, bananas, plums, and sundry fruit and food in another. "Bankers—they say good times are just around the corner, but what corner, there's the rub. The town is full of corners, boys, a man can rub his backside raw against a thousand of 'em."

The two fellers, the sons-in-law, showing their yellow teeth in a sugary smile, had to admit that the Big Chief had a very clever mind, he knew how to turn a phrase or two, the old boy did. And when the old gent told them how the warehouse business was dropping off, how the loads were dwindling, how the freight reports indicated a sharp decline in shipping and that a few of the hands would have to be laid off, why they listened seriously, the lanky sons-in-law did. One of them stroked his long knees in silence, the other tapped the end of his cigar gently, freeing it from ash.

In the kitchen the women were cleaning up, finishing the after-labor of the heavy meal. The kids were bawling there, quarreling and tugging at their mothers' skirts. The oldest, a five-year old, had to have his ears boxed. He howled and cried, then all was quiet again.

Dusk came on. The steam in the radiators made a little, piping sound. One of the kids bent down, crouched and cocked his ear near the pipes. "Tweet, tweet, little birdie," he said, thinking of the sparrows, "tweet, tweet." The radiators piped their busy little lay.

Laying aside the butt of his fifteen-center, Old Running Water spoke to his short old dame, spoke in a monotone, in a low voice so that the kiddies wouldn't catch the wordies. The old woman, looking sly, smiling, went into the pantry and returned with a bottle. The sons-in-law grew watery about the mouth, they had sampled the old man's stuff before. The old boy poured out three drinks gurgle-gurgle into short glasses ("Women shouldn't touch a drop," was his motto in life), while the kiddies looked on.

"What's that, grandpop?" asked the five-year old, a curious lad.

"Grape juice," answered the Big Chief right away.

The sons-in-law, like a small Greek chorus, repeated. "He-he, grape juice," and sniffed hungrily, foretasting the strong, good drink.

The men drank, the women sat by and looked. The five-year old, watching the men's faces keenly, pawed his grandpa's lap and begged for a sip, just a little sip and, laughing genially, the folds of his belly rolling like oily waves, the old man complied. The kid's tongue darted out, he made a face. The whole room sat back and rocked and roared as the kid clawed his mouth. This was the bright spot of the evening; the sons-in-law sat laughing the longest, casting sidelong glances at the bottle half full yet.

But the old boy's beefy arm did not move, didn't even budge; there he sat like a gigantic pot-roast, solid and heavy in the bowl of the chair. Afterwards the kids were given toys and presents, the old grandmother stood by with watery eyes and kissed them as they came running up to show her the gifts. She wore false plates of teeth in her mouth and her lips were indrawn as if sucking in the air. She stood there, old and happy.

And as night fell, the two young, lanky fellers, stroking their legs with their long pale hands, looked toward their wives, asking with their eyes that they go home now. But the girls sat on for a while longer, the kids were still talking excitedly to the old grandmother.

At last, when Old Running Water's heavy head was falling breastward, the women rose, dressed the kids, got everything ready, and finally stood in the front room. The old dame shook her husband gently. The Big Chief stirred. The sons-in-law, standing in hats and overcoats, gave a few last sugary smiles, showing yellow teeth, thanking the Big Chief for the dinner, thinking of his cozy bankroll.

The front door banged at last, the kids hollered in the hallway. When they reached the street, they looked back and saw the colored Christmas lights in the evergreen tree at the front window, and waved their chubby mittened fists at the building. By this time Old Running Water, spittle dribbling from one corner of his relaxed mouth, was snoring away. But at the window his good dame continued to stand there watching the kids, waving back at them with quick, feeble, loving motions of the hand until they passed the second arc lamp down the street. Then she lost them in the darkness.

Coming back into the center of the room she stood old and quiet before her snoring husband, thinking of their fading years. His tremendously swollen limbs lay slackly sprawled like sawed-off logs dumped this way and that. Walking up, approaching him in silence, the old woman took out her handkerchief and wiped the wet corner of the old man's mouth. Then she stood looking at him again, thinking of their fading years. Her nose went moist and her eyes puckered, she wondered if there was enough chicken left over to do for supper tomorrow night. In the quiet room, standing before the heavy old man sprawled in the green Cogswell chair, she thought the matter over. The light from the floor lamp fell upon the golden fuzz of the Big Chief's forearm.

Time went—tick and tock, and the old man mumbled in his sleep.

## VIII

AT NINE-THIRTY Mr. Boardman and his daughter Milly came out of the Roxy Theater and began walking down Seventh Avenue, taking their time. In the lobby of the big movie palace Mr. Boardman had had to wait a bit, until his daughter paid a visit to the women's rest-rooms. She returned smiling at him, looking at him quizzically, tilting her head to one side, and he smiled back as a matter of course, not knowing why she smiled. She hooked her arm through his as they started walking down the street. The lights of the great white way flashed on and off, traffic hummed and roared up and down the Times Square sector.

"Are you tired, papa, do you want to go back to the hotel?"

"Do you?" he asked, patting her arm.

"I'm asking you," she said. "You've got to answer me, I've asked you first."

"We'll walk a while yet, Milly." So they went along, his cane tapping the sidewalk occasionally, his young daughter on his arm. They made a good appearance, some folks turned to stare.

"I bet they think we're married," the daughter said, squeezing his arm, feeling happy. "I bet they do."

Mr. Boardman smiled.

"But I wouldn't have an old papa like you," she pouted. "You're horrid, anyway," little bits of love hidden behind her girlish words. "This summer I'm coming to live with you in town, and that's all there is to it. You hear?"

"We'll think it over, Milly."

"No, we won't, papa. My mind is made up. You're not to give the matter another thought."

"It's getting dampish out," he said, seeing the bluish haze about the big electric signs.

They kept on walking. At Forty-Sixth Street he suddenly thought of something, and cleared his throat.

"I've got to make a phone call, dear. I almost forgot about it."

"I'll go with you," his daughter said, and they entered a drug store. Now he was sorry he hadn't phoned while Milly had visited the rest-rooms, he could have done it very easily then.

He went up to the cashier and changed a dime for two nickels, then locked himself in a phone booth. Milly, humming softly to herself, stood near the perfume counter, looking at the pretty bottles. She took a small mirror from her purse, held it to her face and started smiling at herself. No, he hadn't noticed yet.

In the booth Mr. Boardman dropped a nickel in the slot and gave a number. The phone rang for a long time. Then the coin returned. His heart began to hammer slowly, heavily. Wasn't she in, was she out? Once more he inserted the nickel into the slot, heard the pleasant ping and gave the number and this time he heard the phone ring at the other end for a very long time, longer than the previous attempt. At last, just as he was about to hang up, he heard a click, then a woman's voice, a slow, sleepy, lazy hello.

"Hello-o," and there it was, that throaty voice he knew so well. Someone else was laughing somewhere.

"Hello-o," the woman said again, loud and getting cross, but still good-natured. Mr. Boardman, his brow damp in the little, stuffy booth, his ear alert, could hear, very faintly, a man's voice somewhere. A crossed wire, or a man at her side? Which? His face went gray, he wet his lips again.

"Hello," he said.

"Oh, it's you," came the throaty answer, and the man's voice somewhere was cut short immediately, only the even quiet humming of a good connection reached Mr. Boardman's ear. Margie started complaining about a noise, about the bum wire, about voices, and made her own voice irritated. "There's a buzzing, dear, and I seem to hear another party talking. Can you hear me, can you hear my voice?"

Mr. Boardman, his heart hammering very heavy now, said he could.

"Try and get a clear wire, Boardie, I can hardly hear you."

Mr. Boardman clicked up and down a few times, caught the attention of the operator and asked for a clearer wire.

"The wire is clear, sir," came the answer after a while.

"Thank you," said Mr. Boardman. He wet his lips again and spoke to Margie. "Can you hear me now?"

"Yes, that's much better," she said.

"I just called up to see how you were and to wish you a very merry Christmas."

She thanked him and told him it was very thoughtful of him, sending her those flowers that had arrived in the morning. He replied he hoped she liked them. Then, in a plaintive voice, in a tone borrowed from the talking pictures, she murmured she was oh so lonely, and she missed him, and her arms were aching, and when was his child going back to school? She kissed twice with her lips over the miles of wire. "I love you, honey, you know I do." That throaty, croony voice. "My God, what a wire we've got!" Mr. Boardman thought he heard smothered laughter.

When he hung up, his thoughts were lulled a little, but not much. He was no fool. He walked from the stuffy phone booth and wiped his brow with his handkerchief, his heartbeat going back to normal. At the perfume counter his daughter was talking with the young woman clerk there and looking at some pretty bottles with silk bows tied around their necks. She turned as soon as he came out and faced him smilingly.

"What kept you so long, was it very important?"

"No," he answered, "just a little call I had to make."

Finally, blocks down, walking along pleasant Fifth Avenue with buses and lamplights and shops on all sides, the girl could contain herself no longer and stopped before a mirror in a millinery store.

"Well, haven't you noticed anything?" she asked, frowning and smiling expectantly at the same time.

Noticed? No, his eyes were turned inward upon himself now, toward the darkness of his mind. He hadn't noticed anything, he was still listening to that smothered laughter, to a man's voice urging a woman to please hang up and come over again on his knee where she belonged. He tapped the sidewalk sharply a few times with the tip of his cane.

"Papa, you're not looking at my face."

He looked, and saw nothing, only her half-frowning, half-smiling stare.

"Don't you notice anything, papa, don't you see anything new or different?"

Her lower lip began to tremble with disappointment, he noticed nothing after all.

"I've put some lip rouge on," she said softly, almost in a whisper. "I put it on when I left you in the lobby of the show, you haven't noticed me at all."

And then he saw—her lips were carefully penciled and now he noticed she was quite grown up, a graceful young lady. He stood there looking at her, seeing her, his mind on other things. His stare was blank.

"I'll take it off if you don't like it," she said quickly, seeing how gray and vacant he looked. "If you don't like me like this I'll take it off," and she opened her purse for her handkerchief.

"That's all right," he said as they started walking.

"No, it isn't. I'll take it off." She spat upon her handkerchief, then began rubbing her mouth vigorously.

"There," she said, "I'm just the same as ever, papa, you've got no fault to find at all with me!"

## IX

ON CHRISTMAS DAY Mr. Franconi kept to his rooms —all day. In the morning he sat near the front windows reading the papers, turning the pages slowly, allowing his eye and mind to wander occasionally. By swinging his glance to the side he could command a good view of the street below.

This was a good way to spend the day. House-slippers were upon his feet and a silk lounging robe was wrapped about his body. When he grew tired reading the news of the day, he lay quietly upon the sofa, relaxed, and stared thoughtfully up at the dull tone of the ceiling. He started thinking of his life, of the years just passed.

He remembered the ship he had come over to America in. It was a big clumsy boat and there had been a storm on the way over. That was thirteen years ago, he had been what is known as a "greenhorn" then. He remembered many scenes, many pictures, and felt, now, as though he had come a very long way. Much water had hurried under his private bridge since the old days. He remembered that a relative had met him at the gangplank of the boat where all the immigrants had been shoved cattle-like down upon the shores of America and the relative had pumped and pumped his hand, a glad look on his honest face. In a big, bare room the immigrants were herded, segregated, and tagged, then the relative who waited outside took him by subway to a cold, drafty flat somewhere near Canal Street, and that night friends and more relatives pumped his hand, smiled gladly at him, and asked him many questions about Bessano. But already their words were flavored foreignly and they injected American words into their Italian which he did not understand. When he asked questions, they laughed and clapped him hard and friendly upon the shoulder. Later on the relative who had met him at the dock, a third cousin and a good man, though he had stabbed somebody at a festival back in Italy, took him aside and began talking over plans for the future.

In the end, after he had learned a few American words and terms, Mr. Franconi had been apprenticed to a barber on lower Third Avenue. He learned how to say, "Shave?" "Haircut?" "A good tonic?" and acquired the knack of slightly raising his eyebrows while questioning. More words and terms came, in due time. He was conscientious, he worked carefully, he wanted the customer to feel satisfied. By slow degrees, always doing good work, he worked himself up into the better shops, subduing his voice, raising his eyebrows in a more refined manner, "Shave?" "Haircut?" "A good tonic for the scalp?" Now he worked in a Wall Street barber shop, one of the best in town, had a following of his own and made a decent living.

Thinking about his slow but steady progress up the tonsorial ladder took Mr. Franconi's mind away from other things. It took his mind away from his first years here in this country, when he had gone the rounds of dance halls and amusement parks, had dressed like all the other Latin jazz-hounds and had had only one thing on his mind—women. He had been a wild buck and had had his share, mostly American girls, all kinds of them, blondes, brunettes, red-heads, and once or twice had gone into the Harlem jungle for a change of scenery. He had burned himself out. He was tainted, too.

"I think we will have it arrested in a few more treatments," Dr. Morrison, who had offices on Madison Avenue, said after almost every visit. "However, we must not be too optimistic as yet. You must continue taking treatments."

In the neighborhood the bells rang off and on, the echoes fading over the cloudy town. Mr. Franconi could hear, faintly, phonograph music. The young "Russian" couple who lived on the floor above were entertaining, spending a "Russian" Christmas day at home. The record being played was a merry *metelitza*, a Russian dance. Vanya and Natasha, host and hostess in the Russian manner, were at home to their guests, a young artistic couple living on Charles Street in the Village. They were telling the guests all about the knickknacks on the mantelpiece, the perfect flow of Turgenevian and Gogolian prose, also about the quaint customs of White and Little Russia, where the peasants sang as they stacked the wheat and hay and the tolling of the chimes floated sweetly over the fields.

"Then you're communists?" inquired the guests, noting the knickknacks, seeing a samovar on the little parlor table.

"No," came the answer quietly. "What we admire is the old Russia, the tsareviches, the troikas, and the singing peasants under the barins."

"Oh," said the guests, making a round O with their mouths, admiring the shiny copper belly of the samovar.

Vanya, beaming, went over to the phonograph and put on the merry *metilitza* again.

Downstairs Mr. Franconi heard it as he lay quiet on the sofa. Later he got up and stood at the window. Church bells were ringing again. Against the front walls of the Catholic school across the street there were no shadows, the wide strong front loomed up like the set face of a heavy, gloomy man. The big doors of the garage next to it were grimly closed against the street.

Mr. Franconi thought of himself as a staunch Catholic but had long since stopped going to church. Why, he did not just know. America. He had stopped going, that was all. He stood at the window a long time and stared down the length of empty street which ran dead end into Fourth Avenue. He was still standing there when the doorbell buzzed. He wondered who it could be and stood quiet, thinking. Then he went to answer it.

"Hello," he spoke down into the hallway.

The answer, almost a half-shout, came back quickly in Italian.

Mr. Franconi was somewhat astonished. "Gregorio?"

"Si, Andre," and Gregorio came inside, a short, powerful man with the shoulders of a wrestler, a fellow member of the Italia Club. He came in smiling, shook Andre's hand with vigor and stood in the doorway, twirling his hat. He had a big, round, shiny face.

"Come in."

He came inside and saw the quiet, tastefully furnished apartment. He had never paid Andre a visit before. He stood there playing with his hat, smiling, his face more shiny than ever.

"Sit down," said Andre.

Gregorio, grinning broadly, set the edge of his healthy rump on the edge of the sofa. Mr. Franconi held out cigarettes and struck a match. Through the first bluish haze of smoke he saw the round face of his friend and wondered at the visit.

Then Mr. Franconi remembered to give Christmas greetings. The men shook hands again, Gregorio warmly, spouting Italian greetings by the yard, goodness all over his moon-face. He had a hearty voice. Blowing a huge cloud of cigarette smoke straight ahead, starting to sweat, his eyes popping, Gregorio blurted out, "Why don't you come up to my home for the evening, Andre? People will be there. My brother Joe is bringing his mandolin. There will be wine and food, good wine. . . ."

Now he was sweating good, and blew another cloud of smoke. Andre, his head tilted pleasantly to one side, a friendly look in his eyes, waited for more.

". . . Ai, the wine will be good, Andre. And besides, there will be girls. . . ."

Gregorio grinned broader than ever. Andre, looking rougish, smiled back, the cat was out of the bag now. He knew. One of the young women he had danced with at the Italia Club had been Gregorio's sister, a squat, robust girl whose thighs had quivered against his all through the dancing. Mr. Franconi understood, she was of a marriageable age, her folks had her on the auction block, she herself was hot and ready for a man.

Mr. Franconi, reaching over, lit a cigarette for himself. He and Gregorio continued to smile at each other, but all the while Gregorio sensed that Andre would not come over to his folks' house. He sat there with a set smile on his full, firm face, and called himself a fool, imagining that the great Andre, that wolf of a fellow, would waste time at the home of his people, or with his sister.

Finally he made a jest and both men laughed heartily, smiling at each other, grinning at each other's eyes. Mr. Franconi went into the kitchen and came back with a bottle and poured wine into two small glasses. He held the first glass out to Gregorio and they clinked to each other, then drank. The wine was excellent. Mr. Franconi poured another. Gregorio stood up, ready to go. He stood there stocky and thoughtful.

"I should have told you sooner, Andre. A man like you, you must have made arrangements days ago." Once more his eyes swept over the flat. "You have a nice place here," he said simply.

At the door they shook hands, Gregorio with much vigor, his face shiny, his eyes slightly fiery from the wine.

"Be sure to give your family my Christmas greetings," said Mr. Franconi, speaking in Italian. "Give your sister Teresa my regards too."

"I will, Andre, I will." He shook hands again, then hesitated. "Who is coming up this evening, Andre?" Half his body out the doorway, he twirled his hat on a short finger and leered obscenely into the flat.

Mr. Franconi gave his practiced, pleasant smile for answer. ("Shave?" "Haircut?" "A good tonic for the scalp?") The hat went round Gregorio's stubby finger at a quick pace.

"A blond one, Andre?"

Andre smiled back, his lip muscles set.

"A good thing I did not drop in later, Andre. I would have come upon you at the critical moment, eh? Ha, ha, ha. Greetings from my sister, be sure to come to the club soon again, Andre." He stuck his fist out impulsively and for the third time shook hands hard.

Mr. Franconi stood at the door until the entrance door closed below. There was a gentle bang. Then he closed the apartment door against the hallway. He walked into the bathroom, clicked on the light, and standing before the mirror over the sink began stroking slowly the sides of his face. Allowing the cold water to flow for a long time, he finally placed a brown pill upon his tongue, followed by a quick, expert gulp of water.

Then he clicked all the lights of the flat out and with legs, arms, chest, belly and mind relaxed, lay quiet on the sofa, thinking slow thoughts in the dark and in this way enjoyed a certain peace of mind. This is how Mr. Andre Franconi spent Christmas day.

# X

"THAT GUY'S dropping cards again," said Officer McGuffy, going toward his comrade Hajek. "This time it's about war, something about men and war, but he's got a long word in it I don't just understand. I ought to run him in."

"Oh, he's just another nut," said Hajek, motioning to the north-south traffic to get a move on, to advance a bit more snappily. McGuffy, standing near his pal, stared at the windows of the shops across the way, which already were taking on a post-Christmas look, though from the distance the cotton still resembled snow. The Fourteenth Street sidewalks were still crowded, in front of Loft's a jam of folk were waiting for the traffic lights to change.

"Well, guess I'll stroll around," McGuffy said and crossed over, twirling his nightstick behind his back, just for the exercise of it. At the curb he slowed down, eased his pace as a young woman stepped up into a trolley, then sauntered on, whistling as he went.

Everything was peaceful. He walked northward, turned west, and came back from his patrol. All quiet on the East Side front. In the sky there were no stars, he could feel a dampness in the raw air. Later on, he flashed his light into doorways, tried a few knobs, saw that everything was O.K.

The big clock in the public utilities building struck the quarter-hour. A truck, loaded with the early morning papers, came to a dead stop near the subway entrance and a stocky helper threw off four bundles, big, heavy, whopping pancakes dumped upon the Fourteenth Street jungle track. In his stall, the newsdealer, a small, fat, cranky blind man in an old cap, counted the papers over, found one short, and began swearing, then counted again. This time the amount was correct, so he took the strings off and put the papers on the stand. Then, filling his lungs with air, a hard, gray, filmy stare in his blind eyes, his brain thinking about something else, he yelled out: "Papeh, papeh, what dya read, what dya read? Papeh, papeh!"

Window-dressers in felt slippers were already crawling into the shop windows and taking away the displays, getting ready for the big post-Christmas sales. They took down the fake holly wreaths, cotton, silver dust and spoke choppily to each other, their mouths full of pins.

The dummies they shoved around, getting a kick out of smacking the stylish stout wax models on protruding parts. Signs and cards were hung: "For a limited time only, two dresses for $5, values up to $35, buy now."

A few blocks south, broken men were snoring in the 15–20–30c flop-houses; each man had a tiny booth, sprawled on a hard iron cot, and if he wasn't drunk spent most of the night scratching himself until he drew blood. All the mattresses were old, discolored, spattered with years of tobacco stain, nasal excretion, and vomit; and bedbugs, like systematic squads of marines, scoured each hairy leg and chest.

The Yuletide was going on. The lights in front of the mission were put out, all except one single bulb which burned brightly above the doorway near a gilt sign which read: "JESUS SAVES." Inside, in a corner, the tin cups used for stew were piled up on the floor, and a few feet away the folding chairs were lined up. The twenty-dollar upright piano, used for hymn-singing purposes was locked tight, the manager had the key; it swung from a shiny, silver ring and hung inside his vest near the navel. On the sidewalk in front of the mission, half obliterated by the dampness of the weather, was a passage from the Scriptures printed in many colors of chalk, red, green, purple, white, and old rose: "WHAT DOTH THE LORD REQUIRE OF THEE BUT TO LOVE MERCY, DO JUSTICE, AND WALK HUMBLY . . ."

Toward midnight the air grew damper, the chalk marks blurred, running together, and all that was visible was "WALK DUMBLY . . ." No more, no less. The three golden balls above Uncle Beagle's began to sway when the wind shifted. Two old bums stood on the corner. "Where you goin'?" the first one said. "Me?" "Yeah, you." "I'm goin' to sleep," the second one answered, and walked into the doorway of the barber-college next door. "Where you goin'?" he said, stretching out on the damp tiles, moving his bones around to find a nice, soft tile or two. "I'm gonna sleep too," the first one said and ambled up, shuffling his old varicose legs, settling down before his pal. Across the way the bulb burned brightly: "JESUS SAVES." The light was in their eyes, they turned their rumps toward it.

In the west a few beacons on the Jersey City shore twinkled in the darkness. The radio stations began signing off: "Until tomorrow, ladies and gentlemen of our radio audience. Here atop our golden tower of the new giant Goodie-Cookie Building we bid you good-night, hoping you will buy the famous Goodie-Cookies at your neighborhood grocery store. Remember, only the best ingredients and utmost care go into each and every cake. Scientists have labored long over this patent formula so that you, madam, and you, sir, shall be protected. Buy a package tomorrow, you won't know sorrow. And now, good night, star bright, sleep tight . . ."

Midnight came. All the clocks began hammering out the hour, heralding the new day. Twelve bells, twelve o'clock.

Like a gray wolf, Christmas slunk from town, running swiftly down the streets, keeping close to buildings. By the time the last thunderous peal had died upon the air, the animal was already near the Battery and, with one last desperate leap, cleared the iron railing and tore on silently, crossing the water rapidly in the fog, running a neck-and-neck race with the fading echo. Pretty soon you couldn't see him any more, he was gone—swallowed up in mist and darkness.

Then two tugboats snorted, and the echoes were like baying.

# FIVE

## I

THE NEW YEAR arrived like a fast delivery truck turning a corner on two careening wheels. All at once the big stores began running gigantic, cut-rate sales, slashing prices "to the bone," putting full-page advertisements in the newspapers, giving the public downright bargains. The citizenry must be served, your majesty the people are our masters. So ran the advertisement copy, printed in tall, black letters followed by many exclamation marks, with drawings of furniture, underwear, hot-water bottles, electric heaters, diapers, and high school suits with two pair of trousers, the seams reinforced at the crotch.

In the square, business was also on the boom. Competition among the pretzel venders became very keen and bitter, some sold three pretzels for a nickel, but the conservative faction still clung to the old price, two for five, please buy by me, I need the dough. New articles began to be hawked, Soviet candy in Soviet wrappers, direct from Soviet Russia. At Klein's a woman had to be a football player to get near the racks of dresses; on some days the jams were so fierce there that, when a dame finally procured an empty booth to try on a garment, she found her limbs moist from the struggle, the silk clinging to her belly and her back; but she bought the dress anyway, the price was cheap enough, and no lie.

At the north end of the square a new pavilion was going up, cool gray pillars in the Grecian manner. Many people did not know just what kind of a building it would be—some said it would turn out an up-to-date hot-dog and orange-juice stand, others felt it would be a public comfort station. "After all," went the argument, "it's on the city's ground, the public must be served." Turning the corner on two wheels, the new year thus whizzed into sight. Ragged men stood above the subway grating, feeling the warm, dank air flowing up their chilly legs. And now the matinee performances at the burlesk and vaudeville houses were packed to the doors, jammed to the rafters; if you didn't buy your ticket early enough, there was only standing room to be had. On the stage the famous Happiness Boys gave the folks their famous Happiness Ditties, crooning softly, giving the house their happy, million-dollar, tooth-paste smiles.

Several newspapers began running editorials about the unemployment situation, and a few of them started printing weekly budget lists, showing how an average American family of five could eat fairly substantial food on eight dollars and twelve cents a week. The help-wanted columns dwindled down to a few fake "come-on" ads for agents or canvassers. At the agencies the girls at the desks shook their heads briskly and told you not to trouble yourself making out an application. Folks walked the streets, a man with a steady job was a lucky dog indeed.

And into this seething broil of strife and woe came the gentlemen of the platform, unshaven fellows who donned blue or khaki work shirts and harangued from soap-boxes, telling the apathetic people all about the class struggle. In the square these fellows spoke, one after the other—as soon as a man's voice gave out, another jumped up to take his place. Small crowds of fifty to a hundred stood about and listened: old men, young men, all with blank beaten faces, while on the outskirts a few comrades tried to sell copies of proletarian papers. The raw wind blew dust up the street, while off to one side, at the army recruiting booth, a warmly dressed recruiter walked slowly at his ease. The wind nibbled at the flapping paper poster: GO PLACES, DO THINGS. Under a warm and glowing halftone sky, files of khakied figures marched in order along a Filipino road. Join Now, Service in Foreign Parts. The tall, well-fed recruiter thought about the island climate. He had a yearning for a nice, hot plate of beans.

## II

HANK AUSTIN was laid off at the ninth of the month, just as the big sales were climbing to their peaks. A note pinned to his time-card gave Hank his news of freedom. When he punched in from lunch, the note was not there, but at five-fifteen Old Running Water's office boy went out and pinned four notes upon four time-cards, using metal clips, then came back to read his book again. The clips held the paper to the time-cards firmly.

> Owing to present business conditions, it is necessary for us to inform you that your services are no longer required as truckman in the receiving department.
> THE CONSOLIDATED WAREHOUSES.

That's what the notes said, the four of them. Two were carbon copies; there was no sense for the faithful lad in the office to type twice as much as was necessary, when a sheet of carbon lay handy in a drawer.

Time went, tick and tock. At five-twenty Old Running Water, a little uneasy under the eyeballs, called the foreman into the office and told him to take charge of the floor until quitting time. "My kidney trouble again," explained the old gaffer, his glance queasy, his plump hands resting awkwardly upon his hefty thighs. "My kidney trouble again, you take charge." He got up, faking a painful sigh, slipped his overcoat on, grunted, and went out, passing the men who were still rolling the loads from the big freight elevators, not looking at them, staring intently into space, as if contemplating the abstract, or a heavy shipment due to arrive on some vague tomorrow.

Back in the office the foreman stood quiet near the Big Chief's desk. "So four of the boys are getting the air," he said to the kid, to the lad who now had that nose of his buried into his mystery novel, now that Old Running Water was gone for sure.

The youth, reading how the famous detective was out detecting further clews, made no answer.

"So the Chief didn't have the nerve to stick around until five-thirty, so he didn't have the guts to face the boys, eh?" the foreman muttered musingly, hearing the ticking of the office clock, noting that the minute hand was now near the 5 figure, twenty-four after five, six more minutes to go.

At five-twenty-nine, a gentle gnawing at his bowels, the foreman went to stand in the office doorway, which was five or six feet from the time-card racks. And a minute later, when the machinery of the clock whirred and clicked inside, he started staring toward the floor.

Far down, near the wall to the left, where a huge shipment of boxed herring and sardines from Norway (for the coming Lenten season) stood neatly piled, the truckmen came talking and laughing and jostling, heading for the time-clock. The first man, shouting something over his shoulder, punched out with a sharp ping and stuck his card into the OUT rack. The third man, seeing a piece of paper pinned to his card, punched out, then with slow fingers and a fast-going heart took the clip off. . . . The foreman, his eyes downcast, noted the shadow of the fellow upon the floor suddenly go stationary, not wavering or moving an inch. The feeling as if two or three tiny mice were gnawing gently at his bowels grew more acute.

Four stood behind, looking with burnt-out eyes at the foreman, the others, silent, went down the iron stairway to the street.

"Well, boys," said the foreman, his voice a sympathetic half-mutter, his eyes dead and quiet, "well, boys . . ." and said no more.

For a while the four discharged hustlers stood slack before the foreman, as if driven into the iron floor, or like four old pier posts standing upright in muddy, sluggish water. Each man held the note between his fingers, feeling the metal clip small and firm against his thumb. The foreman, a post himself, said nothing further, his eyes were drilling futile holes into the floor. Over his shoulder the truckmen could see the empty chair of Old Running Water, the wide empty chair that was smooth and shiny on the seat from years of rump friction. The office kid was placing a leather covering over the typewriter, so that the covered machine resembled a small, black tombstone. Then the kid clicked out the light over the Big Chief's desk, and gloom, a blank gloom, settled down upon the office.

In half-darkness the four hustlers went toward the iron

stairway and started walking down the metal stairs. All of them were a bit gray about the mouth, all were married and had a kid or two. When they reached the street, they stood and looked at the traffic with dead eyes, and mumbled in an undertone a few words about things which were unrelated and unimportant. They made it a point not to look at one another's eyes.

Five minutes passed like that, just standing there with bowed shoulders, then each man went his own way, not shaking hands, no good-bye, just going off, the muddy, sluggish water finally getting at him, working him loose and carrying him downstream at last. . . .

Before he climbed the tenement stairs Hank Austin thought out some words, how he would look at his wife, how and when he would spring the news and the exact pitch of his voice. Standing there in the drafty hallway, he silently rehearsed his rôle. The skin on his face felt like dry, old wrapping paper. He made a few faces suddenly, grinned silently, rubbed his cheeks with his paws, set the blood going, then cleared his throat. All set now, he began going up the stairs. There he goes, slowly.

The kids, hearing his hand on the knob, get in formation for the nightly football rush. As soon as Hank opens the door, they run at his knees, growling like bulldogs, and Hank, mighty Hank of the iron shoulder-blades, drags them across the floor like so much seaweed, a funny grin on his face. He even lifts the smallest kid high into the air and speaks a gentle word or two. Then he sets the lad down, throws his leather jacket toward a chair, sits, stretches out his legs, and waits for the meal. His wife, short and sturdy on her healthy legs, bends over the stove, her plump back toward him. When she turns around, a big dish steaming in her hands, he sees a thin sweat on her face, and also a wifely glow. He forces himself to nip her buttocks, when the children aren't looking. Then, reaching out for a tablespoon, he starts swallowing the thick, hot Yankee bean soup, and lifts and swallows, and forces it down, though all appetite is gone forever now.

Later on, when the kids got in bed, when it was quiet in the flat, when his missus sat on the other side of the kitchen table, her sleeves rolled to the elbow, Hank wet his lips, but no words came. In the hallway the door banged, the ten-cent lock rattled on the rusty staple, and Hank, forcing himself to look alert, pricked his ears, a coltish gesture, but there was no fire in his eyes, no thunder in his voice now, as he shouted and jerked his head toward the door.

His voice died inside his throat, a dry echo. Under the kitchen table his great legs sprawled out weakly, as if someone had struck him stunning blows high on his thighs. His wife, her reddened hands mutely folded, the fingers interlocked, sat staring quietly at the pattern on the tablecloth. She was a good woman, and faithful, too. Hank wet his lips, frowned a bit, but when the missus glanced up he gave a funny grin and moved his great legs slightly, stirring them under the table. One of his boots happened to graze her ankle.

"Hank," she said, getting red all the way down her throat, starting to breathe fast, keeping her eyelids down, her glance on her shiny knuckles. "Hank."

And Hank? He wet his lips again, but the words stuck in his throat. In the other room the kids were sleeping. The gas-heater burned evenly, the heat flowed pleasantly toward his face. For the last time Hank wet his lips, made an effort. Another funny grin was the result.

Then, rising, he faked a yawn, trying to drive the old,

wrapping paper feeling from his face, trying to set his blood pulsing faster. In the end he gave a grunt, and postponed the matter; today was Saturday, there was plenty of time yet.

Unbuttoning his shirt at the collar, he went to the sink and took a long drink of cold water, and when he set the glass down his wife was still sitting quietly at the table, a modest, faithful dame. Her straight, ash-colored hair was tied in a tight, neat knot in the back of her head, her ears were small and pink; she sat with her bust touching the edge of the table. Hank planked himself down in a chair and bent away over to untie his shoelaces, grunting as he stooped, wetting his lips, forcing his brain to go forward at a normal pace.

"Well," he grunted, his shaggy head down, his fingers fumbling at his shoes. "Well . . ." he said, and that was all.

His left sock had a hole at the heel.

His wife rose quietly and turned the gas-heater off.

## III

FIVE MINUTES LATER Leon Fisher—artist and communist—put his overcoat on and clicked out the light in his room, then went downstairs. As he was descending the last few stairs in the hallway, a door under the staircase opened and Celia came out, walking quietly and rapidly toward the bird-cage, to adjust the cloth.

Leon said, "Hello."

"It's so chilly in the hallway, I thought I'd come out and see if the canary is covered properly," said Celia, and she gave him a crooked, childish smile, drawing her lips carefully over that tooth of hers, giving him her sweet, frozen face.

Leon, pausing, smiled back at her. He said the bird must be used to the temperature of the house by this time.

"Is it a male or a female bird?" he asked Celia.

She turned quickly toward the cage again, and her hands fluttered at the cloth.

"I don't know. I think it's a female, she has such a high voice . . ."

"Well, females stand the cold better than the males," said Leon. "That's a well-known scientific fact. Look at human beings. A man wears an overcoat and shivers while a woman puts on a light silk wrap and doesn't feel anything."

"It's not as bad as that."

It wasn't, eh? The little painter gave her more facts, even quoting figures. He had plenty of time to keep a certain appointment, so he could afford to kill a few minutes here in the hall. Speaking authoritatively, he mentioned the fashion plates of certain magazines, which showed the tiny frocks women put on in winter, spoke about the gowns the movie queens wore in their pictures, and, as a crushing blow, called attention to the window displays along Fourteenth Street, "where," he said, "you could crumble up a lady's garment into your fist and stuff it into your pocket as a handkerchief."

To this Celia had nothing to say.

"However, that's not what I was thinking about as I closed the door of my room," Leon went on.

No?

"No," he said. "I was thinking of the chances of my picture at the exhibition being sold and bringing a fair price."

The girl whirled suddenly, lifting puzzled brows at him. His picture at the exhibition? What exhibition? In a flash Leon realized that he hadn't told her about his stroke of luck, he hadn't mentioned a word to her about it. And yet, she was the one who had posed for it, had refused the canvas as a gift, and had urged him to send it away. Leon stood there, his face going red, his eyes wandering.

"I really don't know why I didn't tell you," he said, fumbling about, trying to look at ease before her glance, and he told her that the picture she had posed for had been accepted for exhibition at the Pennsylvania National Academy and would be displayed when the show opened soon. "They sent me a special-delivery letter telling me about it," he said.

The brows shot up, higher.

"On Christmas?"

Leon cleared his throat, and coughed gently. Yes, that was it.

"My aunt told me you had a letter then," the girl said.

Again Leon coughed gently and stared at the covered bird-cage. Then he remembered something else and the feeling of guilt increased more than ever. "Thanks for the necktie you placed on my dresser," he said. "It was very nice of you."

"Did you like it?"

He said he did.

"That was nothing," she told him, "but it was all I could afford."

Then it seemed that Leon's coughing troubled him so much that he had to take his handkerchief from his pocket and place it to his mouth and, flushed in the face, hating himself, he made quickly for the door and was outside on the street. He put his handkerchief away and started walking grimly, forcing all thoughts out of his mind.

He turned up Irving Place and, going south, passed the burlesk show, one eye toward the photos of the undressed ladies, the other on the lights of Fourteenth Street up ahead. Near the box-office the little barker with the hooked nose was croaking hoarsely, as though his throat were lined with coal dust. "You can't go wrong folks . . . plenty of young, bee-ootiful girls, dancing, shaking, singing . . . comedy and laughter for old and young. You can't go wrong, smoking in boxes . . ."

The words of the barker floated behind Leon's back until he reached Fourteenth Street, where he slowed his pace a little. Finally he came up to the doorway of Twenty-Door City, stood there hesitating, stood there undecided whether to go in, to stay out, to wait a while, or return back to his room. Finally, dry-throated and with his palms going damp, he went inside the building. Above the door in the rear he saw a glow against the filmy transom window. He raised a hand and knocked softly.

The door opened just a little; José stuck his head out.

"Is Helen in, comrade?" Leon tried to make his voice pleasant.

The Mexican, only his head out in the hallway, shook his head vigorously and frowned. "She's not home, went out somewhere."

Leon felt the man was lying. The big round head of the Mexican continued to stick out into the hall, like a giant sunflower nodding on a stem. "Did you tell her you were coming here?" José said, not asking Leon inside, not acting friendly.

Leon hesitated, then said no—no, he wasn't expected.

"She's not home—not here," said José again, and slammed the door in Leon's face.

Leon stood there, feeling small and hollow. He walked toward the entrance and for a while stood looking at the lights of Webster Hall across the street. Little by little the lights stopped blurring, until he could distinguish each separate bulb, and then he knew his eyes were dry again. He stood there thinking. Then, because he had nothing to do, because he did not want to return to his room and go to sleep, he re-entered the building and started climbing the flights to Jason's rooms. On the way up he did a "Hank Austin transformation," he rearranged his facial muscles as well as he was able.

"Where have you been, my proud bee-ooty?" said the ex-poet, who was scanning a draft of a story he was thinking of sending out. "I haven't seen you for over a week now, Comrade Leon."

"I had to do some Party work," said Leon. "It kept me pretty busy."

"You're a liar, Leon. You've been on the hop, skip, and jump for that comrade down on the main floor, for that dizzy blonde."

Leon's body contracted, as if he had suddenly received a blow in the face. The ex-poet's face was set.

"Why walk five flights up when you can be entertained on the ground floor? That is the question, Comrade Leon, the big issue that confronts us here. I grant you the floor, you may answer at your leisure," and he turned to scan his typed sheets again.

Leon didn't answer, didn't say a word, didn't sit down, though Jason had motioned to a chair. Finally, no words coming forth, the ex-poet glanced up.

"Down below you could have listened to sweet laughter and viewed a pair of twinkling dimples and also dimpled twinklings, you know what I mean, comrade; she sure has a pair of dimpled twinklings and I don't mean maybe, while up here you have only my sour face to gaze upon."

Leon, hurt, didn't know what to do now, Jason had never gone as far as this before. Staring about, he saw a mouse trap near a hole in a corner. Jason followed his friend's glance.

"Yes," he observed, "I have become troubled lately by nocturnal prowlings. Yesterday I caught two visitors, little fellows they were, with nice, sensitive tails. Today I trapped one. Business, you see, is not good, not so bad."

"Is bread good bait?" asked Leon, glad that his friend was off on another subject now. The trap had a bread pellet.

The ex-poet raised his brows. Good bait? Why, he himself ate the bread, it was so good. "What kind does the blond Venus eat? Bread made from golden dough, or does she prefer muffins?"

Leon crept further within himself. Why Jason was hurting him so much, he didn't know.

"Unless you stop talking like that, I'll have to leave," he finally told the ex-poet.

"Go ahead," answered Jason, "but don't slam the door, my nerves are sensitive tonight, I have just completed another epic, a tale of Miranda Hastings, who comes to New York, gets a job in a speakeasy, and finally marries Dick Hathaway, son of the Macedonian consul, who is off on a spree from Bulgaria. They meet in a coffee-pot on Eighth Avenue. However, I might have to revise my tale a bit, maybe I didn't make Miranda hot enough for the editor, and you can't blame the editor if he turns the epic down. Who wants a cold woman, anyhow? I should have made Miranda like Comrade Helen, a big, hot baby."

Now Leon's mouth was twitching, his legs were quivering too. He whirled around and gripped the doorknob and was going out when Jason's voice rang out with a clear command.

"Here, you! Sit down, come back here!"

Leon, still quivering, closed the door and sat down quietly. Jason, his face changing, laid the sheets aside and stared toward an empty bottle on the floor; when he spoke to Leon his voice was calm and quiet.

"Leon, I understand you're making a fool of yourself. I hear you're calling on the blonde downstairs almost every day when the greaser's not around and you're hanging around her like a puppy. Believe me, Leon, she's not worth it, she's just a stuffed doll with the face of a simple farmer girl. I'll admit she's got a body, if you like that kind of a shape, but she's too big for you to tackle, and besides, I doubt if she'd hand herself over to you. She's playing with you, kidding you along."

Leon's heart was hammering hard, going like a triphammer against his ribs.

"You ought to stop chasing her before she gets too strong a hold on you," Jason said.

Then the little fellow found his voice, words spurted from his mouth as from a fountain pen. "And what about yourself?" he demanded harshly, two spots showing on his cheeks. "You've made a wreck out of yourself over a girl, then she threw you down. How can you talk and advise me, how do you have the nerve to do so?" He shrilled the last words.

"I don't count," said Jason. "And anyway, the girl didn't wreck me, she tried to build me up, but there was nothing there to build up."

"You're a liar," screamed Leon from his chair.

"No," said Jason calmly, "I'm not," and he smiled,

one of his rare smiles that touched his bitter mouth with something that wrenched at Leon's heart.

"I'm your friend," said Jason. "Don't forget that."

Leon sat there. He pulled out his handkerchief and blew his nose violently. Jason turned his head and for a long time stared off at some sheets of paper on the bed. When he turned around, Leon was all right again, smiling faintly, calmed down, but his eyes were still bright with a strange, dry fire.

"What I came up for," said Leon after a pause, "was to ask you to go with me to a meeting a week from next Sunday. It's going to be held across the street, at Webster Hall."

Jason said he wasn't interested.

"But this isn't strictly a Party meeting," Leon argued. "This is a mass meeting, the public is going to be invited. It's about the striking miners down in Kentucky."

Again Jason said he wasn't interested.

"I'll be around anyway," said Leon, getting ready to go, and stood at the doorway, staring at the face of his friend, sorry he had touched the ex-poet's sore spot. "That room across the hall," he said, making conversation, "is it rented yet, did someone take it?"

"Rent that room? Don't make me laugh. Why, it's colder there than here. Who'd want to live in an ice-box?"

"That means that your gin would freeze there if you rented it," Leon said, starting to smile.

Gin? Jason was sober now, his cash was all gone, his bill at Pete's was very big and for the past few days all the ex-poet had ordered was doughnuts and coffee because Pete had stood there clawing thoughtfully at the cheese holes of his leathered face, clearing his throat, hesitating to speak on a topic very tender to both of them. "No, I'm not interested in gin right now," said Jason to Leon. "I'm thinking of taking a bus trip, just for a change of climate. Maybe I'll go down to Philadelphia, I don't know yet."

"If you go there next week, you can drop in at the Academy and see my picture," Leon said.

Jason snorted. "Your picture? Who the hell told you you could paint? I could do better drawing with my left hand. How did it get in the show, anyway?"

Leon grinned back at him. "I'll count on your coming to that meeting," he said before he left. "I'll come up here and call for you. The admission is only twenty-five cents."

"Twenty-five cents! I can buy four cans of beans for that. No, don't trouble yourself, comrade. Twenty-five cents! I can get three pairs of socks for that. Nope, not for me."

Jason was still shouting as Leon closed the door, but when it was shut his face changed, his voice dropped, and he stared thoughtfully at the sheets of paper scattered about on the cot.

In the hallway Leon was going down the stairs, feeling pretty good again. He took the narrow turnings slowly, the steps were treacherous. He knew the building. When he reached the ground floor, he didn't look back in the rear but continued on his way, heading for the entrance, and when he reached the front door he saw a gray-mustached man with a worried look under the eyes leading a small dog by the strap.

At that moment Sid Turner came up to the building, Sid Turner who was a good friend of Leon's. Sid was a nice, quiet fellow. They stood talking in the hallway, in the entrance of the tenement.

"Just coming from Helen?" said Sid sociably.

Leon, his head going into his shoulders, tried to change

the subject. He said he had just come from Jason's place.

Sid looked at Leon quickly, queerly. "Helen was expecting you. Just before I left the flat about an hour ago, she said you told her you were coming over. Didn't you have an appointment with her, Leon?"

Now the little fellow was trapped, his eyes took on that strange, dry fire again. He wet his lips, opened up his mouth.

"I did knock, but José said she wasn't in."

"Was that you who knocked about an hour ago?"

Leon nodded. Across the street the lights of Webster Hall started blurring again. Sid was talking, his words reached Leon faintly, as through a windstorm.

"José told us that the agent was in the hallway asking for the rent. He said he told the agent to come around tomorrow."

Then Sid saw that Leon had begun to shiver. "Say," he said, "you're cold, you'd better come inside and warm up for a while," and he took the little fellow by the arm.

But Leon, his face horribly distorted now, wrenched himself away, and, emitting a short, hoarse cry, started running up the street.

At the corner he passed the gray-faced man with the gray mustache and in his haste almost stepped upon the yapping dog.

## IV

MR. BOARDMAN, seeing Leon going by, gave the strap a tug, and the dog, bracing its legs, calmed down, growling in a smothered fashion. When Mr. Boardman jerked gently at the strap again, the animal trotted meekly at his heels.

Reaching the entrance of the Glen Cove Apartments, Mr. Boardman paused a moment. Before mounting the stairs he wet his lips and in the hallway practiced smiling a few times. Then he walked up the stairs, carrying the dog under his arm.

Margie, in pale blue pajamas, was stretched out on the sofa, belly down, reading a confessional magazine and smoking a cigarette from a long ivory holder. Mr. Boardman closed the door quietly, set the animal down, then took his hat and coat off. The small dog trotted around the room, dragging his strap, and began yapping shrilly.

"Dodo mustn't," said Margie, not looking away from the magazine, not taking her mind off the story, only her lips moving. "Dodo mustn't." She grew irritated quickly if her reading was interrupted. Right now she was in the thick of the story, right in the spot where Bruce McCrae has June out in a lonely shack and starts taking off June's one-piece bathing suit, when the honking of an automobile sounds faintly from down the road near the lake. Margie was in the thick of it, her eyes were racing on ahead, she wanted to find out if Bruce succeeds in taking off that one-piece bathing suit. The dog kept on yapping.

"Boardie," she shouted, bouncing up, her face going livid. "Boardie, throw that goddamed hound out the window. Throw him out or cut his neck with the bread-knife. Shut him up!"

Mr. Boardman came forward, bent down, picked up the animal, patted the little head, stroked the silken ears, and soon the doggie was grinning, his mouth open, his tongue lolling out contentedly like a maple leaf in an April breeze. Mr. Boardman took him into the bedroom and placed him upon the deep, soft hide of the polar bear near the bed. The dog lay silent, still grinning as Mr. Boardman went out. Mr. Boardman closed the bedroom door quietly. Margie, her stare hard upon the print ahead, spoke, hardly moving her lips.

"You saw I was reading, you knew damn well I didn't want to be disturbed."

"I was taking my coat off, dear. The dog is quiet now."

Margie finished the story. The auto had raced up the road just in time, just as the stitches of June's bathing suit were beginning to rip. In the auto had been Tom Holliday, one-time football star at Princeton. It was a fairly good story. Reaching out, moving her arms and yawning, Margie took the cigarette from the holder and slowly crushed the burning end of it against the polished top of the expensive mahogany table. She knew that Boardie was watching. When she looked up, however, he was staring at the rug. She yawned slowly, stretching like a leopard, feeling nice and lazy.

"I feel rotten lately," she said, yawning again. "I get the blues so damned often now, I don't know what's the matter with me. All I feel like doing is swearing all day. Honest to Christ, that's the way I feel lately. I tell you, I'm going nuts!"

"Maybe we should have taken in a show tonight," said Mr. Boardman, staring thoughtfully at the polished points of his shoes. "I could have phoned for the tickets."

"Shows, hell. We don't see any people, that's the trouble. We have no friends."

Mr. Boardman winced a bit.

"But it was your wish that we live quietly," he said.

"Well, I'm sick and tired of it now. My wishing days are over."

"You yourself said you didn't care to meet my friends. You said you knew you wouldn't like them."

"And I haven't changed my mind either. But why can't we get in touch with some live people? Why can't we step out once in a while with a crowd, with a party?"

Mr. Boardman did not know any lively folks—folks suited to Margie's temperament. He told her so, speaking quietly, his glance shifting from his shoe points to the fine crease of his trousers.

Margie, lighting a fresh cigarette, said that wasn't her fault. There was a pause.

"We could go out some time with your friend Daisy," Mr. Boardman said, his glance still averted. He had no use for Daisy, and this concession cost him quite an effort. Margie had been waiting for the news.

"Daisy used to be my best friend," she said. "It wasn't her fault she got mixed up in that hotel suicide last summer. She's a swell kid."

"All right," said Mr. Boardman, "we could go out with her and her gentleman friend some time then."

There was another long pause.

"I haven't seen Daze for a long time," said Margie, musing.

Later on, feeling peppy, she rose from the sofa, and, with the thin transparent material of the pajamas flapping about, she executed a few steps of a tap-dance, a relic of her hostess days, jogged lightly up and down until her cheeks grew rosy, then, breathless, slid onto Boardie's knees and started kissing and biting his face, stroking back his iron hair, murmuring baby-talk, pulling his ears, and, in short, making him feel cozy-cozy.

Then she jumped up, went into the pantry for tall glasses, and made highballs. They drank drink after drink, Mr. Boardman sipping slowly, feeling the rooms blur; and pretty soon the drunken girl on his knee began telling disgusting stories, one right after another, but his brain was not clear enough to revolt against them; at the telling of the filthiest tale his brain cleared for the fraction of a second and suddenly he thought of his sixteen-year-old daughter, remembering faintly that the last three letters from Milly had not been answered yet; he was always postponing it, he would write her from the office in the morning.

But when the next day came, he did not write. He did not write because the day was Sunday, because he had a slight headache, and because he did not want to draw paper out of the drawer and have Margie looking over his shoulder. He sat around reading the Sunday papers.

Margie made a long-winded telephone call and late in the afternoon, when Daisy and her gentleman friend came over for a little social visit, Mr. Boardman felt more than ever that he was waging a losing fight.

## V

DOWN THE BLOCK the owner of the small Hungarian restaurant stood waiting in the rear of the store, cracking his fingers nervously, his hands behind his back. He had very dry joints, and if he waited another half-hour he could make the cracking sounds all over again.

Pretty soon a big man with his hat pulled low entered the store and slammed the door shut with a bang. He carried a long black suitcase, the weight of which pulled his left arm down.

"Anybody here?" the big man asked, looking around, his eye hard upon the Hungarian.

"Only my wife, in the kitchen."

The big man grunted, went behind the counter, and opened up the grip. "Better bolt the door, there's no business on Sunday anyway."

The Hungarian walked toward the front of the store, drew the dark curtain across the window of the door, then shot the brass bolt into place. When he returned, he went to stand behind the counter in the rear where the big man was staring thoughtfully into the large, black grip.

"How did the stuff go?" the big fellow asked gruffly.

The Hungarian didn't answer right away, so the big man had to repeat the question. "Well, how'd it go, how'd the stuff go?"

"All right. But I'm starting to feel nervous now."

The big man gave a short laugh. "You began it, you can't back out now. Here, I've got some other stuff for you now. This sells for a dime more a shot, but it's better stuff, the trade won't kick." He held up a quart bottle and wiped the fine dust from the neck of it. "Right from Cuba, it don't come better."

Out of sight, standing stocky in the kitchen, the Hungarian's wife heard every word and stood twisting the edge of her apron. In her small, brown eyes there was a frightened glaze, as if a bug were about to drop down her neck from the ceiling.

"You got to talk to the trade more," she heard the big man telling her husband. "Don't be afraid to tell 'em you're handling the stuff, they all want it. It'll mean more business for the restaurant too, you'll be making gravy from both ends then. Get me?"

"But maybe I shouldn't handle so much so soon."

The big man, taking out the bottles, laughed a short, hard laugh. After that, the Hungarian decided to do very little talking.

"I'll be around Friday night," the big man said, striking a match to his cigar. A curl of bluish smoke went slowly upward. "We'll see how the stuff goes, don't be afraid to tell the trade. After the first week you won't have to talk to them, they'll do all the asking. Well, I'll be seein' you."

The Hungarian walked with him toward the front and unbolted the door. Cold air hit him square in the face. The wide back of the big man, going up the street, seemed very broad and compelling indeed. About forty feet away or so a long blue car was parked. The limousine started off with a powerful sputter, like an airplane motor.

The Hungarian, bolting the door again, came back and hid the bottles in a packing case behind the counter, hiding them carefully. He placed another case on top of the first one. Then he went toward the front again and, breathing easier, lifted the shade at the door and released the bolt. Just as he was finished, a fellow who roomed a few doors away came in, a steady customer, and sat down, and ordered a forty-cent dinner, and muttered a few words into the Hungarian's ear. The Hungarian, not used to it yet, nodded nervously and came back with a tumbler filled to the top, good measure. The customer tossed it off, smacked his lips, then was ready for the soup. In the kitchen the owner's wife, with an unsteady hand, was poking the roast around in the big pot.

When the customer was gone, the Hungarian went back there and stood over the pots sniffing, from habit. Now that the store was empty again, his wife stopped twisting the edge of her apron. She had a broad, faithful face, was sturdily built, and before coming to America had worked in the fields on her father's land.

Darkness came on, the arc lamp outside lit up. Neither spoke for a long while. Finally the Hungarian lifted the lid from the pot again, sipped the gravy with puckered lips, then sprayed salt over it and stirred with a big spoon afterwards.

Then there was nothing more to do. Both stood, though there were a few boxes in the rear to sit upon. In the end the Hungarian began pacing the store again, pausing up in front, where he could see the arc lamp swaying in the wind outside. The light shone against the quartered windows of the Catholic school, and the building rose huge and solid in the wintry dusk. Placing his hands behind his back, he began exerting pressure again and pretty soon was rewarded with a dry cracking sound.

In the kitchen he spoke to his wife, his head away from her. "You can buy Vincent that pair of shoes tomorrow. And while you're at it, you can buy yourself a pair of woolen drawers you said you needed. Go to the marketplace, you get things cheaper there." He spoke in Hungarian, in a low, subdued voice.

Meek and stolid, her round, dull face as expressionless as a peasant listening to the village priest, the woman stared at her husband's cheek, because his eyes were still turned from her.

# VI

A FEW BLOCKS farther north the cracked printer was talking to Pete about the maneuverings of the ancient Roman legions. His left eyelid jerked, and in his excitement the coffee ran in a thin stream from a corner of his mouth, like pale tobacco juice.

"In Justinian's time the legions developed a new mode of attack," the printer said. "They devised the frontal formation, bringing both ends of the column round like the corners of a handkerchief, thus surrounding the enemies. Like this," and he took an old soiled rag from his pocket, a rag used for wiping ink from type and rubber rollers. "The center withstood the attack while the ends went swiftly around and encircled the foe. Of course, it took a lot of training and didn't always work."

Pete scratched his forearm, the rash was gone—sites of old wounds. He was tired of the fellow's twaddle, but by now had perfected a front of his own: he knew how to stare at a man without listening to a single word spoken to him.

"While making the attack the men stand shoulder to shoulder, so that their shields present an unbroken front," the printer said. "The enemies' spears bounced off like toy arrows, it was like a pup biting at a big turtle's back."

The front door opened, a man came in for doughnuts and coffee. The printer, taking a piece of paper from an inner pocket, began drawing diagrams. He made squares and circles and at the bottom drew the four points of the compass. All the while, his left eyelid was jerking. With his free hand he fumbled in another pocket and brought out three more pencil stubs, all of different colors. Pete was pouring the customer a second cup of the Crystal Lunchroom's famous coffee and stood on his thin, bowed legs, staring at the iron supports of the elevated outside. For Sunday business was fair, as usual; he had had a slight run on meat-balls in the early afternoon. Feeling his pockmarked face, he wondered if he should run a liver special tomorrow, or maybe a pork chop with beans and mashed on the side. He thought the matter over. In the rear the jumpy dish-washer broke a plate on the floor and began coughing loudly, trying to hide the fact. Pete heard.

"Was it a dinner plate?" he asked in a clear voice, in a clear, loud, ringing voice.

A pause . . . then came the mumbled answer. The old man's shiny, bluish skull shot out the wicket. "It was a small saucer, boss, one of those small ones. It had a crack in it, anyway."

The cook cackled, out of sight, and waited for the boss to fly off the handle. Nothing happened, Pete was calm about it. After that, the old man took more care, and gave a whining smile toward the dirty floor. The cook, grouchy and disappointed, rattled his pans harder than ever.

"The frontal flank formation is the only method," the printer was saying, "only it takes a lot of practice. A united front, that's the best thing," and he drew a few more circles with a colored pencil.

The customer down the counter finished the second cup of coffee, picked up, with his fingernails, the last few crumbs on the plate from the two crullers, wiped his lips with his palm, got up and paid the bill. The cash register went *ping;* Pete shut the drawer smartly. 15c.

Down the block the dime-movie house was showing two features, a gangster film and a western, see how Hickey Savo and his gang could not outwit the fighting state's attorney, also Buck Jones riding, shooting, and rounding up the hoss thieves in GUARDING THE RANGE, a fast-moving thriller of the days that was. In the box-office, which was the size of a miniature outhouse, a hefty dame of fifty winters (her hennaed hair frizzled and burnt around the edges) sat upon a hard, oaken stool, and shifted position, and chewed her wad of gum, rolling it from cheek to cheek, giving all her teeth a chance. At five-minute intervals the boss came out, a small, bandy-legged man with a pot belly and a dark mustache, and he looked up and down the street for customers, his nostrils twitching, but the street (Third Avenue) was dead and gloomy. Dusk settled over the city, a wintry gloom. Inside the smelly movie the sixty patrons yawned and nodded. Most of them were sitting through the show for the third and fourth time, not looking at the screen—a dime was cheap to rest your bones.

By this time Daisy and her gentleman friend had arrived at the Boardman apartment a few blocks south. They took their hats and coats off and started to make themselves at home. Margie and Daisy hadn't seen each other for a long time, so they had a lot to talk about, and stood there, bright-eyed, speaking quickly, brittlely and with due length, while the men, all out of it, sat quiet, occasionally glancing at each other.

Daisy's gentleman friend was named Mr. Blatz; a stubby, stocky German of fifty, bald, but with plenty of coal-black hair over his ears. His mild eyes, set in a heavy Teutonic face, stared vacantly about, and his wide, meaty hands rested plump upon his knees. He wore a black suit, a dark blue tie, and a hard collar; a conservative, trusty-looking man. In his lapel a small yellow rose stood out, firm and wax-like, with a pert tilt to its head. Mr. Boardman learned, later on, that Herr Blatz was in the picture-framing business.

"I have sixteen men working in my shop," Mr. Blatz said later on. "A year ago I have over forty men. People don't buy so much pictures now."

The girls, through gassing, sat down all gassed out. They looked alike, only Daisy's hair was dyed a flaming red. Both were tall, slim, firmly fleshed, and had long, slender legs. Conversation was hard getting started (this was a mixed group), but the girls, gassing again, prodded it on, and the men dropped a few words now and then, flat-voiced, just sitting there, trying to look and act pleasant.

Finally, at five-thirty, when darkness had at last settled fully over the town—like a magician's black cloak over a table of apples—when the demented printer had gone to his Thirteenth Street basement abode to write in his journal of the frontal flank formation, when Pete's old dish-washer (his seamy face steamed up from the hot suds) took time out to gnaw a sandwich (he had four teeth left in his mouth)—at that time, Margie rose to her slim, sinewy height, her cool, maddening height, walked over to the phone on her high sixteen-dollar heels, and called up a swanky delicatessen store over on University Place and gave the gent at the other end of the wire a juicy order. Mr. Boardman, listening, stirred slightly in his chair.

Twenty minutes later a delivery boy (coming on foot, his legs swishing through the sifting lanes of air), a lad with a starched white jacket, brought up quite a heavy basket filled with varied kinds of food, a whole roast chicken, olives, celery, jam, rye bread, cookies, and a lot of other items. Mr. Boardman, rising, dug into his pocket. The lad put the money away slowly, hanging around, looking at the floor. Mr. Boardman gave him a coin.

In the kitchen the girls were getting a kick out of fussing around, preparing the supper. They twittered above the food like a couple of canary birds. Just a night at home, an evening of comfy, wholesome home life to warm the cockles of yer 'eart.

In the living room the men sat quietly, listening to the talking, the giggling, the heel-rapping of the girls. Mr. Blatz, a man with a roving eye, was a bit puzzled at the blackened spots all over the wooden arm-rests of the chairs and also on the tables. The furniture looked to be expensive. He rubbed his moist thumb over the marks; the blackened spots remained. Mr. Boardman, glancing away, was coughing gently. In the kitchen, more shrill talk, more giggling.

"Do you eat uptown or downtown?" Mr. Boardman said at last, being amiable.

Mr. Blatz, who liked Mr. Boardman the instant they had met, said sometimes he ate downtown, sometimes he ate uptown. "It depends on what calls I have to make."

At that, Mr. Boardman gave Mr. Blatz his card and invited Mr. Blatz to take luncheon with him whenever he came downtown.

"I'll phone you first," said Mr. Blatz, holding the card between his fingers.

"It isn't necessary," said Mr. Boardman pleasantly. "Just drop in around one o'clock, I'm in at that hour."

Mr. Blatz, putting the card away and making up his mind that he would like to dine with Mr. Boardman, said that he would do so.

The girls came in, carrying food.

The meal dragged. Once more the girls started gassing, and prodded the talk on, trying to get a real hilarious feeling going, but the men sat there like patient steers, their horns lowered in quiet stolidity. The table they sat at was small, and it was crowded eating there, and Mr. Boardman, because the girls had forgotten a few items, had to make frequent trips to the kitchen to get them. Mr. Blatz, a healthy man, had a healthy appetite. The small sandwiches and knickknacks of food went into his mouth like a disappearing act, his heavy jaw moved up, down, up, down; and the food was gone; on both sides of his forehead was a powerful, swelling, chewing movement, like that of a horse.

The drinks followed. Daisy, who was an expert, knew a new combination highball and did a bit of scientific pouring. Marge, not to be outdone, shook the cocktail shaker for a good five minutes, and served cocktails. Mr. Blatz, who liked wine with White Rock in it, did not go after the hard stuff very much; still, the drinks were pretty fair; he drank them. Again he rubbed a moist thumb over a blackened spot on the arm of his chair, but the burnt surface remained; he couldn't figure it out.

When the eating and the drinking was over, when everybody felt a full, a tingling feeling somewhere near the navel, when Herr Blatz and Mr. Boardman complimented the girls on their supper, dead-voiced, flatly-pleasant, trying hard, though, they sat around the dirty dishes, and the girls started putting their cigarette butts into the coffee cups, into the half-filled cups. The girls hinted that they were tired, so the men rose (Mr. Blatz grunting) and together both men carried the dishes back to the kitchen and piled them in the sink while the girls sat around. The maid was due tomorrow.

From then on the evening dragged very much indeed. The men, seeing each other's counterpart in each other's eyes, noting that the girls were alike in face, build, and manner, had very little to say and did not look cheerful. They tried, but failed. Middle age was in their bones, old age was coming on. One thought about his daughter, the other about the picture-framing business.

To liven things up Margie put a record on the phonograph, and the girls started dancing, but it was hard going on account of the carpet, on account of the heavy, thoughtful faces of the men, on account of everything, so Margie, glaring toward Boardie, shut the machine off.

The evening passed somehow. The hard, brittle faces of the girls were offset by the sad, lost countenances of the men. The evening was a flop, irritation crept into Margie's face like a rash. Toward the end she started talking harshly, loudly to her friend Daisy, cutting words and phrases, remarks about bedroom slippers by the old fireside, old age, early-to-bed and early-to-rise. Mr. Boardman, his face going gray, rose from his chair and walked slowly toward the front windows, to see what kind of a night it was. His back quivered. Down below a file of cabs was dragging by, the lights of Webster Hall blazed on the street.

Finally Mr. Blatz, who was a man of honor, whose round face had been growing gradually pink at Margie's words, coughed three or four times, warning coughs. Daisy gave Margie the eye immediately, she knew the danger signals. Margie took the hint and, winded and blowing, stopped her talking. From then on the flat was decently quiet and Mr. Boardman came back from the windows and sat down again.

Soon after, the visitors left, it was getting late. Mr. Blatz, his brown eyes going hard, had been staring intently at Daisy for some time. Margie got their hats and coats, Mr. Boardman rose, and all went toward the door. The girls kissed quickly, Marge whispering rapid words into Daze's ears when the men weren't looking.

Shaking of hands, words and talk, the open hallway, the yawning stairs below. At the door Mr. Boardman looked as if he wanted to say something to Mr. Blatz, and Mr. Blatz was waiting, but all at once the girls stiffened, alert, and Mr. Boardman merely coughed gently behind his hand.

As the door closed, however, Mr. Boardman felt quite sure that Mr. Blatz would call up to take lunch with him some time soon.

"That Dutchman gives me a pain," Margie said as soon as they were alone. "How Daze stands him, I don't know. He ought to be behind the counter selling pork chops."

"I thought he was a very pleasant man," said Mr. Boardman. "He spoke pleasantly while he was here."

"The hell he did. Why, he didn't speak at all, he sat there like an old cow, that's what he did."

"I could find nothing wrong with him," Mr. Boardman said.

Five minutes later a real argument was going, Margie firing shells on all fronts, Mr. Boardman's lines making no attacks at all. Margie began shouting so loud that Mr. Boardman grew afraid the neighbors would complain. Across the hall Vanya and Natasha, their ears glued to the door, were listening.

Once more Mr. Boardman stood at the front windows, his back toward the flat, his head bowed as he stared down upon the street. Margie kept hollering until he faced around and, when he did so, she took her burning cigarette and put it out against the small mahogany end-table, the one he had bought just last week, the one which had no black marks on it as yet. Turning her wrist vigorously, like the heel of a boot grinding out the life in a worm, she ground the fiery end of the butt into the polished wood and whirled toward him, her face grim. Mr. Boardman said nothing. His silence infuriated her. She began shouting louder than ever, her hands stiff at her sides, clenching and unclenching her fists, then started striding up and back and finally, shouting, "I'm going nuts in this goddamned flat!" she went with long, angry strides into the bedroom. When she came out, she was fiercely shoving her arms into her overcoat sleeves.

She slammed the door. Mr. Boardman could hear her going rapidly down the steps of the hallway. When he thought she must have reached the entrance door, he stared from the front windows again, waiting.

Pretty soon he saw her down below. He saw her cross the street in a hurry, shake the sleepy arm of a taxi driver, then step inside the cab. He saw the chauffeur's arm reach out, then heard the door bang shut.

A second later Mr. Boardman saw the cab roll briskly up the street.

## VII

THE NEXT day dawned clear and cold. At half-past seven Grandma Volga and Mr. Feibelman, running a neck-and-neck race all the way from First Avenue, arrived at the square in a dead-heat, and there ensued one of the fiercest battles along the turbulent Fourteenth Street frontier. Grandma Volga, breathing hoarsely from the sprint (she was an oldish dame, a wheezy mare that had seen her best days a score of years ago)—Grandma Volga emptied all her Russian invectives square upon the chestnut vender's round fedora and in the end had to resort to spittle, but in vain. By a clever maneuver (leave it to Mr. Feibelman!), the chestnut vender had gained his objective, and none too soon. As the traffic light changed, both had rushed forward over the cobbles, wheeling their carts at a breakneck pace toward the coveted position near the main B.M.T. subway entrance, keeping neck and neck, pretty winded now, their eyes bright with battle as the prize loomed near; and then Mr. Feibelman, gathering his loins together, as the saying goes, taking a deep breath of the Monday morning air of Union Square, heaved the front wheels of his little wagon over the curbing and, with one last, heroic shove, his trained hands directing, pushed the wagon forward on its oiled wheels, and the cart rolled snugly into place, a split second before his rival's entry. It was a bit of slick strategy. Sweating and breathing hard, the little chestnut vender smiled proudly toward the statue of the Frenchman: "Lafayette, I am here," he seemed to say, this vender of the cart marked CheTnutZ.

The greenish bronze sword of Lafayette, poised in a stiff, frost-bitten gesture, grinned back at Mr. Feibelman. Officer Terence McGuffy, rounding out the last half-hour of his night-beat, came over to see what the squabble was about, came over to settle any disputes among the venders in his charge. He came swinging his nightstick behind his back as he sauntered over, a good, husky lad with a seventeen-inch collar. In his belly was a pretty fair remnant of a midnight snack (eaten at Thompson's), three cups of hot coffee, and two ham sandwiches, also a big rosy apple "donated" by an early-bird apple vender when dawn had come marching clear and cold over the iron-hooved town.

In a trice the dispute was settled, the authoritative figure of the cop squelched all boisterousness. Grumbling, rubbing her purple gums together in a mumble, Grandma Volga unloaded all her troubles onto McGuffy, then handed the officer a nice, twisted pretzel, one with a lot of hard salt sprinkled on it. Mr. Feibelman, hunting suddenly in his pot, finally came across with a couple of nuts (slightly burnt, but then, he had the burnt sides turned the other way), and McGuffy took both offerings. The woman and the little man watched him walking off, and after the cop had gone thirty paces Grandma Volga whirled fiercely, and made an unclean gesture, and spat, and Mr. Feibelman, gazing mildly across the now surging square, murmured a short prayer to himself, wondering how long the old woman would live; he put some newspaper in the tin bucket and started the fire.

Across the street the citizenry were being treated to the sight of a newcomer, The Man Who Walks Backwards. A crowd followed the fellow, even the cops stopped and stared. Tapping a stout, blackened cane against the sidewalk, a lean-faced man of forty was walking backwards at a pretty natural and rapid pace; there was nothing hesitant about the gaffer, he had a lot of confidence in his ability and kept on going backwards. Even the blind beggars in the block were somewhat astonished. The newcomer wore strange-looking spectacles, horn-rimmed glasses with neat, tiny mirrors adjusted to them, so that he could see where he was going. On his back, which faced you as he came your way, was pinned a sign: THE MAN WHO WALKS BACKWARDS, ALL THE WAY FROM LOS ANGELES LIKE THIS. And beneath this legend was a small metal cup. People started dropping coins inside it. And even when he paused to stare at shop windows, his back faced the displays, and a little kid, looking up, looking puzzled, tugged at his mama's sleeve and asked, "Mama, does the man eat backwards, mama, does he sleep backwards, too?" His mother hushed him, life was puzzling enough for her the way things were.

Officer McGuffy, munching on a pretzel, sauntered over and looked the newcomer up and down, down and up. When his curiosity was satisfied, he walked away.

The Man Who Walks Backwards, a thin-lipped smile on his lean, clean-shaven face, hesitated for the fraction of a second each time a good dame made ready to open her purse. The coins, mostly nickels, hit the bottom of the cup with a clink.

Over the iron-hooved town the day was marching. Clear and cold it came. Folks flowed by in a heavy, Monday-morning tide, going toward the stores, the subway entrances, or merely killing time by walking to and fro. The dime movies had not yet thrown open their proud portals to the eager patrons, the five-and-ten-cent stores were not yet due to welcome the mob until nine-thirty. Up and down the crowds went, tramp, tramp, tramp. Every time a subway train came to a halt below, you could hear the roar of wheels coming through the iron grating of the sidewalk. Porters were washing the windows of Luchow's, the refuse trucks were hoisting up big cans of garbage from the restaurants. On Third Avenue, Pete was just about to paste up a very important announcement against the front windows, informing the gentry that for 30c a veal cutlet and two vegetables could be had, served in that famous Crystal Lunchroom manner with plenty of gravy seething all over the plate and maybe some of it overflowing onto your pants; be careful.

Smoke from big buildings hung above the rooftops. Over the town rolled the roar and petty strife of millions. Merchants slashed their prices for the trade, workers took cuts in wages to hold onto their jobs, girls without families who had to meet their room rent or get thrown out upon the street stayed a little later in the offices if the bosses demanded it, stayed to take "dictation" and swallowed hard, and made no outcry, there in the darkness, when the boss clicked the lights out. There was stiff competition on all fronts, selling out below cost, come in and look around, last few days, please let me go, Mr. Goldman, please, please, please, oh, I got to go home now . . . The neon lights flashed on and off. The flavor lasts. In the square, at the orange-juice stand, the attendant, casting a sharp glance around, bent over and poured a gallon of pure cold water into the hold, then stirred the contents with a wooden ladle; a few wisps of orange peel, like small, dead fishes, floated slowly to the surface. Putting on an honest look, the attendant wiped his hands, drew a deep breath and shouted: "Orange drink, orandri', or-range, fi-ive cents here, hot frank on a ro-oll, fi-ive cents here, gettum while they're hot, or-range, orange!"

The clock in the tall tower of the public utilities building struck eight times, *bong, bong, bong, bong, bong, bong, bong, bong.* Officer Terence McGuffy, his mind alert, counted. Eight times it was. Tightening his belt, he swung across the street, free from duty now, an easy, off-duty smile on his faithful, beefsteak face. Feeling pretty good, he opened the little iron phone box near the bank, knocked off work, called up, and, waving his hand leisurely at another cop coming from the opposite corner, turned his broad, smooth back and sauntered from the square, the blare and noise striking the rear of his head like little, playful, cotton balls.

At eight-thirty Hank Austin, discharged from duty Saturday last, was still walking aimlessly around the square, a hollow, beaten feeling in his Yankee bones.

He had said good-bye to his wife and kids in the customary manner, as if leaving for work, and by the time he was going down the stairs of the tenement he himself half-believed that he still had a job, that he was due to punch IN soon, due to slam and expertly dump the boxes around, due to say hello to the boys and maybe catch a look of Old Running Water coming in, trailed by a curl of thin, blue cigar smoke like a thinnish piece of silk over those fat, plump shoulders of the boss. Hank clumped down the tenement stairs and began walking up the street, half-believing he still had a job. Millions were out of work, but he still had a job. He swung along. But by the time he covered a full block he knew damn well he couldn't fool himself any longer, and, his chest growing suddenly heavy, his great legs started dragging, his shoulders sank. People walked by, heading for the square. Some were in a hurry, a lot had plenty of time. The heaviness crept up his limbs like a chill, as if he were wading in some kind of deepening water and pretty soon the cold feeling was in his thighs and climbed on higher. Shoving his hands deep into his pockets, Hank walked along.

Over the iron-hooved town the day was marching. The square now swarmed with people, every sidewalk was crowded. Women, on their way to the big East Side markets, carried shopping bags, salesmen held briefcases under their arms, affecting a jaunty pre-depression, American manner, and waitresses going on duty at Child's turned smartly up the street and entered the tiled doorway. A big special was running today, roast turkey sandwich with cranberry sauce, accompanied by our famous chick-peas. In the window a neat jane was neatly flapping flapjacks.

Hank Austin, waiting for the traffic lights like the others, crossed over with the flowing tide and surged high and dry upon the other sidewalk. The early morning sunlight struck the forehead of George Washington's powerful charger with a sharp shaft of golden light. A white-wing, using his brush energetically (it was Monday morning and the supervisor was due to come coasting along in his Ford any minute now), sent a cloud of dust rolling toward the horse's eyeballs, but the steed didn't bat a lash. "Come what may," he seemed to say, this charger with the swelling buttocks.

Again the big clock in the tower bonged, a solemn tone. Time and tide wait for no man, the traffic lights changed once more, the big thick minute hand clicked forward. Never put off today what you can do tomorrow. Hank Austin, raised in the public schools, felt the heavy flow now well up into his chest, and crossed over and, aimlessly, began following the low, thick wall. Sunlight struck the back of his leather jacket; the cloud of dust had settled long ago. With a roar, a big Mack truck went tearing up the street. In the windows of the Manufacturer's Trust Company Bank was a new poster, a polite sign which arrested the roving eye: "Are you going abroad? Please step inside and inquire about our check service."

When he had walked around the square twice, following the wall, Hank saw the bootblacks arriving; they came hurrying into position and by some mutual unspoken law took their posts about ten feet apart; and there was no crowding, either. Some of the "boys" were old and gray, and had shapeless faces, as if hammer blows had been struck them, right between the eyes, on the nose, all over. That's the way they looked. Their knees were ragged from kneeling on the sidewalk while they gave you shines, s'r, shines, s'r, only 5c.

Time and tide. By ten o'clock Hank was sick and tired of walking around the square. There were crowds crossing all the while, and new faces, but he got tired looking at them and also tired of counting sidewalk cracks. In the center of the square a gang of men were standing around a big, empty ash-can because a fire was going there, and the men were chilly and shabby, and Hank saw an old geezer taking off his hat, hold it over the blaze, then clamp it onto his dome quickly. The man was old, was bald, and did this many times, then rubbed his hands with a sort of glee.

Hank struck west. He walked westward on Fourteenth Street, but when he saw the swank of Fifth Avenue, the long cool flanks of gray buildings on each side of the street, he turned back and headed east.

He came up to Third Avenue after blocks of more walking, noted the brand of gentry ambling by with creased faces, and felt more at home. Walking south, he soon passed Eleventh Street and went briskly, in case his missus was out shopping; he passed pawn-shops, barber colleges, hash-houses, Gus Abrams' Store For Fat Men (get your oversize underwear here!), the famous Crystal Lunchroom, "cider" stores, Italian groceries, and a dim doorway where a gypsy woman of generous build, who was giving her small child the breast, went "tsk, tsk, tsk" to the men passing by, yearning to read their palms; and pretty soon Hank reached the Bowery. Here he took his time, he was a man among men here; the heavy flow was still in his chest now, but because it had been there for some time it did not feel so cold.

The bums and unemployed stood on the west side of the street, standing in the sun. The east side was cool and shady, no one walked there at all. The elevated roared overhead. Hank took his time.

By noon he had an unemployed feeling in his bones. He passed a few soup-lines and saw men shoving and arguing to keep their places. The line went raggedly around two corners, like a long, disjointed tapeworm. All was meekness, all was humbleness. The sign, JESUS SAVES, was not lit up, it was daylight now. Those who came out of the soup-kitchen walked smartly for a half a dozen paces or so, then slouched along, their eyes sniffing at the curbing hungrily for cigarette butts.

In so short a time Hank became educated in the humanities, in all the social sciences; he knew what he was up against. A walk through the illustrated corridors of Bowery University was a mighty instructive course. Exhibit A and B and also C were on view, guys in varied stages of decay, illuminating matter on the situation of our times.

Noon arrived over the iron-hooved town, the sun hung brightly brilliant over the rooftops; a wintry day. Hank's legs grew tired from walking, his mind grew tired out from thinking. He turned west again, taking slow, sluggish breaths, and made for home. There was no other place to go; he couldn't run away from it, sooner or later there must be a showdown. Bending his head, staring at sidewalk cracks again, he walked west.

It was ten after twelve when he entered the doorway of Twenty-Door City, ten minutes after twelve by all the correct clocks in town. In the flat his kids were already eating, their heads bent over, their mouths close to the spoons, while Hank's missus was dishing out the food. The oldest tried to get a bigger helping and got slapped over the wrist sharply; and after that the lad was quiet. In the other room the youngest, the infant (nine months old now), was gurgling in his little bed, an old silver spoon clutched in his hands, gurgling to the walls. In the kitchen steam rose from the pot.

Outside, in the hallway, Hank stood there. His breathing was labored, his broad chest rose and fell unevenly, as if he had just unloaded an extra heavy hand-truck piled with pig-iron. He stood there, no thoughts at all in his head. At last, placing a heavy fist on the doorknob, he went inside.

His wife gave a little cry, a startled half-scream, as if she had just seen a ghost or something. The kids, their spoons midway to their mouths, turned gapingly, but didn't take it in such a spectacular manner, Hank's dramatic entrance. There he stood, at the threshold, in the center of the Austin stage. He came inside with averted eyes. There was a good, rosy color in his cheeks from walking all morning in the cold air, he looked healthy all right, but oh Christ, how heavy his legs felt, especially up in the thighs. He was fagged out, his eyes were dead. Missus Austin, squat, faithful, sturdy, loyal Missus Austin, couldn't get it through her head that her man Hank was home at noon. She stood there like a statue, a dipper in her hand, her eyes fixed, all her robust body hard and firm as wood, her brain stopped short like a stationary train on a railroad track.

"Hank," she said at last, clear and cold like pure icewater.

And Hank stood dumb, stood dumbly in all his powerful Yankee frame. He took his cap off, and his dry hair rose slowly upward like needles on a porcupine's back.

"Hank," his missus said again, her brain coming alive, the hard wood feeling melting from her flesh, leaving it weak as water. The kids, thinking their old man had a bit of a vacation, turned to their bowls and went on eating, shoveling the food in.

Hank went slowly to the sink and washed his hands. The hot water felt strange and scalding against the chilled flesh. He wiped each mitt carefully, there was no sense getting his skin chapped this time of the year. His wife, her forehead wrinkled between her brows, grew so nervous she almost dropped the dipper loaded with hot soup over the eldest's head.

Hank pulled up a chair and sat down. He set his elbows on the edge of the kitchen table and stared vacantly ahead. One of the kids kicked his shin playfully under the table, grinned, and waved his spoon, but Hank didn't notice, didn't even feel the blow at all. The kid, disappointed, sniffled, then dug into the bowl again with the shovel of his big tablespoon. The missus put down another plate.

After a few hot gulps of pea soup Hank said, his voice dead, that he had no job. The kids stared pop-eyed. No job? That meant that papa would have something else to do then, that's what it meant.

Little by little, as the soup went down hotly, as the boiled beef was crushed to a dampish, softish mush between his jaws, it all came out. "I was laid off Saturday," Hank told his missus simply. "There were four of us."

Missus Austin sat there with hard, frightened, startled body, every muscle set. "For good? Is the lay-off for good?"

"Don't know," said Hank, the meat-mush warm and tasteless in his mouth. The kids got excited and pounded him with questions but received no answers. The sight of him in the flat when there was school, when they were due back to the classes soon, sent them up in the air. Pa's home, he's sitting right with us now, right in the middle of the day. One of them, going back into the smaller room to get a good start, rushed growling forward at his father's knees, snapping like a bulldog; the impact almost threw Hank off his chair. He sat dead, not speaking. Then the kids grew silent, and hung around like old-faced, little men, like mournful Jews praying in a synagogue, their little faces sagging.

"Pa ain't got a job," they said solemnly to each other as they went out the door, as they went toward school again. "He ain't working any more, he ain't got a job." Missus Austin, her eyes wet and glassy, buttoned their coats with fumbling fingers. As soon as they were gone, she closed the door and started crying quietly. In the other room the infant gurgled to the walls.

Hank sat on in silence, staring at the floor. After a while his missus' tears started gushing more freely and she had to blow her nose often. She started asking questions but the way she bawled he couldn't understand half of them. His answers were dead and hollow.

He got up and washed his hands at the sink again and dried them carefully, no sense getting them chapped in this kind of weather. And hours later, when the kids came home, they found him there, and they jumped upon him, and pulled his long arms, pinched his back, and forced him to crawl on the floor. They did not see their father's face, they didn't see his eyes. In the other room near the sleeping infant Hank's missus was weeping quietly. She was standing in a dark corner, away from the kitchen light, her hands half hiding her face; and both her palms were wet and sticky from her tears.

Darkness came on, a cold blue frost. Over the iron-hooved town the last part of the day went marching, tramping up the cold, gray streets. Please step inside and inquire about our check service.

In a flat next door a young couple were getting ready to take in a Broadway show.

# VIII

THEY WERE PUTTING ON their hats and coats, the "Russians" were. Vanya shoved his arms through the sleeves of his overcoat and grunted like a great fellow, like a lusty Russian councilor, frowning as he did so. Natasha, thinking a while, musing over the matter, finally put on her smart Russian boots, stamped a bit, tugged at the leather tops, then smiled at her slim, booted legs in the full-length closet mirror. All set now, they went out into the East Side night, into the cold blue frost.

As far as the corner they walked chattering to each other, blowing vapor from their mouths, walking away from the Glen Cove Apartments; and when they turned north on Fourth Avenue a draft of cold air struck them squarely and into Vanya's chest there crept the old, old plaint.

"Natasha," he said, bending his body forward, bracing his short, fat legs against the gust, "Natasha." But Natasha had all she could do to keep herself upright against the howling breeze; her coat and skirt flapped against her leather boots, her nose grew rosy as a little cherry plucked too soon.

"Natasha," Vanya said again; and cold air drove into his opened mouth. Natasha didn't hear. Bending his head still lower, Vanya walked on, thinking and thinking—thinking how, when he had come home from work this evening he had seen Natasha coming out of the I.R.T. subway entrance on Fourteenth Street with a strange man; and the man had been using his elbow for a rudder, steering an uncharted course through the surging home-going crowd. The man was tall, tall and slim, and all at once Vanya knew he must be that assistant manager who worked in the basement of the Bronx department store with Natasha.

Averting his face, crossing Fourteenth Street in the teeth of a withering cross-fire of traffic, going against the lights and the yells of Officer Frank Hajek, Vanya had hurried home, arriving breathless; and five minutes later, when Natasha came in, her face rosy from the cold, he got busy trying to open up a can of sardines and smiled with trembling lips as Natasha spoke cheerfully of the day at the store.

They had half-rate tickets for the show, Natasha had gotten them from the store. On and on, through wind and breeze, they struggled to the square, to the subway entrance.

"Natasha," said Vanya as the traffic lights changed, as they passed Officer Hajek who was still at the helm, highlights on his grinning, Slavic cheek-bones, "Natasha, we'll have to hurry, the show will start soon."

And down into the subway entrance they went. Vanya stuck two nickels in the slot.

"Have you got the tickets?" said Natasha when they were on the platform, waiting for a train.

Vanya, touching a pocket at his breast, nodded.

"And the little package?"

Again Vanya nodded, a small smile creeping into the corners of his loyal "Russian" mouth. He touched another pocket, at the hip. (A packet of sunflower seeds was there.)

Fifteen minutes later they were in the show, inside where it was warm and cozy, where other people sat in rows and tiers, leaning forward all, eyes glued on the stage, ears cocked, mustn't miss a single word.

The curtain rose; a tragedy in three acts, life in a small town, the wife of the small-town doctor, her yearning for the higher things of life, for beauty, for love; and for a child (the last yearning touchingly presented: gazing at a picture-book). The small-town doctor was a faithful lad, but too much wrapped up in his work and the community, open at all hours, I am here to serve the people, a benefactor of humanity, and all that stuff. See him walk across the stage, a neat black satchel in his hand, wearing a quiet gray suit, trim spectacles (by Hunkel's, Broadway's favorite oculist, see program), his gaze serious, a thoughtful drawing-together of his carefully trimmed Broadway eyebrows. He's a busy, indispensable professional man, and no lie, and the town needs him, right now he's working on the case of Mrs. Beekman's recently grown-up daughter, the one who had such sharp pains in her breasts not so long ago. In Act II, no smoking on the stairs, please, a stranger came to town, a strong, quiet engineer recently back from the pampas of the Argentine. "I have been busy building dams and bridges," he tells the town, sitting strong and manly on his rump. "I have had fever, have withstood the onslaughts of savages and native women, endured the poisonous snakes and summer rains, have grown a half-beard down there in the tropic jungle. All night long the jaguars howled, it was terrific, a life where man is pitted against the elements. Ah, my friends, I am lucky to be alive. Well, here I am, look me over," and he lights a cigarette expertly, fingers trained in the pampa way, a steady hand for a steady lad. In the audience the women heave sighs, the actor has some profile, what a nose, what a nose, my dear! And please note (not *nose*) the cut of that coat, tailored in Bond Street, straight from London. The wife of the small-town doctor, making her entrance from center left, noting the stranger, walked across the stage from left to right, to center front, in her gracious, small-town way. Introductions, a slight bow on her part. Rising from his chair, his manly spine as straight and powerful as a granite column, the stranger rose to kiss her hand. "Ah, madam," whispers he, bending low over the soft, pale hand. And into each other's eyes they looked a long, long time. The yearning for a child, a piercing pain, turned slowly within her breast like little hatchets. The town folk talk, tea is served, more adventures about the pampas, the ladies wanting to know about the horrors of the jungles, the few men present dying to find out about the onslaughts of the native women. Time passes, aye, time and tide etc. . . . The lamps are low, all alone now, the small-town doc's wife, the pampas engineer. The doc's wife stands center front, her bosom heaving just a little; and the engineer comes toward her from behind, strong and silent he comes, like a jaguar stalking a deer, only the wife is waiting, waiting, she feels him coming; and turns around, toward him. "Oh, Kenneth, at last you have come," she softly breathes and is ready to swoon when he rushes forward, holds her tenderly, closely, the emoting muscles on his face emoting on all twelve cylinders; and slowly the lights of the stage dim (in the wings the head electrician is squirting tobacco juice at the floor, his hand on the switch-lever), the lights dim more, dim down so low you can hardly see Kenneth carrying the doc's wife tenderly to the couch at right center. And as they embrace there, comfy now, the curtain falls, and up in the gallery an old maid of forty winters screams spitefully, silently to herself: "I bet she's going to have a baby in Act III." More time and tide. . . . Act III, the doctor patiently pacing, Vanya and Natasha leaning forward with the others, cracking their sunflower seeds, chewing, spitting the emptied shells to the floor, Vanya reaching out and holding Natasha's free hand tightly, tightly. A phone rings, yes, Missus

Beekman, open at all hours, your daughter again? She has pains in her legs now? I'll be right over, duty, I am here to serve you, the public, a benefactor to humanity, please pay your bills promptly, after all, I have to live, too. Walking thoughtfully across the stage from left to right he exits, drawing his thoughtful brows together, his satchel in his hands. The door closes with a little noise behind him, another opens silently. "Oh, Kenneth, he's gone, he's gone, dear." "Darling." Clinching, kissing, shoving their faces at each other in a goody-goody fashion, no rough, realistic pawing, you know, doesn't pay to make the scene too lifelike. In the gallery the old maid feels sure the kid is due soon (the program says five months later, autumn, dead leaves outside the window). "Oh, Kenneth, Kenneth." "But I must go, darling, the pampas are calling, there's a bridge waiting for me, a pretty high one at that." "But . . . but . . ." and the doc's wife says no more. 'Tis the child, the child for sure, screams the old maid in the gallery silently, voicelessly to herself. And as they clinch for the last time the door at left opens slowly, cautiously, and the doctor (who's not the fool he looks to be, cheers for him!) sees and knows all. They draw back startled. The engineer, thinking fast, engineers a strong, manly look upon his powdered face, he shoves his jaw out, draws the wife snugly into the crook of his arm. "Do what you will," he seems to say, engineering himself into the spotlight, his profile to the dames all over the house. "Do what you will, we love each other." Anyhow, the whole business gets straightened out before the final curtain, the author saw to that, the play is half-sold to the movie people and it looks like a real money-maker all around. But time and tide, the play must go on. "My place is with my husband," the small-town wife of the small-town doctor says, going to her legal man.

"My place is with Tom." And the engineer understands, besides, he's getting a little tired of the third act by this time and has a dinner date at twelve sharp at the Lido. "Then I must return to the Argentine alone?" But he knows the answer, the crafty hound. "And . . . and the . . . ?" A long, long pause, the old maid in the gallery knows what he means, he can't fool her, he can't. "I have told Tom all," the wife answers, simply, humbly. "We shall name him Kenneth." Slow exit for the engineer, showing his smooth, well-tailored back, the marcel waves on the rear of his head. Back to the pampa bridges for him, back to the savages, back to the onslaughts of the native women. The men in the audience stir slightly. "Oh, Tom," says the wife when alone with the doc, "oh, Tom . . ." A long, long husband-and-wife kiss, a happy sigh from her. And as they walk slowly across the stage the phone rings, the doc goes over. "Yes? Missus Beekman? Your daughter has pains in her ears? I'll be right over," and he makes ready to go. Duty, that's the ticket, duty. He must go. He went. Taking up his satchel, he crossed the stage, from left to right, then returned to deposit a kiss upon his wife's brow, then out into the night for him, into the small-town surge and flow. Duty. Standing alone, clasping her hands to her breast, a happy smile on her face, eyes lifted toward the balcony, the gallery, to see what kind of a house she had been playing to, the small-town wife brought the drama to a close. Off-stage the whistle of a steamboat, a liner bound for the Argentine, flutter of handkerchiefs, all this by clever suggestion. The curtain fell, the small-town wife stood at center, her hands still clasped, smiling at the gallery. Gowns by Mme. Dupons, don't run in case of fire, keep cool, choose your exit. Lights; and the bang of seats.

It was all over now. Vanya helped Natasha with her coat, squinting in the light. Both thought the show was a corker; they smiled at each other. There was so much tragedy in life, but a wife had to remain faithful and do her duty, Vanya said. Natasha, thinking of the engineer's profile, that nose, nodded vaguely. As they rose from the seats, the shells of many sunflower seeds fell to the floor from their laps, as in the cinemas of Moscow. Vanya brushed them from his trousers, Natasha shook her coat out briskly. It was cold walking to the subway. They got in a train and sat close together, in the hurrying car, thinking of the play, Vanya still talking about the duties of a wife. Then his mind turned a sharp corner.

"But, of course, it's not as good as the Russian drama," he said. "Not as good as Chekhov."

"Ah, *The Cherry Orchard*, Vanya, who can write with so much sadness?"

"Ah, *The Cherry Orchard*, Natasha, that last scene where the woodcutters are chopping down the cherry trees and the old faithful servant is left behind. Who can write plays like Chekhov?"

And "Ah," they said together.

At Union Square they got out, climbed up to the street and once more were walking in the cold, the cold blue frost; and as another gust hit them squarely, Natasha, thinking of all the sad, dead things in life, holding onto her husband's arm, said softly, "Oh, Vanya, how much pain there is in life, how much pain!"

Just then a shabby little fellow came up and asked for a dime in a piteous whine. He said he was hungry, he had no place to go. The young "Russian" couple started walking faster, their hearts fluttering as the little shabby fellow followed a few paces, then by brisk walking, by looking sternly straight ahead, they finally left the fellow behind. The remainder of the distance to the apartment they walked without speaking.

And just before retiring, Natasha, thinking again of all the sad, dead things in life, thinking of the melancholy plays of Chekhov, said, "Oh, Vanya, how much pain there is in life, how much pain!"

Vanya, looking sadly toward the floor, his back to the copper belly of the samovar, nodded slowly. In his breast there rose the old, old plaint. Grunting, rolling over, he clicked out the little table lamp, then snuggled deep under the covers; and heard, across the hall, a door bang sharply.

Margie had come back again.

## IX

THE ECHO of the banging door faded in the hallway. After one day and night, Margie had returned.

Mr. Boardman, sitting in the deep chair drawn up to the table, writing a letter to his sixteen-year-old daughter at last, raised his head quietly. At the door, tall, silent, waiting, her face slightly tortured, slightly pleading, stood Margie. With a hasty movement, Mr. Boardman swept the half-finished letter quickly into the pocket of his smoking jacket, and laid his fountain pen aside. His lips moved, but no words came. Margie stood there.

"Well, I'm back," she said softly, staring at his eyes. She came over quietly and took her things off. "Do you want me back, can you stand the sight of me?" She still spoke softly, still stood staring at his eyes; and in the long, long silence she read his answer; his stare was lonely, the corners of his mouth tightened a bit, then quivered. She came over quickly then, a little, moaning cry breaking from her, every bit of goodness she possessed melting from her eyes. She was crying a little; and sat on the wide arm of the deep chair, and buried her face in his shoulder, and started rubbing slowly the breast of his jacket, sobbing just a little.

"I was at Daisy's, I stayed there all last night." She blew her nose. "I don't know what's the matter with me, dear, I guess I'm goofy. Kiss me. Oh, for Christ's sake, kiss me!" He kissed her. "Kiss me again, I can't stand this!" She pulled his head down and gave him her hot, quivering mouth; and all the while she clutched the breast of his smoking jacket, and cried a little, and said, over and over, "I don't know what's wrong with me, I guess I'm goofy." Her whole body was trembling.

Then she lay quiet against him, still in the chair, and stroked slowly the smooth, silk lapels of his smoking jacket, and grew calmer. She sat with his head pressed against the left side of her breast and he could hear the heartbeats growing slower. In the kitchen the alarm clock ticked, tick and tock, just like her heartbeat.

"Oh, my God, Boardie," she said and began crying all over again, with more violence, cuddling his head in her arms, covering his face with tiny, impulsive kisses. Later on, when she was calm again, Mr. Boardman started to say something, but she put her finger to his lips, then kissed him quietly. They sat on in silence. Her weight was pleasant at first, then heavy in his lap.

They sat on. Toward one o'clock in the morning they were still sitting like that. His right leg had long since fallen asleep, but he did not notice. They sat on until gray light spread softly through the front-room windows, until dawn broke over the frosty town. Neither spoke, her cheek still lay quietly against his face. So calm, so still.

And when at last they rose, stiffened, they stood and smiled at each other, wan smiles, and gave each other long, quiet, thirsty, happy looks. Then Margie found her voice. She went into the kitchen singing, her dress crumpled from so much sitting, and made a pot of hot coffee and over the steaming cups they looked at each other and, turning, saw the dawn grow clearer. Outside, on the fire-escape, a cat was sleeping; the wind moved its fur a bit. Over the rooftops of the city the morning climbed, the hum of Fourth Avenue traffic floated toward the building.

When it was time for him to go, time for him to start for the office, Margie helped him with his coat and ran to fetch his hat; and at the door she clung to him, kissing him passionately, almost sobbing again. Both of them were very moved and happy.

She didn't close the door until she heard the entrance door below bang shut. Then she went to stand at the front windows.

Pretty soon she saw him cross over to the other side of the street and start walking westward. He walked briskly, with a hint of jauntiness to his stride. She watched him as he walked firmly up the street and saw him strike at the sidewalk occasionally with the tip of his cane, lightly. Then he turned smartly, out of sight.

The street was empty. She must have stood at the window for a long while after that, because pretty soon she saw the first few kids going into the Catholic school across the street and then, leaning her brow against the cool pane of the window, she began sobbing quietly and had to go into the next room for her handkerchief.

# X

A FEW MINUTES later the lower door of the Glen Cove Apartment opened and Mr. Franconi came forth. The kids were still playing on the street in front of the school, they ran and shouted on ahead of him. Drawing on his gloves, Mr. Franconi stared at the hooded sisters in the doorway, walked briskly past the gathered unemployed in front of the cooks-and-waiters' agencies and headed for the Fourteenth Street subway station.

When he reached the barber-shop, the porters were mopping up the floor. He stepped carefully across the puddled water, where the suds had gathered in the slight hollows around the chairs (caused by walking round and round a chair a hundred million times or so), took his hat and coat off, slipped into a clean white jacket, and went to stand before the mirror, combing back his hair. Only a few barbers were about, it was very early yet; and these few were in the rear, near the "sanctum," and were scanning the latest racing-form, doping out a sure winner.

The front door opened and the first of the manicure girls arrived (the shop had three), a peppy little kid with a good shape; she slapped her gloves down, took off her coat, pulled her stockings up tight while the Negro porters, bent down, swishing the heavy mops over the tiles, grinned slyly at the floor.

"Hi, Andre," she said briskly, pleasantly. "Hi."

Mr. Franconi, busy combing his hair, smiled into the mirror, and so she received it in reflection. She walked briskly back toward the rear of the store, her high heels rapping smartly against the tiles, her small, rounded buttocks quivering, humming a tune all the way back there. When she returned, she was wearing a short frock of clinging material, jersey silk, no sleeves, a low-cut *V* neck, a garment for the trade. All the girls in the shop wore that type of dress. She slowed down and came up to Mr. Franconi, who was still combing, stood beside him, and he, looking at her in the mirror, noted a rashy area of skin on her neck and under her left ear. The girl saw that he noticed, and gave a short laugh.

"That's where he rubbed his chin last night, Andre."

Mr. Franconi, running the comb again through his smooth black hair, smiled in the glass.

"You should have given him a shave first, Andre. Christ, what a brute he was, he couldn't wait."

"He was a wild man, eh?"

"And how! And how, Andre!" She went over to her table, opened the drawer, and took out snippers, files, orange-sticks and nail-polish, getting things ready. Up ahead, in the front of the store, the porters were finishing up the mopping, dry-mopping now, taking their time, speaking in low Negro voices to each other. Outside, going past the window briskly, men and women hurried to work.

"Well, Andre," said the girl softly, coming over, nuzzling her cheek against the back of his shoulder as he stood there combing, "well, Andre, when are you giving me a break, when are we going out together?"

Mr. Franconi, smiling suavely, saw her looking up at him with large, pleading, bedroom eyes.

"Eh, Doris," he said, "you're too hot for me," and laughed a little as he said it. Doris was a new girl, this was her second week at the shop. Up in front the Negroes, swishing with long, lazy strokes, grinned slyly at the floor again.

"Ole Andre, he's got a way wid 'um," they said. "He's

smart, he gets 'um coming and going, they sure falls hard."

Two more barbers came in and took their coats off and blew on their hands, then went back to the "sanctum" in the rear to study the racing sheet, to see how the ponies were running. In fifteen minutes the boss arrived, Mr. Hugo Flenckner himself, six feet two, forty-eight inches around the waist, an eighteen-inch collar. All the barbers, sixteen of them, fussed around their cabinets; they stood alert, moved briskly, got their razors and scissors ready, and laid up a fresh supply of towels. One man turned the hot water on and felt it with his finger, another stood frowning at his sharpening-stone. Mr. Hugo Flenckner, casting keen, piggy eyes up and down the line of empty chairs, cleared his throat, a business-like gleam stealing into his foxy stare. His blond hair, cropped close, rose shortly up like a bristly scrub-brush; his face was pink and healthy-looking. One of the porters hurriedly swabbed the first chair with a damp rag, from top to bottom, all around. The two other manicurists came in later, hardly looking at the boss; they were the old hands, had their following, and Hugo treated them with kid gloves. Many of his customers came into the shop solely to talk to the girls; neither was young any more, but they were pleasant, hefty women, nice to gab to about home and business while one of the boys ran a razor down your cheek.

The day started. By half-past ten half the chairs were filled. You could hear the firm smack of cloth as the porters bent low over the customers' shoes, giving the gents a good shine. Steam rose from the sinks, hot towels lay wet and heavy over the Wall Street faces. Mr. Franconi, working suavely, expertly, moving his hands like an artist, was taking care of Mr. B. Sackheim, a big-time advertising man with offices in the Herald-Tribune Building. Doris was giving Sackheim a manicure, looking up at Mr. Franconi in the pauses.

"A lousy week," Sackheim was saying, a generous, good-natured man, a swell tipper, too. "Andre, I happen to belong to that great class of suckers known as the American advertising man. Once upon a time, Andre, I wanted to own a small country newspaper." A wet, steaming towel, descending upon his face, interrupted the homily for a second. Doris changed her stool and started on his left hand. "Yes, Andre, I could have been a big shot back in Wheeling by this time, but here in New York I'm just a little belch in a big gale."

Mr. Franconi was a good listener. He smiled and said a few words. Sackheim grunted, he liked his steady barber.

"I bet you, too, wanted to be something else, hey, Andre?"

"Me, I cannot kick. I am a modest man."

"Aw nerts, Andre. The hell you are. Look here, what town in Italy did you come from?"

"From Bessano."

"Bessano? Never heard of it. Anyway, Andre, you should have stayed there. What have you got here? Well, what have you got? Just a razor in your hand and a couple of hot towels on my mug. Believe me, Andre, you and I should be back in Bessano drinking up the wine."

Mr. Franconi, placing his palms soothingly against Mr. Sackheim's jowls, began shaving. "Business, it is still not so good?"

"Good? It's lousy, Andre. Bessano is the place, my business should be in Bessano. Ask the girl if she was ever in Bessano, Andre."

The barber turned. "Doris, have you ever been in Bessano?"

"The only foreign country I've ever been to is Buffalo."

"Ha, ha," said Sackheim, and then they had a good, three-cornered conversation going, all talking, all taking turns. Mr. Hugo Flenckner, looking keenly down the line, saw that his best man, Andre, was giving the gent "the works," a haircut, shave, message, shampoo, and a dose of the best tonic. He eased up the aisle, old Hugo did, his belly bulging from out his starched, white jacket.

"Everything all right, Mr. Sackheim?" he inquired in passing.

"Hunh? Oh, sure, Andre is the best guy in the dump."

Hugo smiled, went back toward the "sanctum" in the rear, sat there at his ease, strained a little, and in due time walked up the aisle again, rubbing his plump hands slowly together, as if he had a lump of sweet-smelling fat between his palms.

Andre gave Mr. Sackheim the final touches, and combed back the advertising man's hair. Sackheim stepped heavily from the chair, a porter ran for his coat, started whacking the air with a big whisk-broom, and, after leaving tips all around, Mr. Sackheim walked out, a wide trail of tonic hanging in his wake.

The little, peppy manicurist came over.

"Andre, that friend of yours, that big palooka, he pinched me twice on the leg when you were at the sink with your back turned."

"Mr. Sackheim is a very fine man. He is a married man, Doris."

"Well, he gave my leg a feel just the same. . . ." And later: "Andre, I'm not doing a thing tonight. How about it?"

But the boss was watching. Drawing her brows together in a frown, the manicurist brought her bowl and instruments over to another customer and started working. The two other women, busy over hands, were watching narrowly.

The day passed, the shop closed; the lights went out, a wintry gloom outside. At the corner, walking toward the subway, Andre turned and found the little manicurist trailing him. He stopped, and for a second stood there irritated. She was a young kid, not more than nineteen or so.

"Well, Andre?" she said, and hooked her arm into his saucily. "Like me, like me just a little?"

He smiled, hiding his irritation, thinking hard, feeling a trapped sensation in his bones. He began arguing good-naturedly with her at first, then seriously. People were passing them on all sides, going down into the subway.

"But I have an appointment," he told her again and again. "Do you want me to be late?"

She stood there hanging on his arm tightly, smiling at him; she shook her head and said he was lying.

In the end he took her to a restaurant nearby. They sat eating, Doris looking lively-eyed at him, nibbling at the food, star-gazing, reaching over occasionally and holding his hand, when people weren't looking. Andre smiled, but his face was becoming drawn. He ate, but had no hunger; and kept thinking how he could extricate himself without a forfeiture of honor. He sat there quietly, his brain racing; and cursed himself and all the glamour that friends had cast over him down at the barber-shop and at the Italia Club. He sat at the table and called himself a fool. The waiter came over. Andre ran his glance down the lists of desserts on the menu. Chocolate custard, lemon cream pie, or our famous Southern spice-cake, all goods made on the premises. He ordered the custard.

The waiter walked off. Then, addressing Doris, smiling and begging her pardon, he rose, excused himself and headed toward a door in the rear marked GENTLEMEN. The door was behind the cloak rack. He called the head waiter over, whispered hurriedly, appeased the man by paying the check with an extra good tip topping it, then slipped his arms into his overcoat. The head waiter, alert, called a busboy over, spoke in a low tone, and the kid led Mr. Franconi through the kitchen, around two wooden barrels of slops, past the dish-washing department, and out upon the street by the employee's entrance. Mr. Franconi gave the boy a coin, then turned up the collar of his coat.

It was raining outside, thinly. At the corner Mr. Franconi picked up a cab and rode on home.

The next morning the two older manicure girls arrived first on the scene, for a change. They had been with the barber-shop for years, had made a play for Andre, and had long since given up hope of snagging him. They hung around the front of the store until the boss came in, then poured a lot of hot, whispered talk straight into Hugo's porky ears. Hugo Flenckner looked up and down the long store. Doris had not yet arrived. He nodded curtly at the two pleasant, hefty women; and five minutes later, when Doris came in, Old Hugo's big bulk blocked her entrance. In a few seconds, in a few words, he told her he didn't stand for affairs among his help. "That's all," he said. "Come around Saturday and we'll settle up."

The two other manicurists happened to have their backs turned all the while, as soon as the door had opened.

Andre was a trifle disturbed over the matter when the

boss eased up later and told him softly all about it, but in the end he felt thankful and very much relieved. His reputation among his fellow barbers rose higher than ever and for the next few days the two manicurists, Alice and Margaret, looked pleasantly his way, working up the old hopeless, yearning feeling, then the shop settled down, another girl was hired, and time flowed firmly on.

## XI

ON WEDNESDAY Jason decided to make a little trip to Philadelphia. He had received a small check for another story, paid Pete five dollars on the bill, another five against rent due, and had a little over. The bus fare for a round trip was about three-fifty.

He went out and got a haircut, bought a toothbrush and scrubbed his greenish teeth, then, because he had received another card from Miss Allen, met the young nurse in the doorway of the hospital in the afternoon. Behind his horn-rimmed glasses his gray eyes stared forth thoughtfully. He took her to a movie at the Sheridan, stopped in a lunchroom for a sandwich and coffee, and when they came out upon the street darkness was falling. Traffic tore up Seventh Avenue. Big buses bound for Newark and Jersey City rolled swiftly by, humming heavily.

"Well," he said, "I'm leaving town for a few days, I'm going to Philly."

Miss Allen asked no questions. She had noticed his haircut, his clean shirt, and when they had eaten in the lunchroom had seen that he had tried to clean his fingernails.

"There's a lot of people and a lot of houses down there," said Jason. "I'm going to take a look around, just a change of scenery."

"Oh."

"Maybe I'll drop you a card when I get there."

"I wish you would," she said, and then there was nothing more to say. They walked toward the hospital, she was due for duty soon.

"Will you stay there long?"

"Can't tell. Maybe a day, maybe a week, maybe an hour."

"Well, take care of yourself then, get plenty of sleep," she said, then good-bye and went inside.

The next day it rained. The wind, blowing in from the Battery, sent sheets of thin water hissing against the sides of buildings. In his room Jason stood near the windows, looking at the dripping fire-escapes across the yard. Noon came, and it was still raining. The rain fell hard and steady now, blurring the panes of glass. Jason stood looking at the wet walls of the tenements across the way for a long time. Then, suddenly putting on his hat and coat, he slammed the door and took the subway to the bus terminal, where he bought a ticket and hung around until the Philadelphia bus pulled up alongside the curb.

The road leading out across New Jersey cut across rolling country. Hills rose and fell and the land slipped away before the silent wheels of the hurrying bus. In the distance a mist was always hanging over the fields, because the rain was falling steadily, and as the bus sped on the mist receded, sometimes blue and sometimes gray in color, but the thin haze was always there. Jason, his stare fixed upon the cold, wet landscape, sat hunched in front, near the driver, shaking gently from side to side. Every so often he rubbed the misted pane with his palm.

It was raining over five seaboard states that day. It rained back in New York, over the five boroughs of the city, upon the spanning bridges and the deserted docks. Ships came and dumped their loads and the loads were covered with tarpaulins; the perishable goods were hustled away by fast-working longshoremen. The rain drove hard down the streets and sent the venders and peddlers from the square. People did not venture against the traffic lights now, but stood well back upon the sidewalks, because in the hollows of the street was water, and when traffic went by a swish of dirty liquid went spurting at your clothes. The traffic cops, in the middle of the street, stood salient in their rubber boots and coats, rubber covering their caps, too, and water fell from their rubbered, shiny shoulders. They stamped and sloshed about and waved their arms and blew their whistles.

Darkness came on early. The rain thinned out, a sifting drizzle; from the inside of a house, looking out, you could not tell if the rain had stopped or not. The arc lamps shone brilliantly as the air cleared. Then the drizzle stopped, the wind went up and down the town, swinging all the signboards, whipping the wet streets dry, sneaking around the corners. On Third Avenue Pete poked his head from his front door, stuck out his palm, and it came back dry; no rain. Then he came back and stood thinking about the next day's menu, wondering and thinking hard. He had his troubles, that pock-marked Serbian had.

## XII

A LITTLE LATER, at seven o'clock, the streets of the town were bone-dry.

At seven-fifteen, as the clocks were striking the quarter-hour, Celia put her hat and coat on, held her purse tightly, told her aunt she was going to the library on Second Avenue, and left the house quickly.

Three blocks away she slowed her pace. Above a drug store (and she had passed and stared up many times) there hung a sign, a big, gilt sign with two strong electric bulbs glaring toward the print: "Painless Dentist, First-Class Work, Lowest Rates, Plates and Crowns, also Gas Administered." Celia stood hesitating before the doorway, then turned the heavy knob and found herself inside the hall. She started climbing. In her purse was seven dollars and sixty cents—a few singles, the rest small change.

The dentist, hearing footsteps, darted into the next room and came out wearing a short white jacket and also a busy frown. He snatched up an artificial plate and as the door opened was scowling thoughtfully at the dental work in his hands. He was a very young man, recently graduated, but he knew a thing or two. Swinging around, as if just noticing the young girl for the first time, he set the plate down, still frowning.

"Good evening, madam," and he smiled quietly.

Celia smiled back and stood there feeling her purse and, in a gush, told him she had broken off a front tooth over two years ago and she wanted a new one and she had seven dollars and sixty cents to pay for it.

The dentist, touching the plate with his fingertips, looked serious, and gave his whole attention to the business at hand.

"Sit in the chair," he said.

Celia took her hat and coat off and sat.

"Now open your mouth."

Her mouth went open, wide open. He poked here and there with a cold metal instrument.

"Ah," he said at last, straightening up, glancing

sharply round the room. He picked up another instrument and looked some more. "You have a very bad tooth there, miss, a ticklish job."

Celia, her mouth still open, swallowed.

"You may close your mouth," he said.

Then she lay back, panting a little, staring at the ceiling, wondering if she had enough money, if she had come to the right place, wondering and thinking all about it. The doctor's diploma hung in a frame a little to the left, and right in front of her (she couldn't miss it) was a small neat card: "A cash deposit required on all work begun." The doctor, his back toward her, was standing at the cabinet, looking for something, humming. When he turned around he had several loose false teeth, samples, in his hand which he held close to Celia's mouth, trying to get a good match.

"How long will it take?" said Celia, still lying there, still staring at the ceiling. The dentist, looking for another sample tooth, began his humming again. Celia plucked the edge of her dress down, why, she had been sitting with too much of her shapely little legs showing! When the dentist came over again, with a new tooth, she asked once more, "How long will it take?"

He turned the tooth slowly between thumb and forefinger.

"You have a bad tooth there, a ticklish job, miss. How long has it been broken off?"

And Celia answered, still wondering if she had enough money, if she had come to the right place, maybe she should have shopped around first, prices were cheaper at other places maybe.

"I'll have to reinforce the new tooth with posts behind and then attach it to your other teeth," said the dentist.

"A ticklish job, but leave it to me, I'll do it so neatly no one will know you've got a false tooth there."

"How much will it cost?"

He placed the tooth down, picked it up, then placed it down again.

"For twenty-five dollars I'll do a first-class job."

Celia almost bounced out of the chair. Twenty-five dollars? Why—she had seen advertisements in the paper where you could get two whole new plates, upper and lower, for seven-fifty each. The dentist explained, smiling a little, thinking fast. If he did the job a different way he could do it for ten dollars; that meant filing down the tooth on each side and attaching the new one by a cap, not so neat but easier to do, and quicker.

"I can make the job for twelve-fifty, if you want me to. However, I'll have to use a rear band, not the posts to hold the tooth in place."

Twelve-fifty? For one tooth?

"I'll tell you what, for ten dollars I'll handle the job. I'll file down a tooth on either side tonight, the pulling won't take a second, the tooth is loose and is ready to fall out any day by itself."

All right. The price was agreed. The young man swung into action, and scratched his mustache (grown to make him look older), and as he worked he talked a bit, finding out if the patient had a family, sniffing around for new customers. He hummed, talked pleasantly; and a half-hour later, feeling the raw gum near the new socket with the point of her tongue, Celia walked up the windy street toward home, feeling very daring and very happy. It hadn't hurt much, why, hardly anything at all; and no blood to speak of, either.

She walked rapidly toward the rooming house, stood

near the front door hunting for her key, then remembered she was supposed to have gone to the library on Second Avenue. Running down the stairs quickly, she hurried east, walked the few blocks, reached the library just before closing time and snatched the first book from the shelves her hands touched, from the shelf marked: TRAVEL; and when she returned home, her aunt, looking up from her reading, glancing up from a last year's number of the *National Geographic Magazine* (she had a friend who had a brother-in-law who was a missionary over in India), wanted to know what book Celia had brought from the library, and reached a long bony arm across the table. Her brows shot up, she started smiling pleasantly, and turned the first few leaves. *"From Delhi to Peshawar by Elephant,* ah, I've heard of this book. Can I read it, Celia, when you're finished?"

Celia said she could, then went into her room, and for the next half-hour stood before her mirror, practicing silently how to talk and smile without showing that new hole in the front of her mouth.

## XIII

JASON CAME BACK to New York the next day, in the afternoon, gray in the face, silent. He sat in his room thinking for a while, then went out and in a basement joint in the Village bought a quart of gin. In his room again he started drinking, but the uplift was slow in coming. He corked the bottle, laid it aside.

He went out again. The second building south had a brown door. . . .

When Leon came up he knocked, and receiving no response, turned the knob and walked in. Jason lay flat on his back, dead drunk. The ex-poet's relaxed face, the loosened, softened mouth, the glasses awry low on the nose, wrenched at the painter's heart. Going over, he shook Jason gently, but Jason didn't move. Leon bent down, and drew back, startled. The drawn lids had a sickly bluish tint, the temples, too, were bluish gray. He snatched his handkerchief from his pocket, wet it at the small, dirty sink in the corner and applied it to Jason's brow. Then he shook Jason. Jason lay like a sack of wheat. Leon, all excited now, hurried downstairs and phoned Miss Allen at the hospital.

Ten minutes later, alarmed, out of breath, the young nurse climbed the five flights (her first time here), and came into the ex-poet's quarters. She was still on duty, but had begged a few minutes off from the head nurse by saying she had an uncle who was in trouble somewhere. She came in her uniform hidden under a long winter coat.

In ten minutes she had Jason's eyes open. She sent Leon out for a bottle of rubbing alcohol and cotton and started massaging Jason behind the ears, at the base of his neck, his temples. He came to. She slapped him smartly on either cheek while Leon stood near, holding the opened bottle and the cotton. Leon started smiling when he saw a weak grin spreading Jason's mouth slightly wider. The nurse, looking up, smiled, too.

"How did you know where to reach me?"

"He spoke about you once or twice."

The young girl was curious. "What did he say?"

But Leon didn't answer. The truth was, Jason had said he was being pestered by a young kid from some farm upstate, just a kid, and she's a nurse over at St. Vincent's.

The nurse rubbed some more, not so vigorously now, and in a little while Jason was able to sit up and began complaining he had a splitting headache. He was still a little drunk. Seeing Miss Allen start cleaning up the place, sweeping the floor, picking up old bottles and papers, he half-rose on his elbow, swore under his breath, and told her to leave things alone, then lay down again and stared at the ceiling. Leon left a little while later.

Later on, when she was through cleaning up, when he felt a bit better and lay quiet, breathing easier, she came over to the cot and looked at him, and spoke to him, and lifted up his hand to feel his wrist. Then she gave a sharp, startled cry. She rolled his sleeve up quickly.

"Dope—you've been taking dope!" she cried and stared at the raw, red-looking little scars all over his forearm. Her professional composure left her, she was just a weepy kid from an upstate farm. He lay there like a stick listening to her, not moving, not answering, just lying there. After a while she got a grip on herself and washed his arms above the elbow with the rest of the alcohol. Then, rolling him over, she undressed him completely and, making many trips to the sink, gave him a very thorough sponge bath, using the alcohol sparingly so that it would last. He protested at first, then said nothing. Afterwards she helped him on with his clothes and he said he felt better. He looked around, but she had put the bottle of gin away, out of sight.

He lay down peacefully and fell into a deep, sweet sleep.

That night, when Leon came up again to see how his pal was getting on, he found Jason looking very well indeed. In fact Jason was feeling so well that, as soon as Leon came in, the ex-poet started a hot argument, and, of course, it had to center around communism again, as that was Leon's tender spot.

"Well, Leon," Jason said, "how's the tempo going along on Fourteenth Street? Anything new along the heroic East Side frontier?"

Leon sat up stiffly, tried to change the subject, made up his mind he would not be ensnared again, but Jason continued prodding.

"The trouble with those speakers in Union Square is that they're all a bunch of small peanuts and petty soreheads," said Jason. "They stand up there bitter-faced, screaming, pointing across the Atlantic to Russia, talking about Tom Mooney until you get an earache, and telling the crowd it's a bunch of suckers. That's no way to turn the trick, you can't afford to make the masses feel uncomfortable and stand there squirming. Why, I've seen plenty of men come up and at first stand around interested, but the orator turns on his bitter, sarcastic spout, starts to calling everybody who isn't a communist a dirty name and pretty soon the newcomers start squirming, feel a bit revolted, and walk off. And who's left behind listening? Why, a few old panhandlers from the Bowery and a half a dozen venders with their carts drawn up close, hollering peanuts, shoestrings, hot chestnuts, or maybe a cheap brand of razor blades. Every time I pause in front of a speaker I recognize the same faces and hear the same speech. It gets to be like one of those piano exercises, two notes up, two notes down, all on the loud pedal."

"The masses have to be made class-conscious," said Leon quietly, snared at last, answering.

"The way the Party is functioning here, it'll take two hundred years to get the people class-conscious. Why, comrade, they talk about being militant, always about being militant, but they haven't the sense to realize that being militant is just a small part of the matter. What's needed is careful planning, clear thinking, a definite five-, ten-, or fifteen-year plan of agitation. Being militant isn't enough. A small kid who doesn't like castor oil can be militant toward his parents and endure a spanking bravely. Brains, that's what's needed, but alas, little Leon, little comrade mine, brains are not forthcoming."

Leon shifted in his chair.

"Let's go out for a walk," he said quietly, and Jason said he could stand some air.

On the way downstairs the ex-poet again swung back to the subject. "The trouble with you communists is that you lack a sense of humor; you eat, sleep, think, and breathe communism twenty-four hours a day, and no man can keep that up for any length of time without going batty in the belfry. Take it from me, a guy has to have a sense of humor. For instance, he has to fall in love with the wrong girl every so often." Jason lit his cigarette and threw the burning match on the stairs. Leon, who was walking behind, stepped on it. "Sure," said Jason, "here I went to Philadelphia yesterday—"

"Did you see my painting?" Leon broke in eagerly.

"Your painting? To hell with it! As I was saying, here I went to Philadelphia for a change of scenery, for a chance to meet a certain party, and what did it get me? I made a fool out of myself, with her silence she spat upon me. I stayed in the town for one night because I missed a bus back home. Why, good Christ, man, she barely looked at me, she was staring at the floor all the while. And I had a haircut and a shave. 'Sylvia,' I says, 'I am a changed man.' Aye, I spoke like the movie lads, low and quiet. 'Sylvia,' I says, but she just sits there, and when her nose goes red and it looks like she's about to start crying, why, I leave."

They were out on the street now and walked northward toward the square.

Someone was speaking there, haranguing away, none other than Comrade Irving Rosenblum, who was giving the citizenry the lowdown on the whole rotten situation, telling them all about the inner workings of Tammany Hall and how different things were going on in Russia. He also threw a few words in about Tom Mooney—"Tom Mooney, fellow workers, who rots away in a California prison while the capitalists grow fat and greasy on his life-blood!"

Jason and Leon paused a while. Rosie was sure going strong, and no mistake; his throat was quivering as if a fish were flopping inside near the throttle.

"Take the Government," he shouted, flinging out his fist, glaring at the heads below, "take the Government. They know bad times are here, but what are they doing about it? Comrades, what are they doing about it? Ah, don't worry, things will straighten out—like hell they will! Fellow workers. Fellow workers, here in America, in the richest country in the world, with warehouses overflowing with food and clothing, ten million unemployed stalk the land and millions more are going hungry. . . ."

And Rosie told them all about it. "Now, in Russia," and his voice rose, "in Russia, fellow workers, there is no . . ." and he had to scream because a Fourteenth Street trolley was going by.

"Peanuts, five cents a big bag," sang out a vender softly, so as not to intrude upon the speaker, and a few other peddlers began combing the small crowd. One or two citizens bought, the rest stood in the cold with their hands in their pockets. "Peanuts, five cents a bag," sang out the vender softly, and wiped his watery nose on the hard, glossy sleeve of his shabby overcoat.

"Fellow workers," Rosie was shouting, winding up at the finish, calling all to the red banner. But at that moment a man in the crowd, a hawk-eyed fellow who saw Rosie glancing at his watch, at his gold watch, raised his voice and shouted to the crowd:

"He talks about workingmen, about the masses, but he's got a gold watch!" he screamed. "He's got gold in his palm and he talks about starving workers!"

The crowd whirled around, stiffened, thought in a flash, and swung over to the stranger's side. Rosie stood there gasping, high and dry, his face flaming, his mouth opened, stuttering.

Then a clear voice came from the outskirts, from the edge of the crowd.

"You fools! Does communism stand or fall just because a man owns a gold watch? If a poor worker has one little gold filling in his mouth, would you line him up against a wall and shoot him? And what the hell has a fellow's gold watch got to do with communism, anyway?"

The crowd whirled again, stiffened, thought in a flash, and swung back to Rosie. The hawk-eyed gent edged off, slinking as he went. The crowd looked toward the last speaker, a pale young fellow wearing horn-rimmed glasses.

"As our fellow worker in the audience pointed out," yelled Rosie, recovering quickly, going better than ever now, "as our comrade in the crowd pointed out . . ." and he told the citizenry all about it.

Jason and Leon, walking away, could hear the orator's shouting long after they had drawn away. Leon looked straight ahead, but his eyes were shining, and he was smiling a little.

Suddenly Jason, feeling old and hollow, thinking of Philadelphia, of his hack-writing, whirled around and hollered into Leon's face.

"What are you grinning for?" he shouted. "I put my nose in just for the sake of logic, just to show the crowd up for a pack of fools. Don't think I give a damn about anything else," and, staring straight ahead, his eyes hard and dry, he said no more.

## XIV

NIGHT ON THE SQUARE . . . a wintry night. Jason and Leon walked around the square in silence a few more times, then went their ways. From the south, the Man Who Walks Backwards came, heard the orator's words, stood about a while, then made off, tapping with his stout, blackened stick, his active eyes reflected in the mirrors attached to his glasses. He walked backwards, following the low, thick wall. Officer Terence McGuffy spotted him, let him go, just another freak, another nut, besides, McGuffy had seen him before, the novelty was worn off.

A few blocks south, in the Hungarian restaurant, another officer, Mike Kelly, who had been hauled on the carpet not so long ago, spoke threateningly to the frightened owner, and the Hungarian went back behind the counter and counted out some bills, cleaning himself out. "Is this enough, is this enough so that I won't get into trouble?" In the kitchen, standing meek and stolid near the stove, his wife heard every word, and her legs started trembling. Officer Kelly, with his light blue eyes, looked darkly at the money, held it in his fist, glared at the quivering little Hungarian, then shoved the bills into an inner pocket. "Now, let's have a taste of the stuff," he said. He sat down and took his hat off (there was a pink, circular welt on his forehead from the stiff sweatband). Two drinks went down, he smacked his lips, smiled. "O.K." he said. "I'll be around next week, every Friday from now on, no one'll bother you, nothing to worry about," and he went out. The door banged, the cop went marching up the street, plowing on to duty. In the kitchen the Hungarian stood looking at his stocky wife, then both stared toward the floor; a cat was sniffing at a peel of onion, and sneezed loudly in the quietness, the stillness.

Cold air tore into the slums. Around the kitchen stoves sat families, and fed the fuel in sparingly, like handing scraps to hungry dogs. Those rooms which were not in use were locked off, to save the heat, and the rooms which had no doors had old, grubby blankets nailed to the tops of the doorways, and there they hung, like tent-flaps; that helped a little. On the Hudson River, Skipper Jim Hawkins, master of an up-and-back ferry, walked from stern to port side, thinking of a piece he had read in the papers some time ago which called upon all Americans, all loyal American citizens to take their money out of hoarding and put it into banks. Another ferry passed, going the other way, snorting, groaning. Looking aloft, staring at the wintry, evening sky, Jim Hawkins made his way toward the bow, trying to make up his mind if he should take his few dollars out of that White Owl cigarbox in his Jersey City room and deposit in some safe savings bank. Waves slapped the sides of the boat, ahead were the lights of Manhattan, glittering like a spray of radium beads.

Now, though it was mid-January, no snow had fallen yet. There had been occasional flurries but always the flakes had quickly turned to rain and the streets of the city had not known whiteness. Fog hung often over the town, and smoke, and roar, and the petty hate and strife of millions. From the river you could see the skyline through a blur.

One night Bill came over—Hank's friend, Hank's buddy—and sat and talked a while about the days of yore, dodging the unemployment situation, but he couldn't do it for long, the dodging. No, Hank hadn't found a job yet, his savings were melting pretty fast. Three families in the tenement were already living on charity, but not for Hank, no, not for yours truly. It was a good thing he had his money in a reliable bank, you can't tell what'll happen these days, in these times. All in all, after years of honest sweat and toil, Hank had a bank account with a hundred and eighty dollars to his name. And the family yawned for food, the stove yawned, the landlord yawned, Hank was busy shoveling out the appeasing fuel, seeing his pile growing smaller and smaller. He walked the town every day ("If a man really wants work, he'll find it," he recalled having heard), and found nothing. The agencies were bluff and brisk, they took your deposit and didn't make a definite promise, while outside, in the corridors, more men, old and young, kids, too, stood blank-faced, slouched against the walls because there were only a few shiny chairs. Bad times, bad times. Each day when Hank came home from tramping, his missus stared quickly at his face; and saw the same grim, set, blank look; he'd pull himself up a chair, whip off his cap, grunt; then silence. His shoulders had never felt so powerful before, he came home with a huge, shouting appetite now; and, in bed at night, was more a man than ever. But there was no work, he got no job. Loafing made him strong and lazy, made him surly, but still he was good-natured.

When Bill came over Hank sat around. Bill still had a job, he looked a little tired, but he was working; Bill had a job. Hank stared away. They shuffled gossip for a while. Bill tried to speak the right words, tried to look as bad off as Hank, sang the blues, but before the evening was over he sensed that Hank wanted to be left alone.

After Bill was gone, Hank stared round the flat with beaten eyes. His wife, her face contracting as if she had a toothache, sat with bowed head, looking at her shiny knuckles. Time passed, tick and tock. In the other room the kids were sleeping. Rearing himself up, Hank went to stand slouched against the kitchen sink. He couldn't stand it when his missus began to bawl; her tears fell with little splashes upon her fists, and ran down over the fingers, into the cheap cotton tablecloth. Hank cleared his throat and took a long slow drink of ice-cold water. He set the empty glass down with a little noise.

Time and tide. Wind and rain. Come unto me all ye who are heavy-laden, and I shall give you rest. Gray dawns and gray days, heavy legs lifting and falling, arms slackly swinging, shop windows going by, trolleys passing, women with hard, calculating stares shopping around for bargains, pinching pennies, saving nickels. The American people, facing this crisis as they have faced many other crises before . . . *Crises,* a foreign sound, a strange word to roll off the tongue.

And next door, in the Glen Cove Apartments, things were not much better with a few tenants, though the question of money was not paramount. Andre Franconi, urged in every letter from California, finally sent a snapshot to Florina, a photo taken during the summer-time, showing his smooth, black hair, his opened collar; and she had written back, gushing and happily, that he looked so well, then complained about her lot, and yearned and yearned for freedom.

On the floor above, Mr. Boardman had his troubles, too. For the first few days and nights after Margie's return there had been a bit of heaven in the Boardman apartment, all the hidden sweetness of the young woman had risen to the surface, but now her supply was exhausted, and once more hell was there, inside her. During the day, when he was at the office, she stood at the front windows for hours, staring up the street, thinking and thinking. When he came home, she took his hat and coat, set the table (they had taken to eating a few meals in now), and, after the delicatessen meal, piled up the dirty plates in the sink, came back to the living room, and, later, after a long silence would burst out shouting and screaming in his face. Her hate for him was terrible, her face grew hideous, livid.

Boardie once more hit the depths, he had torn up that letter to his daughter and now would have to write another. He sat there with set face, bleeding inside, as Margie's darts found their marks. When he couldn't stand it any longer, he went to stare down upon the street from the front windows, her invectives at his back. He began to feel old, though he was not really a man of many years. Within a few days all the untouched furniture was heavily marred with round, burnt marks. There were even blackened holes in the velour sofa, as if bullets had been fired into the cushions, and these holes were large enough to stick the point of your little finger into; and when you sat down, a few fine, downy feathers would float briskly toward the ceiling.

Then one night, when he came home, there were no scenes. Everything was calm. They went out to eat, took in a movie, and did not quarrel. In Margie's eyes there was a heavy, veiled look, her lips drooped full and drowsy.

Riding home in a cab, his hands clasped on the handle of his cane, Mr. Boardman tried to choke off his intuition, but was unsuccessful. The movement of the speeding cab set their shoulders touching. They rode on in silence. There were no scenes either when they reached the flat.

As they climbed the stairs, as he helped Margie with her coat, Mr. Boardman felt quite sure she had formed connections with another man. He had no proof, but knew that this was so. They sat around calmly, Margie placed an ash-tray near his hand, picked up a magazine, started reading, set it down with a yawn, and soon the little metal clock on the table struck the half-hour with a fine, soft bong. Margie extinguished her cigarette against the glass bottom of the ash-tray, stretched and yawned lazily, and went into the bedroom. Mr. Boardman, smoking quietly, sat alone in the front room until long past midnight.

The next day at the office there was a phone call from Mr. Blatz, Daisy's gentleman friend. Mr. Blatz said he had a call to make downtown and, if it was convenient, they could take lunch together perhaps. His thick, slow German voice floated over the wire.

They ate in a French restaurant in a side street off lower Broadway. The food was good. The waitress cleared the plates away and with his fingernail Mr. Boardman made invisible tracings against the linen tablecloth. Mr.

Blatz, smoking, following his friend's fingernail tracings, thought that Mr. Boardman was a very fine man, a gentleman. Afterwards they talked. Mr. Blatz told Mr. Boardman about his son who was in a southern military academy, Mr. Boardman said he had a daughter in a Massachusetts finishing school.

"How old is your daughter?" asked Mr. Blatz politely.

"About sixteen, I believe."

"My boy is seventeen, he's getting big and strong. Look," and from an inner pocket he drew a snapshot of a tall, rather stout young boy standing stiffly in a cadet's uniform. Mr. Boardman glanced at the photo and said a few words while Mr. Blatz stared proudly; then Mr. Boardman, with the same fingernail again, began making little, delicate tracings on the tablecloth.

Finally, speaking quietly, he asked Mr. Blatz if Margie had spent the night with Daisy on a certain evening only recently. Mr. Blatz, not sensing what was up at first, put his son's photo back and said, why no, Daisy had had no girl friend over for a long, long time. There was a lengthy silence after that, then Mr. Boardman glanced at his watch, saw time was wearing on, and called for the check. He insisted on paying; and not until they were walking toward the door did the German begin to understand the drawn look around Mr. Boardman's mouth. He swung the talk to other topics. They went up the street and at the corner shook hands in a friendly fashion. It was chilly standing there. Mr. Boardman went north toward his office, Mr. Blatz said he was turning east to make a call. They smiled and parted. Cold air was coming in from the Battery.

## XV

ON SUNDAY Leon walked up the five flights to Jason's room and reminded the ex-poet that he had called to take him to the mass meeting across the street in Webster Hall.

"We've got some miners from Kentucky who'll speak, you promised me you'd come along."

"Who, me? I said so?" and the ex-poet smiled mockingly while Leon, small and quiet, stood at the door looking into the room with his warm, sad stare.

In the end Jason went—it was only across the street anyway. On their way to the hall Leon stopped on the first floor of the tenement to call for Comrade Helen and the others. Everybody was going, the Turner brothers and José, too; they all crossed the street together, the six of them, and went inside.

The hall filled rapidly. By eight-fifteen the place was packed. Talk buzzed, cigarette smoke floated upward, comrades were going through the audience trying to sell proletarian magazines.

At eight-thirty the lights upon the stage lit up and about a dozen men and women walked from the wings to sit in a semicircle of chairs—the speakers, the writers' committee who had gone down into Kentucky to "investigate" the situation. A few Party men joined them, sitting down with the others.

Jason turned his head. Comrade Helen sat between José and Leon and, while the Mexican kept quiet, the little painter was constantly turning to talk to the girl. After that Christmas evening hope had sprung up in Leon's chest like a weed, watered by her words, ". . . if you want me to . . ." but since that date Comrade Helen had never mentioned the subject of posing, and Leon, timid, did not speak about it either. Jason sat next to

Leon and smoked cigarette after cigarette; when Comrade Helen turned his way he saw teeth-marks on the left side of her neck.

One of the Party men on the stage rose to take charge of the meeting. The hall settled slowly. The chairman lifted his hand.

"Comrades and friends," he said and spoke quietly. The hall grew silent. Then, in a few words, the chairman told the purpose of this mass meeting. He told the packed hall that down in Kentucky the rights of a certain class of people had been snatched away, that in those mountains a vicious class-war was going on, with murder stalking the hills. He gave the facts briefly, still speaking in an even quiet tone of voice, and the mere recital of incidents gave the audience a vivid picture of the stark brutality of the current Kentucky scene. "We have here tonight some miners from those hills. Some of them have brought their guitars along, some their voices, and all the story of their struggle upon their faces. We have here, also, the members of the writers' committee who went into Bell County. Some of them were thrown into jail and a few received brutal treatment. They are here tonight to tell you about Kentucky 'liberty' and 'freedom.' But before they do, however, we will hear from the Kentucky miners' orchestra."

The hall cheered. From the wings came seven or eight men, dressed in overalls and old overcoats, wearing miners' caps with small lamps at their foreheads. All of them were tall and gaunt, the old mountaineer stock, men of the long blue rifles and the days of Dan'l Boone; they looked out upon the massed heads with dead, dull stares. They came shuffling across the stage, sat down, shifted into good positions with their instruments, then one of the men slapped his foot against the floor and all swung into action.

Such bleak, homespun music the hall had never heard before—hill tunes and barn-dance numbers, the whining twang of steel guitar strings. The men kept staring blankly at the huge, packed hall, their fingers plucking at their instruments.

When the music stopped, the hall shouted and cheered. There was a stamping of feet. Here was the genuine stuff, workers beaten down into the ground, silent, plucking their instruments—men starved and gaunt with toil. The clapping and cheering increased. The chairman, rising, motioned to the miners who had risen and had slouched off into the wings. The miners came out and bowed awkwardly, from the hips. None of them smiled. They were cheered so long that they sat down and played one more tune, a fast, dreary piece, a haunting, twangy number that ended trickily and neatly. The ending was so abrupt that it left the hall speechless, then the crowd poured forth more applause. Again the miners rose and bowed stiffly, with frozen faces, then slouched off into the wings.

The hall grew quiet again, the chairman rose. In a few words the first speaker was introduced, a young writer known to be a communist sympathizer.

The young writer faced the hall, the huge, silent hall. Years ago he had written modernistic verse, had lived in Paris for a while, had learned to drink, to look bored, to feel himself as belonging to the "lost generation," and had gone heavy for the Dada acrobatics. He was a nice young fellow, came from a fairly well-to-do family that had lost heavily in the Wall Street crash, and had entered literary activity straight from college. Now he stood facing the huge, silent hall.

When he began speaking he felt instantly the hollowness of his past; he faltered often, searching for the right words, and knew he was making a poor address. He told the hall how the writers had gone down into Kentucky, what brutal treatment they had encountered, and also spoke about the wretched living conditions of the poor miners. At the end of his speech he managed to whip himself up a little and ended his talk on a militant note. The hall clapped, but not enthusiastically.

Other writers spoke. They gave the facts, but what they said did not seem very important after the hall had seen the gaunt faces of the miners' orchestra just a moment ago. Those in the audience who were workers wanted to see the miners again.

Writer after writer took the floor, all telling the same story, giving their versions of the trip down into Kentucky. At last the chairman, sensing the hall was growing restless, slipped the writer who now had the floor a note and the writer chopped his speech short, got red in the face, and sat down.

Then the chairman rose and faced the hall. He told the crowd he had another speaker to introduce, a young man from the mines, a worker who had recently turned agitator among his own people. He faced the wings and beckoned and a young, blond fellow came out, also in a miner's slouchy stride, dressed in a cheap, ten-dollar store suit. He had yellow, shiny hair and faced the audience awkwardly, with hands dangling, but he was very young and so he started smiling a little. The audience warmed to him right away. He held up a palm for quiet, like a preacher.

"Folks," he said, "I'm here to make a speech to you-all, and I hope I make a good one. The people back home want me to make a good showin' here. I'm from the Kentucky hills, my ancestors have lived there for nigh onto a hunderd and fifty years. Since I wuz thirteen I worked in them mines and brought my pay home to feed my ma and three sisters younger than myself. My pa was killed in a cave-in eight years back, so since then I had to be the pappy of the fambly." The kid cleared his throat, fought his nervousness down, and took to striding up and back the stage. The hall was dead quiet. Then the lad remembered the coaching he had received from the Party and he started shouting his words, barking them out, facing the audience squarely. "Folks," he shouted, "I want to sa-ay that there have been hard times in our homes. I want to sa-ay that none of us back there has had a good, full meal for years. I want to sa-ay to you-all that you cain't buy milk for babies there, only out of cans, canned milk. We have to buy at the company stores, and if we be broke we have to go a-whinin' up to the side door and say sugary-like: 'Mr. Bookkeeper, can us-all have a bit of credit till next payday?' We have to do that." Now he was going good, shouting, his body taut, looking at the ceiling occasionally, as he had once seen a country preacher do. "Folks! For twelve years, my friends, I, a mere boy, not turned twenty-five yet, have gone down into them there mines to dig out a livin', for twelve years I walked two miles underground, stooping down so low in the tunnels that I walked like an ape-man, like this," and he started going across the hall, his arms dangling, his head bent as if walking underground in darkness. The hall, bent forward, all eyes front, stirred with subdued excitement. The boy faced them again, his face grim. And from his lips there flowed the story of his black days, his black years, and the black lives of his family.

The speaker held the floor for a long time. He spoke about sanitary conditions, malnutrition, rickets among the children, dysentery among the grown-ups, starvation, filth and misery on all sides. He used simple words. When he finished, he gave a short bow, stiffly, and sat down.

Shouting and stamping broke out all over the house, on the main floor, in the aisles, up in the balconies. The thunder rolled stageward in huge waves. The young man was forced to take over a dozen bows and at the end he started smiling, and then the cheering of the crowd grew more deafening than ever. On the stage the writers were smiling, too, and the Party men there were busy talking among themselves.

The chairman rose, and while the cheering was still in progress, spoke into the boy's ear. The boy nodded, then held up a palm and in a quiet voice thanked the crowd for its demonstration.

After that a collection was taken up, girls went among the audience, combing the crowd thoroughly while the chairman upon the stage kept whipping things up, telling the people to give and give again. He kept on talking all the while the girls were making collections, all the while the plates and baskets were going up and down the rows of seats. Many people started leaving.

After that, more speakers spoke, more writers, and these fellows gave the same old speeches. Their talk was flat and unconvincing. The hall grew restless and more people started leaving while talking broke out all over the floor.

In the balcony, seated with the others, Jason felt the meeting should be closed, and turned to Leon. "Say," he said, "why do the communists make their meetings last so long that they have to drag the people out on stretchers after a session?"

Leon, stirring, made no answer, and turned to talk to Comrade Helen.

"Well, if you don't like it, you can go home," answered a young woman sitting in the row ahead.

"Who hollered, 'fish'?" said Jason, giving her a hard stare.

This got the woman sore and pretty soon she threatened to have Jason thrown out of the hall. At the ex-poet's side the little painter sat sweating.

"When I holler, 'fish,' you can answer, madam comrade," said Jason again. "In the meantime the back of your head looks better than your face."

On the platform the chairman was pounding his gavel. More people started leaving. Those comrades who had peddled their left-wing magazines before the meeting had opened, now began shouting their wares again. Twenty fellows in dirty white jackets were selling soda-pop for a nickel a bottle and "please hand me back the empty bottle, comrade."

Finally a lot of people left, but still the meeting continued. The writers had finished talking a long time ago and now the Party men had the floor. The Party men were still haranguing when the Twenty-Door City comrades left, accompanied by Leon. It was almost twelve o'clock when they reached the sidewalk, and José said he was tired. The others stood on the front stairs of Webster Hall and watched him crossing the street and enter the tenement. Sid and Harry Turner said they were tired, too, then followed, also crossing the street.

At the curb stood a long line of cabs, but business was

bad. People were coming from the hall all the while and still Jason, Leon, and Comrade Helen stood there. Then someone else said there was a gathering at 444, an old tenement frequently called the Kremlin.

"Come on, let's go," everybody said, and the first few comrades started walking up the street. Leon, looking at Comrade Helen, looking at Jason, said he wasn't tired, wasn't tired at all, and stood there waiting. Jason yawned. Comrade Helen, smiling at the little fellow, said she wasn't tired either. Leon stood looking at the ex-poet with his sad, warm stare. He urged Jason to join them, took the ex-poet's arm and finally dragged Jason a few paces while others, who were also going, gave Jason's back a shove.

The ex-poet found himself going along. He walked the few blocks in silence, listening to the talking and the laughter of the others all the way.

## XVI

444(frequently called the Kremlin) was a huge tenement house condemned by the city authorities many years ago, taken over by a real estate company, remodeled cheaply into "studios," and rented out to young painters, writers, and musicians at low rates. There was no heat or hot water, but the doors had been given two coats of orange and black paint and the young artists flocked to the old quarters, which soon became well known in East Side artistic circles.

The tenement did not face the street but was reached by a narrow passageway which went through a few old buildings until you came to a small, square cement courtyard, and then, all at once, you saw the Kremlin, huge and sagging, with rotted wood at the window ledges, but—the doors were orange and black. Dank stairways tunneled the old building and the smell of ancient plumbing, softwood floors, decaying plaster, and hollowed-out stairs had an odor all its own.

Jason had heard about the place often but had never paid a visit to the venerable old building. In the courtyard burned a small electric bulb and over the central door there was printed "444," the street number. He looked up and saw many lights burning in the windows; there was the sound of screechy violin music, laughter, and a few loud-voiced arguments going strong. The single electric bulb in the courtyard cast thick shadows across a narrow row of box-like affairs, which stood up like coffins, or narrow telephone booths.

"What're those?" someone asked.

A few girls started tittering.

"The toilets," a fellow answered. "That's the only bad feature of this place, the toilets are out in the cold."

The comrades went into the central doorway single file, the girls still tittering; a quip was on Jason's lips, but he suppressed it for a while. As they started climbing a creaky stairway inside, Jason spoke.

"Comrades," he said, his voice ringing up the hallway as they ascended, "I move that the inmates of the Kremlin march in a body to the City Hall next Saturday and demand from the mayor that these, er, these, er—well these artistic outhouses be removed inside the walls. I move that they demand this from the mayor in the name of health, economy of foot-movement, and the betterment of mankind in general."

Everybody was laughing as they climbed the stairs. They passed doorways and on some were tacked numbers and on some were tacked cards; and on one was tacked a card which read: "Eli Dorfman, worker." Jason snorted, then followed after Leon and Comrade Helen who were waiting.

Three narrow, winding flights of stairs had to be climbed, and the soles of their shoes felt the hollows all the way up, as if treading tracks. When they reached the third floor, they heard screaming and loud talking, then came the sharp bang of a door and a girl was hurled from a room, clutching a half-closed suitcase filled with jammed-in clothes. She picked herself up from the hallway, swung round defiantly, and yelled at a young fellow who stood glaring at her in the doorway. "You're not the only one I can live with," she screamed, her face boiling. "Don't think you're the only man on the face of the earth," and trying to close the bulging suitcase she kept shrilling loudly. Jason thought he recognized her. Wasn't she the girl, the would-be poetess who had come up to his place over a year ago to show him a sheaf of her very mediocre verse, asking for an opinion? She was. He had told her her stuff was bad, and she had slammed his door upon leaving. Now she stood before him in the hallway of the famous Kremlin, a rebellious girl with dark curls, her full red mouth drawn angrily, sensuously down at the corners, tossing her hips like a young mare. She wore no stockings. Jason, looking sympathetic, coming to the rescue of the fair damsel now outcast, cleared his throat and spoke.

"Hello, Sadie, what's wrong?" said he.

She whirled around. "Sadie? My name is Sonya," she answered shortly. "I can take care of my own business."

Jason bowed, in the Sabatini tradition, and stroked his upper lip, as if a mustache were there. The other comrades, going up the hall, turned out of sight while Jason hesitated until he saw the ejected girl gather up her baggage, knock at another door up the hall, then turn the knob, and enter. Then Jason followed the others.

Finally the comrades reached the right "studio." One of the fellows knocked and all filed into a large square room. Voices burst upon them, they had come in at the midst of a reading or recital. Jason looked around while Leon helped Comrade Helen with her coat. The place was warm, two small coal stoves were going. On the walls were several muddy-looking paintings and in a corner stood a few easels. The newcomers were greeted boisterously.

"We were just beginning to listen to some proletarian poetry," said a girl sitting on the floor, on a cushion. "You've interrupted us."

Jason looked around the room with his sniffing eyes, trying to locate the "healing balm." He stood around until someone told him to take off his hat and coat, then sat down on a couch and waited for the party to get going again. On the other side of the room a young fellow nodded and Jason nodded back, and in a few minutes, by quick whispering, word got around that Jason Wheeler, at one time one of the most promising poets of the last ten years, was in the place. Jason looked bored, scowled hard at the walls, and grumbled to himself as he felt the others look his way. "What the hell are they gaping for?" he said to himself. "What did I have to come up here for, anyway?" Then his stare, wandering about, came to rest upon a small table in a far corner where half a dozen bottles stood, all full. He felt a bit more cheerful.

"Well, resume, resume, comrade," said a few voices, and a young man, after quiet was restored, continued reading from his manuscripts. The words buzzed in Jason's ears like the drone of flies.

Afterwards he heard his name mentioned, all were looking his way.

"We would like to have Comrade Wheeler's opinion of the poems," someone was saying.

"I wasn't listening," Jason answered. "I was thinking about something," and he continued to stare toward the bottles at the far end of the room.

The last few poems were read over again, for his benefit. On the other side of the room, sitting next to Comrade Helen and staring proudly at Jason, Leon sat looking happy because everybody was paying so much attention to his friend.

"Well, what do you think of them?" came the question again, after the poems were recited.

"Pretty rotten," said Jason, still staring at the bottles.

"Why? Why do you say that?"

"Why? Why is a rotten apple rotten, my friend? Why does limburger cheese have a cheesy smell?"

Instantly Jason found himself the pivot of a hot argument. "Give real reasons," all cried. "You've answered cleverly, but that's all," a girl shouted at him. "What we want is your opinion, not a wise-crack."

"The poems aren't worth a good opinion."

More fury came down upon him. The two poets who had just finished reading from their manuscripts, hurt by Jason's words, shuffled their sheets and sat in silence. In a few minutes there was so much heated discussion going on that the "studio" was bedlam. Jason, a dry, mocking smile faintly touching his lips, stared at Leon, who turned quickly and began talking to Comrade Helen about something. Leon knew his friend had started the commotion on purpose.

Pretty soon the room was so disorderly that someone suggested that a chairman be appointed and, all acclaiming that this motion was sensible, a chairman was appointed, none other than the young fellow who lived in this "studio," the master-mind of the muddy paintings now adorning these walls. He was appointed chairman by popular acclaim. He stood in the center of the large, square room, held a ruler in his hand, and rapped on the back of a chair for order. The place became quiet.

"Comrade Wheeler, do you care to address the floor?"

"Care? I have nothing to say," said Jason.

"But you made a few remarks just a while ago that need an explanation," the chairman said. "All of us here feel you should be able and willing to back up your statements."

"I'm not interested," Jason answered.

The room grew hostile. Leon, sitting nervously, once more turned to Comrade Helen and started talking about something. Finally the little fellow, his palms going damp, couldn't stand it any longer and turning sharply toward the others said: "Can't you see he doesn't mean what he says to you? He's toying with you."

"I meant every word," Jason replied in a ringing voice. "Every word. The poetry I heard was bad. It stank to high heaven."

The comrades in the room let out a grumbling roar, and once more the chairman had to rap his ruler against the back of a chair for order. "Throw him out," someone shouted. "If he sits here condemning the poems for no good reason, throw him out." More noise, and the chairman had to shout the others down.

Finally, his face working, Jason got up and stood against the wall, and instantly the room went quiet. All heads turned his way, those sitting on the floor raised their hostile faces.

"All right," said Jason, "ask me as many questions as you want."

"Now we're getting somewhere," said the chairman quietly and made a few remarks to the floor, then called for questions. A few in the audience took out paper or old envelopes, and got ready to jot down notes, ready to trip Jason up if he erred.

The first few questions addressed to the speaker came hot and heavy, in loud, angry voices, and before Jason could answer fully, more queries were shot at him. Finally Jason turned to the chairman for relief.

"Comrades," shouted the painter (master-mind of the muddy pictures now adorning these ancient walls), "comrades, give Comrade Wheeler a chance to reply."

"No, let them fire their questions, all of them, in one barrage," said Jason. "I'll answer them all at once then."

Everybody was satisfied with that and for a full five minutes Jason, his head bowed thoughtfully, received each question with a curt nod until the room exhausted all its queries, and then the place grew very silent indeed.

"Well, is that all, are there any more questions?" asked Jason, making his voice ring, looking the whole room over, swinging his glance around. No one spoke.

No one spoke and no one moved. For the first time the room sensed the sneering fire of the comrade they had just bombarded. There he stood, a lank, sour-faced fellow in horn-rimmed glasses, the corners of his mouth twisted as one would twist the ends of a handkerchief, and he stared coldly at them through his thick spectacles.

"Comrades," he said, speaking slowly in the quiet room, "you have honored me by asking many questions, some of which I will take the trouble to answer. First of all, I must repeat my original statement: The poetry recited in this historic amphitheater stank to high heaven. I shall now proceed. Comrades, you of the new day, of the new dawn, you have not been listening to proletarian poetry, you have not been listening to good bourgeois verse. On ships, when the seamen dump out old, used water over the side, when they heave the stuff overboard in buckets and barrels with a grunt, they take no notice where the water goes, because it is unimportant. They call it bilge. That's what you have been listening to. A great many of you here are no more 'proletarian' writers or painters than I am the pilot of a zeppelin. Think you, O comrades, that because you have aligned yourselves with the communist movement that instantly all your work becomes proletarian and stems from the masses? Think you, O comrades, that because you have memorized a few Marxist slogans, such as *opportunism, capitalism, Leninism,* the *proletarian state, revolutionary, petty bourgeoisie,* and a few other catchwords that automatically you become heralds of a new 'workers' art'? You're all wet, you're all wrong, my friends."

"What are you driving at?" someone shouted from the floor.

"Shut up!" said Jason. "I'm talking now, it's my turn. Comrades, if you will allow me to say so, all of us here are nothing more or less than parasites, we're barnacles on the bottom of a boat. The Revolution doesn't need us at all, what it needs is militant workers, militant, intelligent workers. You saw that demonstrated at the mass meeting tonight. After all those well-known, well-meaning writers

were through talking, it took just one worker from the
mines to electrify the crowd. Why? Because he really feels
what he's fighting for. He cares nothing about the latest
ideology, nothing about Marxism, but he knows he's up
against starvation and exploitation and eviction and he's
putting up a battle."

"Would you have the movement without the intellectuals then?"

"Shut up! Yes and no. You people here are not good
writers or good painters or good thinkers, you go along
with the movement like little fishes with the tide. Most of
you are New Yorkers right from college, most of you have
never had a calloused palm in your life, except maybe
from stroking a girl's leg. You have never worked in
shops, factories, or on farms; few of you have even worked
in offices. You know nothing of the mental make-up of the
masses you're always writing about. In fact, comrades,
you're just a lot of ordinary bohemians."

The room burst into uproar. The chairman, rapping
loudly, had to shout the others down. "Comrades, comrades, let him finish, let him finish, pleeease!"

"I repeat: You're all bohemians! Fifteen or twenty
years ago you would, if you had been born earlier, been
living in Greenwich Village, fighting for the 'new freedom,' free love, and all that sort of stuff. But what's
happened, what's happened, comrades? Why, the bourgeoisie has stolen your ancient thunder; every shopgirl,
every fifteen-dollar-a-week clerk believes in free love and
freedom now. The single standard business is old stuff
now. Even in the movies the heroine no longer has to be
virgin before the hero will take her in his manly arms and
whisper wedding bells into her ear; and, in fact, a movie
star nowadays can't make a hit with the fans unless she

has sinned through four-fifths of the film before the hero goes broad-minded and forgives all. And look at the confessional magazines now, all of them have the heroine sinning and finding happiness at the end. Alas, my friends, you have been left high and dry, stranded, so you've shoved off with the Party."

Two or three in the crowd rose from the floor and tried to shout the ex-poet down.

"You call yourselves radicals," Jason went on, speaking louder. "Well, what of it, what does that label make you, a ham sandwich? Any young writer or painter of any promise at all has to be a radical. This isn't new, this radical business. But not only do you call yourselves radicals, but you paste a second label on and add the word, *revolutionaries*. Why? Whoever told you you knew what the Revolution is about, anyway? What have you done that justifies the name you call yourselves, proletarian writers and artists? What have you done, what are you doing that is helping the movement in America?"

"We're making the masses class-conscious," someone hollered.

"Pah! Do you think they stop to read your bilge or look at your paintings? What does a worker care for these messy things against the walls? What does a factory hand, a farmer, a white-collar slave care about tricky verse shot through with 'new dawn,' stereotyped sloganisms?"

"Then you say we are of no use?" the chairman asked quietly.

"Good writers and good painters are always useful," Jason said. "I have a friend who is a capable painter. But does he go around showing the masses his portraits, his still lifes, his landscapes? No. He draws well-conceived, fiery, striking posters for the Party so that they can carry them in parades and demonstrations."

The whole room looked at Leon, they knew whom Jason had reference to.

"He's made himself of some use to the Party, he's no parasite."

"And what about yourself?" someone demanded.

"Me? That's another story, that has nothing to do with this argument," answered Jason, his stare going hard.

"You write sex-stories for the cheap magazines now, you yourself must be a parasite then."

"Yes, but I don't deny it," Jason shot back. "I am a parasite of the lowest order, almost as low as yourself."

"Comrades, comrades!" The chairman rapped loudly for order, the floor was in confusion again.

"He has been telling us half-truths," a girl said, the one who had spoken before.

"We demand that he be more explicit," another comrade put in, a little fellow with soft, rolling collar and a black necktie, the fellow who had nodded to Jason at the beginning of the meeting.

"Aren't you Eli Dorfman?" said Jason, beginning to smile, beginning to show a dry, mocking smile.

The comrade said he was, and looked uneasy.

"I happened to pass by your door as I came in," said Jason, "and I saw a neat card tacked up. It read: Eli Dorfman, worker. Well, comrade, just what kind of work do you do?"

Dorfman, sitting near a girl whom he had been kissing earlier in the evening, grew red in the face. "I am a poet," he answered. "Several of my poems have appeared in proletarian magazines."

"And who reads these little arty, 'proletarian' magazines, comrade? The masses?"

No answer.

"Well, what kind of work do you do?"

"I'm at work on a novel now," Comrade Dorfman answered.

Jason gave a short laugh. Most of the comrades in the room knew that Dorfman was living with a young schoolteacher who made enough to keep them both. The young girl Dorfman had been kissing was not the schoolteacher.

"Pardon me, comrade," Jason said, in mock apology. "You are working on the great American proletarian novel, therefore you must be a worker. Pardon me."

Other young men in the room began squirming. Fully thirty per cent of the male comrades at the gathering were being "subsidized" by typists, teachers, shopgirls, or sympathetic part-time mistresses.

The floor was quiet for a long time.

"But we're all very young," a girl finally said. "None of us makes the statement that he or she is a great writer or painter. We're trying hard to accomplish something."

"Why don't you join the Party then, not merely be sympathizers?" Jason demanded. "Why don't you canvass for aid, agitate, why don't you submit your services to the sub-committees?"

"We feel that by making the workers class-conscious we can help the movement better."

This brought the argument back to a previous statement and Jason said they were talking in circles. "The chances are, the Party wouldn't have you."

"Stick to the point," cried several voices. "Tell us what's wrong with the poetry."

The chairman looked at Jason. Jason was growing weary of it all.

"Bad poetry is bad poetry whether it's proletarian or bourgeois verse," said Jason. "Not one single line read tonight was worth the good paper it was written on. You comrades here are not willing to serve your apprenticeships, you want to wallow in heroic, epic, revolutionary stuff right away. Writing is a craft, painting is a craft, and there are no short-cuts to artistry. Before you can hope to do good work, you'll have to serve your time and knuckle under and learn certain fundamentals; and in the end, the chances are you won't do anything worthwhile anyway, because real talent doesn't grow on bushes like blueberries. You think you have talent. All right. But you have the wrong slant on the whole business if you think you can run shouting along with the movement and by acting enthusiastic over the masses thus give your work the hallmark of merit. My friends, I speak sincerely when I say that the poems read here tonight are bilge. They are badly constructed and pointless, they lack centralized ideas, in short, they must have been tossed off like a five-cent drink of coca-cola."

"But don't you think they show promise?" the serious girl asked. She had been "subsidizing" one of the poets and she wanted to get the lowdown on the lad's output.

"No," said Jason. "For one thing, you comrades who are living here in New York are handicapped from the start. You are living in a 'literary' town where everybody either writes or paints or has some other cock-eyed urge just to be in the swim of things. Small fry are all around you who have a superficial smattering of all the arts, in conversation, and everything disintegrates into gossip and petty shop-talk. And as soon as one of you gets a poem or short story published in an obscure magazine, as soon as one of you gets a painting hung in some tiny gallery, you set yourselves up as full-fledged artists. Most of you talk too much. And most of you are poseurs."

A rumble went through the room, but Jason continued.

"For three years, before I hit the great isle of Manhattan, I knocked around the country, earning my way by doing part-time, full-time, or any kind of jobs. I was a dish-washer in Seattle, a steward on a Great Lakes excursion liner, I worked with a pipe-laying crew for a gas company down in Texas, did road work in Iowa until my health broke down, I was a busboy in Chicago, and not once did I ever meet a worker who handed out business cards, not once did I find a laborer who tacked against the door of his room in some cheap boarding house: Jim Jones, worker, or Tom Brown, truck driver. Not once, comrades."

Now the room was dead quiet, no one stirred at all. On the floor, almost out of sight in a corner, Comrade Dorfman sat gazing at his shoes.

In the rear a fellow who had been taking a lot of notes broke the silence.

"I wish to call you to account for stating a certain remark, Comrade Wheeler. Would you want all painters to draw posters, would you want all writers to compose handbills for the Party?"

"I'm getting tired of answering all your five-cent questions," Jason shot back. "What I say, and I say it for the last time, is, that, if you want to help the movement, you must first be capable in your craft. The Party doesn't want bad posters, in fact, the movement really doesn't need you at all. Two or three intelligent, articulate workers could do more good than a whole hall full of 'class-conscious' painters or writers. What you've got to get through your heads is that the Revolution must be a workers' revolution and not a rising by the intelligentsia. What the hell do workers care about art? And why should they be made conscious of your so-called 'proletarian' twaddle about the masses rising up to greet a new workers' culture. You can't have a workers' culture without a workers' revolution, and if the workers do stage a revolution they'll be too busy changing things to worry their noodles about art. Of course, if a writer or painter springs direct from the workers, if he has a background other than Manhattanized communism, if he has real talent and knows what the struggle is all about and can translate it effectively through his medium, why that's another story. But, so far, this country has produced no first-rate proletarian writers or artists, it has produced few enough second-raters."

"You're too hard," said the serious girl.

"What are those bottles doing over there?" Jason put in.

"He's given us destructive criticism," someone hollered from the floor, springing up. "I demand, comrade chairman, that he deal sensibly with the issue."

"Those bottles—are they full?" said Jason, his mind on more important business. He went back to the couch and did not answer any more questions.

The place was full of discussion, but Jason took no further part in it, even though they called on him. He pulled up a chair and, while talk raged hotly all around, he sipped the "healing balm" and got himself well pickled. Talk buzzed in his ears like the heavy drone of late summer flies.

Time and tide. At three o'clock in the morning the first few comrades, almost exhausted by the session of arguing, began leaving. Leon, sitting at Comrade Helen's side, had been talking as hotly as the others, defending the ex-poet's remarks as well as he was able. He told the comrades of the record Jason had made at a large mid-western university, how Jason had won prizes, how various front-line critics had predicted a brilliant future for Jason in poetry.

"But he's doing nothing now," the comrades told Leon. "We haven't seen a poem of his printed in over a year now."

It was cold and dark when Leon and Comrade Helen, holding Jason on either side, helped the ex-poet down the narrow stairs. As they approached the staircase, a door was flung open and Sonya (Sadie in the days of yore) came out into the hall, dressed in soiled red pajamas, and hammered with her fists upon the door across the way.

"Gustaf," she shouted, "let me in for a second. I've come back for my syringe. Gustaf! Don't think I want to come back to you, I'm only asking for my syringe, it cost me eighty-nine cents. It's behind the couch, hand it to me then. Gustaf! Gus, Gus!"

The door did not open. She kept on pounding. Finally she went angrily back into the room across the hall she had just come from, and slammed the door, and left a hard, angry atmosphere trailing in the corridor. Jason, held under the armpits, rattled off a few remarks.

"Life among the Kremlin artists. In again and out again, my name is Hymie Finnegan. You have now witnessed the last act of our stirring drama, folks, where the heroine slams the door and disappears in high dudgeon. Curtain, curtain, avast there!"

They helped him down the stairs. In the courtyard the

cold revived him, he stood leaning against the brick wall breathing in long breaths of air. In the windows of the Kremlin many lights were still burning. Someone had a radio going softly, and from a second- or third-floor window came the sound of a girl sobbing. Jason, standing away from the wall, said he could walk unaided, and the three plunged into the darkness of the narrow passageway which led toward the street.

They turned west and walked in silence. Over the town hung a cold blue frost. Cats were running up and down the chilly street, and the wind swung the arc lamps up and back. It was now half-past three in the morning.

At Second Avenue Jason turned to Leon and told the little fellow, who had been walking shivering, to go on home. "I'll see Comrade Helen safely to her door; you beat it and get some sleep."

Leon stood in his tracks and objected a little, but Jason cut him short. The little fellow stood there looking at the girl.

"Comrade Helen and I live in the same house," said Jason, getting sore. "You don't have to be afraid, I won't harm her."

Leon smiled, his teeth chattering. He looked up at the girl, at the large, well-rounded, buxom comrade, gave her his sad, warm stare and asked if it was all right if Jason saw her home. She said it was. He stood there a while, undecided yet, and chilly.

"Go on, beat it!" shouted Jason, and at last the little fellow, like an obedient poodle, turned and headed quickly for his rooming house while Jason and the girl stood watching. When he had turned the first corner, Jason and the girl walked west toward the tenement.

The first block they walked without speaking a word. A

brisk wind was driving in their faces. Then Jason, speaking throatily, as if he had his chin deep inside his overcoat, told Comrade Helen from New Orleans a thing or two. He told the buxom girl that Leon was his best friend, that the little painter was fool enough to believe heart and soul in a certain person who did not and could not return the feeling, and he added, his voice sounding more than ever as if it came from deep within his overcoat, that if anything happened that would cause Comrade Leon any suffering, there would be hell to pay.

Comrade Helen, keeping step with Jason, her full, vigorous body a good mark to the brisk wind, answered without turning her head.

"I've told José to keep silent," she said quietly.

"And see to it that he does, Comrade Helen. If I ever find out that either you or José lets the news break, if I ever learn that through you he hurts himself, I'll take a club and beat you until I break every bone in your body."

Now Jason's voice was very thick, and when they reached the tenement Comrade Helen had to wait a moment in the doorway while the ex-poet, leaning heavily against the lamp-post for support, coughed up large, heavy pieces of slime upon the sidewalk. After he was finished, Jason weakly wiped his lips. Then, in silence, they went into the tenement, walked up the drafty hallway, and without saying good-night parted at the foot of the staircase.

# XVII

MORNINGS CAME AND WENT, and Hank Austin took to wandering around the square because it was nice and sunny there and there were strong, wide benches to sit upon. To the low, sad voices of the bootblack boys he acquired the knack of curtly shaking his head, which saved him the trouble of opening his mouth. And to the orators he did not lend his ears. No, Hank didn't think much of the guys who spoke, urging the workers to unite, to come one and all under the banner of the hammer and scythe. Most of the haranguers were sawed-off, unshaven runts with small, mean eyes, and Hank knew damn well they couldn't wheel or unload a hefty hand-truck. Not for me, Hank told himself, nope, not for yours truly.

Besides, I'm an American, says Hank to himself, and those guys should go back to the old country, that's where they belong. To be sure, Hank saw, here and there, a few fellers sitting or standing around who looked to be Yanks, but they didn't count; anyway, they were merely curious, like himself, he figured. Hank didn't trust these spouting gents, no sir! Not for yours truly.

He sat around in the sun, in the cold bright early January sun, and half-heartedly went looking for work. Once or twice he scanned the want-ad columns of the morning papers and, if there did happen to be one solitary ad, why, he'd run for it, but always when he got there there'd be a gang of three or four hundred other fellows ahead of him, all standing around, all silent, all after that one job, all hating each other for wanting that job too.

So he did not chase the want-ads any more, and in the agencies the girls at the outer desks shook their heads shortly without looking up, and he knew there were no jobs around. He found nothing. His mind settled, slowly, to that fact. He sat around in the sun. His thoughts took queer turns and twists, went back five, ten, and even twenty-five years, sitting in the sun, to his kid days, his schooldays, and his months in the Army and in the far-off trenches of France. At the east of the square Lafayette stood facing the hurrying Fourth Avenue traffic, standing in a graceful pose like a ballet-master.

Hank thought about a lot of things, but his thinking was not clear-cut or scientific. He started smoking a pipe and bought cheap tins of tobacco because it was nice to grip something warm between your teeth as you sat on a cold bench under the sun. And now, when he came home to eat lunch, he made it a point to arrive on the scene after the noon hour, after the kids had eaten and gone back to school. He'd open the door slowly and craftily, also guiltily, then, putting on a gruff front, his eyes on the floor, would ease in and make for the sink and spend a long time there, washing his hands, doing a very thorough job of it. He'd sit down at the table finally, and his missus would lay out a big plate of hot food for him and, not looking up, his head bent down, he'd eat the stuff, scowling and frowning. Christ, what an appetite he now had, he could have masticated coffin-nails. Fresh air makes you hungry, he told himself. In the next room the kid in the bed lay on its back, cooing happily at the ceiling. Missus Austin tried very hard not to look weepy when Hank was around, but her cheeks were often puffy and red now.

Days passed, wintry days. There were a few more charity drives, posters and placards were stuck into windows to aid the good cause, and some of the biggest and most public-spirited businessmen in town joined in the movement to lend their support in urging one and all to ship cast-off clothing to headquarters for the needy and destitute of our great city.

"While these times may have caused a bit of suffering among the people, it has no doubt brought to the fore their better qualities, such as patience and forbearance," a great man told the press, who quoted him in full. "All of us are learning what true co-operation means, we are putting our shoulders to the wheel so that the heavy wagon of good times will once more be on the roll. No one has starved yet this winter, better times are bound to come soon. The American nation, facing the future courageously, will emerge from this crisis bigger and stronger than ever; it will emerge with . . ."

The great man's picture was underneath, a hearty fellow, three underchins and stocks and bonds all over South America and Europe; and he was pretty shaky on his pins himself.

Wind blew over the town, rain and fog, the sun rose up and went down again, sinking into the icy waters of the Hudson. Every morning Mr. Quincy Boardman left his apartment more firmly convinced than ever that he was waging a losing battle. He felt it in his bones, in his blood, in his mind. No more scenes took place; over the flat had settled an outward calm. Margie was now sweet and gentle enough for anybody, but in her sweetness he could taste the bitter tang of cuckoldry. Every morning, going to the office, he had to get a fresh grip on himself before he reached his desk, and in the subway, as he rode to work, he'd carry on inner conversations with himself about unimportant things; and always there was that gnawing, gnawing, gnawing at his mind. His cheeks grew a trifle hollow and, if he applied too much talcum after shaving, his face would appear very pale and corpse-like. The Eastern manager, a close friend of Mr. Boardman, came over to the desk one day and in an undertone, speaking sympathetically, wanted to know if anything was wrong. "Have you invested unwisely, is it your daughter?"

Mr. Boardman, after the Eastern manager went back into his own office, started. His daughter? Good God, he hadn't answered her letters for a long time now. He kept sending her her allowance, but never wrote her a line because he found he couldn't bring himself to put down on paper anything which did not give a hint as to his inner feelings. The last letter he received from Milly showed she was worried, she wanted to know if he was still so busy he couldn't drop her a little letter, not just those checks alone.

Mr. Boardman called his secretary over and started dictating. The Eastern manager had gone back into his office quite a few minutes ago. Maybe he has stomach trouble, the Eastern manager thought, and gave his attention to important matters, to the production manager's weekly report. Sales had fallen off sharply, but the production was holding up. He sat staring out over the river, at the rooftops which were like boxes and masts below, and finally dictated a letter to the production manager, shaving off production.

Two offices away, Mr. Boardman was also dictating, trying to get a good-sized order out of an old house, using the time-honored words, the time-honored phrases. He got a headache later on and felt a heavy throbbing in his temples.

At night, when Mr. Boardman came back to the apartment, he did not have to stand outside the door and change the muscles on his face; the muscles had rearranged themselves as he had walked up the steps, he was an expert at the business now; and he'd walk inside the flat, Margie would kiss him lightly on the cheek, and she'd even take his hat and coat from him now. When her back was turned, he found himself sniffing—sniffing for a man-smell, or a different kind of cigarette smell—and would run a hand over the sofa arms in search of black hairs (Margie was a blonde). But he learned nothing, found out nothing. Every night they went out to eat now. He took Dodo out for short strolls and did not walk the doggie far in the cold, did not go east to Third Avenue as the roar of the elevated had begun to frighten Dodo lately.

And over the town passed wind and rain, fog and the muffled bellows from the ocean liners. The mayor sat in his fine offices in City Hall. Janitors swept the front stone stairs clean every morning, and there were always a few reporters and photographers hanging around. The Broadway cars went past City Hall Park for a way, traveled to the Battery, went round in a semicircle and came back, rolling northward again. Conductors rang up fares, the wheels clicked over the tracks below.

Celia saved her nickels, dimes, and quarters. The dentist was progressing with the work, the job was coming along all right, pretty soon she would have a perfect row of front teeth; and that meant she could smile without feeling ill at ease, without pulling her lip carefully down so that her sweet, little face looked twisted and frozen at you. That meant that Leon could see that now all her teeth were perfect up in front.

As for Leon, why the little fellow was mighty busy these days, he was busy making posters and placards for the Party. The communists were planning to stage a big demonstration in Union Square pretty soon and they would have need of fiery banners. Leon worked hard every day at it. Sometimes, when he came back to his room after going out for lunch or breakfast, he'd see a rose stuck in a glass of water on his bureau, and then he'd think of Celia, but he was pretty busy working and couldn't think about her very much, and when he wasn't working, why his thoughts centered about Comrade Helen, whose full, firm, vigorous form now began bothering him in bed at night, though he tried hard not to have certain visions.

By this time Leon's funds were running low, so one day he called upon the manager of the engraving house and wanted to know if there was a chance to get back on the job again in a few weeks or so. The manager, who liked Leon, looked thoughtful for a while, said he didn't know, he'd have to think it over, but all the while he knew he'd call Leon back again (there was a big catalogue job coming in in a few days and he'd need Leon then for sure). "I think I might be able to use you again," the foreman said slowly, as if half-decided, as if not at all sure of it yet.

Leon left the place happy. After all, that was something. He went up to Jason to tell him all about it and found the ex-poet gloomy and surlier than usual. Jason was having his own troubles, was hacking his way through his own wilderness. He started writing letters to Philadelphia again, though he knew he was wasting his time, hoping against hope. After he had written three, four, five of them, he received a reply, a brief note telling him to try and not think about her any more. A five-dollar bill was enclosed, though no mention of it had been written in the letter.

Leon didn't stay in Jason's room long, he went down the stairs quietly and returned to his room to work on those posters again. Besides, Jason had hinted that he had a date with someone, and in half an hour, half timidly, there came a knocking on the door and Miss Allen came in, and sat there, and did not take her hat and coat off, and cleaned around, putting things in order, while Jason sat like a wooden man, no warmth in his eyes. After a while the young nurse left, but at the door turned toward the ex-poet. From her eyes there flowed her love for him, she stood there as Leon had stood there many times before, giving Jason her sad, warm stare.

"Take care of yourself," she said quietly, and hesitated. "Don't take any more dope, Jason. Promise me you won't take any more."

"Rats," said Jason. "I'm not promising anything." But the truth was he had not knocked on that brown door for a long time now; he got no kick from it any more, so he had dropped the habit. At first there had been a sharp uplift, but the terrific let-down afterwards was too severe, it wasn't worth it. So Jason returned to the "healing balm" and applied himself assiduously to it, and it did not fail him.

The old fat janitress, leaning on her broom, told the ex-poet that the gray-haired, gray-mustached man who lived in the Glen Cove Apartments next door looked more worried than ever.

"Something must be preying on his mind," the ancient dame told Jason. "He looks so nice, too, he's a gentleman, Mister Wheeler, you can always tell." The old girl warmed to the topic, she had a big heart, a heart as big as her stomach, the old girl had. "And just think," she said, "he came up to me last night when he was taking the snipe out for a walk and he says to me, he says, 'Is there a room for rent in your place?' He says, 'Have you got a vacancy?' At first I thought he must be joking, Mister Wheeler, but he wasn't. So I told him I had a room, a vacancy as he calls it. 'Does it face the rear?' he asks, 'does it give a view at the building to the right?' Imagine him asking me that. I musta smiled, Mister Wheeler, because all of a sudden he tips his hat quickly and makes off that the little snipe is tugging at the strap. Now I ask you, I ask you what does he want with a room in this old tenement?"

"You're not to rent it to him," said Jason, putting on a stern front, feeling tired and hollow, whipping himself up a little for the old girl's sake. "Dont rent the room to him, that's to be my gin-chamber when I get my first million dollars."

"Hee-hee," laughed the old janitress, and her big stomach quivered, as if a trickle of ice-water had gone running down her ancient back. "Hee-hee. Hee-hee-hee."

## XVIII

THE DAY BEFORE the big demonstration was held in Union Square, the communists ran a meeting and final plans were laid. The sub-committee chairmen gave their reports and mentioned the names of the various comrades who had been chosen to lead the parade, to address the crowds when the marchers would be assembled in the square, and to see that the whole affair would run off smoothly. The police department had already granted a permit for the parade and had also granted the use of the square for the afternoon.

"We intend to be orderly," the chairman said. "We must watch ourselves, comrades, there will be thousands of the public there. If the police disguise themselves as workers and try to incite the crowd, we must not be ensnared."

A chairman of a sub-committee rose and reported that microphones had been obtained for the meeting, so that the whole square would be able to hear the speakers. This announcement caused some talk and several orators wondered which speakers would be picked to talk before the microphones.

Then came discussion concerning the parade itself, the line of march, and the order in which various divisions would assemble. It was finally agreed that the demonstrators would gather on upper Fifth Avenue at a little before noon.

"Have the strongest comrades carry the posters," someone said. "At the last parade some of our comrades grew tired out and the placards wobbled so much that the people couldn't read them. They should be carried upright."

"That means that the women will have to hand the posters over to the men," a female comrade said, objecting. More argument followed.

In the rear, sitting next to Comrade Helen, Leon followed the talk like a hawk. He had been painting and lettering placards for days and days, and his work had been praised by the central committee. While everybody was arguing and discussing the line of march, he sat restlessly, listening. Finally he raised his hand and the chairman acknowledged him.

"A comrade in the rear wishes to speak," the chairman said. The floor grew quiet, heads turned.

Leon rose, his face going pale, his hands damp, while at his side, sitting, Comrade Helen was watching. Wetting his lips, speaking in a high, loud voice to make himself heard, Leon said:

"I suggest that the posters and banners be carried scattered all along the column of march with the scattering thickest at the front and rear of the line. Formerly, when we have paraded, all the placards have been carried in front. I believe this is not the best way. After the head of the column passes, the people on the sidewalks see only the heads of the marchers, their eyes have nothing to read, the end of the column goes by with nothing to show and gives the finish of the line of march a flat look. I suggest that signs be scattered throughout, with the end of the column holding something in their hands for the people to read."

He sat down sweating. The hall immediately buzzed with talk, the suggestion was keen, apt, and curtly put. A score of comrades instantly jumped up and seconded the motion.

"As Comrade Fisher has stated," they said, and amplified the little painter's remarks. Leon, still sweating, glowed as he heard his name. "As Comrade Fisher has stated . . ." and they went on to talk about his suggestion. Comrade Helen was looking proudly at him, but he continued to stare straight ahead, his forehead shiny with perspiration, his eyes blazing. Several more comrades turned around and smiled at him, and this made him sweat all the harder.

The chairman rapped for order. A vote was taken, Leon's suggestion was put into the form of a motion and was passed by a show of hands. Comrade Helen shot her palm away up high, then sat a little closer to Leon, so that their knees touched. She whispered something softly, but he did not hear; his head was buzzing, as if a power-driven saw was whirling its teeth through a block of lumber.

Before the meeting was over, Comrade Edward Lukotas rose and gave one of his customary fiery orations, but no one listened and he sat down, red in the face and panting. The chairman stared vacantly at Comrade Lukotas's large, moving mouth. Over to the left Comrade Bessie Silvers was speaking, gossiping a bit with a few other girls. She had been on picket duty last week again, and the cops had tried to get fresh with her, she said. Leon caught some of the words. "Just as I was walking down Twenty-Seventh Street, this cop comes up and starts shoving the crowd back, and when he sees the picket signs pinned to my front and rear why he goes for me, but I don't budge. So he starts pushing and tries to take the sign from me, but he sticks his fingers on one of the pins, then he gets sore and tries to tear the sign off, but he shoves his hand into my blouse . . . bzzzzz . . . you know them kind of cops, and he makes out he's just pushing me . . . bzzzzz . . . and he works his hand inside there, so I spit right in his face, all over his nose, and while he's wiping hisself I ran off. He was a gray-haired cop, anyway . . ." Bessie Silvers speaking, a worker in a sweat-shop, a girl with a sturdy build, and she knows it.

Finally the meeting was over. There was a scraping of chairs, talk, small groups formed, then the rear lights in the hall were put out.

Leon walked Comrade Helen to the tenement. It was cold going up the street, and he had his hands in his pockets. At the corner Comrade Helen took his arm on account of the traffic, and did not release it when they had crossed safely over. Leon, his heart fluttering, felt his brow going damp in the cold. Comrade Helen kept up a chatter all the way and returned to his speech many times. She said she was proud of him.

"That was nothing," he stammered, liking the soft, firm feel of her arm in his, liking to be walking on this frosty night with her; and, when they reached the tenement, he hesitated in the doorway (it was late and he thought she wanted to go to sleep right away), but she said, "Well, aren't you going to walk me to my door, aren't you going to see me safely home?"

He spluttered something, confused and happy, and they entered the old tenement and went up the long, dim hallway. A light shone on the transom window, they knew José was inside. For a few minutes they stood talking in a whisper, then Comrade Helen, still feeling proud of Leon, reached out to say good-night and gave his hand a squeeze, fumbling for it in the half-dark of the hallway. He returned her pressure so impulsively, so quiveringly that the girl, deeply moved for the first time, stared at him with shiny eyes, then, bending forward, kissed him quickly on his mouth. He stood there speechless.

"That's because I'm proud of you," she whispered, and gave his hand another squeeze, then opened the door quietly and went inside.

Leon stood there. Warm tears of happiness were running down his face. Then, hugging her words, her kiss, the pressure of her hand to himself, he headed rapidly for his rooming house, a strange gurgle in his throat, a tight, happy feeling in his chest.

As soon as Leon had closed the front door of his rooming house, another door under the staircase opened and Celia came out, came out to see if the canary was properly taken care of, came out to see if the cloth covered the cage. She came from her little room with a serious frown on her face.

Leon, his face still sticky with happy tears, was glad to see her; he had a singing feeling in his body for everybody in the whole, wide world right now. He chattered to her.

"Why, you've been crying!" she said quickly, looking at his cheeks.

Crying? No. He brushed his face quickly. "It's the cold

outside, sometimes my eyes get watery," he said. But his eyes had a shine she had never seen there before. And all at once he began talking to her, low and rapidly, about the glory of the Party movement, about the vision of Marx, of Engels, of Lenin. He spoke low and rapidly, his eyes staring at her, through her, beyond her, and it sounded as if he were praying happily. Celia glanced around, to see if anybody else was listening, it was so late.

"Are you sure you weren't crying?" she asked seriously, interrupting him.

Crying? Leon Fisher came down to earth with a bang. Here he had been pouring out his soul about communism, and she had asked if he were crying. He answered cuttingly. Irritation showed on his face and, turning away, he started climbing the stairs to his room. Down below, with trembling fingers, with trembling lips, Celia continued to move the cloth over the cage a bit, fussing with the fringe.

But before Leon reached the top of the stairs, his anger had passed and, looking down the flight at the girl still standing meekly at the cage, he cleared his throat.

"Comrade," he whispered, "forgive me. I'm sorry I talked to you like that."

The small dark head below turned toward him, he saw her sweet, frozen smile, the way her lips hid the cavity up in front.

"I'm sorry," he whispered again.

Something choked in her throat; the light above his figure threw a long, grotesque shadow of his body upon the opposite wall, so that his head, elongated, sat flush upon his narrow shoulders as if he were a hunchback, as if he were a little peddler carrying a sack on his shoulders.

"That's all right," she whispered back, and then he smiled down at her and said good-night.

Back in the tenement Comrade Helen was sitting at the kitchen table drinking *tequila* with José. As soon as she had come into the flat she had seen that José already was half drunk, had asked him why he had not attended the Party meeting tonight, and wanted to know what was in the bottle.

"My cousin from Vera Cruz was here," José answered thickly, grinning. "He brought this drink along, a Mexican drink, a real drink. Here, sit down." He poured out half a drinking glass full of the liquid, and Comrade Helen, after taking off her coat, sipped some. It tasted fiery, she made a face. José struck her a glancing blow on the cheek and told her to finish it. She sat down quietly and by the time she finished it got to like it. He grinned at her and poured another. In a half an hour both were very drunk. Comrade Helen, her mouth slack and sloppy, her hair disarranged, was clumsily pawing José's black Mexican hair, mumbling something about a parade on the morrow. When Sid and Harry Turner came in, they undressed the girl and the Mexican and dumped them into the double bed in the little room off the kitchen. Both the Turner brothers were getting a little tired of the couple. They undressed and in quiet voices spoke about breaking up the ménage pretty soon if things didn't change around the flat. They were tired, also, of Comrade Helen's sloppy housekeeping. The flat had gone untended since Leon had been busy working on his posters.

Finally Sid clicked out the light; the brothers spoke to each other in the dark for a while, about trivial things, then dropped off to sleep.

The windows of the old building shook in their sockets, wind blew over the town. Blockhouse shadows lay thick against the pavements. The wife of a certain captain of police had a headache and rose in the wee hours to get herself an aspirin tablet. The cops walked their beats. In the press-rooms the presses were grinding out the morning editions. Life must go on, we must face the future. There are children to be born. Men with shaggy heads and a hankering for a real stiff drink wrote stirring editorials and finally got the staff artist to make a drawing for the head of the column. Pretty soon the copy-boys went out after pots of coffee, went out into the cold, into the chill of the wee dark hours. Time and tide. The kids came back and collected the nickels, the building shook as the heavy presses below roared on.

Dawn came into town, sowing grayness. In the sky wide arms of pale light moved slowly up and back as if weakened searchlights were playing there. Toward seven o'clock, when people started to hurry along the streets, the heavens were of one dull tone, like a sheet of unbleached muslin, and various citizens, going down into the subways, looked at the weather report.

"Cold and windy," the forecaster stated. "Cloudy and overcast all day. Probably snow or hail by nightfall; diminishing northwest winds becoming southerly tonight and increasing tomorrow. Stormy conditions continue over the Newfoundland area. Light snows are reported from the Lower Lake region, also from the northern tier of states west of Wisconsin and light rains from the Pacific coast. Flying forecast: Northwest winds surface and aloft; fresh in low flying level, strong above low clouds, high overcast; broken clouds, city smoke and indifferent visibility."

In another column of the paper the statement was made that the fall in temperature had caused frosts as far south as Atlanta.

# SIX

**I**

THE CAPTAIN of police, a big man with a powerful jaw, swung round in his swivel chair and told his male secretary to call in Smith, Bowen, and Oldenheimer, three lieutenants. The secretary, laying his pen down, got up and walked around the captain's desk, shoved the door back, and went out into the outer office. He wore rubber heels and made no sound. When he returned, the three lieutenants were walking at his back; two of them cleared their throats before they reached the door, the third stopped to put his hat on straighter; all came in frowning, in a stern and business-like manner, the city's finest, we are here to serve you.

"Lieutenants, the Reds are due to march today, this afternoon," the captain said, his cold blue eyes flashing in their cold blue flashing manner. "Smith, you're to take charge of the rifle squad; Bowen, you handle the machine-gun squadron; have your boys lined up at University Place and Fourteenth Street, a machine-gun in every sidecar, but don't bother about ammunition, we won't use any. Oldenheimer," (and Oldie, a heavy-faced man with sagging cheeks, stiffened), "Oldenheimer, you direct the mounted division. Have the boys swing from the west end of the square, from the northwest maybe, one half up the block on Sixteenth Street, the other half up Fifteenth, or maybe Seventeenth, use your own judgment. Tell them they're not to shoot, no man is to fire a bullet, they can use their riot-clubs. Now, umph, lieutenants, this'll be a big day, the parade has been ballyhooed all over town, the press has got wind of it. The press'll have their camera boys and reporters on the job, you know, umph, what to do. The public will be there. So will the fire department. And, umph, thassall."

The secretary, writing out the previous day's report, was bent over busily as the captain finished, but he had an ear cocked for any forthcoming command. And the command came. Clearing his throat like a commissioner, the captain told his secretary to show Welch and his five patrolmen in. The secretary, laying down his pen, walked around the captain's desk (his rubber heels making no sound), shoved the door back, and went into the outer office; and when he returned, Sergeant Welch with five patrolmen at his heels came filing into the private office, the patrolmen very serious about the ears and eyes, the sergeant coughing gently as he stood stiffly before his chief.

"Have you got some old clothes ready, sergeant?"

"I have, sir," answered Welch, making his report.

"Fine," said the captain and swung round to speak to the five patrolmen who still stood looking serious about the ears and eyes. "Boys, you know what to do, you did a pretty good job in October under the same, umph, circumstances. Any questions you care to ask will be answered by Sergeant Welch. Thassall."

The five patrolmen followed their sergeant out, keeping their serious looks until they hit the outer office, then their faces melted and all felt relief. They went down into a room in the basement and put on old clothes. Two of them pulled on floppy caps, the other three put on shapeless hats which had been stamped upon to make them appear more authentic and shapeless.

In the captain's office upstairs the three lieutenants, after receiving final instructions, were dismissed. As soon as they were gone, the captain phoned his wife to find out if her headache was any better, if the pain over her eyes had gone away yet. He spoke very soothingly over the wire, sitting firm and solid in the wide chair.

The secretary, glancing up from his work, noticed that as the three lieutenants had gone out the last one had left the door slightly ajar, so, laying his pen down, he walked around the captain's chair, came up to the door, and closed it quietly. Then he returned to his desk where he resumed his writing.

The captain, his face close to the mouthpiece of the telephone as if kissing quietly a woman's cheek, was still talking soothingly to his wife. Otherwise the office was very silent.

## II

ACROSS THE STREET from Twenty-Door City the first few children were entering the doorway of the Catholic school. Two gentle-looking sisters stood upon the topmost stair, gazing up the street. At the end of the block, at Third Avenue, the traffic cop assigned to the school had placed an iron notification which barred all traffic from using the thoroughfare until after nine o'clock, when the last bell would ring and all children would be safely indoors and at their desks.

The cop's broad back was toward the two staring sisters, who were curious to see if he were Officer Mike Kelly or not. Their long black habits fluttered in the dull gray morning air. Pretty soon the tall young father with the little protuberant stomach came to stand with them, smiling as he did so, then looking serious as was his wont. He wore glasses now, his eyes had lately felt strained and weak, perhaps from too much reading of the *Lives of the Saints*.

When the first bell rang, the two sisters and the young father went inside the building; it had been rather cold outside, waiting for the children. As soon as all were inside the school, one of the sisters released the catch, and the ponderous door shut with a slow, heavy movement.

By this time the old janitress of the tenement was dragging the two big garbage cans down into the basement, using the sidewalk entrance. She came up again, puffing, and felt a little weak in the legs, so she stood leaning heavily upon her reliable broom.

Up the street came the Jolly Postman, a sack of mail upon his aged back. When he reached the entrance of Twenty-Door City, he frowned heavily, then smiled at the old janitress. He was a bachelor, so consequently he had an ingrained sense of gallantry. "Thirty winters have I trod these blocks," quoth he, "aye, thirty winters," and looked across the street at the garage where a Firestone advertisement hung yellow in the wind: TIME TO RETIRE?

"Any mail?" asked the old janitress looking perky, looking amiable.

The Jolly Postman was busy shoving gas bills into the old battered boxes. "Just bills, that's all, and they ain't mail."

The janitress started a conversation going, but, gallant

man or no gallant man, the Jolly Postman had no time and waddled off.

Pretty soon Hank Austin came down, stuck his fingers into the mail-box, took out the gas bill, and shoved it into his hip pocket with a grunt. He started walking toward the square, away from the tenement, away from home, wondering how he could kill another morning. His money was melting fast, he could hold out only a short while longer now.

Jason came back from his morning cup of coffee at the Crystal Lunchroom and looked to see what the Jolly Postman had brought. No mail for him, only a gas bill, too.

"Well, Mister Wheeler," the old janitress chirped, a bit of flash coming into her ancient eyes, her bloated face wrinkling into some kind of a goodly smile, "did you sell any more of your stories, did you get some checks in the mail?"

"Aye," said Jason cheerfully. "Here's a check for two thousand square feet of gas, you can see for yourself, madam," and he held forth the gas bill, showing the meter reading. "See," he said, pointing to the figures, "big money at last. I'll be able to rent that room for my gin-chamber pretty soon."

"Hee-hee. Hee-hee-hee."

Jason, pretty tired of her hee-hee-hee, turned into the tenement and climbed slowly the five flights to his room.

From the next building—the Glen Cove Apartments—the tenants were going to work, Vanya and Natasha, Mr. Boardman, and two or three other couples. They came from the doorway and out upon the street.

The morning was cloudy. In the papers there was a write-up stating that a famous transcontinental flyer had broken an endurance record and was due in New York in the afternoon for a welcome by the city officials. The mayor sat in his fine offices in the City Hall. On the lawns the sparrows were drilling the pavement, hunting for old seed in the cracks, pecking at the faded grass. And by this time the Jolly Postman had crossed the street and was now almost up to Second Avenue, still sticking mail into the boxes.

Five minutes later Mr. Andre Franconi, who had not been feeling very well for the past few days, closed the door of his apartment and started going down the stairs. In the vestibule he looked through the small glass peep-hole of his mail-box and, seeing mail there, took his keys out. He found three letters, a gas bill and two others. While he opened them, he stared through the entrance door toward the street, and the gloominess of the morning depressed him. Two small boys, late for school, whooped by, playing cowboy-and-Indian. Mr. Franconi could hear their shouts as he put the gas bill away and gave his attention to the other mail.

One letter was from Doctor Morrison, the other was from California, from Florina. Mr. Franconi, starting to feel nervous, went back into his apartment and read both of them.

When he finished Doctor Morrison's letter, he had a heavy, leaden feeling in the pit of his stomach. The note was cautiously written, nothing definite was stated, but Mr. Franconi knew at last that there was no hope. Doctor Morrison wrote that the last blood test showed positive, but he felt quite sure that a cure was being effected. He signed his name politely and did not enclose the customary bill. A gentle let-down. The second letter Mr. Franconi tore open slowly, almost uninterested, but he had not read more than a few lines when he became galvanized. In wild, passionate language, Florina wrote that her husband had given her a terrible beating two days ago, that now with Father Tortinas gone back to Spain she had no one to advise or comfort her; and besides this, Joe had hired the young Swedish widow as housekeeper, dismissed the Mexican servant who went to town after the mail, and then had moved into the widow's bed. "Now I cannot receive letters from you, Andre, I have no one to make the trip to the post office. Adultery goes on under the same roof, in my own house. The children stand around whispering. Andre . . ." The whole sheet was scrawled with powerful, erratic writing; he could picture her moving her firm arm up and back across the writing paper. And down at the bottom of the sheet came the explosions. "Andre, I take the train to you, to New York on Tuesday. I have enough money of my own hidden away to pay for the fare. I am coming to you, Andre. I throw myself upon your mercy, God help me now. I will find the way to your place, I will give your number to the taxi driver." Then came her signature, written firmly. No gentle hand now, her words were high as mountains on the page.

When he finished her letter, Mr. Franconi's face was cold and damp, and the heavy, leaden feeling in his stomach seemed to overturn, as if some undigested food there were stirring slowly. He read the letter over carefully, and by the time he came to the bottom of the sheet he was gnawing his nails, a thing he had never done before in his life. The second reading was as explosive as the first, and the finality of her tone struck him harder. Then he picked up Doctor Morrison's letter. His brow was wet and his temples had begun pounding. He took his overcoat off and laid it across a chair. Then he sat down to think things over, trying to slow his thoughts down so that his brain would stop singing like a thin saw-blade whining through a block of wood. He got up and drank a glass of water, then sat down again. Out on the street he could hear the two small boys playing, shouting to each other. "Bang, bang," one of them said, and the other whooped like an Indian racing across the plains. Mr. Franconi felt his thoughts slow down, but his temples were pounding so hard now that his face ached all the way down to his jaws. He sat relaxed, but this did not help the pounding very much. Finally he couldn't stand it any longer and went into the bathroom to look at himself in the mirror. On the little glass shelf his razor, lying with its blade opened, glittered in the light. He closed it, then started stroking the sides of his face. The pounding in his temples decreased a bit, but came with more frequency. He saw that the trap was perfect; whole sentences from Florina's letter flew before his eyes like a burst of buckshot; then came the slow, measured sentences of the doctor's note, like after-smoke, floating.

Finally he went into the living room and with his head still aching called up the barber-shop and told one of the girls who answered the phone that he couldn't come down to work today. When he had completed the call, he took his vest and jacket off, also his collar and tie. He felt very weak. For five minutes he sat there. He grew calmer. What he was going to do did not seem so terrible to him after he thought it over. He rose and went to his writing table and made out a few checks. He even took out the gas bill just arrived and made out a check for that, too. One of the letters was addressed to Bessano, Italy, and because he had no one-cent stamps he stuck on three two-centers. Then he went to the front windows, opened one of them, and called down to the two small boys playing in the street. He asked them if they wanted to earn a dime. Their little faces, raised up toward him, nodded vigorously. They caught the letters which floated down to them and after a dime rang against the pavement they dived for the coin. Mr. Franconi dropped another dime because they had started squabbling, then watched them running toward the post office on Fourth Avenue and Thirteenth Street.

He went into the bathroom again. He turned on the light once more and combed back his smooth black hair, felt the sides of his face and bared his teeth, looking at the gums. For a fraction of a second he thought his gums had a decayed, purplish tinge to them, but in a little while, still staring intently, he realized it was his imagination.

Reaching over with his foot he brought the bathroom stool into place, sat down and turned on both faucets of the sink, regulating them until he had the water flowing evenly. The water went down almost silently.

He turned his wrists up and under the strong light above the mirror saw the fine blue veins beneath the skin.

Then he opened up the blade and, with two firm, determined strokes, he slashed himself. From the right wrist the blood pumped rhythmically, from the left a thin needle-spray of red leaped up, then flowed forth evenly. There was no pain.

Five minutes later, the room growing dim, the flow and bubble in his ears growing faint, the two small boys came back from the post office and on the street once more began playing their cowboy-and-Indian game.

"Bang-bang," one of them said. "Bang, bang, you're dead."

For a moment the water coming from the faucets swelled to a bubbling roar, then stopped as if the pressure had been shut off.

"Bang, bang." The words rattled against the window-panes of all the buildings.

No sun came out, the air was cold and damp. On Third Avenue the elevated thundered by and the old iron supports, driven into the street, trembled like the legs of elephants, shaky under a heavy load.

Toward eleven o'clock Comrade Leon Fisher knocked on the ex-poet's door, came inside, and told Jason that a big demonstration was to be held in the square. He asked the ex-poet to be present.

"We're even going to have microphones," the little painter said proudly.

"Just like the Tammany politicians," Jason shot back, baiting his friend.

"What's wrong with having amplifiers? What's counter-revolutionary about that?"

"I cannot attend the performance," the ex-poet answered. "I have a date for this afternoon. If you come two-and-a-half paces closer you will note that right now I am about nineteen per cent intoxicated and on the uphill, comrade, on the upgrade."

"Miss Allen coming?"

"I am sorry I cannot attend the vaudeville bill in the square," said Jason. "Very sorry indeed. You may give my seat on the aisle to somebody else, I am very sorry I will be unable to lend my presence at the première."

And when Leon was gone, the ex-poet took a very long gurgling drink, then sat grimly before the typewriter, staring at the keys, whipping himself on, flaying his brain. But he couldn't get started, so in the end shut the machine with a bang, slamming the leather case down, then applied himself to some more of the "healing balm."

Leon, after he left his pal the ex-poet, went quickly

down the flights of stairs and on the ground floor hesitated, wondering if he should ask Comrade Helen to be sure and march alongside him in the parade. A light blurred through the transom window. Walking back there he knocked softly. No answer. He knocked again, softly. Still no answer.

Then, telling himself that they must have forgotten to put out the light in the flat, he hurried toward the tenement entrance and when he reached the street walked quickly westward to official headquarters, where he sorted out the many signs and posters he had worked so laboriously at.

## III

IN THE SQUARE the early morning surge and flow was lapping steadily over the sidewalks. A squad of men came lugging lumber and, after marking off with pencil, held the posts erect, then drove in the long spikes firmly—the temporary speakers' platforms. Several minutes later a small closed truck rolled up with amplifiers and batteries. The chauffeur slammed the door, and the two electricians riding with him carried the supplies over to the raw-looking little wooden stages.

A few yards away, a casual stare in his casual eyes, the recruiting officer, pacing slowly before his recruiting booth, watched the men fixing the horns into place.

In this world things move on apace. Progress overleaps all barriers. Obstacles must be surmounted. Never put off today what you cannot do on the fateful tomorrow. Nothing is impossible. Where there's a will, there is a way.

Where there is a will . . . In front of the Bank of Manhattan a sign, neatly lettered, stared at the passing citizenry: HAVE YOU MADE OUT YOUR WILL YET? DON'T DELAY. REMEMBER YOUR LOVED ONES. AMPLE RESOURCES, WE CAN TAKE CARE OF YOU.

No sun came out, no flood of golden hue. Cloudy and overcast, that was the predicted turn of weather. Indifferent visibility. See Hunkel, Broadway's favorite oculist. The signs along the square blurred; if you passed them in the street car, if you passed them in your auto, they ran blurring, blurring fastly past you, and you caught only a letter here, a letter there, but you knew what you were reading because a fleeting glance was all you needed.

The platforms were completed, the horns stood in place. A few curious men, mostly unemployed, shuffled about, watching. One of them stared toward the east where, hard by the firm bronze doors of the Union Square Savings Bank, a porter (or official) was opening the glass, steel-rimmed cages and changing the advertising matter there. The porter (or official) took out two pictures of bathing beauties in a Florida contest and substituted in their places a couple of views of war-torn China, showing coolies and refugees huddled near a bunch of shot-shattered shacks near a railroad track. Above the sign there read: "Save now, interest compounded quarterly." At the bottom, under the war-torn photoed scenes, an educational note was printed, a bit of information that the eager public was bound to appreciate: *"The Chinese were the first to use handkerchiefs.* Long before the Christian era, a delicate silk tissue and paper form of handkerchief was used commonly in the land of the lotus flower, and was held in high regard as a sort of talisman." From the photos the beaten eyes of the homeless coolies stared fixed and dull toward the restless square.

No sun came out, no flood of golden hue. The sky was now the color of a sheet of cold steel. At the main B.M.T. subway entrance Grandma Volga and Mr. Feibelman had long since taken their stations. From the chestnut vender's cart there came a curl of bluish smoke; he shook the metal pan, rolling the nuts over so that all might bake evenly.

The whole square seemed more alive than ever. Everybody knew a communist demonstration was to be held in the afternoon. The hot-chestnut and pretzel venders had all put in extra rounds of supplies, hoping and praying that the day would be a sell-out for them. Communist demonstrations did not come often enough for these shrewd, far-sighted merchants of the square. Other hawkers and venders were on the scene in increased numbers, and stood about taking things easy until the appointed time.

Toward noon people began arriving. Toward noon the press boys and cameramen put in their appearance, important looking gentlemen who fraternized with the cops on the corners. Young girls and boys—kids of twelve or so—were combing the crowd and trying to sell copies of the *Daily Worker*, and put serious, frowning looks on their little faces, and shouted lustily, and told the folks all about the class-struggle, "Workers, unite to protect the Soviet Union." These were the Young Pioneers, and they told the public what was what, all right. No stopping them, a phonograph in each and every little chest.

So far, the main body of police detailed for the demonstration had not yet put in its appearance. Officer Terence McGuffy, shunted back to the day-shift for today (all hands on deck, commissioner's orders!), sauntered around the square, the whirl and roar of traffic at his broad, heroic back. Casting a keen, discerning eye toward the comrades who were tinkering with the amplifiers on the central platform, he wondered what kind of a show the Reds would put on today. Walking on, his roving eye taking in the situation, he followed the low thick wall and continued as far as Broadway before he headed south again.

More people gathered. Some stopped to stare up at the Great Alaska Fur Company windows where a half-dozen manikins (heavily rouged, artificially smiling) walked about in a small, slow circle, showing what a beautiful lining the garments had, while, out of sight, his bald head behind the grinning face of an imitation white-fox fur, the store manager stared through the tusked teeth down at the heads below to see if many women were looking at the bargains above. Every fur in the house had been sharply reduced in price and he was very anxious that the trade should know it.

Hank sat on a bench near the tall flagpole, near the heavy metal base (heavily ornamented with bas-relief work showing the struggle of a people heroically moving their loins), and read a few lines of the Declaration of Independence, which was printed in raised bronze type on a big tablet. Hank's nose was cold, but his hands which were in his pockets were all right. Before he had left the flat he had shaved, and now his jaw was firm and smooth, with a Yankee steely glint to it. He sat waiting for the speeches, a small sneer already turning down the left corner of his honest Yankee mouth. Looking aloft he saw a few cameramen taking their stations in the windows of the tall buildings surrounding the square, and from the distance the men looked small; and as they climbed out upon the wider window ledges, dragging their cameras, they looked like snipers setting up machine-guns at vantage points. Soon all the best windows were taken up by the cameramen while the reporters (safety first!) took their press cards from their pockets and stuck them in their hatbands, strutting about like cocks with stiffened combs. The air continued cold; whenever a wind started up, it blew the cigarette smoke from the cameramen high up on the window ledges sharply away, like white puffs from musket firing.

Around one o'clock the report was circulated that the communists had already started their march somewhere on upper Fifth Avenue and were now heading south for Union Square. The crowds, increasing, waited for the head of the column to show up on Broadway, and because it was chilly standing in one spot many people began stamping and slapping their sides briskly. All heads were turned toward the north, waiting.

Folks looked aloft suddenly when they heard a dull, sputtering drone, but they saw no airplanes in the sky. It was only the squadron of motorcycle police drawing up in formation at University Place and Fourteenth Street with Licutenant Bowen in command.

## IV

THE COMMUNISTS were marching. They swung south down Fifth Avenue, passing the fine shops and parked limousines at the curbs, while high up in the tall buildings flanking each side of the street people stared down at them from windows, seeing the long uneven ranks moving against the gray cement like a dark advancing shadow. No one cheered or threw down ticker-tape paper, no one leaned far out and shouted, "Onward, onward." No bands played. Against the hard smooth street the brittle trot of prancy horses did not sound. There were no battle-flags or silken banners with rayon tassels in the cold, gray wind. The chill air tore southward from the north, flapping the cardboard placards as the comrades tramped. The communists were marching, a dark, advancing shadow against the flat gray of the street below.

The file wound slowly southward, passing the curious massed people on the sidewalks. Well-dressed ladies leading small, expensive dogs stared at the column; at the windows above were stenographers, office-boys, clerks, executives, porters, and a few buyers, all thoughtful-eyed. At the parked limousines which stood groomed and shiny at the curbs the stalwart chauffeurs in quiet livery stared straight ahead like true aristocrats, and one or two of them snorted.

Some of the comrades had old shoes, others wore no gloves and had to hold the posters aloft with one hand, taking turns at warming the free fists in their coat pockets. Tramp, tramp, tramp, the communists were marching. At the intersecting corners, their arms spread wide as eagles' wings in flight, keeping the crowds back, stood the police, giving the communists the right of way.

The column passed unevenly. Posters and placards were carried all along the line, pictures of fat-faced, piggy-eyed bosses smoking cigars and sitting on a poor devil called Labor, National Guards with bayoneted guns staving off gaunt, starving women and children, hollow-eyed, hollow-cheeked men in a long wavering line waiting for soup, with here and there a caustic bit of print: "Hoover prosperity, no one is starving." Leon's signs drew admiration from the people, he had put all the fire, all the passion of his body into his work. Some of the bigger placards were carried by two comrades, a post in each fist, and this was stiff marching for the wind drove hard against the sign.

When the communists reached Thirty-Fourth Street, a few young women up in front began singing in the ranks. The driving wind shot their voices back over their heads to the others behind, and pretty soon the whole column was singing. There was something thrilling about it. From many of the comrades' faces there shone the light of a new religion. Many of the girls and young women wore no hats and the wind blew the hair back from their foreheads. Singing in time to their tramp they swung along, little curly-headed garment-workers, pants-pressers, millinery-workers, house-painters with no houses to paint, drifters who had drifted into the Party, unemployed of all the lower walks of life.

With the singing continuing, the file started marching better, shouting stronger, getting a swing to their stride. Faces continued to stare down from the windows of the tall buildings.

The column swung along toward Twenty-Third Street. Tramp, tramp, tramp. The women were marching with the men. There were Negroes, too, and these sang the loudest, lifting up their faces and shouting out with half-closed eyes.

At Twenty-Third Street the column turned into Broadway, walking upon the car tracks. The wind from the north was broken a little by the buildings, it was easier to carry the posters now. When the communists came up to Twentieth Street, they were able, by looking southward, to see the square in the distance, and all at once the singing grew louder and sustained, the whole column quivered, as if coming to life, and the walls on both sides of Broadway shot the echoes back. The sidewalks here were black with people.

At Eighteenth Street the square was very close, only a short block away, and then everybody began shouting and singing as if insane, and when the communists passed Seventeenth Street and marched into Union Square the roar of their united voices struck the waiting crowds like the sound of pounding seas.

## V

BY TWO O'CLOCK the speakers on the platform were in full stride, haranguing the multitude, giving the thickly massed citizenry the lowdown on the whole rotten system here at hand. With mouths close to the microphones, shouting, the orators amplified their ideas through the amplifiers. Every once in a while, when a speaker stood too close, a squawk issued forth.

A small boy with a strong sense of curiosity covered his ears with his palms, using them as mufflers, exerting and relaxing pressure so that at one moment he heard what was said, and at another he heard nothing but the blood singing in his ears: "Comrades and fellow workers . . . worldwide problem which is . . . and I say, down with them all and to . . . yes, over in Russia where every worker has . . . and is . . . *squawk* . . . the perfect proletar . . . a militant platform and . . . economics . . . exploiting, grinding us down under this capi . . . no, no, no, that is . . . self-determinism and . . . minorities . . . so can you all . . . Russia has solved and is . . . militant . . . imperialism . . . opportunism . . . Soviet Union will be . . ." After a while the small boy with the strong sense of curiosity took his hands away from his ears because he was getting tired of his game and, besides, he felt an earache coming on. From then on he heard the speeches complete as they flowed forth from the tinny horns.

A tall, lanky comrade with big feet was now addressing the multitude from the central platform: ". . . the workers are becoming class-conscious, they are waking up, they are thinking. *They are thinking.* They want to know why ninety-five per cent of the wealth of this nation is owned by but five per cent of the population. *They are thinking.* They want to know! Fellow workers, the capitalistic system is crumbling, the breaking point is upon us. All over the world unrest is seething. Kings and dictators keep their thrones only with the assistance of large, powerful armies. Our great middle class, which we used to talk about, is rapidly melting away . . ."

The sun came out for a moment, a thin glaring shine, then went away for good. At their vantage points the cameramen ground out a few feet of film, just to get some preliminary shots, saving the rest of the reel for snappier stuff. Looking downward they could see their co-workers, the reporters who strode cockily amidst the throng with press cards stuck in hatbands, viewing the scene with keen reportorial eyes, trying to think of "human interest" touches. "We are here to get the news," the reporters seemed to say, looking about, proud that the public stared curiously at their hatbands. "We are here to give the nation the news, the news as we see fit to report it. Lafayette, we are here," they seemed to say, gazing across the closely packed square toward the gallant Frenchman and his pointed sword.

"Needles, shoelaces, socks, peanuts . . ." barked out

the combing venders in their low, sad barks. "Tooth-paste, balloons, imported toys . . . peanuts . . ." They shoved their merchandise under the public's noses. Buy now, selling out, tomorrow might be too late, only a nickel, misters and missuses. . . . The husky cops looked on, occasionally stroking their beefsteak faces.

In this world things move on apace. Progress overleaps all barriers. On Third Avenue Pete applied a lighted match to the opened jet of his gas-burner and lo, a flame issued forth. He turned over a rather messy-looking omelet, stared out upon the street, and wondered why so few people were walking past his windows. Then the customer waiting for the omelet said the Reds were holding a meeting in Union Square. This explained everything. Pete, his mind alert, flipped the omelet onto a greasy plate. Through the front door came another customer, and he sat down and ordered roast loin of pork with peas and mashed on the side. Pete, turning his head around his neck, like you would twist a doorknob, yelled the order to the cook who re-echoed it back in a clear, low grunt. Pete, scratching behind his ear: "Poppy-seed rolls, bread?" he inquired. The roast-loin-of-pork customer, thinking the matter over, ordered rye bread. "I'm a vegetarian," he said, "I don't eat white bread often." Pete stared toward the wicket. In the rear the cook rattled his pans. In the square the orators were still giving the massed citizenry the lowdown on the whole rotten situation here at hand. Time and tide. The front door opened again and James Nicholson—cracked printer, student of Roman history, thinker, and philosopher—came in, sat down, chewed gingerly on a ham sandwich and, hearing that the communists were in the square, hearing that about a billion people were there, dropped the sandwich down upon the plate, jumped up, said he'd be back later, then rushed to his rooms, where he stuffed his pockets full of printed cards until they bulged. Then he went out and hurried to the square and, when he arrived on the scene, a speaker with a powerful voice was addressing the crowds.

". . . the class-struggle . . . you must unite, you must fight the bosses who are exploiting and . . ." The small boy with the strong sense of curiosity was pressing his hands against his ears again. ". . . the bourgeoisie must . . . in Russia we find that . . . so-called opportun . . . wealth and resources will be . . . yes, yes, yes. The Communist Party of America is the only militant organization with a definite economic program. In Russia——"

"Why don't you go back there?" someone in the crowd suddenly yelled out.

"In Russia——" the orator continued.

"Why-don't-you-go-back-there?" came the hue and cry again, from several voices now, beating in tempo.

"I am an American, comrade! This is my country, I want to better it, I want . . ."

"Boo-oo-oooooo." Jeers and Bronx cheers floated toward the central platform. On the smaller platforms, which were scattered throughout the throngs and which had no amplifiers, other orators were hammering away, trying to knock facts and figures into the thick ivory heads of the public. Once in a while a man in the crowd would shout "agitator," "Red," or "racketeer" but for the most part the multitude stood quietly, listening with blank, unalive faces. The cameramen ground out a few more feet of film. The wind kept flapping the cardboard posters, and every so often a few comrades in the crowd would cheer, but their outcries rose thinly in the chill gray air. Comrade Edward Lukotas, holding up a placard, yelled until he grew hoarse; a policeman, standing near, looked his way quickly.

"Five-cent candy, shoelaces, needles, peanuts . . ." croaked the venders in their sad, hoarse, croaking barks. On the Fourth Avenue side of the square an old shabby gent with a running cold in his nose shuffled along at the outskirts and sniffled at every few paces. He passed the glass advertising cases in front of the Union Square Savings Bank. The Chinese were the first to use handkerchiefs. In the side streets west of the square the mounted police were gathering. They came clumping up on their steeds in ones and twos and pretty soon there was quite a company there; all sat their horses gracefully, out of sight, a block away, and joked and talked together, the city's finest, we are here to serve you.

On the small scattered platforms the orators had to shout very loud because they had no amplifiers. They made their speeches short, for a fellow couldn't keep up that burning pace for very long. Finally Comrade Irving Rosenblum (Rosie to his pals) got up on one of them and he told the citizenry something, he sure did, and no mistake. Facts and figures, that's what they want. On the central platform were the major speakers of the Party and Rosie wished he could be up there shouting, but here he was, so he did the best he could.

"Comrades and fellow workers," he said, speaking slowly at first, getting steamed up gradually, wafting his searching glance from face to face as he paused to get his wind, "you are living in the richest city in the richest country in the whole world. You are . . ." and he shouted on, no stopping the lad now, each man his own loudspeaker and amplifier to the best of his ability. But if only he had a chance at the microphones, he'd show the central committee what he could do, he sure would. "Look, Rosie at the mike," his pals would have said, "Rosie at the mike!"

Pale light came down from a windy dirty sky. At the southwest corner of the square the motorcycle squadron sat at ease, one man in the saddle, another in the side-car. Crowds of bargain-hunters plodded along on Fourteenth Street, business was going on as usual, folks saw the multitude in the square but the business of stretching your dollars was more important than standing listening to just a lot of hollow talk. Nope, not for me, the bargain-hunters said, and keenly looked the 39c brassieres over and wondered how long the thin silk would last against the heavy burden of a pair of sagging breasts.

In the crowd Leon Fisher grew tired holding up his poster and had to motion to another comrade for assistance. "I have a pain in my back," Leon said. "I'm sorry I'm not stronger," he apologized, while the relieving comrade, a big fellow, hoisted up the placard higher than ever. Leon, his eyes bright, a tempest surging in his narrow-chested bosom, stamped for warmth upon the sidewalk and sank his head between his young thin shoulders. He thought about Comrade Helen and wondered in what part of the crowd she was standing. Turning about he saw a big, husky fellow moving away from the platform, and the little painter recognized the man as one of the tenants of Twenty-Door City. It was Hank—Hank Austin.

Hank wandered from speaker to speaker, his hands shoved in his pockets, the words of the orators rolling around crazily inside the bowl of his skull like ivory dice. He wrinkled his nose and he wrinkled his brows and he tried to think the shouted phrases out. *Capitalism, imperialism, class-consciousness, economics, communism,*

*Marxism* . . . what did the words mean? Occasionally he heard the phrase, "Down with the bosses!" and for a second his brain grew alive, he knew what that meant, all right. Old Running Water. But in another minute, like a snowflake melting on the windowsill, the feeling disappeared; his mind, like a spent swimmer, sank back exhausted into the cool green well of the waves. He walked around, his feet trod stone.

"Comrades . . . fellow workers . . . brotherhood . . ." Hank walked on.

In front of his recruiting booth the sergeant stuck a piece of candy into his military mouth and continued to roll it from cheek to cheek, wearing it down, acting aggressive about it. Perseverance, that's the ticket, get your man. The sergeant, his fleshy neck bubbling over the harsh, stiff collar of his overcoat, wondered if the rash he had on the soft undersides of his buttocks was due to his woolen winter underwear or maybe from eating too much fatty foods. He paced his beat, four to the left, a turn, and four to the right, lots of time. A new poster had been pasted to the billboard today, a poster showing half a dozen scenes of maneuvers: scouting signalers waving flags, an artillery squad behind a six-inch gun, airplanes wheeling high in air, skirmishers spreading fanwise as they advanced into "enemy" territory, and Old Glory flying and whipping on some mizzenmast. SEE ACTION, GO PLACES, DO THINGS. When the piece of candy was gone, worn away by constant rubbing, the sergeant popped another hunk into his mouth.

Things do move on apace. At three o'clock the Man Who Walks Backwards put in his appearance, walking backwards from Broadway and Twelfth until he reached the square, standing with his back facing the speakers, listening, his active eyes staring hard and bright at the tiny mirrors attached to the glasses he wore. Folks stared, but he was not embarrassed. Tapping his stout cane he made his way from platform to platform, always with his back facing the speakers, as if his shoulder-blades had ears. The back of his neck looked stiffly attentive, no getting away from that.

Each man is his own loud-speaker, let him amplify his views. What this country needs is more tinny horns, no sense squawking about that. "Needles, five-cent candy, shoelaces, Soviet chocolates, peanuts . . ." in low, sad, croaking barks.

At three o'clock Grandma Volga (all sold out) had to leave the scene and go after a fresh load of supplies, and soon after Mr. Feibelman, his pants pockets heavy with a load of small coins, also rolled an empty wagon away and hurried for more chestnuts, pushing his buggy on ahead, no time to lose, customers waiting, I'll be back soon, don't buy until my return, I got the best nuts, misters and missuses.

The big clock in the tower of the public utilities building struck the hour, a trio of solemn, stately bongs. Three o'clock. At the southwest corner of the square Lieutenant Brown, in charge of the motorcycle squadron, spoke to another lieutenant close by. "I estimate the turnout as well above fifty thousand," he said.

Far down the block two hose-trucks from the fire department drew up silently.

The small boy with the strong sense of curiosity was trying his ear-muffler game again.

"Sir, would you like a first-class shine on your shoes?" an old "boy" of fifty winters asked Hank Austin who was standing by. Hank shook his head. The mayor was sitting in his fine offices and thinking about important business. The famous transcontinental flyer was due soon. Was the tugboat *Macon* ready?

At ten minutes after three Miss Allen knocked timidly on the door of the ex-poet's "abode," and Jason, setting a bottle heavily down, got up from his chair and gripped the doorknob with his fist.

## VI

"IT'S NO USE," the little Hungarian was saying to his stocky stolid wife. "It's no use," he was saying and in a low voice argued hotly that the protection money he was paying Officer Mike Kelly was eating up all his profits. "It's no use," he said again, speaking in Hungarian to his meek and docile dame. "Every time the front door opens I think federal men are coming in. It's no use." On the stove the goulash slowly boiled. His wife, standing quietly, watched the roast and poked it gently with a long, sharp fork. Her hands were damp from dish-washing.

Through the passes and steep canyons blew the chill and bitter wind. The massed citizenry, huddled close together under the dull gray of the sky, stood stolid like a small thick forest of stubby trees.

The orators rattled on. The cops, shifting on their bully legs, faced the platforms with large, set faces, like silent bulldogs, ready to growl, ready to rip off the seat of a man's pants from the rear. Comrade Bessie Silvers (a solid build) gripped the handle of her poster, stared hard at three cops who were fifteen yards away, and allowed her glance to linger on the youngest one, whose jaw was brutal but whose mouth was full and soft. "I don't mind him, but if the others get fresh with me . . ." This in a muttered undertone, to herself; Bessie Silvers thinking, a hefty kid with a beefy can. Yours truly.

Rolling their buggies furiously, Grandma Volga and Mr. Feibelman arrived on the scene and from each chest was torn their battle-cries: "Pretzels, two-for-five, buy by me," "hot CheTnutZ, I got the best, misters and missuses," in low, croaking barks.

The thick black minute hand clicked one notch forward. Time. Two miles south of the square, in his downtown office, Mr. Boardman looked from the windows and made little markings with his pencil upon a pad of paper. His secretary, busy writing a letter to a firm in Toledo, glanced his way occasionally, not stopping her tap-tap-tap of the keys. Toward three-fifteen Mr. Boardman, raising a hand to feel his brow, complained of a headache, spoke to the girl about it, then went into the manager's office, looking pretty bad. His face was gray and drawn, he had been losing weight steadily for a few weeks now. The manager, an understanding man, told Mr. Boardman he ought to go home and call a doctor. Mr. Boardman, tired out and gray-faced, said, yes, that was what he would have to do.

When he came back to his own office, he told his secretary he was leaving for the day. The girl looked up sympathetically and advised him to take a certain brand of headache pills.

"Take one every hour, my aunt always uses them," she said. "If it doesn't pass away, take two after the fourth hour."

He put his hat and coat on, took his cane, and left quietly; and when he reached the street he found a cab standing idle at the curb. He stepped in.

Through the passes and steep canyons the chill and bitter wind still blew; a raw and gloomy day. The mayor sat in his fine offices in the City Hall. "I regret to state," he said, dictating to a secretary, "that I will be unable to appear before the Coney Island Ben-Zion Boosters because of a dinner date as guest speaker at a banquet of the Sacred Blood of the Sacred Heart Brotherhood. But be it known that as your mayor my heartfelt so-and-so, you know the rest, Miss Kennedy, bring it in and I'll sign it." The sparrows in the park outside were drilling in between the sidewalk cracks. The tugboat *Macon* was working up steam, plenty of time yet.

In the ex-poet's "abode" Miss Allen, standing quietly, finally took her hat and coat off.

"What I came up for, was to see how you looked, to find out about your health," she said, not used to lying, speaking with a halt in her voice.

Jason was pouring out a couple of drinks. She said she didn't drink and——

"Drink," grunted Jason and she started sipping. She made a face, the gin was strong stuff.

Jason tossed his off and poured another. He spoke heartily, with a blur. He was pretty drunk already and told Miss Allen she shouldn't worry about his health, he was feeling fine, feeling as fit as a couple of cracked fiddles. As he stood leaning against the wall he could see, by looking down into the waste-basket, all the pink letters he had received from Philadelphia, neatly torn to bits, torn carefully. They lay quiet on the bottom of the basket like the fallen petals of a faded rose.

"Let me see your arm," Miss Allen said, the nurse now.

He held out a thin, limp hand and, while she glanced at her wristwatch, he could feel her cool finger above his beating pulse. She rolled his shirt sleeve up and saw that the tiny reddish marks were gone; a few gray dots the size of needle-points remained, and these too were rapidly fading.

"So you did mind me," she said softly, rubbing his arm, cooling it with her own cool palm. "You did stop taking it."

"Rats," said Jason shortly. "I make no promises to anybody."

"But you stopped," she said, smiling at him warmly.

"Rats!"

And later, on the bed, lolling sleepily, his face sagged; and from bleared eyes he stared out at her. "What are you hanging around me for? You're wasting your time, I'm just a drunken bum. You're not the first that has tried to uplift the human race by taking me in hand, but you're wasting your time. I'm just an old second-hand sparkplug, kid, and my sparking days are over. I oughta be on the dump heap, that's where I belong. All right, quit bawling."

The girl blew her nose softly.

"I've got a new dress on, you didn't even notice it."

"Is that so?" said Jason, speaking loudly. He set his glass down and it rolled around the floor. "I spotted it as soon as you came in," and he reached out (she was sitting at the foot of the bed, he was reclining), and felt the material. "Silk," he said, "and a high grade silk at that."

"It's satin," she told him.

"I said satin, don't contradict me." He rolled the stuff between thumb and forefinger, like an expert. He lay there, looking at her meekly bowed head as she sat. Her heart was beating wildly. Jason did not move; then, all at once (the bareness of the room, the bleakness of the day working on her), the girl leaned toward him impulsively and gripped his hand. Her palm was hot and moist, her brow was lumpy and distorted.

Jason did not move. He could smell the perfume she had put on her dress before she came up, perfume like faded roses, a thin, faint, pleasant odor. He reared himself slowly and sat up, side by side, tired out and still bleary-eyed, but his brain was clear and quiet. His gaze swept slowly round the room, round the old brown dirty walls.

Then, all her dammed feeling for him flooding to the surface and over, he felt her weeping against him, leaning against his chest as they sat, and in the silent room her sobs broke slowly, rippling from her throat. Her whole body started trembling. Jason did not move.

She told him she was so sorry for him and she couldn't get him out of her mind and she wanted so much to take care of him and make him happy. Her words were echoes, he had heard them from someone else before. He sat there as if posing for a photographer, his throat harsh and dry, his stare straight ahead; he wanted to talk, but said nothing. She went on crying, wiping the tears slowly from her face with her palms, a quiet, even weeping without sorrow, without body racking; and little by little (from force of habit perhaps, the old, old feeling) he started stroking her back slowly, to calm her. The girl grew quiet, grew heavy against him as they sat, and her heart hammered strongly against his chest.

They sat holding hands. Through the filmy window the ex-poet saw the sagging clotheslines swinging in the soft gray air. The girl muzzled her mouth slowly against his shoulder and, with half-closed eyes, began to breathe and exhale hoarsely, all her muscles quivering.

For a long while Jason did not move. Then, rising, he

went to the window, drew the shade, and, when he returned to the cot, he found her waiting.

The room was pretty dark now, and he had to feel around for her.

## VII

A HALF-HOUR LATER (the girl was gone, she had dressed and left him dozing) Jason walked slowly down the stairs and at the bottom was about to drop his half-finished cigarette in the hallway when he saw, looking toward the entrance of the tenement, the old janitress talking to Mr. Boardman, who lived next door in the Glen Cove Apartments. The old janitress liked to keep the hallway tidy. Toward the left the door leading down into the basement was open.

Jason tossed his cigarette into the darkness there.

He went forward toward the entrance and from his battered mail-box took out a small pink letter which he shoved deep into his hip pocket, then passed on, walking toward the square.

Mr. Boardman, looking very bad, was speaking with a quiet nervousness. "That vacant room on the top floor, is it still unrented, has it been taken yet?"

The old janitress, warming up, said it wasn't taken yet, no, and she couldn't understand just why the fine-looking gentleman wanted to see the vacancy. "It's cold there, there's no heat, and the windows need fixing."

Mr. Boardman, his face fatigued and drawn, tapping his cane against the dry, splintered flooring of the hallway, said that that was all right. The old woman couldn't understand it.

"And besides, don't you live next door, haven't you got a steam-heated apartment there?"

Mr. Boardman, impatient but well in hand, tapped his cane against the dry, splintered flooring again. He followed the old janitress back into the long dim hallway, back to her rooms in the rear where she started hunting for the right key, which was pretty hard to find. She said she was looking for an especially rusty key, and her fingers, like claws, scratched around inside an old cigar-box. She grew gabby. "That young man who just passed us occupies the room across the hall from the vacancy. He's a writer, he writes for magazines. If you want a place to write, why it's kinda quiet up there."

Mr. Boardman, waiting for her to find the right key, said that he wrote once in a while, and also stated he was on the lookout for a quiet room.

Finally she found the key and gave it to him, but when she thought of climbing those five flights she groaned and started complaining about her old age.

"I ain't so young any more. It's the top floor, rear east. You take the key, you'll be doing me a big favor, I don't think my legs'll hold out if I climb them stairs. Do you think you can find it by yourself, do you think so?"

Mr. Boardman, taking the key from her, said he believed he could. He thanked her for her trouble, walked into the hallway, smelt again the slightly sour odor of the old building, and began climbing the stairs, one hand upon the banister as he ascended.

When he found the rail was dusty, he took his hand away and, walking in the center of the stairs, his shoes feeling the hollows as he climbed, he continued upward, his eyes growing slowly accustomed to the dimness.

# VIII

THE MOB was growing restless in the square. They were patient citizens, but the speeches were many and all were sung to the same tune. The cops stood off, shifting weight from one foot to the other, twirling vacantly their clubs behind their stalwart backs. Across the sea of heads, as over a swell of countless bobbing corks, you could discern, by glancing upward, the manikins still walking slowly in small, graceful circles in the second-floor windows of the Great Alaska Fur Company. Venders and hawkers (low, sad, croaking barks) combed the crowd for business, but their voices were becoming tired and old.

It was now after four o'clock, and the sky was beginning to darken. From the north side of the square five tall burly men in old cast-off clothes got out of an automobile and began mixing with the spectators, shoving and pushing with their shoulders.

Jason, after he reached the square, walked slowly around the outskirts of the crowd, keeping on the Fourth Avenue side near the B.M.T. subway entrance. He shoved a hand into his hip pocket and finally took out the pink envelope, and with the hum and restless drone of the crowd in his ears stood looking at the handwriting, reading his name. "Needles, Soviet candy, shoelaces, razor blades, ticklers, peanuts . . ." The dull noise of the restless mob beat upon his ears. Without opening the envelope, without reading what was inside, he tore the letter carefully into many equal parts, and, as he dropped the pieces to the sidewalk, a subway train roared by below, the speed of the cars sending up a warm draft of dank air. The bits of paper, fluttering downward, were caught—seized by a sudden gust, and shot on forward, whirling and spinning crazily, pink bits separating from green; a five-dollar bill had been enclosed. The ex-poet watched the pieces settle to the sidewalk, then strolled on, going deeper into the crowd.

At the microphone, on the central platform, a fiery orator was at the helm, trying to whip up the multitude, trying to get things going. But the citizenry, unlike a bowl of cream, did not froth in response, but stood stolid, like a squat forest of stubby trees, staring blankly, their hands shoved in their pockets. Through the passes and steep canyons a chill and bitter wind was blowing.

"Here in America we have solved the problem of production for the first time in the history of the world," the orator was shouting. "Yes, for the first time in history a people can produce as much, and more, than its own people can consume. And yet . . . and yet, fellow workers, comrades, and yet, ten million people are unemployed and hunger stalks the land. Now, in Russia . . ."

"Why-don't-you-go-back-there?" the hue and cry again.

". . . now in Russia, comrades, in Russia . . ."

"Boo-ooooooo," a restless, chanting drone.

Suddenly small disturbances broke out in the crowd, in four or five places. The cops started shoving a few burly-looking men around. Instantly the speaker at the microphones shouted louder and a bunch of squawks barked from the horns. People started laughing and booing, but were good-natured about it. The orator, his eyes roving nervously, began talking more calmly, but still in a good loud voice, all right. The cops kept on shoving the four or five burly fellows who were shouldering their way here and there and causing a little commotion. Suddenly one of the husky men pulled a placard from a comrade's hands, the comrade sought to get it back again, both sawed to and fro, the comrade's voice rising harshly, and folks were thrown back a bit.

In a flash the various speakers on the scattered platforms spoke louder than ever, looking uneasy, turning their faces away, but glancing sideways toward the spots which began to seethe. At the east end of the square three patrol wagons drew up, with members of the police rifle squad inside, but they were on hand only in case an emergency should arise, and all of them knew the emergency would not arise.

Hank, pretty tired of walking and feeling foggy-brained from speech-listening, stood with heavy legs in the crowd, the gloominess of the cloudy afternoon weighing down upon him. From under heavy brows he looked toward the west and saw, up Sixteenth and up Seventeenth Streets, the mounted cops drawing their reins in sharply, sitting erect, as if waiting for something. One or two of them pulled out watches. They sat their mounts stiffly, waiting for the first hum, the first rumble of the mob.

It was not long in coming.

A big burly fellow in cast-off clothing lunged at a cop who swung back at him, but missed. The burly man lunged again, throwing the cop back against some people who now started growing nervous, and again the cop missed; and again the fellow lunged. Immediately a space was cleared around the spot, folks shoved back, clawed their way through the press, and a jam ensued. A few women screamed, there was more shoving, three more cops eased over and strange as it appeared the burly man causing all the commotion was devilishly clever in dodging blows from the officers of the law. Then one cop collared the fellow and made as if to strike, when, from under closely knit brows, the man grunted something, and the cop's stick cut a broad swath through the cloudy air. By this time many women, panic-stricken, were screaming and shoving, and pretty soon the fever, rippling the crowd, caught the whole square. The speakers, almost all at the same time, jumped from the platforms down into the mob, where everybody was shoving and pushing to get out of the jam.

Folks fell down and were trampled upon, the posters and placards crying out for mass freedom whirled down into the dirt; it was each man for himself. Buttons were ripped from coats and dresses, and women, their bosoms partly exposed, breasted the tide and pushed on for freedom, yelling, clawing, screaming hysterically.

At the northwest point of the square the motorcycle squadron, like off-stage sound effects, began tuning up their motors until the engines roared like a race-track, but the cars did not move, did not budge an inch. The cops on foot, scattered all over the square, dotting the pressed mob, started blowing whistles all at once, as if on a signal, and, with upraised riot-sticks held aloft like long clubs of heavy bologna, shook and waved for quelling authority; and at the second loud blowing of police whistles the mounted cops, four abreast, came charging out of the canyons of Sixteenth and Seventeenth Streets, the heads of their horses tossing in excitement, the hooves ringing hard against the firm cement. They came charging to the fray, galloping up to the scene in all their splendid, brutal power, a nightstick in each and every hand, jaws set, one fist tightly gripping the reins.

At the sight of the charging horses the women in the press began screaming louder than ever. But even so, though there was pushing and clawing and shoving, the mêlée had not yet grown into a riot. The comrades ducked, all but Comrade Edward Lukotas, who, with breast heaving with the fiery slogans of the orators, reared up his head like a charger as of yore, gripped his placard tighter, and shouted out his battle-cry: "Workers of the world, unite. *Workers of the world, unite!*" The words burst from his mouth with a roar and, with head proudly rearing and tossing, he held his poster higher up than ever. "*Workers of the world, unite!*" Two cops, busy fussing with a big burly fellow in an old cap, left their man and started work on Comrade Lukotas: one of the cops had had his eye on Comrade Lukotas for a long, long time. The two officers, advancing from either side, crushed Lukotas between them and, while one gripped the poor devil by the coat collar firmly, the other kept striking the communist about the head with his riot-club. The fellow, held helplessly, began screaming. The burly man in the old floppy cap disappeared into the crowd.

From then on all was disorder. Hank found himself in a big jam; he pushed this way and that, wanting to get out of the trouble, trying to find an egress, but the police, forming a cordon, were shoving the people more tightly together. Hank used those mighty shoulders of his, and tore and plunged, but could not break to freedom. He started sweating.

On the outskirts, away from the flying nightsticks, a cracked little gent, digging into his bulging pockets, began dropping cards, flinging them out, over the heads of the mob, his mouth jerking, the left side of his face twitching a bit. He threw handful after handful, and the cards, fluttering downward, resembled huge, square snowflakes. When all his pockets were empty the little gent shook his fist at the cloudy sky, gave a hoarse shout, and hurried safely across the street and out of sight, running.

He reached his basement quarters over on Thirteenth Street and locked his door, banging it against the street, against the world, then sat down and wrote like fury, bent over, crouching like a hunchback:

> Now in the winter a new death rides the mountains. The herdsmen in the hills, with flocks of sheep and goats, are driven by the gale and hurry to the valley over stiffened, frosty grass. The lanes are crowded, the humps of rams, the beards of goats, all dip in unison, swaying in descent; staffs crack and swirl, the hard, dry dirt of autumn scuttles down the mountainside.
>
> Through the passes and steep canyons rush fury, while, massed and huddled on the valley floor, the beasts stand stolid, hearing the faint roar of the coming storm.
>
> Then, from the south, in shock formation, spears in their right fists, shields at ease, come the Romans, big men all, advancing. The standard bearers, with free hands, lead captured lion cubs, who, tugging at the leash, paw and snarl the earth. The dust from prancing stallions rises from the ground while the wind, driven northward, brings the lust and smell of battle to the soldiery behind. Sheep whine and shiver; the goats, hearing the lusty baying of the half-grown lions, look with big, soft eyes at the nervous shepherds.
>
> Then, with a thunderous shout, the first ten phalanxes reach the scene and sniff the foredoomed slaughter. The cold sides of the mountain walls send the echoes of their war-cries back. The air rains spears, steeds rear and snort; and at a command all

leashes are loosed, the young lions bound forward to the fray, growling, snapping, crunching with their dripping powerful jaws. Sorrow and woe, woe and sorrow. In the turmoil the shepherds scatter and, seeing all is lost, run crouching swiftly through the mass, parting a lamb here, a goat there, hearing the bleating on all sides until, skirting the slaughter and free at last, they reach the first rise, where the wind blows free and strong; here, not looking back, they dart into the mountain passes and run and run and run, fleeing, until the roar of the fray behind fades slowly and a faint, low drone like sleepy bees hangs softly in the air.

*—This from the fifth volume, from the home and print-shop of a man of parts.*

The turmoil grew. Officer Terence McGuffy, on the edge of the mob where it was comparatively quiet yet (the center was seething with a mighty boil by now), picked up a few of the cracked printer's cards and laughed with a mutter to himself. Then, his brain becoming alert, he faced the surging mob and braced his powerful legs, keeping an eye out for folk who looked to be communists. And when he saw a person who had a "Reddish" look about him, he closed in, using his nightstick expertly. By some uncanny sixth sense many cops judged their victims correctly, and even if they didn't, you couldn't hold them responsible, for after all, we all make occasional errors, and, say we all, "cops are human like the rest of us!" McGuffy, a valuable man on this occasion because he knew all about Soviet maneuvers, followed the rules of his Code Book and did his duty. He struck out expertly. "I have met the enemy and he got a crack on the skull!" he shouted to his nearest fellow officer a few feet away, grinning. Officer Terence McGuffy was famous up and down Fourteenth Street for his quiet humor.

In this world things go on apace. Near the motorcycle squadron (their engines still droning loudly like a bunch of airplanes), Battalion Chief Joseph Carmichael of Fire Company X2 ordered the two hose-trucks to swing into action, and his boys responded bravely, in their brave and loyal manner. Directing powerful streams of water, which shot out of swelling hoses like live things wriggling frantically for freedom, they sprayed the public, which the police, by a clever bit of maneuvering, forced toward the water hydrants. ("That'll cool 'em off, all right."—LIEUTENANT SMITH.)

Above, on all the window ledges, the cameramen were grinding furiously, and one fellow up there had his hat turned around like a jockey. They had to work fast because the light was fading rapidly. A chill and bitter gust shot across the square; it sent the water up in a quick, thin spray, so the cops shoved the herded communists around the other way while the firemen maneuvered the hoses in a new position.

On all sides men and women were running. The venders and hawkers, dodging the spray so as not to get their precious wares wet, ran with huddled bodies, hugging their merchandise close, and whined for quarter. Don't squirt me, mister, I got to live, I got to make my living, too. The cold wind blew hats off, whirling them high and doing freaky tricks with the lids; even a few hats of the doughty gentlemen of the press were whisked off and these gents, frightened, clapped their hands to their domes, hatless, then sought escape, no badge now. Some of the reporters had covered the October riot a bit too sympathetically and now the constabulary, seeing the lads were hatless, paid off old scores expertly. The cops hit all and sundry. They rushed toward cameramen who were scattered in the crowd and smashed the lenses to bits with their nightsticks and, when the photographers sought to read their badge numbers, the cops covered their shiny stars with their palms. The press boys started to protest, then took to running, coat tails flying.

The seething increased. In all the husky beefsteak faces the red juice of life and fury was overflowing, and the communists got spattered with the gravy.

In the end one man was laid low, permanently crippled in the spine, a mere spectator, a man out of work, a worker without a job. He had come to the square earlier in the day just to hang around, but before dusk closed in he had paid the price. He went down fighting, fighting for the Revolution, for the Great October, but he was unaware of the great cause he had served. He was Hank Austin, a husky lad of pure and loyal Yankee stock. He had seen service in the trenches overseas, had voted the straight Democratic ticket in all elections, and had a wife and four kids. He had the shoulders of a coal-heaver, Hank had, no toothpick of a man was he, a *man*, a staunch, ivory-headed American workingman.

Hank was still shoving to get out of the mess, he didn't want to have a thing to do with it. Off to one side the cops were still swinging at Comrade Lukotas, doing a very thorough job. Comrade Lukotas, held limp now, was moaning, and blood ran from his forehead.

Using those brawny truckman shoulders of his, Hank began shoving harder than ever, grunting and panting, and tore great holes in the mob, but the holes were plugged immediately by more citizens. He kept hard at it, perseverance, that's the ticket.

And so it came about that, because of his worker's strength, he was singled out by the cops and set upon; if he had shoved more gently he would have been more gently treated. He plunged and stamped, working up a glorious, fighting, trenches sweat, and finally tore a wide hole in the crowd, and plunged through, but was too late. From either side the mob parted before his terrific onrush. He was sent forward by his own tremendous impetus and, to save himself from falling, clutched at the coats of a couple of men, holding them hard to keep himself from slipping. One of the men he held was a policeman. The cop blew his whistle smartly on the instant, then struck at Hank.

Two mounted officers plunged up, nightsticks in hand, arms upraised, their beefsteak faces overflowing with the juice of justice, biding their time. Working their horses skillfully, they cornered Hank and began raining blows upon the former truckman's head and shoulders. Stunned and furious, still sweating, Hank sought to defend himself. He was aroused now. He swung forward, growling, and, reaching up, gripped the bit of a cop's horse and almost broke the animal's neck. The rider, a heavy man, rolled off the saddle. Whistles started blowing all around. Hank, his nostrils breathing fury, lunged out again, but two blows behind the right ear stunned him, and, great God, he was fighting the police, he was making a stand against authority! He stopped in his tracks and, with great legs lagging, dangled his hands at his sides. He got the blows from all fronts now. Bent down, seeing the whirling hooves of rearing horses, seeing the flapping sexual organs of a straining mare like the limp sides of an old opened leather pocketbook, he covered his head with his arms and screamed, his head to the ground: "I'm no commoonist, I ain't a Red, I'm an Amerikin!"

The noise of the riot was now terrific, no one heard. Still swinging, still working their horses skillfully, the cops closed in tighter. One steed, frightened, reared high, turning on his hind legs as if on a pivot; the rider gave a hard jerk, the horse snorted, terrified, then struck out. One of the iron-shod hooves struck Hank cruelly in the back, at short range, right on the spinal column. He spun around crazily like an empty barrel, twitching, screaming. They kept striking at his head and down he went, laid low.

Then the cops scattered quickly from the spot, the mob surged over the body.

## IX

DUSK began falling. At the northwest corner, near the sputtering drone of the motorcycles, Lieutenant Bowen, turning to his captain who sat in a closed limousine quietly watching the riot, reported briefly: "Well in hand, sir."

Down the block the hoses were quivering like snakes, wriggling and writhing as if in torture.

Over the iron-hooved town came wind and fog. The temperature began dropping. With a little burst of light the small lamps of the square lit up, and now all you could see were whorling shadows running and ducking; the venders, hugging their wares to their bodies, ran low like Indians, fleeing from the scene.

All this while Comrade Leon Fisher, small as he was, had not been inactive. With bright eyes, he screamed and danced around like mad, he had a little revolution in his chest of his own, and it had been seething quietly there all afternoon while he had been listening to the orations of the speakers.

Darting here and there, he shoved with his puny strength, his eyes on fire, his cheeks going hot and cold by turns. He scratched and clawed. Seeing an officer manhandle a buxom female comrade, he rushed at the man in a blind fury and hammered the fellow's broad back with his little, bony fists. The cop whirled around and with one shove sent the little fellow flying. But Leon came back. He picked himself up from the ground and made another rush. The buxom comrade (none other than Bessie Silvers) spat right at the cop, right in the officer's face, then whirled off in search of further opposition, no stopping her now, there she goes! A solid build.

Leon rushed another cop from the rear who was tearing a poster from a comrade, and the officer, turning smartly, cuffed the little fellow a glancing blow. He grabbed Leon by the collar and was astonished at the slight weight of the little communist. In the moment of astonishment Leon wriggled loose, like a fish freeing itself from a hook; he ran five paces away, then shrilled defiance. The cop started after him, but Leon doubled back on his tracks in the crowd and the pushing mêlée. He ran off snarling like an angry terrier.

By this time the little fellow's face was unrecognizable, strange gibberish came from his throat. Once more he attacked, was repelled gruffly, but before running off he picked up a stone and hit a cop in the back, right between the shoulder-blades. He could see the big fellow wince. Then he ran—ran hard, ran from the mob, out of the square, his blood singing happily, his cheeks hotly glowing from excitement, and his heart throbbed violently. And as he ran, he screamed at the empty air ahead of him:

"But I hit him, I hit him, I hit him!" He didn't know he was safely out of the square until he found himself across the car tracks and on the east side of Fourth Avenue.

Jason, who had been standing off all the while at a safe distance, caught sight of his fleeing friend and shouted, but Leon, rushing on screamingly, did not hear. The little fellow ran southward up Fourth Avenue, dodging in and out of crowded sidewalk traffic.

On the window ledges the cameramen folded up their machines. It was too dark to take any more pictures. The riot died away. The hoses shut off. The crowds began breaking up and scattering briskly while the cops, in good humor now, merely pushed and shoved you back. Wheeling and dancing on their sensitive legs, the horses went here and there, guided by the mounted cops who used the sides of the animals to shove the masses back.

On the south side of Fourteenth Street, where the sidewalks had been black with safe-at-a-distance citizens, the venders had resumed their business, no dampening that kind of mercantile folk. "Needles, Soviet candies, brass polish for your doorknobs, shoelaces, razor blades, peanuts . . . " in low, sad, croaking barks.

The wind whipped a stray card across the car tracks, and a small boy with a strong sense of curiosity picked it up and read it:

> **For a United Front!**

The kid threw it away, down into the subway grating, then turned to watch the firemen rolling up the flattened, heavy hoses.

The Man Who Walks Backwards, underneath the

second floor windows of the Great Alaska Fur Company, had his back toward the square so that he could see just how the cops were expertly breaking up the fast-melting throngs. He didn't miss a single thing; his trained eyes swept the scene like a pair of military field-glasses, he saw what was what, all right.

The mayor sat in his fine offices in City Hall. The transcontinental flyer with some kind of a new record under his belt was late. Was the tugboat *Macon* ready? "He isn't coming from Europe, Your Honor, he flew across the continent," said Miss Kennedy, slim and thirty and very efficient, she orders all the mayor's candied fruits. The mayor frowned. "Then call up Captain Quirt, I thought the flyer was coming in from Quarantine." The secretary, walking quietly away, called up from the outer office in a low voice, no sense vexing the chief. Captain Quirt, wearing a new stiff collar, carefully shaven, was ready at the tugboat *Macon*. "Not coming in?" says he. "Not coming, you say?" The wire clicked. He ordered steam to be shut off, a ton and a half of coal was used up already.

Life must go on, we must face the future; there are children to be born, and some will cry when life cuts through their tender skin. Celia was walking quickly from the rooming house, on her way to the dentist's for the final visit, for the tooth. Her heart fluttered happily, she walked along, her shapely, little legs twinkling up the street. Blocks south, in a small, mean, chilly room life was cutting through a tender skin. No child though. Mr. Boardman, holding a rusty key in his hand, peered from the clouded window and saw the evidence of his cuckoldry. He stood staring toward the windows of his flat where, sitting in the wide chair near the floor-lamp, was a big man with Margie on his knees. The shades were not drawn, the view was good. With his free hand (the other was firmly squeezing Margie's waist), the man in the big, soft chair was tugging at the knot of his tie and pretty soon had it loosened, then, still tugging, got his shirt off too. Margie, feeling his bare skin, slid her hands swiftly up and down the muscles (the man was young, a healthy specimen) and started kissing him all over his bare, smooth shoulders. Then she got her dress loose herself, so that after a while it was skin against skin, no use having clothes blocking the way, dulling the sensation, y'understand.

Mr. Boardman, standing alone in the small, mean, chilly room, did not shift his gaze. He saw how happy Margie was, there in the young man's arms, how she fairly worshiped the fellow's body. He saw that, all right. He stood looking from the dirty dimness of the little room and saw everything. Finally they took to pulling off each other's clothes. Then, leaping up, both got off the chair and the room went dark. That was all Mr. Boardman saw for a while.

He waited. He stood there in the chilly darkness. Dusk was falling. He counted up to a hundred, then made it two hundred. Still no light, only the blank dark windowpanes below. He counted up to two more hundred, this time very slowly, his mind clicking off the numbers like an old, wheezy clock, very, very slowly.

Finally the light came on again. The man was combing his hair and had his shirt on again, though no tie. Margie came into the line of vision, in pajamas, in those pale purple ones he had bought her only a week ago. While the young man was buttoning his shirt Margie grabbed him around the waist from behind; and stood there teasing him, and kissed him on the back of his neck; she was laughing, smiling happily. Mr. Boardman, out of sight, saw. Then she held out the young man's tie, and when they looked at it both laughed—laughed like a couple of healthy animals, teeth showing. The necktie was torn, he had unknotted it with too much haste, too much gusto. There it was, dangling in Margie's hand, frayed. She went away and brought him another tie, one of Boardie's, the dark blue one he was so fond of. The young man put it on, felt the material, was satisfied. Then Margie gave him his vest and coat.

After that Mr. Boardman did not see either of them, they must have gone into the living room. One hand holding the rusty key, the other on the handle of his cane, he continued to stand in the dark, mean, chilly room.

The loud chimes of Grace Church struck the hour, five stately bongs. Leon was now running up Fourth Avenue, a fiery, glorious feeling in his breast, cold air against his face as he ran. He felt like shouting and singing out to the world, he was so happy. He wanted to tell all how he had resisted brutal power, how he had fought back at oppression. He rushed running toward Twenty-Door City to tell his friend the ex-poet all about it.

At the door of the tenement he stopped suddenly. A thin smoke came floating from the hallway. He entered the building a few feet and found the smoke thicker. It came rolling up from the basement. Leon stood in his tracks, his mouth popping open. Then, clutching at the banister, he started climbing the stairs like mad, heading for the ex-poet's room. By the time he reached the third floor his legs felt as weak as butter, he could hardly lift them to the next stair, but he fought his way up, a long whistling sound coming from somewhere in his chest, his lungs going like a pair of leaky bellows.

Finally he reached the top floor and staggered back toward the rear. The air was clear here, no smoke at all yet. Leon started hammering against the door, shouting, "Jason, Jason!" hammering hard. No answer.

In the small, chilly room across the hall (the door locked, too) Mr. Boardman heard the knocking across the hall, but did not stir. He was looking from the dirty window at the next building where he saw Margie (alone now) lying upon the sofa, stomach down, swinging her heels in the air, reading a magazine and munching sweets, her hand dipping into the box of candy pretty often.

Leon knocked against the ex-poet's door and, receiving no response, was finally convinced Jason was not in. On his way down he gave the alarm. He pounded on every door, every door except the one across the hall from Jason because he knew that little room there was empty. Folks popped their heads out, sniffed the smoke, and started screaming. They grabbed their kids, dug into mattresses for a few valuables, and fled, sobbing, cuffing and kissing their kids at the same time, grabbing at coats and table covers. Leon pounded on the third floor front very loudly.

"The house is on fire!" Leon screamed and Missus Austin, her jaw dropping suddenly like the bottom of a steam shovel when it lets go a load, let out a long, high screech. She had soup bubbling on the stove, Missus Austin had. She scurried screamingly around the flat, snatching at things, dropping them again, shouting: "My soup, my soup!" then got her senses back and, whimpering quietly to herself, went for the bankbook, for two dollars in small change in the empty pickle jar on the third shelf, grabbed up her youngest kid, hollered at the three other youngsters and, all crying and screaming, dragged their way downstairs. Leon helped her a little, and followed. He tore on down and, when he reached the ground floor, could already hear crackling from the left side of the basement.

Then, once more, he stopped in his tracks. Back in the first floor rear he saw a light coming from the comrades' window, from the square of glass above the door there. He ran back, his eyes smarting a little now, and hammered against the panels. He started screaming.

The door flew open. Comrade Helen, stark naked except for a chemise which she had snatched up to her body, stood in the doorway, and at the smell of smoke took in the situation right away. But Leon, Leon, looking past her, stood transfixed, his mouth open, his next scream gagged at the bottom of his windpipe. Over her smooth naked shoulder he saw, in the room off the kitchen, the powerful, unclothed body of the Mexican, muscled and swarthy, rising lazily and sleepily from the bed. Comrade José was stark naked too, with the exception of heavy shoes, which were on his feet. There were smudges from the soles showing on the bed sheet.

With a scream, his lungs bursting, Leon shouted: "Fire!" The girl and the Mexican were already leaping and bounding about the place, grabbing up a few articles of clothing, and tore past Leon, putting their stuff on as they ran up the smoky hallway.

Leon stood weakly in his tracks, shivering all over. He stood there leaning against the wall. In the darkness of the tenement the entire misery of his lonely life swept over him like a huge, warm wave. His face fell and sagged, he stood there slack and hunched like an old man.

Through the haze of smoke, looking forward, he saw the street at the end of the long hallway. People were shouting and acting excited there. The Italian family across from the Austins were bunched on the sidewalk, about a dozen kids, and the mother, a short fat woman, wanted to go into the building again and save that three-dollar painting of Saint Teresa which hung in the kitchen.

Leon stood there weakly, his soul blasted, burned to an ash, his face an old man's. He didn't want to see Comrade Helen, he could not look at her face any more; he stood there shivering and shuddering as the scene came flickering back again: both of them stark naked, two unclothed bodies, the Mexican tawny, golden, muscled; the girl standing with chemise clutched to her breasts, skin white as milk, all healthy shapeliness. He started sobbing, then cut it short.

Whirling, setting his small jaw, he gripped the knob of the right-hand basement door and went downstairs, down into the damp darkness. It was a little smoky here, but the fire was on the left-hand side. By taking this route he could walk the length of the building and come out upon the street by the sidewalk entrance and so avoid seeing her at the doorway. He felt his way and, as his hands slid against the damp, slimy walls, he started sobbing again, he couldn't hold it back any longer. No light burned. But he knew the building. He knew that all he had to do was to follow the right wall straight ahead all the way up front, then lift the wooden lid and go out upon the street outside. He had seen the old janitress do that a lot of times, as she had set the garbage cans out every night. Half way up front he tripped over an empty coal bucket, fell, and struck his forehead against the iron edge of it. He was stunned sharply, but got up right away, feeling his head; his hand came back wet, he knew it was blood. Then he started walking carefully, reached the front of the basement, felt around in the dark for the flight of wooden stairs, found it and climbed three of them, braced his shoulders against the heavy wooden lid and, creaking, the lid raised. The good fresh air outside struck his face. People were running toward the scene, but no one was looking his way, all had their eyes on the doorway, the mouse-hole of the tenement. With a quick grunt, he lifted the lid a foot higher, scrambled out unnoticed, then cut down the street, running, running, not looking back, starting to sob again, feeling tears rolling down his face. He cut north on Third Avenue, reached his rooming house, slipping inside silently, and went upstairs on swift tip-toes to his room, where he flung his smudged, teary, bloody face face-downward against the bed and, with body racking, lay there crying quietly for a long, long time.

On the sidewalk, outside of the tenement, they were waiting for him to come out of the doorway, puzzled. By this time the town was dark, the lone arc lamp glared down upon the heads. Comrade Helen and José were fully clothed now, safe. The girl stared into the doorway of the tenement which was growing blacker and blacker with smoke. No one came out.

Missus Austin, holding her youngest kid in a Turkish towel, the three others huddled at her skirts, was blubbering something about her soup. The kids at her skirts started bawling, but the infant in her arms, with round, owlish eyes, stared about blankly, no imprint on its mind.

A few minutes later, when the fire, with a long, running bound, had traveled up to the third floor, licking up the dry, splintered woodwork; when the whole rotten inner structure of the building was roaring and crackling away at a good clip, the fire department arrived. Trucks came with a howling of screaming sirens up the windy street. The firemen climbed up on the roofs of the buildings on either side (the house was burning too hotly, they couldn't enter the tenement), and poured streams of water on the roof, so that the flames wouldn't burst through and ignite other property. The boys laid hoses all the way from Fourth Avenue, shutting off traffic, using every available fire hydrant.

The men worked by the light of the nearby arc lamp. From Third Avenue, from Fourth Avenue, from Fourteenth Street and all over, people came on the run, and pretty soon police arrived to keep the hundreds back, using their clubs, shoving the public a good distance off.

But no one came from the doorway. The old janitress, an old coat over her fat ancient shoulders, screwed up her eyes, waiting for Mister Fisher, Mister Wheeler's friend, to come out. The opening of the tenement was fiery with flames now, as if a furnace door had been thrown open. Down the block the Hungarian restaurateur stuck out his head, saw the commotion, and hoped that a few citizens would patronize his establishment. He stuck a bigger sign in his front window, a sign for all to read: "Home-Made Hungarian Goulash, 40c." In the kitchen his wife, patient and docile, added just a trifle of water to the soup. Too thick, Anton.

# X

UP THE STREET, walking from Fourth Avenue, came two serious, determined-looking young women. They came striding up the street with quiet faces, no gloves on their hands, no hats on their heads. With firm shoulders, they worked their way through the crowd. Both wore low-heeled shoes which clicked against the firm cement. One had a mole on her nose, the other started asking questions. No dampening them, they were female comrades.

"Where's Mrs. Austin, does Mrs. Austin live here?"

Finally one of the neighbors pointed toward the other side of the crowd, near the first fire-engine, and the two serious, determined-looking young women, working their shoulders again, made their way forward, their low, flat heels clicking against the hard, gray street.

"Where's Mrs. Austin, does Mrs. Austin live here?"

The old janitress pointed at a short, dumpy woman with four kids on her hands. Then the two female comrades seemed to notice the fire for the first time, though engines were drawn up, though smoke was in the air, though hoses were hissing. They hesitated. They looked toward weepy Missus Austin, who clutched her youngest in that white Turkish towel, which was the whitest, most startling thing on the whole street. Stiffening, the two young women stared at each other. Finally they cleared their throats, walked up, stood before the dumpy woman, took Missus Austin aside, stared at the ground, at the curb, at the quivering hoses, and finally broke the news. " . . . he's in the hospital now, we hired a nurse, he won't be able to work again . . . but the Party is behind you, Mrs. Austin . . . already we are planning to . . ."

One of the girls caught the kid just in time. The old janitress hollered for smelling salts and plowed toward Missus Austin, who lay in a soft heap on the sidewalk.

"We identified him by an unpaid gas bill in his pocket," one of the comrades was saying, in the confusion, while the neighbors came a-running. "He's a victim of the bosses . . . of the whole capitalistic system, it's his spine . . ."

Missus Austin was carried into a neighbor's flat a few houses away, while the old janitress, hovering above her, repeated, "Everything'll be all right, Missus Austin, everything'll be all right." The female comrades shouldered their way in, sat down close to Missus Austin and began talking, hard and firm and quiet, asking questions. Both comrades looked very competent.

"We're here to help you . . . we want to help all workers . . . all . . . everybody who suffers and is exploited . . . the rule of the bosses . . ."

Missus Austin, recently come to, dull-eyed, couldn't think, couldn't say a word, and lay there, helpless.

Out came a pad of paper. "What are your children's names, Mrs. Austin?" The sympathetic touch.

Then the facts struck home, Hank's missus felt the impact. Her screaming and wailing filled the flat, two women had to hold her down. Biting their lips, frowning, the comrades stood off, thinking. They eased off a few paces while neighbors tried to calm the woman. Everybody in the flat heard the siren outside as another firetruck rolled to the scene. A brisk wind was shooting the water back which bounced off the building in a thin spray.

Later on three neighbors left Missus Austin's side and went out upon the street to take up a collection, going through the press. They started to tell Missus Austin's story to each and every one, but that got to be too much trouble, so in the end they worked out a system—they chanted: "She has four children, her house is on fire, her husband was just hurt in an accident." The women carried tin pie-plates, donated to the cause by the Hungarian restaurateur who had his head poked out his door, sniffing for business. They went through the crowd thoroughly, chanting: "She has four children, her house is on fire, her husband was just hurt in an accident." Coins dropped against the tin plates with a musical ring and the silver sparkled in the lamplight. "She has four children, her house is on fire, her husband was just hurt in an accident."

The public responded.

It was still responding when Jason, returning from the square, saw the spectacle, the burning building, and started running up. He tripped over a hose. He shoved and shouldered his way through and, when he came close enough, saw that the burning building was the tenement, was his own dwelling place! Twenty-Door City was in flames.

He tried to push his way closer (there were now thousands on the scene), but a cop shoved him back.

"Don't mind me, officer, I only live in that house, that's all."

The cop grunted, Jason was allowed to shove himself closer. It took him ten minutes to reach the engines in front of the building. Then Comrade Helen caught sight of him, Comrade Helen who had been standing with her eyes glued on the fiery doorway; and all at once her face was a pitiful thing to see. Rushing over, she grabbed Jason's arm, screaming that Leon was inside, inside the burning building. "I told the firemen, but they said they can't reach him! He's inside, he's inside the building!"

The ex-poet stood stock-still, the pavement swayed beneath his feet. With dead eyes he stared at the blazing doorway and as he gazed some spray from the walls dampened his cheeks. Sparks were flying from the charred windows, dancing before his eyes. Comrade Helen, standing at his side and sobbing all her might, grabbed his arm and screamed, "What'll we do, what'll we do?" Jason stood there, staring with slack eyes. Farther back, looking with gloomy, sullen stare, stood the Mexican, his black, oily bare head shiny under the street lamp.

Then, still weeping, Comrade Helen told Jason how it

happened, how Leon had hammered on their door to warn them, how they had run out and had stood waiting for him to come from the entrance, too.

The ex-poet whirled on her.

"Weren't you at the demonstration in the square?" he screamed at her.

Comrade Helen, her face puffy from her crying, shook her head.

"Then where the hell were you?" shouted Jason and swung her violently around, facing him. She couldn't answer for a while, she was crying so hard. People began staring.

"Where the hell were you?" Jason hollered.

Then, in broken phrases, sobbing, Comrade Helen said that she and José had been in all day, hadn't gone out at all. She sobbed out that they had been drinking something which had made both of them very sleepy. "That's all I know, then Leon pounded on the door and woke us. We were sleeping, oh my God, that's all I kno-ow . . ."

In a flash the ex-poet understood everything, knew why Leon did not come out of the building; he pictured the scene vividly, he knew his little friend, all right. His face began to seethe and boil, then he whirled again.

He struck her square between the eyes, all his might, a hammer blow, then kicked her viciously. She dropped immediately, screaming and writhing on the street. A cop rushed forward, people shoved. The officer, looking alert, whirled, but Jason had already ducked into the crowd.

Then the old, fat janitress clapped her hand to her mouth.

"There's a man on the top floor!" she screeched, remembering. "I gave him the key, he went up there to look at a vacancy." Working herself forward, she told the

Battalion Chief all about it. The Chief thought quickly.

"Isn't there a fire-escape at the rear of the house, can't he get down from that?"

"There is, but he's got to get at it from Mister Wheeler's room, from Mister Wheeler's window. And Mister Wheeler wasn't in, I seen him leaving his place."

The Battalion Chief ordered the boys to play the hose higher, to try and reach the top story. The pressure wasn't strong enough; the water fell weakly against the wall a little above the fourth floor windows.

At the edge of the crowd, far down the block, white-faced and quivering, Jason continued to stare at the burning, crackling tenement.

"It started at the basement, they say, someone must have thrown a match or tossed a cigarette," a man was saying, ". . . those old buildings . . . all dried out . . . they go like tinder, they do . . ."

Jason, his knees wobbling, edged off farther, but he couldn't take his eyes from the burning building.

## XI

TWO BLOCKS NORTH, over on Thirteenth Street, the cracked printer, looking from his windows, saw a glow against the sky and rushed outside upon the street. He hurried to the scene, saw the huge press of folk, then went back to his basement quarters and in five minutes returned to the fire with bulging pockets.

The crowd looked aloft as cards were tossed into the air, flung with abandon, twirling and floating downward like big, square snowflakes. Some picked the cards up, then tossed them away again. Nonsense. Rushing off after emptying his pockets, the printer hurried down Third Avenue, passed Pete's joint, cut along smartly and, when he reached his quarters, picked up a metal printer's rule and began fiddling his left arm crazily, as if that limb were a violin. Then he made sure the door was locked, sat down at the desk, pulled his chair up close, and wrote that Rome was burning.

## XII

IN THIS WORLD things move on apace. People who suffer from ailments, from pains, from deformities, no longer have to limp and groan along. Science has come to the rescue. There is wonderful machinery at our command, with a trained staff in readiness. Health and beauty can be had for the asking—for a moderate sum. Progress has overleaped all barriers. At the dental parlor, the young dentist whose business was not very rushing these days was finishing work on little Celia's tooth, giving it the final touches. He tapped it gently with an instrument and saw that the tooth was snugly in place. Everything was in order, a good job. All her teeth in front were perfect now. He placed a mirror in her hand and saw her face glow as she smiled sweetly. After she was gone, the young dentist (no more customers due tonight, the next installment on his dental chair due next week) listened to her rapid, happy footsteps as she went down the stairs.

Westward the chill and bitter wind was blowing. In the square the riot was now all over, no more crowds pushed and shoved about. Along Fourteenth Street men and women, going home from work, knew nothing about the big Red demonstration; they hurried down into the subway stations. The venders were still on the job, chilly, blowing on their fists. Near the main B.M.T. subway entrance Officer Terence McGuffy was helping Grandma Volga and Mr. Feibelman, trying to straighten out the crooked wheels of their buggies; in the mêlée the carts had been overturned, trampled and trod upon. McGuffy took his gloves off, bent down, grunted, and finally, working his thick strong fingers, managed to straighten out most of the wire spokes so that the wheels at least turned on the axles.

Grandma Volga gave him two pretzels, Mr. Feibelman picked out five of his most perfectly roasted nuts, puckering up his face in a shrewd, grinning smile.

At that moment a small plump man wearing a wide black hat, climbing the stairs on stumpy legs, emerged from the subway entrance—none other than Vanya. And he stood in his tracks, rigid. For there on the corner, twenty feet away, was Natasha, his own, and Natasha was talking to a tall pallid man. He hesitated, then went over, and as soon as Natasha saw him she smiled brightly and caught his hand. "Mr. Munson, this is my husband, you heard so much about him," and turning to Vanya, who knew in a flash, who felt in an instant that all his old, old plaints were groundless, that this tall, pallid man was harmless, Natasha said, "Mr. Munson works with me in the basement, he has charge of the next department, he was just telling me about his two-year-old daughter." Vanya pumped the pallid fellow's hand, choking with happiness. Mr. Munson, his eyes tired, let his fingers fall, stood politely for a while, then said good-night. He was a tall thin fellow, narrow at the shoulder-blades, and Vanya watched him crossing the bustling street. Then he took Natasha's arm, took it firmly, and led her between venders, bootblacks, hawkers, shoppers, and home-going workers. His throat was singing silently, his eyes shone ahead like two small cherries. "Natasha," he said, "Natasha," and he squeezed his wife's arm at every seven paces.

They walked up Fourth Avenue, toward their apartment. When they saw the crowd jamming Eleventh Street, they became excited and hurried up the street but, when they reached the middle of the block, they saw that the Glen Cove Apartments were safe and sound and they felt relieved. Vanya still held Natasha's arm, and Natasha did not take her arm away.

In front of the tenement they paused a while and when approached by one of the neighbors, Vanya dug into his pocket and pulled forth a nickel and a dime. Natasha was on the point of opening her purse when she felt an increased pressure on her arm. They went inside the apartment building; the fire was under control now and there was no sense watching it. As they passed Mr. Franconi's door Vanya heard an even flowing sound and, placing his ear against the door, listened. Natasha listened, too.

"He must have left the faucets open," Natasha said; then they went upstairs and ate their supper.

The fire burned out. The blackened walls stood wetly stark, with gaping holes—the empty windows. Gripping axes, the firemen at last were able to enter the doorway of the tenement. They walked cautiously, afraid of falling walls. No body was found in the basement. On the second floor—the three upper floors had caved in, the building was now a hollow shell—they came upon a charred figure, unrecognizable. They broke down doors which gave way like wrapping paper and one of the firemen stumbled over a silver-handled blackened cane. They knocked in more doors and, after smashing through the rear, a draft of clean air blew through the entire tenement and the neighbors outside, standing around, started sniffing, some of them imagining they could smell the odor of burnt flesh. Soon after, the crowd broke up, fire-trucks began steaming slowly down the street.

Over the rooftops stood the chill and cloudy sky. One of the firemen had forgotten to screw on the cap to the water hydrant and now the cap hung limp from its chain, twirling slowly. Water dripped from the lip of the pipe, and in the harsh light coming from the arc lamp each drop was like a pearl falling from a gargoyle's mouth.

No wind blew. The chill damp settled down upon the town like an old cow easing her weight upon her haunches. From the harbor came the echoes of the signals in the fog, with big boats blundering in the thickening mist, going slowly, trying hard not to rub each other's sides as they plowed to and fro in the murky blindness.

All the ferries were run off-schedule. People jammed the piers impatiently, and the guards were busy answering questions. And when the wide, heavy boats finally shoved off, they nosed forward slowly, hardly moving at all, and barked and grunted like homesick bulldogs, sniffing their way toward the slips on the other side.

Far away, somewhere near Boston, the wind was shifting from north to northwest. It came blowing down from Newfoundland, carrying a cold dampness with it. A young girl walked down the hallway of a finishing school dormitory, went into the office, and inquired after mail. The prim lady behind the big desk dipped a hand into the wire IN basket, sorted many letters, but handed none over.

"I'm sorry, Miss Boardman, none for you today."

The girl turned away and went quietly up to her room. Many doors lined the way of the long corridors. Some of the transom windows were open, and she heard the laughter of her friends. In her room she sat at the small desk near the window and, after thinking a long time, began writing a sharp letter to her father. When she read it over, it struck her as being a bit too sharp, so she tore it up and started on another. She tore up three letters. The temperature outside was falling, cold air hurried over the land. At the bottom of the fourth letter she made a lot of little crosses and called her papa a funny name, a name she had called him ever since she had first learned how to talk. "Dear Pika, answer soon," said the third postscript. "Answer right away, Pika. I had such a bad dream last night, papa."

She sealed the letter and then sat looking out upon the darkening Massachusetts landscape. In a little while something struck the glass softly, the first snowflake of the coming storm.

The forecasters were right after all. The storm had come. It swept westward off the sea and blew howling southward down the coastline. The ground became whiter and whiter. The blizzard struck Boston and traveled south, blowing hard over Connecticut, and when the storm reached New York the flakes were whirling in a driving fury. The snow swirled past the arc lamps, driving along the East Side streets. It stuck to walls of old tenements, banked itself on window ledges, and the tops of the garbage cans at the curbs seemed to be covered with fluffy cotton.

In the square the cops were busy knocking down the temporary speakers' platforms, ripping the boards apart, striking lustily at the crude affairs. Women and children stood by, waiting for the kindling wood; every so often they shook themselves, brushing snow from their shoulders.

Toward the left, George Washington's powerful

charger, facing due north, did not bat an eyelash at the whirling flakes. His fetlocks were white with snow, but his rump was still uncovered and dry; the broad back of our first president protected the area there.

## XIII

TOWARD NINE O'CLOCK, when the temperature began rising, the snow grew clinging and moist. Trolleys banged and rattled along Fourteenth Street with trickles of water dripping down their sides. In the middle of the block the lights in front of the Tango Gardens burned brightly, the orchestra swung into their third number; the hostesses, in long, clinging dresses, stood about idly, waiting for the boys to come in. Squinting the side of his face which held the glass eye, the saxophone player started breathing deeply, because he was due for a solo pretty soon. Farther up the block, on the corner of Third Avenue, the Diana Ballroom was also waiting for customers, and had a hot band.

Life must go on, the future must be faced. Children will be born, and some will cry out when life cuts through their tender skin. Dragging his feet through the slush, Jason walked toward Saint Vincent's Hospital to ask Miss Allen for some money for a room. He kept close to buildings, sloshing along. A train of elevated cars thundered above his head as he crossed Sixth Avenue, and he muttered softly to himself a rhyme:

> "Roar trains, roar away,
> The cow's in the pasture,
> The mice are in the hay."

The snow was driving in his face, and some of the flakes entered his mouth. Stopping in a doorway, he took his glasses off and wiped them but, when he started walking again, he couldn't see very well anyway. Something kept bubbling in his throat. Bending lower, he plodded on through the slush and, with wet eyes staring through damp glasses, saw the whirling in a whitish blur.

In this world things move on apace. Progress overleaps all barriers. In a little room under a staircase, glancing at the mirror over her dresser, Celia continued to marvel and wonder at her new tooth, and kept touching it gently with the tips of her fingers. She was waiting for the sound of Leon's footsteps, so that she could go out into the hall with a flashing smile at last. Outside her window, which gave out upon a small rear courtyard, the snow still fell. There was no wind in the yard, because on all four sides were the walls of buildings, and here the flakes fell quietly, settling gently to the ground.

In the hallway, upon the little table which held the mail for the roomers of the house, lay two letters addressed to Leon Fisher. One, a brief note from the Pennsylvania National Academy in Philadelphia, stated that his picture "Celia" would be shipped back to him, charges collect, as soon as the exhibition closed, which was Tuesday. The other letter was from the foreman of the engraving company, asking Leon to report to work tomorrow morning.

Upstairs, hungry, weak from sobbing, miserable, his pillow gnawed viciously at the corners, Leon lay fully clothed, flat on his back in bed, his harsh hot eyes drilling holes into the darkness of the ceiling.

# XIV

AT MIDNIGHT the snow turned to rain, the gutters bubbled with water. The cobbles between the car tracks were nice and shiny.

The downpour lasted all night, washing the slush away. The rain fell upon all the rooftops of Manhattan and also in the square. Lincoln's rugged face was wet. At dawn, when the sky cracked slowly, the storm was over and the temperature started dropping sharply, going down below the freezing point. A hard cold wind went driving up and down the streets, whipping the pavements dry, rattling the windows of the town. Far out at sea a gale was blowing; a big tanker, steaming north with a full load of oil from Tampico, began wallowing, and the skipper, growing nervous, stood ready to instruct his operator to wireless an SOS at any minute now. The wind weakened, however, driving from the east, and when it reached New York the velocity was not more than twenty miles an hour or so.

The day grew lighter. At seven-thirty, when Grandma Volga and Mr. Feibelman arrived breathlessly at the square, running a neck-and-neck race all the way from Second Avenue, Mr. Feibelman winning the coveted position once again by a last heroic shove, The Man Who Walks Backwards appeared upon the scene, bundled up in an old raincoat now, coming north along Fourth Avenue. He stopped in front of the main B.M.T. subway entrance, his back toward the square and, glancing sharply into the tiny mirrors attached to his spectacles, saw a hard glistening drop of ice at the tip of Lafayette's historic sword. He stood staring for a moment at the glittering bead, then turned away and, tapping his stout cane vigorously against the sidewalk, followed the low thick wall.

By the time he had made a complete trip, two nickels and four pennies went clinking into his metal cup and the square was already seething with the early morning crowds. The sidewalks of Fourteenth Street were jammed with folk, unemployed, night-workers, and pushing, plodding bargain-shoppers. In the tall tower of the public utilities building the big clock struck the hour—eight solemn, stately bongs. Mr. Feibelman scratched a match and dropped it upon the split wood and charcoal in his blackened pail, Grandma Volga was busy stuffing pretzels into paper bags.

In this world things move on apace. Life must go on. There are children to be born, and some will cry out when their tender skin is cut. But progress overleaps all barriers. Time does not stop, it moves. The tide comes in and great waves roll toward the shore, and if there're pebbles waiting, why the pebbles are no more. For the future must be faced, no getting away from that, and if you cannot keep apace, you'll be sitting on your hat.

Tramp, tramp, tramp, past Union Square they're clopping. A wooden beat on an iron street, and no telling when they're stopping.